TWILIGHT IMPERIUM

Intergalactic empires fall, but one faction will rise from the ashes to conquer the galaxy.

Once the mighty Lazax Empire ruled all the known galaxy from its capital planet of Mecatol Rex, before treachery and war erased the Lazax from history, plunging a thousand star systems into conflict and uncertainty.

Now the Great Races who span the galaxy look upon their former capital hungrily – the power and secrets of the Lazax await a new emperor...

To lay claim to the throne is a destiny sought by many, yet the shadows of the past serve as a grim warning to those who would follow in their footsteps.

T0064963

TWILIGHT IMPERIUM™

The
VEILED
MASTERS

TIM PRATT

ACONYTE

First published by Aconyte Books in 2022

ISBN 978 1 83908 136 1

Ebook ISBN 978 1 83908 137 8

Cover art by Scott Schomburg

Distributed in North America by Simon & Schuster Inc, New York, USA

Printed in the United States of America

9 8 7 6 5 4 3 2 1

ACONYTE BOOKS

An imprint of Asmodee Entertainment Ltd

Mercury House, Shipstones Business Centre

North Gate, Nottingham NG7 7FN, UK

aconytebooks.com // twitter.com/aconytebooks

For my brother and sister

CHAPTER 1
TERRAK

I am recording this chronicle so that, in the event of my capture and inevitable death, the truth might still come out. I have been accused of a monstrous act, and I am innocent of that crime... although I can't claim to be innocent in a general sense. (Those failings I do possess, and there are many, I will admit to whenever relevant.)

This is how my troubles began.

I stood on the highest floor of Shilsaad Station, at a huge wraparound window overlooking the frozen nova. I swirled a cup of Hacan sunwine and did my best to project an air of knowing, benevolent wisdom. One of the junior diplomats from the Mentak Coalition, a human with high cheekbones and elaborately razor-cut hair named Coralee, strolled over to me, holding a fluted glass of something no doubt less potent than my own libation. The Mentak were organizing this event, so she had more reason to stay sharp than I did.

"Ambassador Terrak," she said, leaning against the railing at the viewport. "I was hoping for the chance to speak with you privately."

I towered over the human by two-thirds of a meter, and surely weighed at least twice as much as she did, but she didn't shy away from me or exhibit nervousness the way many humans do when in such close proximity to my people. The Hacan superficially resemble a nearly extinct predator from the ancestral human homeworld, a large feline called a "lion". Being seen as reminiscent of an intimidating but noble beast can be useful at times when dealing with such people, but this human wasn't from Jord, or even the Federation of Sol. She'd grown up in the multiracial mélange of the Mentak Coalition, which meant she'd lived alongside Hacan her entire life.

The Mentak Coalition was an oddity in the galaxy, with so many different species living closely together in some approximation of harmony. Now her government wanted to expand that coalition to encompass other cultures, including mine, in a grand alliance – and, amazingly, the plan might even succeed. The purpose of this gathering was to discuss final details regarding the rather grandly named "Greater Union", and ours was just one of many preliminary meetings leading up to a major multi-faction summit on the Coalition homeworld of Moll Primus, where the treaty would, in theory, be formally signed. Assuming everything didn't fall apart before that, anyway. Convincing several proud and ancient cultures, some of whom had clashed in the past, to join together in a single grand enterprise was a delicate operation. I was a bit cynical about the whole idea. The Greater Union seemed to me like the sort of plan that would take tens of thousands of hours of collective work in order to achieve, at best, a largely symbolic outcome. But diplomats have to keep busy somehow, and at least such endeavors keep the drinks flowing.

"Am I so famed as a conversationalist?" I said. Before she could answer, I gestured to the vast blur of the frozen nova beyond the viewport, the star stilled forever at the moment of explosive expansion. The nova's true brightness was hidden behind an array of shells, shields, and lenses, so it was possible to look directly upon the stalled stellar devastation. "What's your theory?"

"About the frozen nova?" She shrugged. "Some ancient civilization tried to harness the energy of an exploding star, and that's what remains of their solar battery."

"Ah, the exploitation hypothesis." I swirled my golden wine. "I favor the survival theory myself – that the ancient aliens were local to this system and put the star in stasis to preserve their homeworld from destruction."

She cocked her head. "Surely a civilization capable of halting the expansion of a star and wrapping it in perpetual forcefields could simply pack up and move to a system that *wasn't* about to fall prey to a supernova? It's not as though stars explode without warning – these local aliens would have had time to prepare."

"You underestimate the appeal of defending one's homeland," I said. "Some people are sentimentally attached to the cradle of their civilization, even once that civilization has expanded throughout the galaxy. A homeworld is about heritage, and the root of one's identity as a people. Maintaining that connection can be very important."

Coralee snorted. "Are you making a political point? Since I'm the descendant of prisoners on a penal colony, and grew up on a space station alongside a dozen other species, that means I can't understand cultural identity?"

I blinked at her. "Burning sands, no. I think you overestimate both the subtlety of my wit and my interest in offending you." That statement was half true.

"Oh, I'm not offended." She sipped from her glass, glancing up at me and smiling. "I have great loyalty to my people, ambassador. That loyalty just doesn't have anything to do with our shared connection to any particular ball of dirt and water. Moll Primus is still the center of the Mentak Coalition, but it was our prison, too, long ago, so our relationship with the homeland is... complex. Instead, I'm loyal to our ideals – freedom, of course, but also forging something new and strong from disparate pieces. That's what we're trying to do with the Greater Union."

"I am in sympathy with your stated goals," I said. "But the decision to join was made without my input, so my position never mattered much." I bowed my head. "I am, of course, a humble servant of the Emirates of Hacan... but to be frank, I'm here mostly for the drinks and the chance to catch up with old friends."

"Don't be so modest, Ambassador Terrak. You're a man of influence."

My official title was "Ambassador-at-Large", which was to say, I wasn't ambassador to any place in particular, but represented the Emirates of Hacan in various places and situations as necessary. I did occasionally advise my government on matters of trade, and certainly I had highly placed friends and contacts... but it was no secret I'd secured my largely ceremonial title (and the very real diplomatic privileges that came along with it) by bribing the right officials. Wealth is the source of power, after all, political and otherwise; this is true throughout the galaxy, though only the Hacan acknowledge it openly.

We have a saying back home: "Money is the blood of the world". If money ceases to flow, the world dies. I've spent a lot of time among the other factions and have gradually come to realize they *really mean it* when they insist wealth matters less than diplomacy (as if influence can't be purchased), or military might (when bigger and better weapons can always be bought), or the pursuit of knowledge (which is inevitably used to make money). I used to think those people were naïve. I've come to accept that they're simply *alien*.

My diplomatic credentials accompanied me wherever I roamed, and I led an enjoyable life drifting from one embassy party to another, tagging along on official missions to interesting places, and engaging in a little light favor-trading and bribe-taking here and there. You have to spread around a few credits at strategic moments in order to foster the smooth flow of interstellar trade, after all, and I am one of the people who knows just who to approach, and how to appease them. The purpose of this meeting was ostensibly to discuss the details of free trade areas and cultural exchange programs among Union members, so it was within my sphere... but in reality, everyone from every invited faction was looking for advantages they could gain or weaknesses they could exploit. With a space station full of diplomats and politicians (and, no doubt, a few spies), how could it be otherwise?

I shook my head, mane swaying. "I have contacts in various government offices and can occasionally convince a minister of procurement to look favorably upon one supplier or another. I've been known to arrange an off-the-record meeting with this official or that. But whether the Emirates will join this Greater Union of yours, and what sort of terms will be settled on regarding commerce and so forth... *those* decisions are far above my level."

"Every voice that joins the chorus makes the song that much stronger," Coralee said. "We value your support. We'll all be safer, and richer, if the Greater Union goes forward."

I raised my cup to her. "Your people pour an excellent libation, so consider yourself well on your way to winning me over."

"I'd hoped to appeal to you as a businessman. We've all had trouble with the L1Z1X growing bolder, and the corrosive swarming of the Nekro Virus, but there are also these strange new threats that have arisen recently. These nightmarish invaders on the edge of inhabited space... the stranger-than-usual behavior of the Creuss... the so-called Titans taking over that old mining colony planet... this mysterious information broker on that remote station, buying up influence for reasons no one can ascertain... they all pose a threat to the smooth operation of commerce, don't you think? If we band together, we can form a united front, and stand as one against the coming chaos."

"The nature of the galaxy is change," I said. "And in chaos, there are opportunities for profit. That's something the Mentak Coalition understands. Your raider fleets are always poised to seize the moment when the moment passes by, hmm? I'm not the only one who finds it... peculiar... that you would ask to make alliances with people you have historically boarded and robbed."

She sighed. "Even if you think the Mentak are all pirates, you can see why we'd want to defend the civilized galaxy against existential threats. Pirates prefer nice, predictable trade routes to prey upon. We've all heard the stories of remote worlds being wiped out by mysterious invaders from who-knows-where. No one benefits from that sort of... disruption." Perhaps sensing that this grim turn in the conversation was unlikely to please me, she suddenly grinned. "Besides, we can still ambush and pillage the Letnev. We'd never give up *that* pastime."

"Nor should you." I happened to spot a familiar silhouette across the room – my old friend Qqurant, of the Xxcha, with his distinctive red-and-white striped shell pattern. "If you'll excuse me, I see someone I need to speak to."

Coralee didn't put her hand on me, but she did shift her body to block my smooth escape. "Can we count on your support, ambassador?"

"My support is not worth as much as you seem to think, Coralee, but as I said, I am in sympathy with your goals, and will certainly say as much if anyone bothers to ask."

She hardly seemed satisfied, but she nodded and stepped aside, sparing me the necessity of gently picking her up and moving her.

I strolled across the circular room of windowed walls, the floor dotted with small groups of people, weaving mechanical servers, and hovering drone-trays. Everyone was dressed in their cultural finery: Xxcha shells gleaming with embedded jewels, humans in shimmering gowns or sleek suits, Hylar in elegant mobile tanks (and, in one case, a delicate silvery exo-skeleton; undersecretary Jhuri was one of the amphibious sub-species who could breathe air unassisted), Hacan in formal robes or sashes (the latter a bit daring and modern; that's what I wore, of course), and even a few Yssaril, those being less inconspicuous than usual so no one would trip over them.

The Xxcha Kingdom, the Federation of Sol, the Universities of Jol-Narr, the Emirates of Hacan, and the Yssaril Guild of Spies: if the Mentak Coalition got its way, those factions would join them to form the core of the Greater Union. I'd heard rumors the Mentak had also reached out to the Saar, the Naaz-Rokha, and the Brotherhood of Yin, but if so, those groups hadn't sent any representatives to this particular summit. That was fine by me; the Saar are depressing, the Yin are zealots, and the Naaz-Rokha are just strange, even if the Rokha *are* distant cousins of my people, genetically speaking. My sources told me the Coalition had also attempted to contact the Naalu Collective, through intermediaries in the Yssaril Guild of Spies, who maintained a relationship with the reclusive serpent-folk. The Naalu were aloof, as always, and ignored the call entirely. Just as well. The snakes were said to possess telepathic powers, and I loathed the idea of someone messing about with my mind.

I angled toward Qqurant, who was standing in a corner, holding a tankard and staring at nothing. The Xxcha was a minister of cultural affairs, promoting the art of his people across the galaxy by arranging tours and exhibitions. He was by all accounts an accomplished poet himself, though Xxcha poetry doesn't do much for me; too much water and trees and mournfulness, not enough fire and blood and sex. I wondered what was wrong with him. Qqurant was one of the most animated and gregarious Xxcha I'd ever known. It wouldn't be fair to call him the life of a party – Xxcha don't tend to get drunk, stand on tables, and perform impromptu dances – but he could usually be seen trundling from one group to another, dropping in gravelly witticisms and making wry comments that punctured pomposity and made everyone relax and interact more as *people* than as Representatives of the State. Qqurant and I had known each other for thirty years and been to literally hundreds of these functions together, and I'd never seen him looking so abstract and remote.

"What's wrong, Shelly?" I said. He lifted his beaky face toward me, his eyes glassy and vague. He usually called me "Whiskers", but instead, after a long pause, he said, "Greetings… Ambassador Terrak." A pause. "I hope." A longer pause. "You are having. An enjoyable evening."

I glanced around, and we were out of earshot, so I moved closer. "Blazing stars, Shelly, what's wrong? You've got something on your mind and no mistake. Are the girls all right?" Shelly had been widowed twenty years ago, but he had two daughters, the twin stars his world orbited around.

"The girls... my daughters... they are well. Continuing their studies. Thriving in their... chosen fields. It is kind... of you to. Inquire. After them." Qqurant wasn't quite looking at me. He didn't seem to be looking at *anything*.

I couldn't understand why he'd be so cold and distant. "If I've done something to offend you, old friend..."

Now his gaze focused on me. "Oh. No... please. Accept. My apologies. I have... been ill. Nothing to worry... about. I will be. Fine soon. If you will... excuse me." He toddled away from me but instead of leaving, or talking to someone else, he just took up another solitary post on the other side of the room, watching the others, or else watching nothing at all.

How very strange. I spied another familiar face, a Federation of Sol trade representative named Lillith, just detaching herself from a group of laughing, red-faced humans. She wore a rather daring arrangement of metallic rings held in place by antigravity generators or magnetic resonances or something, and wires woven through her long red hair made her tresses undulate as if in the wind. Lillith tended to dazzle those who weren't used to her, and it took a *long* time to get used to her, which allowed her to make deals that were usually lopsided in her favor. "Lil, you look absolutely bizarre tonight."

She swiveled toward me, smiling. I was taller than her, of course, but she had the long, lean build of someone born outside a gravity well, and she was wearing remarkable heels, so she could nearly look me in the eye. "Terrak, you old reprobate! Is your sash edged in *blue*? What would the revered sages say if they saw you dressed like that?"

"Nothing I haven't heard before." I took her elbow and steered her away from the ears cocked our way. "Have you talked to Shelly tonight?"

"No, I haven't seen him yet, is he here? I never go *looking* for Qqurant, he always bulldozes his way up to me – you know how he is."

I nodded. "Yes, usually. There's something off about him tonight, though. I've never seen him so… distant isn't even the word for it." I gestured with my glass to where Qqurant stood, like a powered-down robot. "He wasn't even like this right after his partner died. He just threw himself into his work then. Have you heard anything that might explain the change?"

Lillith put on a face of concern, but I could see the cogs whirring behind her eyes, trying to figure out how a lapse in Qqurant's focus could be turned to her faction's benefit, but one reason Shelly and Lillith could be uncomplicated friends was because their spheres of influence didn't overlap much. "Not at all. The poor thing. I'll check on him myself, and let you know if I hear anything. I do hope he's all right. I always say he's one of the only truly good souls you're ever likely to meet in our world."

I reared back in mock offense. "What about me?"

Lillith chuckled. "When it comes to goodness, we're not worthy to polish his shell, and you know it."

I thanked her, turned, and almost tripped over an Yssaril I hadn't seen standing so close. You don't usually see Yssaril unless they want you to; that's why the tiny humanoids make such good spies. "Did I overhear you express concern about Minister Qqurant?" she said, voice low. She spoke in my native language rather than the intergalactic argot, which surprised me, though I don't know why. Yssaril operatives are good with languages. Eavesdropping is useless if you can't understand what you overhear. This one was wearing the uniform of station security.

"I was just inquiring after the health of an old friend," I said blandly in the trader's tongue.

She nodded, and switched languages without a blink, and with those large eyes of theirs, you'd notice a blink. "The minister is fine. Just very busy."

How curious. The Xxcha don't make as much use of the guild of spies as other cultures do, favoring open diplomacy over covert evidence-gathering, and anyway, Shelly didn't have anything to do with the kind of operations the Guild would be involved with. "I don't believe we've met before. I'm Ambassador Terrak."

A pause. "This one is Kote Strom."

"And how do you know Shelly?"

"Through… work." She took a half-step away. "I only wanted to reassure you. Do not worry. The minister is fine."

"I am *deeply* reassured." I put a little growling purr into the last word. "Let me reassure *you* on that point."

The Yssaril scurried away, disappearing behind a group of people conversing. How bizarre. I pride myself on knowing what's going on behind the scenes, but there were clearly forces at work here doing things I didn't understand for reasons I couldn't currently imagine. I'd just been warned off investigating Shelly's odd behavior, which, of course, only strengthened my resolve to do just that.

I did a slow circuit of the room, looking around for Shelly, who'd moved on from the last spot. I saw him at last, standing with a peculiar, hunched posture. Was that a *shimmer* beside him, like an Yssaril doing their don't-notice-me trick? Shelley abruptly turned and walked toward the lift platform that led to the complex below us – to the guest quarters, dining halls and meeting rooms of this convention center and luxury hotel.

I considered following him. It wouldn't be difficult to come up with some pretext to tag along after him. But ... what could I hope to accomplish? I'd achieve as much by talking to a stone wall. Something was going on. Was Shelly trying to give me a message by behaving so strangely? The way someone being held captive might say something wildly out of character when answering the door, as a way of signaling that something isn't right, but they can't speak freely? Perhaps my old friend was in trouble. True, he was a cultural minister, not involved in anything more dangerous than rivalries among musicians, but he still walked the halls of power... and the halls of power were filled with trapdoors and pitfalls.

I moved to one side of a crystalline kinetic sculpture, shielded from the eyes of most partygoers and all the security personnel, and pressed an invisible button on one of my bracelets. I subvocalized: "Catriona, I want you to look into a Xxcha cultural minister named Qqurant. Medium-depth investigation, do pattern-matching against the database of known behaviors, and send me a chart of any recent anomalies, particularly financial or intimate-relational. Look into an Yssaril named Kote Strom, too, just a basic dossier, assuming you can find anything – she's here as station security but I wonder if she might be Guild of Spies." I sent the message. It would be encrypted, and then transmit itself disguised as signal noise in routine communication traffic emitting from the space station, to be snagged by one of my consultant's many automated agents. Catriona was a freelance data analyst, and while no one is better at market research, her skills are highly transferrable when it comes to other matters as well. If something was going on with Shelly, assuming it wasn't something happening entirely inside his ellipsoidal scaly head, I'd know soon enough.

I slipped back into my usual role, all bonhomie and knowing

smiles, and circulated throughout the party until it was time for our formal dinner. I ended up at a table with Lillith, so that was fun – she was filled with scandalous tales about old acquaintances. The meal was … peculiar. The Mentak Coalition's culinary tradition is one of fusion, of course, since all the different species living together there had shared their own delicacies for centuries. Our hosts proudly served us dishes that were *almost* familiar, but also all wrong. I'd requested the Hacan-style meat dish, and received a platter of roast caprid, which was all well and good, but the chop was crusted with ground-up arthropod bits and served atop entirely the wrong sort of grain, and worse, the grain was stained deep purple with some kind of discharge from a cephalopod's ink sac. Lillith stared at her plate in open horror. She'd opted for the fish – people who spent as much time at the Universities of Jol-Nar with the Hylar as she did were basically required to develop a fondness for seafood, if only out of self-defense – and the seared protean eel set before her was *technically* a fish, though it looked more like a snake with vestigial fins, and its head was still attached, too. The less said about the sticky reduction dribbled all over it, the better.

Fortunately, the cheese course included several edible varieties, and if you brushed the odd seeds off the bread, that wasn't so bad either, so we didn't starve. Shelly wasn't present at the dinner, despite having the most robust appetite of any Xxcha I've ever met, and I didn't see Kote Strom, either, though that didn't mean she wasn't around. I inquired with one of the Mentak officials circulating the room about Shelly's whereabouts and she said, "Oh, the minister had some urgent business to take care of, but he'll rejoin us for the morning sessions."

Hmm. After the inevitable speeches, I declined several offers of after-dinner alcohols and vapors and teas, claiming I had some reports to go over, and took a lift down to the floor where my room was located. In truth, I wanted to see whether Catriona had found anything about Shelly yet.

I entered my room and turned to face the door to engage the lock. That's when something slammed into the back of my knees, knocking me off balance. I caught myself against the door and tried to turn, but something swarmed up my back. A moment later a hand slammed my head against the wall hard enough to make my vision swim with black dots, and I sank to my knees. My head rang like a bell, and there was pain, but it felt far away. I hadn't been in a fight for a long time and wouldn't have thought someone so small could hurt me so badly. Sometimes it's less about might and more about leverage. I tried to rise, but...

I'll have to pick this up later. My benefactor is shouting questions at me, and when someone saves your life, it's polite to answer.

THE FAITHFUL I

Qqurant lay on the floor of his room, adrift in a peaceful cloud. Thinking was difficult, lately, but then, he was called upon to think less and less. In the early days of his conversion, Qqurant had needed to use his wits, to improvise, to charm and wheedle and insinuate – he was given missions to complete, yes, but he was granted great latitude when it came to *how* he completed them.

Now, he had almost no freedom. He was no longer given missions; he was barely even given tasks, except to be careful, and not arouse suspicion. The last few... days? Weeks? Had been a bit of a blur. Had he seen Whiskers tonight? That old... no, the thought slipped away, as thoughts so often did now. Qqurant didn't mind. He was still permitted to serve, still rewarded for his service, and so, all was right in his world.

That familiar voice, or chorus of voices, spoke in his mind. <*Our faithful servant. We are sorry to see you so diminished.*>

Qqurant stirred. "My... guides?"

<*We are here. We have need of you. One final mission.*>

"My... pleasure. To. Serve."

<*You must make a call,*> his masters whispered, and Qqurant was happy, because such a task was still within his ability, and active obedience was the greatest bliss.

CHAPTER 2
TERRAK

My rescuer is satisfied, and amusing herself while we complete our journey, so I'll resume my account. I would like to send out these missives as I go – Catriona would see they reached the right listeners – but I don't dare risk giving my position away. Catriona never answered my request for information about Shelly, which makes me wonder if my oh-so-encrypted messages were intercepted. If so, I don't dare break my silence now, when half the galaxy is looking for me ...

When I was attacked in my room on Shilsaad Station, head slammed into the door, I growled, fight-or-flight chemicals flooding my system and dispelling my daze. I struggled up from my knees, but the person on my back yanked my hair hard, forcing my head up. A small, long-fingered hand holding a slim black canister appeared on the edge of my vision. Was it poison? A gas to render me unconscious? I didn't want to find out. The weight on my back wasn't heavy, and I flung myself hard to one side, trying to shake off my unwelcome passenger, and falling to my knees again in the process. The canister went flying, bouncing across the floor and out of sight, and small arms locked tightly around my neck.

I was *not* going to be strangled to death in my hotel room. I pulled at my attacker's arms, but despite their diminutive size they were too strong to dislodge, so instead I concentrated on gaining my feet. Once I was upright, I spun and slammed my back against one of the walls as hard as I could, crushing my assailant between my own body mass and the station's bulkhead. The attacker hissed in my ear, but their grip loosened, and I stepped forward, ready to slam myself back again. Instead the figure dropped from my back and scurried away – or so I assumed, since I saw only a shimmer in the air as my door opened and then closed again.

When your attacker is invisible, it's probably Yssaril. Kote Strom? I rubbed my throat, but though it was sore, I detected no real damage. My assailant clearly hadn't been trying to kill me – a blade while I was sleeping would have accomplished that much more easily. What was the purpose, then? To drug me, and take me somewhere else, for some unknown purpose? That thought disturbed me the most, in some ways. I have devoted much of my life to being the insider, to having control over my own small sphere of influence, so being at the mercy of mysterious forces chilled me to the heart. I am in the business of knowledge and influence, and I currently had neither.

Best to correct that and learn what I could. I picked up the canister from the floor. The cylinder was small and black, barely the size of my thumb, with a simple push-button and nozzle on top, and a toggle to open or close the valve. There were no markings or indication at all regarding what substance might be inside. I pushed the safety toggle closed and tucked the canister away in one of the hidden pockets in my tunic. I considered whether or not to call station security. This attack had all the makings of an international incident, and I wasn't sure I wanted to be in the middle of one of *those* as they involve far too much paperwork and long, tedious meetings that detract from the more enjoyable things in life.

A melodious chime sounded from the ceiling. "Ambassador Terrak, you have a message," the room's expert system said.

"What is it?"

A pause, and then a recording of Shelly's voice played. "Old friend... Whiskers... I need your help. Please... come to my room... so I can. Explain. I am on Azimuth Deck... room four. Hurry. As soon. As you... get this." He still sounded strange, but if he was in trouble that could be explained by stress and fear. So. Shelly had gotten mixed up in something, and in the course of asking about his welfare, I'd mixed *myself* up, somehow. Whatever was going on, it was serious to send an Yssaril operative to try and gas me.

I sighed. This summit had seemed so uneventful, and I hadn't been prepared for this level of excitement. But the Hacan have a saying: *There's no use arguing with the desert.* Protest all you want, but the sun will still beat down on you, and the drifting sand will bury you while you complain about the injustice of it all. Sometimes you just have to deal with things as they are. Was someone trying to disrupt the Greater Union? The idea wasn't universally popular, but how could Shelly possibly impact it one way or another? Not to disparage my old friend, but his role in the Kingdom of Xxcha simply wasn't that important.

I considered bringing a weapon, but only ceremonial ones were allowed at the summit, mostly for photographs, and those aren't any good in a fight. My own dune spear – a traditional Hacan weapon – had *never* been wielded in a fight, though I looked quite dashing with it across my back. I decided to leave the spear in the closet; walking around the station with a weapon was sure to draw comment. At least I always have my claws.

I went into the hallway, keeping my eyes open for shimmers in the air. I didn't see anyone suspicious, or actually anyone at all, on my walk to the lift – most of the delegation was probably drinking and talking and making the little side deals that keep international relations interesting. I descended to Azimuth Deck and walked down another empty corridor. Room four was at the end of a hallway – and the door was ajar.

I growled and pushed the door fully open, wishing I *had* brought my dune spear. "Shelly?" There was no answer, and the lights inside were dim. I stepped into the suite's foyer. There was a little sitting room with a chair and stool and a table straight ahead. No sign of Shelly, or anyone else. I turned toward the sleeping quarters, and the door was standing half-open there, too.

I pushed the door wide and looked inside.

Shelly was dead on the floor at the foot of his sleeping pod, his head twisted at a horrible angle… but not because his neck was broken. No, his head was pushed aside by the haft of a spear sticking out of his body. Someone had inserted the point of the spear at the base of his neck, in one of the few places not protected by the shell, and shoved the weapon down, doubtless destroying all sorts of vital organs on the way. How could you even manage such an attack, unless the victim simply sat there and allowed it?

I was so stunned, it took a moment for me to realize the spear looked familiar. It had a red jewel set in the base, and the haft was wrapped with dark blue cloth – the colors of the Emirates of Hacan diplomatic corps. That was *my* dune spear. Someone had stolen my spear from my room and killed my friend with it. Which meant–

"Burning sands." I turned just in time for three people in station security uniforms to rush into the room pointing sidearms at me.

I raised my hands and lowered my head. I'd been in a number of unusual situations over the course of my life and career, but this was the first time I'd ever been framed for murder.

Station security put me in a room. It wasn't a cell – Shilsaad Station was essentially a convention center, not a detainment facility – but it was obviously the closest thing they had, just a table and a couple of chairs and bare walls, with a camera high up in one corner, watching me. I should have been mourning my friend, but I confess, I was a bit more preoccupied with the idea of how to save my own skin… and figuring out who could possibly want to frame me for such a crime. I had enemies, but none of the sort who'd go to these lengths. Time enough for grief when all this was cleared up… or, I supposed, while I was sitting in a prison cell somewhere.

I wondered which branch of officialdom would arrive to interrogate me. The station was owned by a Federation of Sol corporation, so it would probably be their police, but the Mentak Coalition was running this summit, so maybe they'd jump in, or it could be Xxcha, since one of their people was the victim. I wondered how long I'd have to sit here before the various interested parties worked out their jurisdictional issues and sent someone in to ask why I'd murdered my friend of three decades.

It took less than an hour, and when she arrived, she wasn't any of the people I might have expected. She was a human, dressed in a station security uniform – they're white and gray, and make their people look more like custodial staff than the teeth and claws of authority, but again: it's a hotel and convention center. They don't get a lot of murders. She stepped inside and shut the door, and then gave me a grin. I grinned back, because my spirit was not broken, and my teeth are a lot longer. She dropped into the chair on the other side of the table and relaxed, like she was a princeling on a throne. "So. Terrak. How's it going? You need anything?"

"I need to contact the Hacan diplomatic corps so they can send an advocate. As I told your colleagues when they first brought me in."

She snorted. "I meant more, like, do you need a drink of water, or to take a leak, or whatever."

I sighed. "No. I don't."

"Great." She reached into her pocket and removed a small black canister.

I reached across and pinned her wrist to the table, her hand still wrapped around the spray bottle. *Another* attacker? Was all of the station security compromised? If so, my prospects for escaping this situation were even more dismal than I'd realized.

She laughed and patted my gripping hand with her free one. "Relax, big guy, I'm not here to blast you in the face. This is the canister you had in your pocket when they took you in – I filched it out of the evidence locker. Which is really just the security head's *personal* locker, where she keeps a spare shirt and stuff, so it wasn't too hard to get open. Amateurs, right? The security team on this station is *not* equipped to deal with somebody sticking a big spear through a guy. The real authorities are on the way, though. Federation of Sol investigators from the colony world we're orbiting." She looked at my hand, still pinning her wrist. "Go ahead and take the canister and let me go, so we can discuss your options." She opened her fingers, and the canister rolled across the table toward me.

She was clearly not your average security guard. I let her wrist go, picked up the canister, and tucked it away again. It was my only evidence that someone had done anything untoward to me, and I wanted to protect it. "What are you talking about? What options? Who are you?"

"I'm Amina Azad. That's not the name on my official identification, but hey, why should we have any secrets between us?" She laced her hands together on the table. "You've stepped into a big ugly mess, Terrak. Fortunately, I can get you out of it. If you want to help me clean it up, that is. I could use a person with your resources and connections."

I barked a laugh. Was she a spy from another polity, or just an opportunist who wanted to turn my disaster into her personal gain? "My diplomatic credentials aren't much good now that I've been accused of murdering a cultural minister, and I rather doubt I'll have free access to my bank accounts."

She shook her head. "I asked around about you. You know *lots* of people – maybe even as many as I do – and because you've helped a lot of them get richer over the years, they're all happy to see you whenever you come around. Most of my old friends hate my guts, I'm sad to say, and in this part of space, I don't have many people I can reach out to. As for money – come on, Terrak. A guy like you keeps all his money in *official* banks? I don't believe that."

I cleared my throat. "Well. I've made a few arrangements over the years, yes. For tax purposes. But…" I glowered at her. "I'm not *paying* you."

"I'm not asking you to. Funds aren't currently a problem. I was just making a general observation. I believe in honesty and transparency between friends. We should be friends. You sure could use one."

"Who *are* you?" I had suspicions. I've met a few covert operatives in my time. They can be very smug, because they really *do* know more about what's going on than you do.

"I told you who I am. I think what you mean is: what do I *do*?

The answer is, I clean up messes. Discreetly. And if I can't be discreet, I can at least be deniable."

Interesting. "You're telling me you're a covert operation? For the Mentak Coalition? Or the Federation of Sol?"

She made a sour face. "Ugh. Don't talk to me about the Mentak Coalition. You'd think a bunch of pirates and convicts would be more fun. I was born on Jord, but I haven't been back in a while. There's a great big beautiful galaxy out there, and the stars are all the home I need." She pointed at the canister. "Let's focus on your immediate situation. Someone tried to spray you in the face with whatever's in that tube. If they had, I'm pretty sure one of two things would have happened. Either you would have been killed, and replaced with some kind of double, maybe a clone or an android or something, I'm not sure. Or you would have been mind-controlled, hollowed out, and turned into a puppet. One of those things happened to your buddy Qqurant. Don't you want to know which one? I do. I'd like to get a read on the contents of this canister – is it knockout gas, or poison, or some kind of nanotech brain-rewiring stuff, or what? That little spray bottle is the first bit of actual *evidence* I've gotten my hands on regarding this conspiracy. We need to find somebody reliable and trustworthy who knows their way around a chemistry lab to analyze that evidence and see where the information takes us."

"What do you mean, Qqurant was replaced? What *conspiracy*?" Conspiracies are mostly imaginary, in my experience. People aren't that organized, they're terrible at keeping secrets, and they're generally too wrapped up in their personal drama to really commit themselves to collective action, even for nefarious reasons. Most attempts fall apart quickly.

She shrugged. "Maybe not replaced. Maybe brainwashed. I'm not sure yet. I thought about hanging around for the autopsy results, to see if there's anything weird about your dead friend's body, but then I'd miss my chance to recruit you, and a partnership seems more useful. Besides, if I'm being totally honest, I'm not as good at waiting as I should be. I'd rather be making moves."

"You want to recruit me into some investigation you're conducting. Because of my connections." At that moment, I should have been sleeping. I was supposed to wake up in a few hours, have a lavish breakfast, and attend a breakout session on the establishment of free ports. I was not supposed to be sitting in an interrogation room with someone who claimed, in a nebulous and deniable way, to be a spy.

"For your connections, sure, but also because you're highly motivated." Azad leaned forward. "You asked too many questions, Terrak. You got overly nosy. The bad guys tried to compromise you, the way they did Qqurant – the way they've compromised a *lot* of others, believe me. When they couldn't turn you, they fell back on plan B: frame you for murder. You were found standing over the corpse of a known associate, killed by your own decorative spear. If they faked that much, they can fake whatever other evidence they need, but I doubt they'll go to much effort. Why would they? There's no reason to think you'll survive long once you're in custody. If I was running their operation, I'd make sure your transport shuttle had a fatal fault. Or maybe you'll get knifed in the holding facility on that colony planet below us, in a random act of violence. But maybe not. Maybe the puppetmasters will get a few guys to pin your arms and legs while they blast another canister of whatever this is right in your face, and then clear you of all charges, and send you out to do their work."

That was a lot of maybes, but I didn't find any of the options reassuring. I was, however, thrilled to be in the company of someone who at least *claimed* to know what was going on. If I could orient myself, and figure out what the stakes were, perhaps I could find a way to extricate myself from this situation… and maybe even to profit from it. (Unlikely, I know, but I'm a trader at heart, and we can never stop looking for angles.) If she'd just stop being so damnably *vague*. "What work? What's the goal of this supposed conspiracy?"

Azad shook her head. "Wish I knew. I'm supposed to find out. All I know is, the puppetmasters have compromised people in your government, and the Federation, the Coalition, the Universities, the Kingdom, the Guild, everybody involved in the Greater Union. Not just that, but they also have Letnev agents, which makes me think they're involved in the alliance the Barony is putting together, the Legion. Somebody with connections like that could do all kinds of damage."

If this supposed conspiracy could pull the strings of two great opposing factions, they could do almost *anything*. Alter the entire financial structure of the galaxy. Manipulate supply chains, corner markets, vertically integrate every known industry, create multiple monopolies. They could starve any system they wanted, metaphorically *and* literally. You don't have to control the levers of power. Just the people who can reach those levers.

She shook her head. "Sorry. I'm heading off into spirals of speculation."

Same here, I thought.

"That's the problem with investigating a mysterious conspiracy with tendrils in a dozen polities," Azad said. "It tends to be distracting. So, let's focus. You're the latest victim of the conspiracy, and lucky for you, I just happened to be here when you got victimized, pursuing the same lead you stumbled on."

"You were looking into Qqurant?"

"You aren't the only one who noticed he was acting strangely. I've got a shortlist of people who've almost certainly been compromised, and Qqurant was on it."

"Why kill him if they controlled him?"

"Who knows? Maybe things reached the point where Qqurant was more useful to his new masters dead." She squinted. "I think we have about fifteen minutes before the actual cops show up and start asking you polite questions, or hitting you with sticks, or whatever it is they do in this jurisdiction. Do you want to wait around for that, or do you want to leave with me?"

I barked a laugh. "Flee the charges? Become a fugitive? That's the option you're offering me?"

She shrugged. "Fleeing is just step one. Step two is, you help me uncover the conspiracy. Prove your innocence. And maybe save the galaxy. But it's up to you. I could be a lunatic, and this whole murder charge could be a big misunderstanding that gets cleared up as soon as the lawyers get involved. Maybe a few hours from now you'll be walking around free, instead of on your way to getting murdered or mind-controlled. What do *you* think is most likely to happen?"

"Something was… very wrong with Qqurant." *Had* he been replaced by some sort of imposter? That didn't seem quite right. I thought it *was* Shelly, but profoundly traumatized, mentally broken, going through the motions of life and only barely managing that. A wave of despair rose up at the thought of my clever, quick-witted, murdered friend, and I pushed it down. I had to focus on keeping myself alive. "*Very* wrong."

She nodded. "We think he was one of the earliest… whatever. Replacements. Puppets. The early ones, they aren't as convincing, and they seem to get more glassy-eyed and vague and mumbly as time goes by. Maybe the puppetmasters were still working out the glitches with their brain-stealing or body-copying technology or something. The conspiracy started small, compromising people who didn't have a lot of personal security, but who went to *meetings* with the really important players, you know?"

I could see it. "Qqurant doesn't have a lot of power, but he works with people who do."

"Exactly. Maybe your buddy had his own little canister and sprayed it in the faces of his more powerful friends. The puppetmasters turned people like Qqurant, and used them to turn *others*, and so on up the ladder. I'd sure like to know how exactly they're compromising their targets. Seeing what's in that canister might help."

"How do you *know* all this? Where did you get this shortlist of candidates?"

"I am a trained investigator with very smart and well-connected bosses." She rose. "I'm also leaving. Are you coming with me, or are you going to sit there and hope for the best?"

I am, as a rule, a careful person. I study data. I do market research. But, in the end, whatever the numbers say, my decisions ultimately come down to my instincts. Not because I fetishize intuition, but because I trust that my mind is conducting calculations, analysis, and synthesis beyond the level of my conscious understanding. I've walked away from deals that looked great on paper and embraced ones that seemed questionable, and usually, my decisions worked out. Ninety percent of the time, anyway. Maybe eighty-five.

My instincts now were telling me to go with this woman. The worst case if I did was becoming a fugitive from justice, and that was pretty bad. If I stayed here, and she was right... the worst case was ending up dead, and that was much worse.

Except, no. The *worst* case if I stayed was being transformed into a hollow shell of myself and used as a pawn, like Shelly had been.

I stood up.

Azad grinned at me.

Azad had an array of useful override codes, including ones I was pretty sure only the chief of station security should possess. A facility like Shilsaad Station has many public-facing areas, but it also has myriad places the average visitor never sees: service corridors, maintenance tunnels, freight elevators, laundries, kitchens, pantries, and storage rooms. That's the world we passed through now: far less polished but far more functional, full of clanging and rushing and shouting, laughter and loafing and low conversation, stains and scuffs and doors that stuck a little before they slid open. Everything glamorous is built on grimier foundations.

We did not creep through the corridors silently. Azad led me openly through rooms filled with workers of various species, occasionally nodding and smiling at them, but mostly just breezing by. I learned long ago that if you walk with confidence and intent, you can reach all sorts of interesting places without being challenged. Her wearing a security uniform probably didn't hurt. I admired her brashness, though I couldn't share her confidence. Word must have gotten around about the killing, and there weren't *that* many Hacan on the station, so surely someone would wonder…

But no one did. At least, no one that made a fuss about it where we could see. Probably because no one would believe an escaped prisoner would walk around so openly. We made it to one of the hangars, where the station's dart-like security ships were located. The small ships were only big enough for two or three crew members, and were theoretically a last line of defense if the station came under attack ... but in practice they mostly did escort duty for dignitaries on larger ships entering and leaving the area.

"We're escaping in one of these?" I said when she approached one of the fighters. "Surely the station has ways to track their own ships?"

Azad stopped, turned, and stared at me, eyes wide. Her hand went to her mouth, trembling. After a moment, she whispered, "No. Oh, no. I never thought of that. How could I be so *stupid*? After all the years I've spent as a covert operative! Thank Sol I had an elderly merchant here to warn me, or I would have made a terrible mistake!"

I sighed. "Yes. Fine. Point taken."

"Good. Get in the ship, big guy."

"For the record, I'm only *middle-aged* for my species," I grumbled as I obeyed.

THE FAITHFUL II

Kote Strom, head of security on Shilsaad Station and devotee to the great work, sat on the floor with her back against the wall in her quarters and communed with her masters.

Since taking the sacrament, Kote did not feel pain as keenly as she once had, so the sore spots from Terrak slamming her against the wall were only distant aches. The shame of failure hurt far more. "I am sorry, guides, for how things went with the Hacan. Your contingency plan has been enacted, though. Terrak has been framed for the death of Qqurant, and will meet with an accident on the shuttle tomorrow." A misgiving – actually, a pair of misgivings – surfaced in Kote's mind, and because her masters were generally gentle and seldom showed anger, she dared to broach one. "Was he really such a threat, to require such extreme actions?"

The answer emanated through her mind. <*We made inquiries among the faithful. Terrak pretends to be a simple trader, but his influence extends through many factions, like root tendrils hidden in the soil. He is a creature of connections, and if he continues to ask questions at this delicate time, and spurs his associates toward deeper investigations, the faithful might be exposed. Terrak must be thoroughly discredited and removed. We cannot allow anything to endanger the summits on Moll Primus and Arc Prime.*>

"Yes, but … a murder at this meeting is *already* disruptive, isn't it? The Xxcha Kingdom is threatening to leave the negotiations–"

<When Terrak is dead, they will be satisfied. Any who are not satisfied can be bribed or otherwise soothed. The crime will become simply another point in the negotiation – while the discovery of our influence would end the alliance entirely.>

"Yes, guides. I see now."

<Something further troubles you. Let us ease your mind.>

A soothing wave passed through Kote as the sacrament released all the best chemicals in her brain, and she relaxed against the wall as tensions she hadn't realized she was holding bled away. Eyes half-closed in bliss, she said, "Qqurant. I killed him, and he didn't resist, but he barely seemed to understand what was happening. When he recruited me, he was so sharp, and so clever. I understand that he became a… liability to the great work, and had to be removed, but what caused that change in him? Why did he become so… hollow?"

<He was one of the first to accept the sacrament, and our guidance,> the voice, or voices, said in her mind. <After so much time spent in our service there was a certain amount of… degradation. Personality decay. Diminished faculties. It is regrettable.>

"Will that happen to me?" The prospect didn't worry Kote, exactly, but it seemed, to some distant part of her mind, important.

<We have refined our techniques and continue to work on the problem. You will last longer. But more importantly, you will last long enough. And even if your mind or body fail, perishing in the service of the great work is more noble than to live for nothing, is it not?>

"Yes, my guides," Kote murmured, and shivered with the ecstasy of purpose and service.

CHAPTER 3
FELIX

Felix Duval – captain of the cruiser *Temerarious*, leader of the covert operations team nicknamed "Duval's Devils", witness to the infamous "fractured void" experiment, rising star in the Mentak Coalition military – woke with a groan as his cabin lights flashed red and a siren shrieked at him from the ceiling speakers above his bunk. Those were emergency signals. There should not be an emergency here. They were parked in their ship outside Shilsaad Station, doing transport duty for a dignitary visiting the Greater Coalition summit. The biggest crisis around here should be running out of canapés.

He fumbled for the comm-switch beside the bed, but some override protocol had already turned on the viewscreen. Felix blinked into the bulbous face of his superior Fololire Jhuri, the dignitary in question, Undersecretary of Special Projects for the Mentak Coalition. Jhuri's chromatophores were flushed with the yellows of irritation. "Wake up, Felix. Things are falling apart, and we need you to pick up the pieces."

Felix sat up on the side of the bunk and rubbed his face. This was supposed to be his rest-and-recovery shift, and he'd prepared for it by having a drinking competition with Calred, his ship's security officer. (Felix lost, but he didn't mind; he played for love of the game.)

Rubbing his face wasn't working, so he slapped his own cheeks a couple of times, and that helped. He also found the switch that turned off the alarms, which helped more. "Sir. Yes. Present. What?"

Hylar didn't really sigh, not even the amphibious sub-species like Jhuri who could live in air or water, but Felix had grown up among the aliens, and he recognized the body language equivalent – chromatophores shifting to red, tentacles twitching. "Focus, Felix. This is important. Someone murdered one of the Xxcha delegates."

What, here? He looked out the window, at the spindle of the station and the frozen nova beyond. It was hard to imagine someone had died violently in that graceful structure, set against such grandeur. Wait. What did Jhuri want him to do about it? "I'm not much of a detective, but I guess I could–"

"We know who did the killing," Jhuri said. "A Hacan trade ambassador named Terrak. He was taken into custody almost immediately. But then he escaped."

Ahhh. That made more sense. "So you want me to catch him?"

"That's the idea, yes."

Felix managed not to grin; grinning after hearing some fancy official had died was inadvisable. But that disaster meant he had something to *do*, besides sitting here waiting for Jhuri to finish negotiating things, and that was a reason to be cheerful. Felix was happiest when he was in forward motion, in pursuit of some difficult-to-achieve goal, overcoming challenges and engaging in derring-do in the company of his trusted crew – wait. He had a horrible suspicion.

"Will you be joining us?" Felix asked. The *Temerarious* had

transported Jhuri to the summit and having the boss on board
for that long was weird enough. Usually, the undersecretary set
the mission parameters and then sent Duval's Devils to do the
job, with the understanding that if anything went terribly wrong,
Felix and his crew were pretty much on their own. That was life
in the clandestine services. Actually taking their handler on a
mission would be… distracting.

Fortunately, Jhuri gestured in the negative. "No, I'll provide
operational support remotely as needed, and I'll be in touch a *lot*
more than usual."

Ah, well, that was fine. There were always ion storms or
technical difficulties to blame communication delays on if Jhuri
became too intrusive.

"This situation requires a delicate touch," the Hylar went on.
"My superiors are worried this will delay the treaty signing, the
Federation is running around shouting because it happened on
one of their stations, and the Kingdom… well, you know the
Xxcha don't scream and throw things, but they're very, very
unhappy. Speaking of, there's going to be a temporary addition
to your crew."

Felix frowned. He'd had a horrible suspicion about the wrong
thing. He ran a three-person team – himself, Calred, and his
first officer, the Yssaril Tib Pelta – and they worked beautifully
together, a smoothly calibrated team. He didn't want help or
need a babysitter. "If I'm pursuing a fugitive, shouldn't I… start
pursuing? This hardly seems like the right time for new crew
member orientation."

"We don't even have a direction to point you in yet, Felix.
We only just realized Terrak is gone, because the security logs
were tampered with – he must have had inside help, which
suggests an organized plot, maybe one meant to disrupt the

Greater Union, rather than a crime of passion or some personal grudge."

"I still don't see–"

"An Xxcha was killed, Felix," Jhuri said. "The representatives of the Kingdom are insisting – politely, but implacably, you know how they can be – that an Xxcha be included on the mission to hunt Terrak down. They want to be sure you're properly invested and motivated."

"Ah," Felix said. "I guess that makes sense. You're Hylar, I'm human, Cal is Hacan, Tib is Yssaril – add an Xxcha and we're like the Greater Union in microcosm, right?"

"The optics of a team like that are good. And since the overall optics are otherwise terrible, we'll take all the good we can get. I won't say the success of the Greater Union depends on the swift apprehension of Terrak, but… let's just say it would help."

There were a few Xxcha with the Mentak Coalition delegation at the summit, and Felix tried to think of who they'd send with him. "It's not Rrimiel, is it? She's a good systems analyst but she goes *on* and *on* about hydroponic agriculture – we get it, you like lettuce, but that doesn't substitute for a personality–"

"It's not one of our people," Jhuri said. "The ambassador from the Kingdom is sending their personal bodyguard. Her name is Ggorgos Skal."

Felix had known many Xxcha, but they were from his culture, not the Kingdom itself, and while all the various species that called the Mentak Coalition home retained elements of their ancestral cultures, they had more in common with each other than with the modern offshoots of their common ancestors. The denizens of the Kingdom were famed for their diplomacy, their measured approach, their thoughtfulness, and their calm in the midst of chaos. Felix wasn't sure how any of that would be much help in a chase, when speed and rapid responses were requirements. There was something strange, though... "Hold on, did you say Ggorgos Skal, two words? The Xxcha have surnames now?"

"The second name is a sort of qualifier, or signifier," Jhuri said. "Not all the Xxcha use them, and they're not quite ranks, not quite titles... but sometimes they're a job description, or a status revealer – they might translate as 'senior' or 'doctor' or 'the wise' or 'the younger' or other things."

"So what does Skal mean?"

"Ah. You know how the Xxcha are renowned for their placid natures?"

"I do."

"Every culture has its exceptions," Jhuri said. "As best I can tell, 'Skal' means something like 'the righteously violent.'"

"Oh. Well. I can't wait to meet her," Felix said.

Felix stood in the hangar bay of the *Temerarious* with Calred and Tib Pelta. Calred had recently returned from a rest-and-relaxation rotation, and still had colorful beads woven into his mane from the beach resort. (Such decorations were a violation of Coalition Navy uniform order, but part of the fun of being a covert squad was a certain looseness when it came to the niceties of military protocol. Felix himself often kept the top button of his uniform jacket undone.)

They were discussing their new crew member, of course.

Tib Pelta, who was pragmatic by nature, said, "OK, but who's in *charge*?"

"I am," Felix said.

"Jhuri is," Calred said.

Felix sighed. "Well, yes, *ultimately*, but Jhuri gives out the missions, and I decide how to complete them."

"Sure, but this… murder turtle… is outside your chain of command," Tib pointed out. "Is she going to be a good soldier for you, or try to boss you around?"

"She can *try*," Felix said. "But this is my ship, and I make the decisions."

"All the decisions that Jhuri delegates to you," Calred said.

Felix glared. "Which is most of them."

"It could be good, having someone new on board," Calred said. "Maybe she plays cards. Maybe she plays cards *badly*."

"You probably shouldn't cheat someone who has 'righteously violent' in her name," Tib said.

Calred smirked. "I've never met a Xxcha who intimidated me. Someone who hides inside a shell at the first sign of trouble isn't intimidating."

"What about Qqmel?" Tib said. Qqmel was an Xxcha from the Mentak Coalition who ran with the raider fleets and had a shoulder-mounted autocannon; he tended to make a striking impression.

Calred went *hmm*. "All right, Qqmel, I'll grant you, is a little daunting, but Qqmel is a hardened raider, not the babysitter for some ambassador."

"The shuttle's docked," Felix said.

They stood at approximations of attention while the airlock cycled up to pressure. They were meeting a representative of another faction for a difficult cross-cultural mission, and Felix wanted to make a good impression.

Ggorgos Skal emerged from the airlock, carrying a heavy-looking black duffel bag in one clawed hand. Felix swallowed a gasp. Calred made a small sound of surprise that he turned into a cough. Tib Pelta said nothing, but the Yssaril were good at hiding their reactions.

The Xxcha, as a species, resembled immense bipedal tortoises, though in place of hard shells, they had artificial onces, "exo-carapaces", in a variety of designs. Some were painted, some studded with jewels, some smooth and gleaming, some pocked by kinetic fire or scorched by energy weapons in battle with the marks left as badges of honor. Ggorgos's exocarapace was beautiful, in a menacing sort of way: a matte black structure made of interlocking hexagonal panels, constructed of some material Felix couldn't immediately recognize, but which he assumed was highly armored. Her head was scarred, and one eye had been replaced with an embedded metal monocle where an oval lens glowed faintly yellow. "Felix Duval. Captain." Her voice was a rasp, as if her vocal cords were damaged.

Felix realized he had no idea of her rank, or how to refer to her, so he fell back on the basics, and hoped he wouldn't give offense. "Ggorgos Skal. Welcome aboard. We look forward to working with you."

Ggorgos just stared at him, then flicked her eyes – one black and gleaming, one yellow and shining – toward the others. "Calred. Security officer. Tib Pelta. First officer." A grunt. "Duval's Devils." Her rasp made the name sound like a joke, or a mockery, or maybe Felix was just feeling overly sensitive. She gazed at them for a moment, then said, "I need to stow my gear."

"I'll show you to your–" Felix began.

She slung her bag at his feet. "Just put my bag there. You can show me the bunk later. First, I need to review the ship's armaments. Calred, take me to the tactical board."

Felix looked down at the bag. No. This wasn't happening. "Listen. We're perfectly happy to have you on board, but I'm the captain here–"

"A high official of the Xxcha Kingdom was assassinated,"

Ggorgos said. "I will apprehend the killer. You are my support staff."

"I don't think so," Felix said.

"Your thoughts do not interest me. Check with your superior. He must not have explained the situation clearly enough, or perhaps you simply failed to listen. Calred, take me to the security console now."

Calred glanced at Felix, who sighed. "Go ahead. I'll call Jhuri and get this straightened out."

Ggorgos ignored him, just waited impatiently for Calred, until the Hacan shrugged and beckoned her down the corridor.

"She's nice," Tib Pelta said. "Almost makes me miss Thales."

Felix shuddered. Their first covert mission had involved ferrying a truly vile human scientist halfway across the galaxy. "No one is *that* bad."

Jhuri's face appeared on the screen in Felix's ready room. "Ggorgos says *she's* in charge here. Can you set her straight, please?"

"Ah." The Hylar's chromatophores flushed a deep purple. "She is, broadly speaking, in a technical sense... correct."

Felix closed his eyes for a moment. "You might have mentioned that." All he'd ever wanted was to have his own command, and the opportunity to do his nation proud (ideally while enjoying a bit of excitement along the way). He was in the military, and no stranger to taking orders, but to be supplanted on his own *ship*, by someone from an entirely different faction? That was hard to swallow.

"I was hoping it wouldn't be necessary. I just finished a call where I sadly failed to make any headway. When the Xxcha first suggested that Ggorgos lead the mission, we pointed out that we had our best people on the case, and her presence wasn't necessary at all. We thought adding her to your crew was enough of a compromise, but the Xxcha ambassador is… rather implacable. It's like arguing with a very polite stone. The Xxcha are really bothered by this. I gather Qqurant was well liked by a lot of important people. We're counting on the diplomatic ties the Xxcha can provide to make the Greater Union a success, and if they pull out, the whole enterprise could fall apart."

"But to be demoted on my own ship, Jhuri!"

"If Ggorgos tells you to fly into a black hole, you have my permission to mutiny. But as long as her plans are reasonable and tactically sound, why not go along with them? One of their people got killed on our watch, Felix. We can't undo that, but we can try not to make it any worse."

"Understood." Felix clicked off the comms, took a deep breath, and fastened the top button of his uniform. He was an officer of the Mentak Coalition, and he would comport himself with all appropriate dignity, even if, inside, he wanted to stomp his feet and punch the bulkhead.

"I think we got off on the wrong foot," Felix said.

Ggorgos, standing over a navigation panel, grunted.

The two of them were alone on the bridge. Calred was doing a manual check of the torpedo bays because Ggorgos had seen a number on a readout that wasn't perfectly optimal, though it was within acceptable range. Tib was off reviewing the dossier they'd been sent about Terrak's history and known associates so they could try to guess where he might head for sanctuary.

Felix went on, "There was some confusion, on my part, about our arrangements, and I… apologize for that."

This time he didn't even get a grunt. "Set a course for the Rantula sector, captain."

Felix frowned. "I thought we didn't know which way Terrak went?"

"I received an intel update a moment ago. I'm sure the Coalition will have one for you shortly. In the meantime, set the course. Every moment we fall behind is a moment a killer enjoys freedom."

Felix doubted being on the run was very enjoyable, but he took the point and went to the navigation terminal. While he was laying a course, he got the *ping* of a priority update from Jhuri: *Proceed to the Rantula sector.* There was a lot of supporting data included – information about a missing security ship, accounts from other vessels who'd seen a vehicle that couldn't be accounted for by local traffic control – but Felix just skimmed it. "Ggorgos," he said, "would you share your intelligence from the Kingdom with me as soon as you get it? Just so we're all working with the same information at the same time?"

"I see no reason to refuse." The Xxcha didn't look up from her panel, but it was a start.

"We can be more than transportation for you, Ggorgos. We want to catch Terrak as much as you do."

"Doubtful," Ggorgos said. "I will be in my quarters." The Xxcha stomped off the deck.

Felix sank into the captain's chair and sighed. He pulled up the information Tib had compiled on Terrak and the dead cultural minister. Maybe he'd find some useful insight that he could present to Ggorgos. He'd gone from running the ship to trying to find ways to impress the person who was *now* running the ship. The great virtues of the Mentak nation were resilience and adaptability. They were descended from prisoners, transported to a distant planet, considered outcasts and pirates, but they'd united, and risen to the heights of influence and prestige in galactic civilization. If their great founder Erwan Mentak was able to unite the disparate, feuding species of Moll Primus into a unified whole, overcoming their tribal affiliations and old prejudices to make something new, then surely Felix could get along with one brusque and zealous Xxcha. The important thing was the mission.

Also, the sooner Felix *finished* the mission, the sooner he could get rid of Ggorgos.

As Felix perused the details, though, he realized the crime made absolutely no sense. Terrak was by all accounts interested in two things: money and pleasure – and even the money was mostly a way to facilitate more pleasure. The Mentak Coalition had invited Terrak to the summit because he had an outsized level of influence with the leaders of the Emirates, considering his status and rank, because he was a lightly corrupt favor trader who was good at making friends. Felix's bosses thought Terrak could be wined, dined, and wooed into supporting favorable trading terms within the Greater Union, and to bring along some of his highly placed friends. Terrak had seemed happy to enjoy the thinly disguised bribes… until, for some reason, he'd murdered a random Xxcha cultural minister. Terrak and the victim were old friends, so maybe there was some personal reason for the violence hidden in their deep history, but it was hard to imagine what. If Terrak had planned to kill Qqurant, he could have done it in a more subtle way, so it must have been a crime of passion… but if it was a spur-of-the-moment assault, how could you explain that someone was prepared to smuggle Terrak off the station? That suggested planning, even a conspiracy, but to what possible end? To disrupt the formation of the Greater Union? Why would Terrak want to do that so badly he'd sacrifice his own good name and freedom to the cause? Unless someone was just using Terrak for that purpose.

Felix sent a note to Jhuri: Are we sure Terrak is the actual killer?

The response came quickly: He was found standing over the victim, with his spear stuck in the dead minister, so it sure looks that way.

Could be a frame-up, Felix sent. Part of an attempt to disrupt the Greater Union, maybe.

We're considering the possibility, Jhuri said. We're not idiots over here, Felix. The simplest way to find out what's going on is for you to find Terrak and ask him.

If I can keep Ggorgos from killing him first.

Jhuri replied: By all accounts, Ggorgos never kills anyone until she's finished with them first, and she likes to take her time.

"Uh, Felix?" Tib said over the comms. "I think you should come look at this. I found something Shilsaad Station security missed."

Felix went to Tib's office. Her specialties were infiltration and intelligence gathering, and she also had a natural affinity for data analysis. Her office was wall-to-wall screens, and they displayed a dizzying array of data, from loops of video to blown-up still photographs to pages of text with sections highlighted and color-coded according to some arcane system of Tib's own devising. Tib herself sat in a swivel chair in the center of it all, fingers manipulating a tablet in her lap.

"What did you find?" Felix moved a pile of binders off a chair to sit beside her.

"A human member of station security disappeared at the same time Terrak did, and the current theory is that she's the one who helped him escape. Her name is… some human name, it doesn't matter. I assume it's a fake anyway, though so far, the identity stands up to scrutiny, so it must be a really good fake. There are some weird gaps in the station's personnel files – all photographs of her are gone, along with any security footage that might have shown her face."

"She's a professional, then," Felix said.

"You could say that." There was something peculiar in Tib's tone, and Felix knew bad news was coming. "All Jhuri sent us was a description of the woman, and you know how useful *those* are. If she cut and colored her hair and put on high heels and a baggy coat, she wouldn't match the description anymore. I was annoyed by the lack of photos, though, and you know how I get when something annoys me."

"I annoy you, and you became my lifelong best friend."

"OK, the *other* way I get. Stubborn and mildly obsessive, I mean. I kept digging through the station systems and found out the employees set up a secret social media intranet. It's basically a forum for gripes about management and guests and so on. There are some photos there, very informal, including a group shot from some junior officer's going-away party a week before the summit." She tapped her terminal, and one of the screens filled with a crowded shot of about thirty people holding drinks and laughing and jostling each other, some caught frozen in mid-dance-step. "I ran facial recognition to match all the people at the party with the photos in the personnel files," Tib said. "Everyone was accounted for... except one." More tapping at the tablet, and the photo on the screen zoomed in and cropped, isolating a single face, turned partly away from the camera. It was a human woman, her hair buzzed short on one side, her mouth thrown open in a laugh, and–

Felix groaned. "No. It's not. It can't be. It's just a superficial resemblance. Right?"

"All humans look basically alike to me," Tib said. "So, I pulled up one of *our* photos from ship security and ran a comparative analysis. That picture on the screen isn't very high quality, so I can't be absolutely sure, but I got an eighty-seven percent probability match." She sighed. "I'm pretty sure the mystery guest is Amina Azad."

Felix put his head in his hands. Amina Azad was a covert operative from the Federation of Sol. She was a dreadful combination of the unpredictable and the implacable, wickedly good at improvising, and a joyful sower of chaos and confusion. She'd once pursued him across the galaxy, and with the help of an equally horrible Letnev officer named Severyne Dampierre, she'd even seized control of the *Temerarious* for a while. If Felix had to pick, of the two of them, he'd honestly rather face Severyne again – sure, she'd stab him in the neck too, but at least she wouldn't crack jokes while she did it.

"We'd better tell Jhuri," Felix sighed. "We should also tell Ggorgos. I asked her to share information with us, so that should go both ways."

"By 'we' I assume you mean 'you,'" Tib said. "Talking to Ggorgos makes me nervous. When she looks at me it's like she's running down a list of ways to dismember me."

"The burdens of captainhood," Felix muttered.

Not much later, Ggorgos stood in Tib's office, reviewing the data, while Jhuri's face watched from another screen. He'd set up an office on Shilsaad Station, and there was a large fern and a bad painting of a beach in the background. "This Azad," Ggorgos said at last. "She is employed by the Federation of Sol?"

"Not officially," Jhuri said. "She's a former naval officer who left the service many years ago to become an independent security contractor. Unofficially, we know she was employed as a deniable asset by the Federation a few years ago, when Felix tangled with her. She may have actually become a freelancer since then, or she could still be working for the Federation. I'm making inquiries with my counterparts among the humans, but the nature of deniable assets is that the people in charge have a tendency to deny them."

"A Hacan and a human conspired to murder one of my compatriots at a diplomatic summit. We must ascertain whether they did so at the behest of their governments, or for reasons of their own." This was a very long speech for Ggorgos.

"I can't imagine that the Emirates of the Federation directed Terrak and Azad to do this," Jhuri said. "Both those nations have fairly good relations with the Kingdom, and if they wanted to disrupt the Greater Union, they could just pull out of the treaty."

"Governments are not monolithic," Ggorgos said. "There are factions within factions. Perhaps Azad and Terrak represent minority members of their respective governments who wish to see the Greater Union fail. When we apprehend them… we will ask."

"You can't believe anything Amina Azad says," Felix offered. "She's treacherous. And by all accounts Terrak tells lies for a living. He's a trade ambassador with a fondness for bribes."

"I am adept at extracting the truth," Ggorgos said.

"Torture doesn't actually work," Tib said from the corner. "People just tell you what they think you want to hear, so you'll stop hurting them."

"I am aware." Ggorgos's voice was even frostier than usual. "I have experienced torture, at the hands of skilled practitioners. I have my own methods. They have proven effective." She clomped out of the room.

"She's charming, isn't she?" Felix looked at Jhuri. "Do you know how she, ah… got to be the way she is?"

"Her service record is sealed," Jhuri said. "Apparently everything from the moment she enlisted to the day she was assigned as the ambassador's bodyguard is a state secret. I think you can assume she's good at her job, though."

"I'd better make sure we do ours just as well, then. Do we have any idea why Terrak is headed to the Rantula system?"

"Amazingly, yes," Jhuri said. "He has two known associates there. One is an agricultural exporter who specializes in fruit. We think he's an unlikely target. The other is a professional liaison and information broker called the Facilitator – no one's even sure what species they are, or if they're an individual at all. They connect people with other people for a living."

"What, like hired killers, professional thieves, things like that?"

"Certainly," Jhuri said. "But they facilitate legitimate business meetings, too. If you desperately need an audience with someone you have no way to reach, the Facilitator can help, for a price. That's how Terrak knows them – our murderous Hacan can secure audiences with certain Emirate officials, especially in the economic departments, so he's part of the Facilitator's network."

"This Facilitator sounds like the kind of person who could help you disappear," Felix said.

"Or hire you to disrupt a diplomatic summit," Tib said.

"Or first the second, and then the first," Jhuri said. "The Facilitator operates out of a little moon in the Rantula system. That's where you're headed. We don't advise bursting in and blowing things up – the Facilitator is the kind of person you pay off, not the kind of person you beat up – though the specific tactical approach is at Ggorgos's discretion."

"Shouldn't you be telling Ggorgos all this then?" Felix said.

"She knows," Jhuri said. "She received substantially the same intelligence from the Kingdom about half an hour ago, as best I can determine. Their diplomatic connections make them *slightly* faster at finding things out than we are, and they tell Ggorgos everything before they mention any of it to us."

Felix ground his teeth. "She told me she'd share."

"Did she really?" Tib said.

"Well, not in exactly those words," Felix admitted. "She said she couldn't think of a reason *not* to share."

"I guess she must have come up with one," Jhuri said.

THE FAITHFUL III

Kote Strom snarled at her subordinates one last time, slammed the door to her office, and crawled underneath her desk, where it was quiet, and dark, and she could try to think. She had failed the guides, not once, but twice, and *that* was a pain that made her whimper.

<*What has happened?*> the voice in her head said. <*We are too distant to taste your thoughts directly. You must tell us what causes your distress.*>

"Terrak has escaped. We do not know how. Someone helped him. One of my... one of my own people, we think, though we don't know why."

<*He must be captured and killed.*>

"Yes, of course, but I'm not in charge of that operation, guides – station security is in some disgrace now, as you might imagine, with a murder and an escape in the space of barely a day. The Mentak Coalition and the Xxcha Kingdom are coordinating the pursuit. The operation is still being run from here, and as a professional courtesy they're giving me updates, so I can, at least, keep you informed. They've sent a team of operatives to pursue Terrak and his accomplice."

A pulse of pain shot through Kote's head, making her clutch her skull and moan. *<We must have one of the faithful on that ship!>*

"We do, we do!" Kote said. "I checked. If you reach out, you'll find one of us on a ship called the *Temerarious*–"

Calm flooded her mind, and she slouched in relief.

<Yes, we see. Good. Terrak cannot be allowed to tell his story or share any of his speculations. Our operative will kill him on sight.>

"There is, ah… another problem. The canister that holds the sacrament was stolen from my locker. I fear Terrak has it."

A long silence, and then, in a voice as chill as the void: *<We see.>*

"If they find someone to analyze the sacrament, they might be able to trace–"

<The implications are clear to us. We will take further steps to ensure Terrak's capture.>

"What steps, guides?"

<We have other faithful nearby, with other resources. We will mobilize them as well. This Terrak will be pursued from many sides. Escape will be impossible. The great work will succeed.>

"What shall I do, guides?"

<Don't make any more mistakes,> the voice said, and a cascade of pain – needles, teeth, acid, ice – poured through Kote's brain, leaving her curled on the floor of her office… but she was grateful even for that.

She was, at least, still permitted to serve.

CHAPTER 4
TERRAK

"Off to see the Facilitator, then?" Azad said, piloting the little ship through the void toward the Rantula system.

"It seems like an obvious destination for a fugitive and his mysterious benefactor." I'd figured out how to make the co-pilot's seat recline and was resting with a cloth over my eyes.

"Probably not so mysterious anymore. I covered my tracks as best I could, but the Greater Union people will be highly motivated to track us down, and sadly, I've had some past interactions with the Mentak. If I missed a photo, somebody there will recognize me."

That was mildly interesting. I lifted the cloth from my eyes and looked at her. "What was the nature of those past interactions?"

"It's all double-secret classified," Azad said.

"Ah."

"Fortunately, I don't give two craps about that. What happened was, my bosses sent me to steal a guy from a Coalition colony world. The Coalition didn't like that, and they stole him *back*, and then I had to go and steal him *again*, and it was a whole thing. This one Hylar, Jhuri, he was my opposition on that operation. I actually saw him at the summit."

"I am familiar with him," I said. "He has a very vague job title, something about 'special projects', but everyone assumes he commands squads of elite black ops assassins."

Azad snorted. "Maybe he does. I didn't meet any. Just some jerks with a fast ship and better-than-average luck."

"They got the best of you, then?" That wasn't comforting.

She shrugged. "It's more like we all failed *together*. I walked away and kept my job at the end, and looking back, parts of it were pretty fun. Like, I met this girl–"

"Please spare me tales of your romantic adventures," I said.

"Your loss. It's a good story. Two people from different worlds, brought together by circumstance, forced to work as a team, finding common cause in a shared enemy… it's a whole enemies-to-lovers-and-then-back-to-enemies-again sort of thing."

"I'm sure it would make a wonderful serial drama, but I'm more concerned with my future than your past, Azad."

"Fine, be like that. So we'll drop in on the Facilitator – I never met the guy, are they even a guy, or like a consortium, or what?"

"They are a shining black obelisk with a speaker in the side, usually," I said. "I have never seen them or heard their unaltered voice. That's how they operate. In the shadows."

"An entity after my own heart," Azad said. "I love shadows. That's why I set so many fires – you get lots of shadows cast in the light of burning things."

"Let's try to keep any burning to a minimum. Anyway, I just said going to see the Facilitator would make sense. That's why we aren't actually going to *do* it."

Some people are hard to read because they're impassive and blank. You have to watch them carefully to catch fleeting micro-expressions that give away their thoughts, and those are wildly different for every species, not even counting variations within cultures and subcultures. Amina Azad obscured her true feelings in a different way; she was incredibly expressive, always showing *something*, usually a variety of malign delight, and the trick was looking deeper to see what her *true* feelings were, always hidden by the tricksterish mask. I didn't know her well enough at that point to tell if I'd truly surprised her.

She cackled and said, "Beautiful, I love it. Anyone who gets a sense of our bearing and looks at your known associates will assume that's where we're going. So, what's the *actual* destination?"

"My other usual contact in the Rantula system is an agricultural importer and exporter. He has contracts with many colony worlds with fruit orchards, and I've helped him make some useful connections, especially selling his wares to Federation ships in this region of space. Humans are vulnerable to a vitamin deficiency disorder called scurvy, and while there are supplements that can help, your people generally prefer fresh fruit to dry pills."

"Ooh, yeah, scurvy is nasty. Has all kinds of gross effects. Your teeth fall out, your joints go to hell, you're irritable – which is a natural response to having your teeth fall out and your joints hurt, probably, but even beyond that. Do you know what the wildest symptom of scurvy is?"

"I'm sure you'll tell me."

"Scurvy stops your body from producing collagen," she said. "In humans, and maybe Hacan too, collagen is the stuff scar tissue is made of. So, in advanced cases of scurvy, old wounds you thought were totally healed can *open back up again*. It turns out, you never truly recover from the damage you take in this life – you're never *really* as good as new again. You carry your wounds with you forever, and the best you can hope for is that they get hidden away."

I thought about that. "I feel like you're trying to make some kind of philosophical point."

Azad cocked her head. "Nah. That doesn't sound like me. I don't need philosophy. I just do stuff. Thinking about why would only slow me down. Anyway. You were saying. We're going to see your fruit guy? Does he do chemical analysis on the side?"

"We are not, and he does not. I'm sure if anyone realizes we're heading to the Rantula system, they'll send someone to check his warehouse, too. I want to avoid my known associates entirely."

"We're going to an *unknown* associate then. Those are my favorite kind."

"Yes. But I met her through the, as you say, my 'fruit guy'. Lonrah is a chemist, a Hylar, who makes her money from the production of bespoke recreational drugs."

"Ooh."

"Her most expensive wares can be tuned to individual brain and body chemistry, for a variety of species. She acquires many of her raw materials, rare botanicals and organic compounds, from my agricultural friend. I made contact with her years ago, and meet her surreptitiously, under the cover of other appointments."

"Ha, so you're a drug dealer, too?"

"I will sell anything there's a market for," I said. "Assuming there's some profit in it beyond the merely monetary. The Quieron's personal facilitator is a connoisseur of unusual psychedelics and euphorics, and my partnership with Lonrah allowed me to strengthen my relationship with him."

"The Quieron is like the king of your people, right?"

I growled. "The Quieron is an elected representative who speaks for the united emirates of the Hacan and resolves disputes among the clans. We do not have *kings*."

"OK, I didn't mean to stick a thorn in your paw. Take it easy. I knew your shady connections were going to come in handy. This Lonrah can take a look at the stuff in that canister and tell us what we're dealing with, right?"

"That is my hope," I said.

"How do we get a message to her?"

"I generally just turn up," I said. "She's an agoraphobe, so she's always home."

"Why is it called Huntsman's Moon?" Azad asked as we followed the bored traffic controller's instructions to a designated landing zone.

I shrugged. "I have no idea. Probably named after some early settler."

"It's a good thing I don't believe in omens, or I'd say this is a bad one. If there's hunting going on, I prefer to be the predator, and right now, we're mostly the prey."

I had discovered, to my chagrin, that I rather enjoyed Azad's company. She had that human brashness and impulsiveness that can be so invigorating (when it's not irritating), but she'd also proven herself a capable operator. Getting me off that station could not have been easy, but she'd made it look that way. She was worthy of my respect, though not, as yet, my trust. I believed we had a common enemy, at least, and that would have to do for now.

Azad settled the ship onto the surface at the end of a row of other vessels. She'd done something to disguise the ship's transponder, so in theory, we wouldn't be immediately identified as escaped fugitives. "If you need anything from the ship, grab it now. We're going to have to find another ride off the moon."

I spread my hands. "I appear to be fully packed."

"We are traveling pretty light. Maybe we can find you another spear at least."

"I am not particularly adept with spears. We carry them mostly for ceremonial purposes."

"Sure, but when you're a two-and-a-half-meter-tall lion-guy with a polearm on your belt, you don't *have* to be good with it, because nobody bothers you anyway."

"That has been my experience," I agreed. "But it's hardly a priority. We won't need to menace Lonrah to get her help."

We disembarked. I wouldn't miss the cramped little ship, though I missed my *own* vessel, the *Afterparty*. I wondered if I'd ever see her again.

Huntsman's Moon had a breathable atmosphere, though the air was a bit thin and acrid – typical of terraformed worlds engineered to sustain the lives of as many different species as possible.

"Not much of a skyline, is it?" Azad looked at the low cluster of buildings a few hundred meters away from our landing zone.

There were only two major cities on the moon, each near a pole, where water and ice was most plentiful. We were in the northernmost city, Missulena, the oldest settlement on the moon. "Large portions of the city are still underground, and there are even a few domed areas left, from before this place had breathable air. The domes are now full of atmospheres we'd find inhospitable, neighborhoods set aside for those species who don't cope well with what we're breathing."

Azad tilted her head back. "Nice view when you look up, anyway. I grew up near a gas giant, Meginstjarna, so having a huge storm-world hanging over my head always comforts me."

The planet we were orbiting, Tegenaria, was a swirl of orange and blue clouds, and filled nearly a quarter of the sky. No one lived there – the clouds were full of leviathan aliens, unintelligent but hostile, and since they weren't good to eat and their bodily fluids had no useful properties, no one bothered with the planet much. With seventy moons, there was plenty of other real estate available, and you didn't have to rig up floating cities on any of them.

"Did you just reveal something about your personal life?" I said as we walked toward the city.

"I'm an open book! I was trying to tell you about my *love life* before you shushed me earlier. If you're curious now, there was this Letnev–"

"Again, please. My sensibilities are too delicate. Let's just go see Lonrah." There was a transit hub near the landing area, and Azad used a smart ring to acquire day passes for us. "Aren't you worried about leaving a data trail?" I asked her.

She snorted as we pushed through the gate, both of us with hoods up to disguise us from any security cameras, and joined the small crowd waiting on the platform. The travelers were mostly humans with a smattering of Hacan and the odd representative of other species. The station was pretty, with cream-colored pillars carved with representations of the local moons. "I've got a bunch of accounts under a bunch of names and corporate designations, and the ring cycles through them. The encryption is really robust, but even if someone cracks it, they won't find anything useful. My resources are more limited than I'd like – my bosses don't trust me *that* much – but I can safely buy us train fare."

The local mass transit system was less a train and more a series of windowed pods that hovered in magnetic fields, but fair enough. I consulted a wall map – not having a personal terminal, tablet, gauntlet, or even ring of my own was annoying – and found the right place on the platform to wait. Lonrah lived in a distant, industrial part of the city, and since our journey took place outside regular commuting hours, we were alone in our pod. Azad amused herself by reading the graffiti aloud while I sat on a padded bench with my elbows on my knees and my head in my hands, massaging my temples.

The worst part about running for your life is how simultaneously tense and boring it can be. There's a lot of time spent just moving through space, or waiting to do so, with nothing to occupy the mind but one's terrible predicament. Azad said there was a vast conspiracy at work, one that had wormed its way through multiple governments, and that conspiracy was after *me*, because I'd been unlucky enough to stumble into the middle of their operation. Now my only hope for survival was to unravel that conspiracy. No one with knowledge of my official resume would have selected me for a mission like *that*. I had to hope Azad was right, and that I could prove useful to her investigations... because if I *wasn't* useful to her, I had no doubt she would cheerfully abandon me to my fate. There wouldn't even be any malice in the act. I thought she liked me, in fact... but she was a professional, despite her jocular air.

The pod hissed to a stop, and we disembarked. This station was rather less pretty, a low-roofed structure, open to the air on all sides, with trash blowing across the platform. We went through the exit gates, and Azad raised an eyebrow at me. "I don't think we'll have much luck getting a pedi-cab out here, but I can try to steal some ground transportation."

"Lonrah's lab is within walking distance." The air was chilly, and I wished for a heavier coat. I'd have to make Azad use some of her untraceable funds to get me a change of clothes, at least, before we left; there were Hacan shops here. I took off my sash and stuffed it into a pocket. Such an accessory was appropriate for the summit, but here, it would just look like I was trying too hard. The rest of my clothes were unexceptional apart from their fine quality, but they were wrinkled, and would become rank if I wore them too much longer.

We set off along the pavement, past the blank facades of warehouses and fabrication plants and empty lots that were nevertheless warded with chain link and razor wire. After half a kilometer, I led Azad down an alley between two brick buildings to what looked like a large utility box, marred with graffiti and scratches.

I pressed a few seemingly random locations on the box, and the front panel popped open, revealing not wires or controls but a tiny elevator. I squeezed in, and Azad joined me to make it an even tighter squeeze. The doors closed, and we waited.

"Who's your friend, Terrak?" a speaker in the ceiling said. Lonrah's artificial voicebox had a metallic edge. She thought it made her sound menacing, and if you didn't know her, it probably did.

"Her name is Amina Azad," I said. "She's helping me with a problem. We have need of your professional services."

"I heard you murdered someone, Terrak," Lonrah said. "That doesn't sound much like you."

"News travels … faster than I anticipated," I said.

"Oh, it's not trending at the top of the feeds or anything," she said. "I just have alerts set up for basically everyone I've ever met. Because you never know. Knowledge is power and all that."

"I am innocent," I said. "You might be able to help me prove that."

She was silent.

Azad closed her eyes. "Terrak, if you brought me to someone who is going to *turn you in*–"

"Come on down," Lonrah said, and the elevator lurched into motion.

"I wasn't worried about her turning me in," I said. "Lonrah was expelled from the university on Jor for some of her more unconventional experiments. Now she works in areas that are at best quasi-legal and at worst forbidden in major systems. As a result, she doesn't like authorities very much."

"You are an actual *literal* government official," Azad pointed out.

"Yes, and that fact was always something of an impediment to true intimacy between us. I think Lonrah will like me better as a fugitive."

The elevator opened into a long narrow room lined on both sides by shelves filled with jars, which were filled with various things, many of them disgusting.

"This place looks like a museum of medical oddities crossed with an herb shop," Azad said.

"Lonrah collects unusual biological samples, and studies them to see if they have any useful properties. She found the cure for Gungar's Rot in a clump of swamp mud – I think selling that pharmaceutical patent is the way she secured initial funding for her operation. These days, she's less interested in curing unusual fungal infections, and more interested in turning brains into fountains of pure bliss."

"A noble form of employment," Azad said.

We proceeded between the shelves, across the polished floor, made of black stone with little starlike specks of white. Chosen because of how pretty it looked on psychedelic drugs, I'd always assumed. I ducked through a beaded curtain, into a little anteroom lined with shelves full of tea canisters and boxes of crackers and cookies. The next doorway was covered by a plastic flap that unsealed with a *schloop* and then sealed back closed after us. A few short steps through the plastic umbilicus took us to a matching doorway at the other end. "Uh, do we need to be in clean-suits or something?" Azad said. "I'm getting bio-weapons-lab feelings here."

"No," I replied. "This is just a safeguard. She keeps the nastier things well contained. As for any contamination we might bring in – well, if we tracked in some horrible pathogen, Lon's sensors would detect them, and she'd probably be very excited to examine them."

We went on into the lab, a far sleeker, cleaner, and better-lit area than we'd seen so far, with worktables and glass-fronted cabinets and mysterious silver and white equipment everywhere. Lon was small even for a Hylar, and she sat nestled in a mech suit nearly as big as my body, fitted with an array of articulated limbs tipped with delicate pincers and assorted diagnostic equipment.

"Terrak! And your new friend. What can I do for you?" She worked delicate levers with her pseudopods and marched the suit toward us.

"What have you got in the way of human-compatible combat drugs?" Azad said before I could answer.

"Oh, all sorts of stimulants, focus drugs, pain blockers, sensory boosters, the works."

Azad grinned. "I'm gonna want some of all of those."

The idea of Azad on *stimulants* was rather alarming – humans were energetic as a rule, and she was already an extreme outlier on their scale – but I liked the idea of her investing in combat drugs. That meant, if it came to fighting, she'd be the one to leap into action, allowing me to observe, which was the position I preferred.

Lonrah glanced at me. "I can take a blood sample and get started on some personalized items, sure. It'll only take an hour or so to analyze your samples and chem-print the product."

"That's it? You didn't have to take a break from being a fugitive to make introductions for this kind of transaction, Terrak. I thought it was going to be something *weird.*"

"We'll do the weird stuff while we wait for my drugs to be ready," Azad said. "You tell her about the canister, Terrak. I'm going to check out some of these news stories she mentioned and see what I can glean about the state of the investigation." She found a battered crate labeled "DO NOT SHAKE" to sit on, and stabbed at her gauntlet, pulling up the feeds.

I showed Lon the canister. "Someone attacked me and tried to spray me in the face with this. I fought them off, and they escaped. Not long afterward, I was framed for murdering one of my oldest friends. I suspect these events are connected."

One of her mechanical arms uncurled and took the canister from me. "So, you'd like to know what they tried to spray you with. Could just be poison, or something to knock you out, right?"

"Could be," I agreed. "But… we have another theory." I opened my mouth to tell her about how strangely Shelly had acted, and Azad's theory that people were being brainwashed or replaced, but Lonrah held up one of her fleshy pseudopods in a "stop" gesture.

"Don't tell me," she said. "I don't want to be influenced. You can't go around prejudicing the *science*."

"You might not want to, ah, risk inhaling any of it–"

She flushed the colors of amusement. "You'll be shocked to hear I have protocols for dealing with unidentified and potentially deadly substances, Terrak. Let me draw some of your friend's blood, and then I'll get into analyzing this."

"Can I borrow a terminal?" I said. "I'd like to check the feeds myself, and see how much trouble I'm in."

"I don't think you're going to like it at all, actually, but feel free," she said. "My server room is just through that door, and there's a terminal you can use."

I spent a rather demoralizing hour reading about myself. There were quotes from some of my colleagues, expressing shock and dismay, but not nearly enough of them were insisting I must have been framed or was obviously innocent of these scurrilous charges. Being found standing over a corpse with your own spear sticking out of the body tended to dampen such doubts, apparently.

Azad was amusing herself, instead of amusing herself with *me*, so I had nothing to do but read about my perfidy. Azad's name was left out of the accounts, and indeed, there was no suggestion that I'd had help escaping at all, least of all from station security, though I was sure the authorities knew. They were just holding that information back, probably because it made *everyone* look bad.

There were lots of pieces speculating about how my vicious and senseless crime might impact the plans for the Greater Union, with somber quotations from the Xxcha Kingdom and the Mentak Coalition. I was wondering about that myself. It seemed like such a scandal was obviously bad news for the alliance, but at least one respected columnist said: "This Terrak is clearly on the payroll of cowards opposed to the Greater Union. The fact that such treacherous people are opposed to the treaty is a strong argument for moving forward as planned. If we let this disrupt the Union, then we're letting terrorists like Terrak win." I mused, not for the first time, that writers of political opinion pieces could make almost any event an argument for whatever they wanted.

I returned to the lab. "Azad. Who do you think is behind this conspiracy? If they're manipulating the prospective members of the Greater Union, *and* of the Legion, they must belong to some other faction, right? Trying to diminish the effectiveness of those alliances?"

"Like maybe one of the great big bogeymen your Union is supposed to protect against?" Azad said. "Could be. The N'orr don't do subtlety. I've met the Creuss and they're spooky as anything, but I feel like they'd be more likely to fill your guts with frogs or turn you into a cloud of radioactive glitter or something than enact a complex plan based on social engineering. The L1Z1X… maybe. Their whole thing is cybernetics and the mindnet. I'm open to the possibility."

"There are rumors of other forces… nightmarish creatures attacking the edges of the galaxy, though who knows if they even exist…"

"Oh, they do," Azad said. "I've even seen them. But though some of them look a little like spiders, they aren't exactly delicate web spinners. And, yeah, I've considered the other rumors. I'm pretty sure the Mahact are imaginary, and the Titans are more the brute force types, if the stories are true."

"How about this shadowy information dealer I've heard

rumors about? No one knows anything about their true motives, and they're rumored to have agents everywhere."

Azad nodded. "Yeah. That's a possibility I'm considering. One of many, honestly. But I think you're starting off from a faulty premise anyhow."

"In what way?"

"It sounds like you think the conspiracy is trying to disrupt the Greater Union and the Legion, and I've got my doubts. Some of the people I'm pretty sure have been compromised are the ones pushing hardest for those treaties. So, ask yourself: why would someone want to bring all those factions *together*? Don't assume it's an outside group, either. It could be one of the member states of either organization, trying to manipulate the rest. Or it could be some totally unaffiliated bad actors. We just don't know enough yet."

Lonrah reappeared through a door in the rear of the lab. I am not a master of Hylar body language, but I could tell immediately she was troubled. "This is very weird," she said. "How much do you know about the Arborec?"

I shuddered. "More than I'd like." I'd met a lot of species in my business. None had disturbed me so much.

Azad went *hmm*. "They're just about the most *alien* aliens we're actually able to talk to, even compared to the Creuss. Sapient plants. It's pretty impressive they managed to build spaceships, honestly."

"They're native to a planet called Nestphar," Lonrah said. "They're plants, yes, but it's more than that – the Arborec are composed of many species, some ambulatory and some not, with many grown for specialty purposes, but all symbiotically and telepathically linked by a planet-spanning cloud of spores. They call that connection, shared by all living things on the planet, 'the Symphony'. It's better to think of the Arborec as a conscious ecosystem than as a species in the conventional sense."

"So, your basic hive-mind sort of thing," Azad said.

"In a sense, but they can send out representatives who have a sort of temporary individuality, called the Letani. Those are the ones who make contact with the rest of the galaxy's inhabitants, and they carry a miniature version of the Symphony with them, generating their own spore field to allow communication beyond Nestphar. When they return home, I gather they're sort of absorbed, giving the Symphony the knowledge and experience they acquired while they were elsewhere."

"I was in a room with an Arborec representative, once, during a trade negotiation," I said. "It was one of the most unnerving experiences of my life." (And not just because the Arborec barely understand the concepts of ownership or property.) "The Arborec can't speak, by word or gesture – they only communicate telepathically among themselves. So, when they have to talk to other species, the Letani acquire corpses, and reanimate them through some... fungal alchemy, and use those bodies as mouthpieces. It's horrible. Talking to the *corpse* of someone, puppeted around, their original consciousness gone..."

"Yeah, I've heard of those, the Dirzuga," Azad said. "Somebody I know had to... eliminate one, once, to disrupt... well, it's not important. The Dirzuga was using a human body. My colleague stabbed her, and the Dirzuga didn't even react, just stared at her, and then said, 'This is a new sort of conversation'. So, then he started cutting off limbs and stuff, and the Dirzuga kept saying 'Please provide context for this interaction', and honestly it came down to fire and acid to clean the whole mess up." She crossed her arms. "I assume we aren't just sharing our best weird alien stories, though. What's in the canister, Lonrah?"

"Spores," she said. "An engineered variant of a fungus called Arzuga. I've only seen a sample of Arzuga once before, collected by a friend of mine and smuggled to me in the greatest secrecy."

"What's so special about Arzuga?" Azad asked.

"That's the fungus the Arborec implant in the brains of dead bodies to create the Dirzuga."

THE FAITHFUL IV

Doctor Astin Canner wasn't sure what the point of this autopsy was. He stood over the exam table in Shilsaad Station's tiny pathology lab, a space he'd hardly ever had to use before, and which, in his opinion, he didn't really need to use *now*. The victim, some Xxcha cultural minister, had been killed by a spear, which was unusual, but easy to diagnose. The weapon was thrust down vertically through the victim's main body cavity with substantial force, causing massive trauma to the minister's internal organs. The crime hardly needed further investigation, at least when it came to determining cause of death.

But that intense-looking Hylar, Jhuri, had insisted on a thorough examination of the body, and the Xxcha Kingdom officials had agreed, so here Canner was, taken away from his usual duties. Canner was human, but an expert in xenobiology, which was a good fit for the head of medicine on Shilsaad Station, where so many aliens congregated, although the full range of his expertise was seldom called upon. Usually, all Canner had to deal with was bumps, bruises, and the sort of viruses that liked to spread through convention center crowds. Doing an autopsy was admittedly a diversion, but not a pleasant one. He *liked* things simple. That's why he'd taken this job.

There were some intriguing peculiarities, though. The toxicology screening had turned up drastically elevated hormonal levels in the victim's blood – mostly chemicals associated with pleasure and calm, oddly enough, rather than the fear-chemicals you would have expected in someone who was murdered by a spear. Canner didn't know what to make of that data. Jhuri said the victim had exhibited odd behavior, possibly even signs of dementia, on the evening of his death, so maybe there was some sort of issue with brain function that indirectly caused the anomalous readings.

Canner's bone saw whirred, and in a few moments, he had the top of the victim's skull ready for removal. He twisted and pulled away the bone cap, set it aside in a sterile tray, and angled the light to shine on the minister's exposed gray matter.

He hadn't seen the inside of an Xxcha's head since his fellowship, but even someone with no experience at all would have known something was *very* wrong here. For one thing, the gray matter wasn't gray. The dead Xxcha's brain was threaded through with green tendrils, almost mossy in spots, and there were tiny red bulbs nestled in some of the folds. The bulbs looked like miniature versions of the air sacs produced by some aquatic plants like kelp. He let out a low whistle. "Poor creature would have been dead soon even without a spear through the neck," he murmured. It must be some sort of exotic fungal infection. He'd certainly never seen anything like it. Perhaps he could write a paper about it…

Canner picked up a shining steel probe and gently prodded one of the sacs – and it burst with a surprisingly loud "pop", spraying gold-green motes all over Canner's face shield. He gasped and stumbled back. Spores! Some kind of fungal infection! He had his transparent shield, and a mask over his mouth and nose that should keep him from breathing anything in, but damn it, the spores were in the *air*. He'd have to seal the room, go into quarantine until the spores could be identified, notify his second-in-command to take over operations until–

"Welcome, doctor," a voice said from beneath the autopsy table.

Canner frowned and crouched, and station security chief Kote Strom shimmered into visibility. "What are you doing here?" Canner asked.

Kote launched herself at him, knocking him to sprawl on the floor. She knelt on his chest as he gasped, more shocked than hurt. She wrenched the face shield from his head, then tore the mask from his face.

He rolled over – she was tiny, and her weight couldn't hold him – and scuttled away on his hands and knees. "What are you *doing*? There's an infectious agent in the air here!"

"There's a *sacrament*," she said.

Canner looked at her, baffled and alarmed. She was holding up his face shield, still dusted with spores, with its speckled surface parallel to the floor. She took a deep breath and blew across the shield, sending motes spiraling into his face – his nose, his mouth, his eyes, his mucous membranes.

Canner fell back, coughing, as black spots danced before his eyes. He had to get to the eye wash station, had to take anti-fungal drugs, had to notify his colleagues–

<Shhhh,> a voice – or chorus of voices? – whispered in his mind. The sound was faint at first, but soon became clearer. <Be at peace. We are your guides.>

Canner slumped to the floor as his brain unleashed its finest chemical vintages in a sustained rush. Once, before medical school, Canner had accepted a mysterious pill from a man he had a desperate crush on, some designer drug that stimulated the pleasure centers of the brain, and he always remembered it as the most profound physical enjoyment he'd ever experienced, an all-consuming sense of total euphoria.

That pill was nothing compared to this. This was bliss, and peace, yes, but it was also *purpose*.

<Will you be faithful?> his guide whispered.

"Oh, yes," Canner said eagerly. "Anything."

<We are engaged in a great work.>

"What can I do to help?"

<You can start by getting rid of all this evidence,> the guides replied.

CHAPTER 5
SEVERYNE

Severyne Joelle Dampierre – captain of the Barony of Letnev battleship *Grim Countenance*, famed fugitive hunter, highest-ranking survivor of the catastrophic expedition to the World of Light, rising star in the military – sat in a meeting and stifled a yawn.

She sat in a room full of other Letnev captains – most older than her, and largely a bunch of puffed-up toads, deeply uncomfortable in the presence of people they couldn't order around, since they spent most of their time wielding (locally) absolute power on their ships. She despised nearly all of them.

The one advantage was that they weren't with her in person, so she didn't have to smell their various exhalations. Severyne was actually in her ready room on the *Grim Countenance*, immersed in a holographic representation of a meeting room in a government installation beneath the city of Goz (which was already deep underground) on the Letnev homeworld of Arc Prime.

When the call went out to so many high-ranking members of the military, speculation among the captains was rampant. With the imminent formation of the Legion, the treaty organization led by the Letnev in response to the Greater Union, there must be major plans afoot. Were they finally launching all-out war against the Federation of Sol, aided by their new allies? Had the Baron crafted a plan to seize control of Mecatol Rex, and re-establish the empire the Lazax had incompetently lost so long ago? Was the prototype Dark Star – the newest generation of the Letnev version of the Gashlai War Suns – finally operational, and ready to lead the Legion vanguard into battle? Severyne had even found herself caught up in the whirl of speculation.

The lights brightened – though not much, of course; they were Letnev – and a figure shimmered into view on the stage at the front of the room. A mechanical voice said, "Prepare for a briefing by Lady Immental, high admiral of the Prime Fleet."

Everyone straightened up in their seats, even Severyne. Admiral Immental was her boss, but she'd never actually received an order from the woman, or indeed even seen her. In rank, Immental was just below her cousin, the Baron, in the government's hierarchy. If she was here to address them directly, something serious was going on.

The admiral was tall for a Letnev, her back perfectly straight, her uniform so pristine it might never have been worn before, her expression a cool snarl of disdain. She stood before them, hands clasped behind her back, and surveyed the gathering, her eyes resting a moment on each and every one of them. When those dark eyes fixed on Severyne, she had to resist the urge to squirm a little in her chair, even though the woman was actually millions of kilometers away. Severyne seldom found anyone impressive, let alone imposing, but Immental was everything a Letnev official should be, and everything Severyne wished to someday be herself.

"Captains," Immental said at last. "The balance of power in the galaxy is about to radically shift. You've all heard about the negotiations I'm leading on the Baron's behalf, to form a treaty organization with our natural allies against our most persistent rivals. You are here now to learn the part *you'll* play in the Legion's formation. But first… a few words about why the Legion is so necessary."

This should be interesting. Opinions among Letnev officers were sharply divided on the issue, and as far as Severyne could tell, most of the military was opposed to the idea of a treaty. The Letnev were the most capable, most accomplished, and most powerful civilization in the galaxy – why would they bother to ally themselves with lesser races? Severyne herself was relatively open to the idea, having collaborated usefully with people of other species on occasion in the past, but even she was a bit leery of the proposed members of the alliance.

"You might ask yourselves, why would we ally ourselves with lesser races, including factions we've clashed with sometimes in the past?" Immental said. "The reason is simple: our enemies gather against us." Images began to appear on the screen behind her: the twin worlds of Jor and Nal, superimposed with the head of an impassive Hylar; the hated blue-green globe of Jord, overlaid with a sneering human face; the yellow haze of the three principal desert worlds of the Emirates, beneath a hooded Hacan figure, canines bared; the twin planets of the Xxlak star system, a beaked Xxcha squinting disdainfully above them; and finally the shrouded orb of Moll Primus, surrounded by a pirate fleet, inset with a scheming human face and a shifty Yssaril: the Mentak Coalition and the Guild of Spies. "These are the likely members of the so-called Greater Union, led by the Mentak." Her voice dripped with the appropriate scorn. "Their propaganda *claims* it is a strategic alliance, to allow them to join forces against new threats in the galaxy." She shook her head. "They cite fairy tales of the Mahact Kings and the Titans, and rumors of strange new aliens in the outer systems. Obvious nonsense."

Severyne still didn't shift in her chair, but it took some effort. The Mahact Kings... well, she found the idea of their return plausible. Not so long ago, she'd been lost in a deathtrap of a world *created* by one of the Mahact, and where there was one, there might be others. As for the mysterious aliens, she'd heard the same rumors of misshapen monsters descending on remote worlds and outposts. The creatures described in those fragments sounded disturbingly like the entities she'd glimpsed through a rift in space when the rogue scientist Thales attempted to create an artificial wormhole. She'd turned in her reports on those events – slanted, certainly, to show her in the best light, but accurate in their essentials – so Immental must know the threats she cited weren't "obvious nonsense", though the details were highly classified.

Immental paced back and forth, boots clicking. "Why do they gather together, then, if not to defend themselves against these imaginary threats?" She stopped and looked at the holographic audience expectantly.

Severyne knew the answer the admiral probably wanted and was never above a little light favor-currying. "To strike against us!" she called.

Immental nodded. "Precisely. The human government on Jord has long sought to destroy us, in retribution for the humiliations we heaped on them during our many past conflicts, but they could never hope to defeat us alone. We believe the humans reached out to their cousins on Moll Primus and convinced the Mentak Coalition to organize this alliance under a flimsy pretext. The Xxcha still hold a grudge against us for our occupation of Archon Ren. The Hylar are envious of our technological prowess and wish to take our secrets for their own. The Hacan want to seize our colony worlds and all the natural resources and trade opportunities they represent. The Guild of Spies, well… they work in the darkness, and they hate us for our mastery of the dark. All of them despise us, and the true goal of this Greater Union is nothing less than the *annihilation of the Barony itself.*"

Now the captains murmured, and a few even cursed and pounded fists on their desktops. Severyne made a point of looking just as outraged as the rest, but she didn't truly feel it. She had no fondness for the Federation of Sol *or* the Mentak Coalition, but she thought the admiral's presentation of the facts was at least as slanted as Severyne's own reports tended to be. Still, the Greater Union would certainly be a threat to Barony interests, even if their actual focus wasn't the devastation of Severyne's entire species. Maybe Immental was just trying to get the captains fired up.

"Can we defeat such an alliance?" Immental said. "Can we stand against such an array of implacable enemies when all their resources are ranged against us?"

"Yes!" screamed one of the captains, and this set up a whole round of shouting: "For the Barony!" "Letnev reign supreme!" "Death to the humans!" Immental looked at the room coolly, her own thoughts impossible to guess, and gradually the hubbub wound down and the room settled into silence.

A silence that Severyne broke. "Of course we can't defeat them," she said. "They would crush us."

Now *every* eye in the room was on her, some of the older and more hidebound of the captains (which was a relative term – the default was old and hidebound anyway) gasping or scowling or muttering about disloyalty and treason.

"Elaborate," Immental said.

Severyne sighed and stood up. "We'd make the war *cost* them, of course. No one is better at inflicting pain on enemies than the Barony. But if all five – six, counting the Yssaril – factions truly focused on annihilating us, we would have no hope. The balance of power in the galaxy depends on *imbalance*. No one faction is capable of gaining the upper hand over the others. We have all spent the past several decades busily consolidating power and looking for advantages, even small ones, that would allow us to exert sufficient power to force the other nations into accommodation – to turn them into vassal states, so that we might eventually found a new empire to rival the one the Lazax squandered. If our enemies have changed tactics, and are instead *cooperating*, that balance will shift. The Letnev could destroy any one of those factions, with effort. We could, I daresay, destroy two of them, though it might ruin us in the process. But five? With the help of the spies as well?" She shook her head. "I'm sorry, admiral. You will find no greater patriot than myself. But if we were strong enough to crush the Hacan, the Hylar, the Xxcha, the humans, the Mentak Coalition… we would have done so already, and the Baron would be at ease on the throne of Mecatol Rex."

That was heresy, more or less, Severyne knew, but she was ultimately supporting the admiral's point, so she wasn't worried about ending up in a reeducation facility.

Well. Not *overly* worried.

"Captain Dampierre is correct," the admiral said simply.

If the Baron's cousin and their superior officer said something, it probably wasn't treason, so the captains all murmured their agreement. "Well said," the one seated nearest Severyne grunted, though he looked like he could taste his own stomach acid while he said it.

"Faced with such a threat, how can we defend ourselves? How can we retaliate?" Immental looked straight at Severyne.

The answer was, depressingly, obvious. "We form our own strategic alliance," she said. "We form the Legion."

The admiral smiled, thin-lipped, but on her face, it was a show of strong emotion. "That's correct."

The captains cheered. Severyne resisted rolling her eyes. They really did bend whichever way the political winds blew.

"Who will we allow to join our Legion? While negotiations are still ongoing, we can confirm some. First, the Embers of Muaat. No one hates the Hylar more than the Gashlai, and they were eager to join us – they know once the Barony is destroyed, they would be the obvious next target for the Greater Union."

And we could use their War Suns, Severyne thought, since the Dark Star program seems to be infinitely delayed.

"The Sardakk N'orr, too, have no love for the squids, and they have also agreed to join us." Various nods and sounds of approval arose in the audience. The Sardakk N'orr were savage monsters, of course, but their skill at violence was unmatched, and it was better to be on their side than against them. "We have also received a… surprisingly positive response from the L1Z1X."

That set off a different tenor of muttering. They'd heard *rumors*, but to have them confirmed was still troubling. The L1Z1X were a mystery in many ways, but they were generally held to be abominations, the corpse of a once-great race brought to lurching life with cybernetic implants and other horrific forms of technology.

"I know," Immental said. "I find the notion of cooperating with such creatures… unpleasant as well. But the L1Z1X have secrets of Hylar technology that could prove useful, and they have a history of enmity with the Hacan that we could exploit. When faced with a threat like the Greater Union, we must be open to extreme measures." Immental went on, "You assembled captains represent the best and darkest of the Barony military. You will each be sent on a mission to meet with representatives of our new Legion. You will finalize any outstanding points of negotiation – I will provide guidance as necessary – and will further act as honor guards and escorts for the leaders of the other factions. We will all gather for a summit on Arc Prime, attended by the Baron himself, who will sign the treaty and formalize the alliance."

Severyne wrinkled her nose. Babysitting duty? Dreadful. She just hoped she wasn't getting sent to the L1Z1X. The rumors said the people they murdered were the *lucky* ones.

"You'll all receive your individual orders shortly," the admiral said. "You are dismissed."

The captains flickered out of existence as their holographic connections were severed... but Severyne's connection stayed live. The image of the admiral approached her and said, "Captain Dampierre. A word?"

"Yes, admiral." Severyne attempted to remain serene as she rose and stood at attention. Being singled out by an officer of Immental's rank was either wonderful or terrible; there was no inbetween.

"You showed an admirable gasp of the political and strategic realities today," Immental said.

"I have spent some time in the field, and among our enemies," she said. "It gives me a broader perspective than the one visible solely from the captain's chair."

"Indeed. It's your field work that interests me now. I have a special mission for you."

Severyne felt a stir of interest. She'd expected to be sent on a mission of diplomacy. This was potentially more intriguing.

Immental said, "Two days ago, at a Greater Union meeting, a Hacan trade ambassador named Terrak brutally murdered a Xxcha cultural minister. Terrak subsequently escaped with the aid of unknown co-conspirators. You will take the *Grim Countenance*, capture this Terrak, and bring him to me."

Severyne waited, but there didn't seem to be anything else forthcoming. "If I may ask, are there any further details you can share?"

"You will be sent a dossier, though I have already presented you with the essentials."

Severyne composed her next words carefully. Speaking to an officer of Immental's rank was like piloting through an asteroid field scattered with hidden mines. "Of course, admiral. I am honored to be selected for this mission and will fulfill my duties with zeal. But in order to ensure my success, it would be helpful if I knew… some things that might not be included in a standard dossier."

The admiral fixed her with a gaze that could have melted tantalum. Seen up close, there were little flecks of green in her irises. The fidelity of the simulation was really remarkable. "Such as?"

"Admiral, if I may. You chose me for this mission because I have some experience hunting down fugitives, I assume?"

She sniffed. "Some rate your abilities in that area highly. You tracked down the defector Shelma and her associate Thales, yes, for all the good that did. What a disaster." The admiral clucked her tongue. "And you managed to prevent the Xing girl from escaping our grasp, though, again, that mission hardly ended in glory for the Barony."

Interesting. Severyne had gone from favored captain to barely tolerated failure in the span of two sentences, and all because she'd dared to ask a question. That just made her want to know the answers more, but she made every effort to appear abashed and defensive. "Those failures could not be laid at my feet, admiral. I acquitted myself as well as–"

"Yes, yes." Immental flapped a dismissive hand. "The general assessment is that you kept both situations from getting any worse than they might have, though I personally prefer officers who triumph, rather than those who merely mitigate disasters."

"I myself would enjoy an assignment where triumph was possible, admiral," Severyne dared.

Immental stared down her nose at Severyne for a moment… and then her lips quirked in the suggestion of a smile. "You were forced to correct the errors of incompetent superiors on both those missions, weren't you, captain? Fortunately, this time, *I* am sending you on the mission, and I am anything but incompetent."

Severyne was curious about the admiral's attempts to manipulate her emotionally by whiplashing Severyne in and out of favor. Most officers of her rank wouldn't have bothered.

Immental said, "To answer your question: yes. You are the closest thing we have to an expert at hunting down fugitive aliens. What's your point?"

"The reason I am good at what I do is because I make a study of my targets, admiral. I knew Shelma from her time on the facility where I served as security chief, and learned all I could about Thales, and the Coalition crew assigned to protect him. As for Bianca Xing… my success with her was based *entirely* on my understanding of her psychology. Essentially, admiral, if you want me to capture this Hacan, I need to know everything I can about him – including why we're interested in him in the first place. If he murdered this Xxcha, and disrupted a summit of the Greater Union, it seems we should thank him, rather than pursue him."

The admiral looked around, then gestured for Severyne to come close. Immental removed a small black box from her pocket and pressed a button. A low hiss filled the air, and the light seemed to shimmer. "Anti-surveillance technology," the admiral explained. Severyne wondered who she could possibly be keeping secrets from in a bunker on Arc Prime. "Is your location shielded against surveillance?"

"Certain," Severyne said. That was true. No one surpassed her in the logistical applications of paranoia.

"What I'm about to tell you is classified above your level, Captain Dampierre, but I am authorized to reveal the information on a need-to-know basis... and you make a good point. You'll do better work with more data. We want the Hacan because he works for us. He has been a spy in our employ for many years. We sent him to disrupt the Coalition. But rather than follow our escape plan, he fled the station in the company of an unknown individual. We don't know who Terrak is with, or, more importantly, who they *work* for. He is trying to escape not just his murder charges, but to escape his responsibilities to the Barony, and, of course, we cannot abide that."

Severyne nodded. "I understand."

"Terrak will doubtless use resources unrelated to his Barony connections to flee. But perhaps knowing his nature will offer you some insight into his character that will prove useful."

"If you tell me *why* he worked for the Barony, it will," Severyne said. "His motives will reveal much about his nature. Did he help us for ideological reasons? Because we had some leverage over him? Or because of greed?"

"Greed, of course," the admiral said. "We paid him for information. You know how corrupt the Hacan can be."

"Of course, admiral. I'll begin my pursuit immediately."

"We'll send all available information to your ship." Immental turned off the shimmering field, gave Severyne a nod, and severed the holographic connection.

Her ready room flickered back into visibility, and Severyne allowed herself a sigh. It was rather early in the day to become tangled in a web of so many falsehoods.

Severyne sat in her ready room sipping moss tea while Undercommandant Voyou – who had, improbably, become her closest confidante on the ship, which was also to say, in her life – processed the information she'd just shared with him.

"I'm fairly sure I'm not supposed to know data classified at that level," Voyou said.

"I'm fairly sure 'classified data' was a lie anyway," Severyne said.

Voyou took that in, then nodded. "Could you explain why you think so, captain?" Severyne liked Voyou because he was competent, loyal, and had no desire to stab her in the back (literally or metaphorically) in order to take her job. He was also the only other survivor of the disastrous mission to the interior of the World of Light, the Mahact death trap where Severyne's *last* mission involving aliens had gone horrendously wrong. The two of them had gone through something together, and come out the other side alive, and while Severyne certainly didn't *need* Voyou, she could grudgingly admit it was nice having someone around to listen while she talked.

She said, "The admiral claims the Hacan was in our employ, spying on the Greater Union for money. Does that seem plausible to you?"

"Greed is a reasonable explanation for treachery, especially among the honorless, duplicitous races," Voyou said.

Severyne waved her hand. "Yes, of course, but think it through. Would Terrak have murdered another delegate at the summit, merely for money? This was no covert assassination – it was a showy, public mess. Would he kill someone that way, knowing it would destroy his life and make him a fugitive?"

"I see. What good would his wealth do him if he had to leave his entire life behind?"

"Yes. Plus, our Baron ... well ... the government purse strings ..."

"Our rulers are not famously generous paymasters, you mean," Voyou said.

"Exactly. Let's say this Terrak is solely and fanatically motivated by a desire for money. A corrupt Hacan trade ambassador would have many other opportunities to get rich, from graft, skimming, and kickbacks. Anyway, he fled from us after the killing, so if it was murder for hire, he didn't even come to collect his balance. It makes no sense."

"If the admiral had said we'd co-opted this Terrak through blackmail, that would be more believable," Voyou said. "But even then, what secret could we know about him that would be worse than becoming a fugitive murderer?"

There was a reason she kept Voyou around. He was intelligent, and was willing to say things to her that might get him in trouble if a political officer overheard. "Yes. I think the admiral had to answer me on the spot, and just fell back reflexively on the stereotype of Hacans as obsessed by commerce. Her explanation makes perfect sense, if you don't think about it for more than two seconds." Severyne sipped her tea. "Oh well. This isn't the first time we've gone on a mission based on incomplete, or indeed outright false, information."

"The fact that Admiral Immental herself lied *personally* to your face, virtually speaking, is even rather flattering," Voyou said.

She very nearly smiled. "I am appropriately complimented. At any rate, it doesn't matter – the orders are lawful, and the mission is clear. We will track and capture this Terrak."

"And… perhaps… find out the truth along the way," Voyou said.

She sipped the last of her tea. "Well. Sometimes such things are unavoidable."

THE FAITHFUL V

"I speak for the Baron," Immental said.

<*To a point,*> the voice whispered. <*But we wish him to speak for us.*>

"The level of paranoia the Baron has regarding security... he is so very cautious. Even I can't get close enough to administer the sacrament, and we've known each other since we were children. His guards are never alone, so they can never be corrupted."

<*There will be opportunities to turn the Baron, during preparations for the summit on Arc Prime.*>

"Perhaps, guides," Immental said. The summit would involve changes in routine, which could provide opportunities. But the idea of taking action that might be construed as – well, as *treason* – was powerful enough to cause a twinge of discomfort, even in the sea of bliss that accompanied her devotion to the guides.

Her masters sensed her hesitation. <*You fear that your cousin would not want this. You fear that he would kill you if he knew your loyalty was to us, and not him.*>

"Yes, guides," she murmured.

<*But think of it this way, faithful one: you are giving the Baron a great gift. Isn't your life better now, in our care?*>

Immental thought of her existence before she took the sacrament. Striving, scheming, and the exercise of naked ambition; playing her rivals against one another; jockeying for her cousin and supreme leader's favor; amassing as much power for herself as possible. In retrospect, all those enterprises were hollow and empty. Immental had wanted to rule, but now, she knew, true pleasure came from service and devotion. "My cousin... he serves *no one!*" She spoke with the force of revelation. "He has no idea the joy that could be his! If the bonds of duty mean anything to me, then surely it is my duty to share the wonder of the sacrament with my Baron!"

<*Yes. You will give him our blessing, and the great work will proceed.*>

CHAPTER 6
AZAD

"They're turning people into *Dirzuga*?" Terrak said, obviously horrified at the prospect.

Azad shook her head. "No, that can't be it, or not exactly. You've seen Dirzuga – you can tell they're corpses. They don't blink, they don't breathe, they don't move or speak naturally at all, and they don't seem to remember who they were in life. They're basically ventriloquist dummies. I know Qqurant was a little out of it at the meeting, but he wasn't a walking corpse, and plenty of the people who've been compromised don't show any level of impairment at all."

"These samples aren't *exactly* the same as the spores I've seen before, anyway," Lonrah said. "They've clearly been altered, though I couldn't say exactly how."

"Give me your data," Azad said. "I need to make a call."

"To *whom*?" Terrak demanded.

"This isn't some personal crusade I'm on," Azad said. "I'm going to report to my bosses and see what they can make of all this." Lonrah transferred the data, and Azad sent it via encrypted channels, then ducked into a side room for privacy.

When her boss made contact, Azad said, "The mind-control stuff is made of Arborec spores, it looks like. Some modification of the process they use to reanimate corpses. Maybe the spores have been altered to turn *living* people into puppets, but puppets who retain their memories and at least a semblance of their personalities."

Pause.

"Yeah, I spiked you the data, so you can get your science types to look into it."

A longer pause.

Azad sighed. "Well, no, I doubt it's the Arborec. I mean, they're *plants*, they barely even interact with the rest of the galaxy, right? They trade with us, but otherwise, they just keep to themselves, doing... plant stuff. They don't strike me as likely prospects for the secret masters of the galaxy. Nobody even thought about inviting them to the Greater Union *or* the stupid League of the Beleaguered the Letnev are putting together. The Arborec are a power, sure, but they're not a major player in the great game of empires, and nobody gets the sense they really want to be."

A much longer pause.

Talking to the boss was so weird, mostly because it wasn't really *talking*. Azad could have carried on her half of the conversation without saying a word aloud, but she didn't trust her thoughts to stay inside the lines. Better to put her thoughts into words, and be sure she conveyed what she intended, and nothing else.

She grunted. "Sure, but it can't be that hard to get your hands on the spores. The Dirzuga are around. They probably leak the stuff out of every orifice. And once you get some spore samples, they're just plants. Anybody could grow more, tweak them, do some genetic engineering… I don't know. My shortlist would include the Hylar, since this sounds a lot like mad science, and the Brotherhood of Yin, since it sounds like *biological* mad science. The Letnev have a lot of experience with mushroom stuff, too, don't they? This discovery doesn't narrow down the 'who' much, admittedly, but it's something. At least it's a 'how'. We can stop looking for evidence of android duplicates or light-based mirror-neuron manipulators and focus on the spores. You can get your people started on some kind of anti-fungal antidote, right?"

Brief pause.

"Ha, really? What a busy little bioweapons lab you must have." Azad had worked for a lot of people and organizations, but her current employers kept surprising her with the depth and breadth of their resources.

Pause.

"Sure, sure, tweaks, tailoring, I get it. How long?"

Pause.

"Hmm, all right. Terrak's friend can probably produce whatever we need if you send a recipe."

Pause.

Azad was getting a headache. Long conversations with the boss tended to cause those. "That's fine. I enjoy Terrak's company, he's got more contacts than I do in this sector, *and* he's highly motivated to uncover the conspiracy. Why?"

Pause.

Ooh, that idea was nasty, even by her standards. She didn't like it. Fortunately, she had operational authority, so she could brush the suggestion off. "Ha. I mean, yes, we do need a subject, but Terrak has uses beyond acting as a talking petri dish. We can find someone else to experiment on. People will do anything for money. Terrak might object to the testing protocol, though."

A longer pause.

Azad chuckled. "True enough. Once he finds out the alternative is even worse, I'm sure he'll go along."

CHAPTER 7
TERRAK

When Azad returned from the restroom, I said, "Lon thinks, given a few weeks, she might be able to engineer an antidote–"

Azad waved her hand. "Not necessary. I've got people working on the problem, and they'll have answers for us a lot sooner than that."

Lon swiveled in her exoskeleton. "What are you talking about? We just found out what we're dealing with, and even with more resources than I have here, tailoring something to combat these spores will take time."

Azad sat back down on her crate and grinned. "If you're starting from zero, sure. But my employers have already been working on ways to counteract Arborec spores. That's how the big plant monsters *talk*, after all, and you know how much the military likes being able to disrupt enemy communications. You can't use signal jammers on people who don't use signals, so my employers explored other possibilities. They already have a way to neutralize Arborec spores. Of course, they'll have to tweak the recipe, since these spores have been altered, but they seem confident they'll have a working recipe soon. I told them we had access to a compounding pharmacy and chemical supply company all rolled up in one; that's you, Lonnie. Name your rate. Feel free to charge us double for the rush job. My bosses can afford it."

I wondered who her bosses were. The Federation of Sol seemed most likely, still; they were always anticipating future conflicts. My more immediate concern was my colleague's safety, though. I turned to Lonrah. "Are you willing to do this?" She was a professional, and no stranger to shady business practices, but this was a different order of complication, and I wanted her to be sure she understood what she was getting into. "You didn't ask to be dragged into my troubles, and you've already helped so much. The forces arrayed against us seem formidable." Azad scowled at me, but I ignored her.

"I'll do it for you, Terrak," Lonrah said. I felt an unfamiliar surge of warmth. She paused. "Also… for triple my usual fee."

Azad laughed. "It's not my money, so sure. We've got some time to kill, though. What do you do for fun around here?"

"Immersive sims, usually," Lonrah said. "It gets a bit cramped down here, so I like to spread my pseudopods in simulated realms."

Azad said *hmmm*. "There's a non-zero chance we'll be attacked by hostile forces at some point, so I shouldn't fly off into a virtual reality right now."

I closed my eyes briefly. I knew there was a possibility that agents of the conspiracy would track us down and take violent action against us, but hearing Azad state that so matter-of-factly made the dread less abstract and more concrete.

"I would rather not have my lab attacked at all," Lonrah said.

"I don't want to cause you any trouble," I said. "I don't think anyone can connect me to you, but… it's not impossible. Maybe we should find another place to wait, Azad."

Azad shook her head. "If the bad guys – or the local authorities, who are probably working for the bad guys, whether they know it or not – figure out you two know each other, they will come *here*. Wouldn't you rather have us around to protect you if that happens, Lonnie?"

"I don't want some military melee in my laboratory, Azad. I'd rather be able to truthfully say that you aren't here, and I don't know where you are, if the authorities ask."

"Ha. OK. Maybe we can work out a compromise. I get the feeling you're operating a little bit in the gray, legally speaking. So, is there a back way out of here? A secret escape tunnel? Something we can slip out of, if the opposition shows up at your cunningly disguised front door?"

"There is," Lonrah said. "But it's made for me to use as a last resort, so… its usefulness to you depends on how long you can hold your breath."

I groaned. I never liked getting wet. Hacan aren't meant to *submerge*. But if it was a choice between discomfort and death – or, worse, the loss of self and subjugation to the will of another – it was no choice at all, really.

We passed the time waiting for Azad's employers to reach out in various ways. Lonrah studied the spores, which she found fascinating and horrifying. I brooded over news reports about my perfidy, and composed messages to friends and colleagues I didn't dare send. Azad slouched in a corner with headphones on, watching a screen and occasionally giggling. I wondered what she was watching. Zany spaceship crashes? The galaxy's funniest reactor meltdowns? People cooing at cute alien fauna, which subsequently ate them?

Finally, she took her headphones off and said, "I've got a recipe for you, Lonrah. Can you make this?"

Lonrah trundled over in her exoskeleton and took Azad's

tablet, peering at the information on the screen. "Oh, I see, they're combining an array of anti-fungals with hunter-killer phages... oh, that's intriguing, there's a neural growth stimulator, I guess to repair any–"

"Do you have the *ingredients*?" Azad said.

Lonrah looked up. "Hmm? Oh. Yes. What I don't have I can synthesize in a few hours. I have no idea if this will actually work on your... spore-zombies, or whatever... though. It seems plausible, but you won't know for sure until you test it."

"Can't you just see how the cure affects the spores you have here?" I asked. "From the canister?"

Lonrah fluttered a pseudopod. "Sure I can, but killing the spores in a jar is different from killing them in someone's *brain*, without also killing, or even damaging, that brain in the process. I could destroy the spores with acid or bleach, but I wouldn't recommend injecting that into an infected person's brain."

I slumped. "Ah. Right. I have no idea how we can test–"

"What's the delivery mechanism?" Azad cut in.

"It will need to be injected," Lonrah said. "Into a vein, not a muscle."

"I was hoping for an aerosol," Azad muttered. "Failing that, a needle I could just jam anywhere at all. But it is what it is." She stood up. "OK, Lonnie, you get to work making the magic juice. Terrak, let's you and me take a walk."

I frowned. I knew by now that Azad always had plans within plans, and that she wasn't reliable about sharing them in advance, or even while they were happening. I'd never liked surprises, but *Azad* surprises were even worse. "Why? Where are we going?"

"We're going to see someone who can help us with our testing problem. I think, for now, we can still leave by the front door."

•••

We walked the industrial streets, and Azad wasn't any more forthcoming about where we were going, or why. "I didn't think you knew anyone on this moon," I said.

"Oh, I make friends real easy."

"What aren't you telling me?" I demanded.

"About a million things. Listen, it'll be easier if I just show you."

"Easier for *whom*?"

"Easier for me, Terrak. I'm always about making things easier for me."

We wound our way through filthy alleys, occasionally passing vagrants – humans bundled in rags, mainly, but also a Hylar splashing in a dirty puddle and muttering to himself, and a couple of Saar sitting on splintered pallets who bared their teeth and hissed at us until I growled at them and sent them scurrying into the shadows.

"Is your contact homeless?" I asked when we walked through a little settlement made of tarps and packing crates built along the back of a warehouse.

"Probably," Azad said. "That would be ideal." I would say that's when I started to have misgivings, but that would belie the fact that I'd been having those all along. I was horribly afraid she intended to abduct a homeless person and infect them with spores just so she could test the antidote. If she tried that, I would have to stop her, and it would be both the end of our partnership and spoil my best chance at proving my innocence.

We turned a corner and then walked around another warehouse, until we reached a weed-filled vacant lot. Azad grabbed my arm. "Right there. I think that's our guy."

She indicated an elderly, slow-moving Hacan wearing a blue tarp for a cloak. He was hunched over, prodding at the ground with a stick. He grunted, leaned forward, and picked up the butt of a cigar someone had discarded, sniffed it, and put it in his pocket.

"Go on," Azad said. "Say hi."

"Why?"

"Because it's polite," she said. "Don't be prejudiced, Terrak. Any of us could end up where that guy is."

I sighed. Azad was clearly not in the mood to be helpful. I approached the old fellow and said, "Hail, elder."

He startled, then scowled, then growled. "My patch," he snarled. "Mine."

I showed my palms in a gesture of peace. "I don't want your…" I lowered my hands. This was ridiculous. "Azad, what is the meaning of this? Why are we talking to this man?"

She sauntered over. "I thought it'd go more smoothly if initial contact was made by someone from his own socio… cultural… somebody who's the same species, is what I mean, but I guess he's just generally cranky. Well, who can blame him?" She reached into a pocket, and I moved between her and the elder.

"I won't let you hurt him, Azad." If she had a stun gun or a tranquilizer gun, she'd have to hit me with it first, and at least then the old fellow would have a chance to run for it. I have no illusions that I can save everyone, or even *anyone*, but I had to at least try when the potential victim was right behind me.

Azad cocked her head, then chuckled. "Let me sidebar with my associate for a moment, sir." She stepped a little distance away, and I had no choice but to follow. "You thought I was going to take a test subject by force. I get it. I'm not even opposed to the idea in principle, but just logistically, who wants to drag a huge unconscious guy all the way back to the lab? I've got money. He's got desperation. We're a good match."

"I will not be party to this, Azad. You want to infect an innocent person with a mind-control drug? That's monstrous, even if you *do* offer to pay him."

"We're going to cure him after we infect him, Terrak. Come on. That's the whole point. We have to make sure this recipe works. Look, maybe you're feeling some sort of species solidarity with this old wreck, and I understand that, but it's really for the best if our subject is Hacan. Maybe the spores in that canister are multi-purpose and work on anything with a brain, but it's possible they were tailored for your specific biology, so our test subject should be as close to your biology as we can get."

"The idea is monstrous, Azad."

She sighed. "OK, Terrak. Just so you know, refusing to help means you're volunteering to be the test subject yourself. Infecting you is actually the obvious choice – these spores were meant for you in the first place. My employer suggested using you right away, but I said, 'Nah, Terrak's useful, we're in this together, we're a team'. Did I make a mistake? Are we *not* a team?"

I thought things over and raised my hands. "We are a team. I just… wish there was another way." Maybe the old Hacan would refuse. If not… I'd have to figure out something else.

"Hey, I'd love to get an ethics committee involved in this too, but we're on the run and we have limited resources. I understand your reluctance, I really do, but the old guy will be *fine*. My people do good lab work. Tomorrow he'll be good as new and a whole lot richer. OK?"

It wasn't OK, but I stepped aside.

"G'off my patch," the old Hacan snarled at us again.

Azad stepped toward him and said, "Sir, we're recruiting paid test subjects for a clinical trial. I can't go into *too* many details, but it's an experimental drug designed to combat certain cognitive deficiencies."

The old fellow glared at both of us. "Can't do those trials anymore," he muttered. "Won't take me. Not healthy enough. Pre-existing whatnot. Mucks up the results." He turned his head and coughed raggedly, as if to demonstrate.

"That is not a problem in this case," Azad said. "It's a study about mental function, and you seem sharp enough to me."

"The drug is *very* experimental," I said pointedly.

"Which is why the payment is *very* high." Azad reached into her pocket again and came up with a credit stick, then pressed the button to display the shockingly high balance. The Hacan leaned forward, squinted, gasped, and then tried to snag the stick, but she danced out of the way. "Now, now," she said. "You get this one when we get back to the lab, and you get another one just like it after the trial."

"How long will this take?" he said.

"What, you've got somewhere to be? I don't know, probably not more than a day."

He looked from her, to me, and back to her. "You'd pay me that much for a *day*? What's the catch?"

Azad surprised me. She said, "You could die. Your brain could melt out your ears. I'm not saying it isn't a gamble, but that's why the payoff is so big."

He looked at me, and suddenly, there *was* some fellow feeling in his eye; this was a human, making an outlandish offer, but I was a fellow son of the desert, and he wanted to believe he could trust me. "Is this for real?" he said.

I sighed. "Yes. Especially the part about you maybe dying." Except it could be even worse – he could be possessed by a mysterious conspiracy, his volition removed, his will lost forever.

He laughed, harshly. "I deal with *maybe dying* every single day. I'll do it. Where do I sign?"

Azad smiled. "We're more streamlined than that. Paperwork just slows us down. Let's just take a walk back to the lab."

"Who is *that*?" Lon asked over her hidden speaker when we reached the utility box.

"A volunteer," Azad said. "Bring us down."

The Hacan smelled rather ripe in the open air, and worse in the jammed confines of the elevator. We took him into the lab, which he glared at suspiciously.

"You can just hop up on this table here," Azad said.

"You gotta put me under," the Hacan said. "I get medical anxiety. I'm not drug-seeking. People always say that. I'm just going to freak out if you put needles in me and I know about it."

"Why are we putting needles in him?" Lonrah said, trundling over in her exo-suit.

"We're going to dose him with the spores, and then see if our cure works on him," Azad said.

The Hylar was silent for a moment. "Sir? Did they explain…"

"Brains melting out my ears maybe? Yeah." He hopped up onto the table and reached out a hand. "Credit stick now."

Azad handed it over, he pocketed it, then lay down on the table and closed his eyes. "I've done worse for less," he muttered.

"See? A volunteer," Azad said. I stood nearby, arms crossed, glowering.

"I still don't know if I'm totally comfortable…" Lonrah said.

"Nothing is more important to me than your comfort," Azad said. "Wait, no, I meant, nothing is *less* important to me." She stalked over to me, beckoning Lonrah, until we were out of the old Hacan's earshot. "Don't you two get it? Some unknown group is out there using *mind control spores* to infiltrate major governments. Terrak, your buddy the cultural minister didn't have his claws on the levers of power, but he routinely met with people who did. That means he could have sprayed military or political leaders in the face in some executive bathroom, or slipped some spores into the punch bowl at a fancy party, or who knows what? We have no idea how widespread this conspiracy is, and we've only identified a few high-ranking officials in various factions who we're *pretty* sure have been co-opted, based on behavioral analysis and other info. If we can cure them? That changes everything. It means we have a chance at stopping them, exposing them, and actually saving people. We don't know what their plans are, but traditionally, conspirators who infiltrate the highest echelons of intergalactic power don't do it for *nice* reasons. Yes, shooting this guy in the face with spores and then jamming experimental drugs into his veins isn't nice, but he volunteered, and sometimes we have to be nasty to save the galaxy. Really, I am being as *nice as I can be* under the circumstances."

"I feel like I should clap," I said. "What a rousing speech. I understand the stakes, Azad."

"I'd prefer wholehearted effort over grudging cooperation, but whatever." Azad flapped her hand. "Put this guy under and put him in some kind of containment and then we can introduce the spores."

"We don't know how the spores work," I objected. "What if he links up with some malign intelligence and attempts to murder us all? Or spies on us? We don't know how any of this works."

Azad rolled her eyes. "Hence the sedation. I was going to suggest it if he didn't. We'll strap him down, too, just in case he wakes up with super-spore-strength or something. I'll even cover his eyes so they can't use his eyeballs for remote viewing. Terrak, don't worry. I secure people all the time. I've got this."

"And what if he dies?" I demanded again. "We have no idea if this will work!"

"He took the job," Azad said. "Again, the job is *yours* if you'd rather take it instead. Otherwise, shut up."

I shut up.

Once the old Hacan was in blissful sedated slumber, I helped Lonrah set up a tent of overlapping sheets of transparent material over the table. Azad eyed the arrangement critically. "Is that thing spore-tight? I really don't want to inhale any of this stuff."

"I work with dangerous pathogens on a regular basis," Lonrah said. "I cured–"

"Yeah, yeah, I get it. Sorry." She shuddered, a rare sign of weakness, and I wondered if the reaction was genuine, or just another layer of subterfuge. Maybe Azad was subterfuge all the way down. "I just get a little twitchy when it comes to stuff like this. Germs, viruses, spores, all that kind of thing. Give me an enemy I can blast or punch or bite, you know? These invisible tiny monsters don't play fair."

"I think we're ready." Lonrah wheeled over a glass box with manipulator arms on the inside and hooked it up to a flexible tube that led into the tent. "We can trigger the canister inside the containment chamber, and the spores will be pulled into the tube and the tent. And then… well, we'll see what happens."

"We think whatever happens works fast," Azad said. "We're really curious about how exactly it happens, though. Do the spores just make the subject pliable, and then a handler gives them instructions? Do the spores somehow *program* a set of behaviors? Do the victims have a mission, but personal agency when it comes to fulfilling that mission? Or is it some kind of telepathic thing?"

"The Arborec communicate through their spore fields," Lonrah said. "They can only talk to each other when there's a certain concentration of spores in the vicinity. That's the whole reason they have the Letani – those have a degree of individuality, but more than that, they're mobile communications platforms, carrying a cloud of the spores with them wherever they go. But these spores aren't exactly the same as the ones the Arborec use to communicate, or the ones that activate the Dirzuga, so these victims might not be… networked the same way."

"Enough speculation," Azad said. "Let's make observations instead."

Lonrah crossed the room, opened a secure container, and removed the canister of spores. She turned toward the tent and the sleeping innocent within. As I watched her, I thought, *There is a better way.*

Then I snatched the canister from her, darted across the room to her bio-waste incinerator, opened the hatch, and dropped the spores inside.

THE FAITHFUL VI

Lillith was losing money every minute she spent on Shilsaad Station, which was generally the worst thing she could imagine, but in this case, it wasn't even the most annoying part of the situation: the confinement was. She paced back and forth in her (admittedly lovely) rooms, waiting to be released. The whole station was under lockdown, with no indication of when it would end. Her own government wanted her to be released, and the other factions were doubtless applying pressure too, but murder investigations took precedence.

She'd expected this to be a pleasant and profitable meeting, and an opportunity to set up even more lucrative deals she could finalize during the Greater Union summit on Moll Primus, and instead it had turned into a nightmare of death and absurdity. Harmless, charming old Shelly dead, and Terrak blamed for it? What nonsense, how absurd–

"I understand you spoke to the Hylar investigator, Jhuri," a voice said, and Lillith spun. There was an Yssaril standing in the corner of her bedroom, watching her with those enormous eyes.

"How did you get in here?" There were representatives from the Guild of Spies at the summit, and some as part of the Mentak

110

delegation, but she didn't remember meeting this one. There were often Yssaril around you *didn't* see, though.

"I'm the head of security for the station, Kote Strom." She gave a little bow. "I can get in everywhere."

Lillith realized she *had* met Strom before, during the immediate chaos of the killing, but hadn't recognized the Yssaril out of uniform. Why *was* she out of uniform, and wearing that plain gray coverall? "What do you want? I've already talked to the authorities and told them everything I know."

"That's why I'm here. Because of the answers you gave to certain questions." Strom sidled a bit closer to her. "I understand you told Jhuri that Terrak was innocent, and that Qqurant seemed disoriented at the party the night he died."

"Yes? So?"

"So, I'd like you to... refine your statement. Tell Jhuri you were mistaken, speaking out of misguided loyalty, and that you've realized the error of your ways, and accept that Terrak committed this heinous crime."

Lillith snorted. "You want to tamper with the investigation? Under some circumstances I might be amenable, if the price was right, but Terrak is my friend, and Shelly was, too. I'm afraid this is one case where my conscience makes me incorruptible."

"Oh, I'm not proposing a transaction." Strom came a little closer still, in that sideways, insinuating way.

Lillith understood that sneaky people had their uses – she'd made a lot of money from information acquired by the Guild of Spies – but it was still unsettling to have someone sidling up to her like she was a pocket to be picked. She moved a step away.

Strom said, "I want you to willingly change your story, because you know it's the right thing to do."

"Why would I do that?"

"Look what I have here." The Yssaril held up a closed hand.

Did the little toad have some real proof that Terrak was responsible? Lillith didn't want to believe it, but she leaned down to look just the same.

Kote uncurled her fingers, revealing… an empty palm. "What do you think of this?"

"What, of nothing at all?"

"It's small, but it's there." The Yssaril leaned forward and blew across her own palm, and Lillith blinked at the puff of air in her eyes. The room was dim, but she'd seen something swirl off Strom's hand. Oh, stars, she'd heard about people being poisoned by radioactive dust, but surely such an attack would poison Kote too? She staggered back as her head began to spin–

<Shhh,> a chorus of voices, speaking as one, whispered to her. <Be faithful.>

Lillith's body trembled. How had she ended up on the floor? It didn't matter. Nothing mattered except the clouds parting in her head, letting the light suffuse her. She moaned as she pressed her cheek against the carpet, which suddenly felt soft as velvet.

Lillith heard Strom say, "I will need more of the sacrament, guides, if you wish me to recruit further. I had to harvest that dose from the ambassador's brain, and it was barely enough."

<All will be well,> the voice whispered to Lillith, and she knew in every fiber of herself that it was true.

CHAPTER 8
FELIX

"There are almost a hundred moons in this system, and only half of them are even developed," Felix said. "Why did this Facilitator go to the trouble of building a space station? It's not like there's a shortage of available real estate."

"Paranoia," Ggorgos said. "Desire to control every aspect of the environment. Long-term security, too. It's not uncommon for polities to retroactively declare that any natural object in a given system is its sovereign territory, which doesn't go well for the people already living there."

"I suppose if you can afford it, building your own station is worth it for the peace of mind." Felix was beginning to relax a bit around Ggorgos, and Ggorgos, for her part, had become a bit more talkative and slightly less intense since they'd reached the Rantula system. *She's just driven*, he'd decided. Now that they had a lead to pursue, Ggorgos had a place to direct her dark energies, rather than letting them spill over onto everyone else.

They'd received permission to dock their shuttle at the Facilitator's station, which saved them the trouble of insisting with threats of missiles and so forth. That was good. Making too much noise would draw the attention of the local authorities, such as they were. The Rantula system was ostensibly independent, a loose affinity group of moons with a distinct commercial lean toward "specialty goods" – things that could be produced here and exported elsewhere, unencumbered by pesky local regulations. The rumor was that the Hylar supported the system on an off-the-books basis, but there was also a nearby wormhole that led to Letnev-controlled space, so maybe they had a hand in things here, too.

The Facilitator didn't provide specialty goods; they provided specialty services. "Concierge to the stars," Felix muttered. "They say the Facilitator can get anything, for a price."

"It's a sound business model," Ggorgos rumbled. "If there's something you *can't* get, you simply claim the client can't afford it, and your mystique remains undiluted."

Only Felix and Ggorgos were on board the shuttle, as far as the Facilitator knew. Calred had wanted to come, expressing an unusual degree of eagerness to do field work. He was usually happy to stay on the ship, but he said after serving as a transport service for Jhuri, he was eager to do something more interesting. Felix had to leave Calred behind, though. If he'd come along, that would have left the *Temerarious* uncrewed… since Tib Pelta was secretly on board the shuttle, too, ready to slip unseen and stealthily through the station to search for signs of their rogue Hacan.

"The station looks like a sort of black crystal knife, doesn't it?" Felix enhanced the view of the Facilitator's facility as they approached. The station was a simple structure: a central spike, with the pointed end at the bottom (relative to their position), with a wider disc surrounded by windows near the top. The whole structure was oddly faceted and threw off counterintuitive sparkles in the illumination of the star, the planet, the nearby moons, and even the shuttle's lights.

Ggorgos grunted. "Like the ceremonial daggers your ancestors used to cut out the hearts of sacrificial victims."

"*My* ancestors?" Felix said. "That doesn't sound like my ancestors. I'm sure my ancestors were lovely. Wait. Why do you have conversational knowledge of ancient human murder techniques?" Actually, upon reflection, that didn't really surprise him.

"I used to be a xeno-anthropologist," Ggorgos said.

That *did* surprise him. "Why did you go into that line of work?"

"I sought to refine the Kingdom's diplomatic efforts by developing a deeper understanding of the alien cultures we dealt with."

"Really. If you don't mind me asking, how did you, ah… transition from that field of study into your current line of work?"

"I had several difficult interactions with the alien cultures I studied," Ggorgos said. "Those experiences altered my worldview. Now I pursue diplomacy by other means."

"I see." Felix looked at her scars, and wondered what other marks might be hidden beneath her carapace. That kind of trauma would have altered his worldview, too.

The station's docking system sent approach instructions, which the shuttle's computer handled more or less automatically. They approached the center of the spike, where a forcefield wall covered a small hangar bay. The station wasn't immense, but it was pretty big for something owned by a private individual. Of course, it was possible the Facilitator was some kind of consortium. No one really knew.

The forcefield shifted to admit them, and then the shuttle settled to the floor inside. A Rokha wearing a white dress with gold cuffs – a striking look against her void-black fur – approached, arms raised in welcome, as Felix and Ggorgos descended the ramp. Felix looked around, and there was the Naaz, a tiny four-armed creature zipping around on a small hovering platform. The Rokha and Naaz species were closely intertwined, almost symbiotic; they shared a homeworld, and even when they went abroad in the galaxy, you seldom saw one without the other.

The Rokha bowed. "Honored guests. I am Makena." She gestured to the Naaz. "This is my partner, Craic."

The Naaz zipped past them – Ggorgos swiveled to keep an eye on her – and then said, in a buzzing voice, "We did not realize you were bringing a third guest. Hello, friend Yssaril."

Felix managed not to wince. The little Naaz must have some kind of tech that enabled her to see through the natural camouflage of Tib's people.

Tib shimmered into visibility and stepped forward to stand beside the others. "This is my first officer," Felix said. "She decided to come along at the last minute."

"All are welcome!" Makena said. "Come. The Facilitator has only a brief window open in their schedule, but when they heard both the Mentak Coalition *and* the Xxcha Kingdom were requesting an audience, how could they possibly refuse?"

"Very civic-minded," Felix said. Ggorgos grunted, and Tib snorted.

"Please, follow Craic."

As they walked through the hangar, Felix was keenly aware that they were being led by an alien floating in what might very well be a miniature mobile weapons platform, while there was an immense humanoid panther at their backs. "I'm surprised you didn't check us for weapons," Felix said.

"We politely asked you not to bring any," Makena said. "Surely we can trust you?"

"Of course," Felix said. "I just wouldn't expect you to rely on trust."

"I am not worried overmuch for my own safety," Makena said. "And the Facilitator is in no danger from any of you."

While it stung a bit to be dismissed as a threat, Felix had to admit that the Facilitator had something of a home court advantage here.

They were led to a rather nice lift, all dim lights and glittering black walls. "What is the station made of, if you don't mind me asking?" Felix said as they ascended. "I've never seen material like this before."

"Something developed by the Gashlai," Makena said.

"They use this material as armor on their War Suns," Craic added.

"The Facilitator helped the Embers with a… tricky negotiation… and this was the reward they offered," Makena said. "I gather it's the only significant quantity of the material in existence outside Gashlai space."

"I'm surprised people aren't constantly trying to chip off samples to take home for analysis," Felix said.

"That would be rude," Makena said. "Our clients are never rude to the Facilitator."

"It's also rather resistant to chipping," Craic said.

The elevator doors opened, and they were ushered into a round, windowless room, completely empty except for a chest-high (to Felix) pillar of the same glittering, faceted material. "The Facilitator will see you now," Makena said.

Felix looked around. "Will we see the Facilitator?"

Makena and Craic didn't answer, but simply withdrew to the elevator. The doors closed behind them.

"The walls are full of scanners," Ggorgos said, peering around through her artificial eye. "That pillar is entirely opaque to my sensors, though."

The pillar said, "Let a mysterious entity keep a few secrets, would you?" The voice was soothing and neutral, neither low nor high, and clearly artificial.

"Where are you transmitting from?" Ggorgos said.

"No preliminary niceties? All right. It's hard to say where I'm transmitting from. The signal bounces around a bit, and I'm always on the move. It's so hard to keep track. If you'll allow *me* the niceties: welcome, Ggorgos Skal of the Kingdom of Xxcha, and Captain Duval and First Officer Pelta of the Mentak Coalition. I have had no contact with Terrak since the commission of that heinous crime."

"How did you know why we were here?" Felix said.

"Knowing things is half my business, captain. In this case, though, I didn't even require informants, just deduction. You're an international delegation of military personnel, dispatched from a space station where a murder was committed by one of my known associates. I was expecting you sooner."

Ggorgos said, "Did you help arrange Terrak's escape?" Her voice was flat, without particular menace, which was somehow even more menacing than a roar would have been.

"I did not."

Felix sighed. "If you knew we were coming, and knew you had nothing of value to tell us, you might have saved us the trouble of actually coming all this way."

"You *will* tell us everything you know," Ggorgos said. "Your station is impressively armored, but you made the mistake of letting me *inside* it. And–"

"And your carapace is full of drones loaded with horrifying quantities of explosives, yes, I know."

Ggorgos seemed taken aback. "You should not be able to scan beyond the surface of my shell."

"I can't, but I can scan information archives. You were once captured on a Letnev science colony, thoroughly searched, and taken to their secure facility, which promptly exploded. You walked out of the wreckage. You've done the same trick a few other times. Given the patterns of the explosions I've studied, there were multiple ignition points, and in most of those cases you didn't have time to place multiple bombs yourself, so: drones. Threatening me is silly. If you disrupt my operations, *so* many powerful people will be very unhappy with you. Anyway, it's unnecessary. I am susceptible to bribes, not threats."

Just like Jhuri said. "So, you *do* have useful information?" Felix said.

"I do. You have identified two known associates of Terrak's in this system: myself, and an agricultural importer-exporter, correct?"

"You answer *our* questions," Ggorgos said. "You don't get to–"

"Yes," Felix said. Ggorgos glared at him. "That's right. I assume you know something we don't?"

"There is a third associate."

"Tell us who." Ggorgos was vibrating, with rage or eagerness or probably some combination of the two.

"If I give you the information you need to find this associate, what will you give me in return?"

"If you obstruct the lawful investigation of the murder of a member of the Xxcha Kingdom–"

Felix rubbed his forehead. "Ggorgos, a word?" He turned his back on the pillar, and Ggorgos glared before stepping up beside him.

"There's no *privacy* here, Duval. Why are you turning your back on a pedestal with a speaker inside it?"

"For my own psychological comfort, Ggorgos. This is a situation that requires finesse, and possibly a bit of charm, and the soft skills of an equitable negotiation. Perhaps you should let me handle things?"

"Handle them *swiftly*." Ggorgos stomped across the room to stand by Tib Pelta, who was staring off into space, looking bored, which probably meant she was thinking hard.

Felix turned and faced the pillar. "Facilitator. What would you like in exchange for this information?"

"I'm so pleased you asked!" the Facilitator said. "I'd love to have the full unredacted dossier on the Thales affair."

"I have no idea what you're talking about," Felix lied. "Pick something else."

"That's all I want that you can offer. Unless… you'd like to offer me a favor?"

"What kind of favor?"

"Mmmm… for this information … a small favor. Nothing that would compromise your mission, threaten your life, or endanger the interests of the Mentak Coalition."

"I am going to need something more specific than that, Facilitator."

"We're talking about you taking a package from one place to another and making sure no one looks at the contents, including yourself. That sort of thing. You wouldn't even have to go very far out of your way. A secure courier with military credentials is a useful thing to have."

Well, if it was only smuggling, that was fine. "Agreed. Who's the third associate?"

"I am not entirely sure."

"Bombs," Ggorgos said in a voice like lead. "I have so many bombs."

Felix winced. He wouldn't have offered a threat of mass destruction at this juncture, but Ggorgos clearly had her own way of doing things.

"Please, don't be so dramatic," the Facilitator said. "The vagueness of my information is the reason why you only had to offer me a *small* favor. Here's what I know. Terrak tried to cover his tracks, but he often went to Huntsman's Moon when he visited the system. He visited an industrial area on the outskirts of the northern city, but I can't narrow his destination down beyond a two-kilometer radius. It's hard to track someone on foot in such a desolate neighborhood, and since no one was *paying* me to spy on Terrak, I didn't allocate very many resources to the problem. There are half a dozen plausible groups or individuals in that area he could have been meeting with – various engineers and scientists doing work that would be frowned upon in more closely regulated parts of the galaxy."

"That's all you know?" Felix had been hoping for something more. The exact location where Terrak was hiding out, and the details of any security he might have, and why Amina Azad was involved in all this, and, well, lots of other things, really, in a perfect world.

"I just narrowed your search area from seventy moons to six addresses on *one* moon. I'd say I know plenty. I can offer more, though: Terrak frequently visited the moon immediately after meeting with the importer-exporter. I have a high degree of certainty that Terrak met this unknown associate *through* the fruit seller, so if you go ask *him—*"

"Let's go," Ggorgos snapped. "If you have further details, Facilitator, send them to our ship." She stomped out.

Felix bowed to the central pillar. "A pleasure doing business."

"One last thing, captain?"

Ggorgos and Tib were on the elevator, and the doors closed when Felix turned back to the pillar. "What's that?"

"Terrak is probably innocent," the Facilitator said. "I have run multiple simulations, and my confidence level is around ninety-two percent. Terrak is mildly corrupt, yes, but he's much smarter than most people realize. Anyone can be a killer, if pushed the wrong way, but it's highly unlikely Terrak would have committed such a violent crime in such an obvious way."

"People have psychotic breaks," Felix said. "There are crimes of passion. It happens all the time."

"My model accounts for those possibilities, captain. But do people who have psychotic breaks then stage unlikely jailbreaks with the help of unknown associates?"

"If he's not the killer, then he was framed. Who'd want to do that?" Felix said.

"I have no idea."

Felix sighed. "I'm just supposed to apprehend Terrak and bring him to justice. The courts can determine his guilt or innocence."

"If he's being framed, captain, it's because someone wants to discredit him, or remove him from the field of play in a game you don't even know is happening. That means Terrak knows something, or can do something, to disrupt the plans of people who are happy to commit murder. Terrak is frustrating those efforts by going on the run. If he is the victim of a conspiracy, do you think the conspirators will give him the opportunity to testify in court, or even tell his version of events to the authorities? My models suggest he is likely to meet with an accident soon after you apprehend him. What precisely *are* your orders, captain?"

Felix frowned. "I told you. Apprehension. Terrak won't come to any harm while he's in my custody." There were all sorts of mysteries and uncertainties swirling around this business, but Felix was sure of his *own* orders and intentions, at least.

"Mmm. Even if you don't intend to do him harm yourself... can you say the same, with certainty, about everyone else on your crew?"

Felix scowled and, like Ggorgos before him, stomped out of the room in a foul temper.

The fruit seller – a Hacan so physically imposing he made Calred look slight – went flying across the warehouse and crashed into a pile of crates. Wood splintered and broke, and small round green fruits rolled across the warehouse floor. Felix picked one up, took a bite, and frowned. "Sour," he said, and spat it out.

"It's a *lime*, Felix," Tib said. "I'd think you'd recognize it. You see slices of them on the rim of your glasses all the time."

"I assumed it was some sort of exotic fruit," he said. "Since this is an alien fruit warehouse."

"Limes *are* alien and exotic to the Hacan."

"Point," Felix said. They were standing off to one side while Ggorgos ran the... interrogation, for want of a better word.

Ggorgos advanced on the fruit seller, who stood up, groaning. The Hacan put up his fists, still game to fight, though he was a bit unsteady on his feet. "I will ask you again," Ggorgos said. "Tell us the identity of Terrak's other contact."

"You can't come into *my* place of business–"

Ggorgos moved faster than Felix would have expected for someone so heavily armored and shoved the Hacan sprawling back into the crates. Felix wondered if there were cybernetic or chemical enhancements at work. Or... maybe *all* the Xxcha could move that fast if they wanted to, and simply didn't bother, since they were generally an easygoing and phlegmatic culture?

"Answer me," Ggorgos said. Some of the faceted panels of her exocarapace slid open, and small sleek drones rose up, hovering, pointing various nozzles and barrels at the Hacan.

The fruit seller closed his eyes and covered his head. "All right!" he shouted. "It's a Hylar chemist, her name is Lonrah!"

"Why would Terrak go see a chemist?" Tib said.

"No clue," Felix said. He was trying to convince himself he didn't *care* if Terrak was innocent or guilty – that the issue was outside his mission parameters. Unfortunately, Felix had never been good at staying strictly within mission parameters. "Her name is on the list of possibilities the Facilitator gave us, though."

"Back to the ship!" Ggorgos said, and headed toward the shuttle.

Felix and Tib walked over to the fruit seller and helped him up. "Sorry about all that," he said. "You obviously shouldn't call this chemist and warn her, or my Xxcha colleague will be very unhappy."

"Who cares about that?!" he bellowed as he rose. "Look what she did to my warehouse! And my employees!"

Felix looked around. There had been a certain amount of... wastage, in terms of smashed crates and pulped fruit. And a couple of the warehouse laborers, who'd attempted to act as ersatz bodyguards, were moaning on the floor by the door, though they didn't seem irreparably damaged. Felix said, "You can invoice the

Mentak Coalition Embassy on Rex for any damage or medical costs. You can pad the invoice by, oh, fifteen percent, and I'll vouch for its accuracy. All right?"

The fruit seller stood to his full height, nearly a meter taller than Felix, and gazed down at him. He showed his canine teeth. "Twenty percent," he said.

Back on the *Temerarious*, they filled Calred in on their adventures, and set a course for Huntsman's Moon. "Will you let me come for *this* mission?" Calred asked. "I've got a new rifle I haven't had a chance to point at anyone yet."

"I've had enough field trips for the day," Tib Pelta said. "I'll stay on board. Also, I doubt Ggorgos has a tactical plan in mind that would make use of my special abilities. She's more run-and-gun than stealthy sneaking."

Ggorgos was standing at the navigation panel, glaring at it, as if doing so would make the ship go faster. "Your security officer may join us," she said. "His marksmanship record is adequate."

"*Adequate?*" Calred said. He held several fleet records for sharpshooting.

"You have to understand, coming from her, that's the highest possible praise," Felix said. "I *dream* of being adequate."

"I need to make a call." Ggorgos left the bridge.

"I should fill Jhuri in on things, too," Felix said, and headed to his ready room.

"The minister's autopsy didn't turn up anything unusual," Jhuri said.

"Did you expect it to?" Felix said. "I thought, well, big spear through the neck, it all seemed pretty clear."

"I was troubled by the reports of the victim acting strangely before the murder. I thought there might be something there, but we got nothing from toxicology, and no unusual findings from the pathologist, so… maybe the ambassador was just having an off night. Something strange did happen, though. I was questioning the other guests about Terrak and met a woman from the Federation of Sol who's known him for years. In our initial interview she told me, very adamantly, that Terrak was never violent, had a wonderful relationship with the victim, and was certainly innocent of the crime."

"I heard much the same from the Facilitator," Felix said.

"Let me finish. This woman, Lillith, came back to me a few hours ago and said she had a confession to make. Now she claimed that, actually, things had been terribly strained between Terrak and Qqurant, and they'd had a serious falling out. She didn't know the details, but said Terrak and Qqurant had gone from friendly to frosty to vicious in recent months. She said she'd overheard arguments between them that included threats of violence. She told me she'd lied earlier because Terrak was an old friend, and she didn't want to see him in trouble, but that her conscience had been bothering her, and compelled her to come forward with the truth. Her conscience! She's a *trade representative!*"

Not a type famed for their ethical inflexibility, Felix thought. Combined with the Facilitator's claims, it was looking more and more likely that the official narrative about Terrak wasn't the whole story. "What do you think it means?" Felix said. "Was Terrak framed? Did someone reach out to Lillith, and, what, bribe her to change her story?"

"A murder that brazen and obvious is a truly stupid crime," Jhuri mused. "And everyone agrees Terrak is anything but stupid. Slightly corrupt, a bit lazy and self-indulgent, but a sharp operator all the same. I don't know what's going on, Felix, but I'll be very interested to hear what Terrak has to say when you get him in custody."

"Assuming Ggorgos doesn't shoot him first."

"See that she doesn't, Felix. I'll be in touch if I find out more." Jhuri cut the connection, and Felix went to prep his gear for their visit to Huntsman's Moon.

CHAPTER 9
SEVERYNE

The *Grim Countenance* had just transited the wormhole and set a course for the nearby Rantula system when Severyne received a call from the admiral.

"We have new information," Immental said without preamble. "Our rogue asset is currently believed to be on a small satellite called Huntsman's Moon, visiting a chemist."

"It will take us a few hours to reach the moon," Severyne said. "But we'll scramble a landing party as soon as—"

"No, the Mentak Coalition has a team closer, attempting an apprehension. You will take up a hidden position near the moon. Be prepared to capture Terrak if the Coalition team fails."

"And if they succeed, should I take Terrak away from them?"

"That won't be necessary. We have ... other plans in place if the Coalition captures him."

Severyne wondered what that meant. There was no love lost between the Barony and the Mentak Coalition. Did Immental have double agents embedded with the Coalition?

"Just head for the moon and await further instructions," Immental said.

"As you command, admiral."

Immental's face vanished from the screen. Severyne looked across her desk at Undercommandant Voyou. "What do you think?"

He considered the question with his customary seriousness. "I think we are operating with too little information for me to think anything much at all."

"I don't like serving as the safety net for a bunch of Mentak pirates. But we do what we must." She waved her hand. "Go set things in motion. Let me know if there are any noteworthy developments."

A few hours later, Severyne's research on Terrak was interrupted by a call from Voyou on her private priority comms. "We're in sensor range of Huntsman's Moon, captain. We've identified the Mentak Coalition vessel, a cruiser that's currently registered as a diplomatic transport ship. It's odd, but it seems you set a flag in the system? You wanted to be notified if we ever encountered this particular ship–"

Severyne groaned. "Don't tell me it's the *Temerarious*."

"Are you familiar with the ship, captain?" Voyou asked.

"You might say that," Severyne said. "I stole it, once."

THE FAITHFUL VII

"Filthy Gashlai." Captain Rayonner ran a finger beneath the collar of his uniform, sweat running down his face. "Why do they keep it so abominably hot in here, eh?"

Undercommandant Misericore said, "The Embers are savages, sir." She did her best to look uncomfortable, too, though since taking the sacrament she didn't feel extremes of heat or cold as much as she once had. She didn't feel extremes of any kind, really: she was too fully at ease in the sure knowledge of her purpose. Misericore was, ostensibly, a representative of the Barony of Letnev, here to escort the Gashlai leaders to their summit on Arc Prime... but she was really here in service to the guides, to fulfill her small part of the greater plan. She burned with the desire to please her masters.

Since traveling through the wormhole to the Gashlai system, she'd lost intimate contact with the guides, but they'd warned her that would happen: she was in wild lands, now, beyond their caring cultivation. Once she returned home, she was assured, she would once again hear them whispering in her mind, and in the meantime, she had her instructions. The guides didn't have a presence in this system, apart from Misericore and a couple of other faithful elsewhere in the delegation. For some reason, the

Gashlai were incompatible with the sacrament. She felt so very bad for them.

Captain Rayonner strode to the small observation window in the wall of this bare room on the tiny, cramped station. Misericore dutifully followed him, hands clasped behind her back to mirror his own posture. This station was where the Embers met with the more flammable biological species, since their home planet Muaat was inhospitable for most organic beings.

"Look at those things." Rayonner was gazing at the War Suns in orbit above the burning sphere of Muaat, far beneath them. The Suns were dark, thorny orbs, surrounded by swarms of lesser ships coming and going. In truth, the War Suns seemed less like ships at all, and more like space stations – cities of the void, but cities full of weapons, capable of moving great distances under their own power. Other species had variations on the theme – the Barony's own Dark Star program was their latest iteration – but the Gashlai War Suns were legendary. "This whole place used to be shipyards for the Hylar, when the Gashlai were their slaves. The Embers took the technology and turned it against their old masters. Ha. The squids should have known better than to play with fire, eh?" Misericore murmured agreement.

The large doors at the end of the room slid open, and three Gashlai entered, wearing their golden Ember suits. In truth the containment systems were less like suits of armor and more like small, armored vehicles, bristling with sensors and manipulators. The Gashlai were creatures of energy, and small windows set in their armor revealed the glow of molten matter and the flicker of flames within. Misericore wasn't sure if the placid faces gazing at them from each suit were the true faces of the Gashlai, or masks of some kind. The one in the lead spoke in a voice like water sizzling on coals, "You may call me Molash. I am a Flame Warden and speak with the authority of our leaders."

"Molash?" Rayonner scowled. "We're supposed to meet with, eh, what is it, Molt, ah, Sha, lah, ta–"

"Cease defiling my true name," the Warden interrupted. "It does not fit properly in your wet mouth. I have offered you a name of convenience – one that you *can* pronounce."

Rayonner stiffened. "Yes. Very well. I have come to formally extend the Baron's invitation to your ruling tribunal to join us on Arc Prime for the upcoming summit, to sign our treaty and join the Legion as a member state, with full partner status. In the meantime, my crew includes various negotiators and lawyers and advisers and the like, so we can settle all those little details in advance of the meeting."

The Warden said, "I know why you are here. My leaders have agreed to this alliance, in principle, but if I may make a personal observation... it is unlike the Letnev, to seek alliances. The Wardens have found the entire process rather surprising."

Rayonner said, "The Baron, in his wisdom–"

Misericore cleared her throat. Rayonner looked at her. "Captain, if I may?"

Rayonner was here because of his legendary military status – at the helm of the *City Imperishable* he'd razed the colony world of Pax Agricola – but Misericore was present because of her diplomatic skills, and because she'd studied the Gashlai. "Carry on," the captain said.

"May your flame burn eternally, Warden," she said, in her best approximation of the Embers' language. No Letnev could duplicate their tongueless tongue perfectly, but she had practiced.

The Warden made a hissing sound that Misericore knew was

a chuckle of amusement. "And yours as well, Letnev. Or, what do your people say – may the dark embrace you?"

"Just so, Warden." She cleared her throat. "It is true that the Letnev are a proud people, and accustomed to making our own way in the galaxy. But we face an unprecedented threat. Our old enemies, the humans, have joined with your ancient foes, the Hylar. We know the humans seek to spread throughout the galaxy until every world is subsumed in their cultural hegemony. We also know the Hylar care only for the expansion of their technological power. The humans view the Letnev as an obstacle to their expansion. The Hylar view your people as a natural resource, theirs to exploit, which is even worse."

Molash sizzled in agreement.

"The Hylar have joined forces with the humans, expanding their coalition, and it is only a matter of time before they seek to regain that which was lost. This Greater Union will bring overwhelming force to bear, and pick off their old rivals, one at a time… unless we can form a united front and strike them first. The Gashlai have been unable to take revenge on the Hylar for their crimes against your people, because your forces are too evenly matched. If you join with the Barony, and our other allies…" She let a small smile touch her lips. "Then you will see the seas of Jol and Nar *boil*."

"We have heard these explanations before, of course," Molash said. "But it is meaningful to us, to hear them in person, where we can better judge your sincerity. I… find your position compelling." The Warden turned to face Rayonner. "We are also pleased that such a distinguished figure was sent to bring this message and escort our leaders to Arc Prime."

"Eh?" Rayonner said. Anything that didn't directly involve warfare usually failed to keep his attention for long.

"I have studied the burning of Pax Agricola with great interest, captain," the Warden said.

Rayonner brightened, as he always did when the subject of past glories, or the prospect of future ones, came up. "Oh, you liked that, did you? Let me tell you something that *wasn't* in the reports, I think you'll enjoy this..."

Rayonner didn't care about anything but war, Misericore thought, which was very sad; she pitied anyone who lacked her own sense of purpose in service. The guides said there was no need to give Rayonner the sacrament, though.

War, after all, was the only thing they *needed* the captain to care about.

CHAPTER 10
TERRAK

Azad groaned. "Terrak, you idiot, that was *so stupid*, I cannot get over how stupid that was."

I expected her to scream at me, punch me, or even shoot me, but after that initial complaint, Azad was all business. Either she was incredibly pragmatic, or she was saving her revenge for later. I greatly hoped it was the former. She turned to Lonrah. "Do you have any samples of the spores left? Can you, I don't know, replicate what was in that canister?"

"No," Lonrah said. "My analysis was destructive. The samples I took are wholly inert."

"Right. Any chance of recovering something useful from inside that incinerator?"

"It wouldn't be a very good incinerator if there was. The spores… they're all gone."

"I hope that warm glow of righteousness I assume you're feeling right now keeps on comforting you when the entire galaxy is engulfed in war, Terrak," Azad said.

"You said you knew the identities of compromised individuals." I'd given this some thought, in the moments before I acted. I couldn't ruin her plan without proposing an alternative.

Azad frowned. "Yeah, we have a list of a few, with a reasonably high degree of certainty."

I spread my hands. "Then let's go test the cure on one of them. If it doesn't work, we're no worse off than we are now, and if it does work, we've made actual, measurable progress against our enemy, and enlisted new allies to our cause, since I'm sure they'll be grateful to be free. That's a much better plan than injecting a random subject snatched off the street."

Azad rubbed her temples. "The problem, Terrak, is that highly placed government officials who've been co-opted by an enemy conspiracy are *harder to tranquilize and strap to a table* than random subjects snatched off the street."

"If your work was easy, Azad, everyone would do it. Plus, I am perfectly comfortable helping you execute this plan, so it's better for our partnership."

"I should execute *you*. 'Partnership'. What do you bring to this operation, besides impulsiveness and unreliability?"

"For one thing," I said, "I can get us on a ship and off this moon."

"I can, too," Azad said.

"My way won't involve theft or murder."

She wrinkled her nose. "OK. That's probably better." She rolled her neck around on her shoulders. "All right. I'm not big on revenge, or on holding grudges. I'm a believer in dealing with the world as it is and changing with the conditions on the ground instead of complaining that everything isn't exactly how I'd like it to be. That said... if you screw me around like this again, Terrak, I will turn you into a fur rug. Do you understand me?" There was no grin now, no playfulness, and I glimpsed a core of ice within her.

I nodded. "I understand. As long as you understand that I won't condone causing unnecessary harm to innocents."

"You want us to inject mystery drugs into generals and political leaders and industrialists, Terrak." Azad rolled her eyes. "We might have to hurt some nice people to get close enough to the bad people to find a vein."

I shrugged. "Military personnel, bodyguards – they know danger comes with the job. That's different from what you wanted to do with this elder."

Azad shook her head. "People who draw lines like that just baffle me. My line of work is hard enough – why set up a bunch of artificial barriers to success? 'Oh, no, I can't do *that*, I have to stay inside the lines' – why? We're not on a sports field here. All that matters is outcomes. But, sure, fine. I've been burdened with people like you my entire career. I'm used to it. Adaptability." She pointed at Lonrah. "You, get me as much of the cure as you can make, and some syringes and such." She pointed at me. "You, think about ways to make me as happy as possible for as long as possible going forward." She pointed at her own chest. "Me, I'm going to go call my bosses and tell them, oops, there was a lab mishap, the spores got destroyed, and we're going into the field to seek a new test subject. Because if I told them the truth, they'd have me kill you, Terrak. See how nice I am? Maybe they can advise me on the best target for your experiment." She left the room.

I released a slow breath. "I was not at all sure I'd survive that."

"Since you did, can we please get this unconscious Hacan out of my laboratory?" Lonrah said.

I picked him up from the table and took him back to the field where we'd first found him. No one paid me any attention on that part of the journey, either. The old fellow blinked up at me when I let him down, and growled halfheartedly. "What? Did you finish? Where are my brains?"

"Inside your head and unharmed. The experiment was canceled, but you have still been paid." I slipped another credit stick I'd pilfered from Azad into his hand. "Be well, elder."

"My patch," he grumbled. "Get off it."

When I returned to the alley that led to Lonrah's lab, I had a nasty shock. The utility box that hid the elevator was surrounded by a group in tactical armor that included a human, a Hacan, and an Xxcha. The Xxcha was cutting into the box with some sort of large grinding implement, the blade showering sparks.

I drew back before any of them noticed me, and stood around the corner of the adjacent warehouse, back against the wall, my mind racing.

Well, not racing so much as just thinking, "Oh, no," over and over.

CHAPTER 11
AZAD

Azad finished her call. She hadn't actually lied to her boss – that wasn't really a thing she could do – but she'd successfully argued for Terrak's continued usefulness. "At least let me use him to get off the moon, OK?" She'd insisted on operational independence for this mission, so it was her call anyway, but she preferred not to be in opposition with the people who paid the bills.

She returned to Lonrah's lab to find Terrak and the Hacan vagrant both gone. She groaned. "Did he wander off? He's supposed to be making me happy. Going off on his own does not make me happy."

"I asked him to remove the subject." Lonrah approached, carrying a slim black case, zippered shut. "This contains the cure. I made enough for about a dozen doses, though it will vary a bit depending on the species of the subjects – you don't need to give as much to an Yssaril as you do to a Hacan. There's also a drive inside with the recipes, and any disreputable chemist should be able to create more. None of the required components are terribly exotic, though the neural growth promoters are expensive."

"Money, I've got. What I need is a more reliable partner."

"Terrak is extremely flexible, morally, when it comes to matters of commerce," Lonrah said. "But he has a few clear bright lines when it comes to people. It's an unusual combination, and he's not as rich as he could be if he didn't care about hurting anyone, but I admit, it makes him more pleasant to be around, and more comfortable to do business with."

"Baffling," Azad said. "You're all just baffling." She took the bag. "Tell me Terrak will be back soon. That he isn't taking the old guy to a rehab facility or setting him up in a hotel or something–"

An alarm blatted, and Lonrah hurried over to a console. "Oh, no. We have visitors upstairs, and they are wearing very shiny black armor."

Azad cursed. She used one of her very best special occasion curses. "Stall them. And then show me that back entrance you mentioned."

Lonrah pressed a button and said, "Can I help you?"

"You will," a voice crackled back over the loudspeaker. Azad thought it sounded like an Xxcha.

"Is this Lonrah?" a human male voice said. It sounded vaguely familiar… "We'd, ah, like to speak to Terrak."

"I don't know who that is," Lonrah said.

Azad shook her head. The soldiers up there clearly already knew Lonrah was acquainted with Terrak, so a more nuanced lie was really called for. Amateurs.

A sigh. "Look," the voice said. "Could I just speak to Amina Azad for a moment?"

The Hylar looked at her, and she looked back at the Hylar, and then, despite herself, Azad began to laugh. She'd just realized where she knew the man's voice from. This was extremely poor operational security, but it was too amusing *not* to answer him. She reached out for the intercom button. "Is that Felix? Of all the moons in all the galaxy, you land on mine?"

"What can I say, Azad? I have extremely poor luck. I also have a question. Would you like to explain why a Federation of Sol operative is helping a murderer escape justice?"

Azad snorted. "First, who says I'm a Federation of Sol operative? You never proved that. You always put the 'ass' in 'assumptions', don't you, Felix? This guy. I can't believe we even have a prehistoric proto-human common ancestor. Second of all, Terrak isn't a murderer. He's the victim of a conspiracy. So, I have a question for *you*: did the bad guys get to you yet? Are you a puppet? Or are you just mindlessly following orders like usual? Wait, that's just a different kind of puppet–"

"I follow my orders with great mindfulness, Azad." He still sounded so smug and sure of himself. The Thales affair really should have knocked some of that confidence out of him, but apparently Felix had mistaken the fluke of his survival for evidence of his own competence. "What conspiracy are you–"

"Enough." That first, harsher Xxcha voice cut in. "You will surrender yourself, and Terrak."

Azad laughed. "Felix, why don't you tell them how likely that is?"

"I cannot guarantee your safety if you do not comply," the Xxcha said.

"That's fine. I can't guarantee yours if you keep bothering me." She turned off the intercom. "OK, Lon. As much as I'd love the opportunity to punch Felix in the face, the situation isn't *quite* what I'd like it to be, tactically, for that kind of fun. Let's see this escape route. And patch my comms into your intercom system so I can listen to what's happening here after I'm gone, all right?"

CHAPTER 12
TERRAK

I went back to the empty lot, where the Hacan was now upright, and said, "Hello. Could I make you an offer? I'd like to buy your garment."

He laughed at me and said, "Consider it a gift. I can buy something better." He pulled off the filthy tarp and threw it at my feet. I wrapped it around myself and nodded my thanks.

I made my way to the outskirts of a homeless encampment, one where broken-down Hacan sipped from green glass bottles, and a few Saar scuffled at the dirt, and a N'orr missing half its limbs lurched along, picking at a pile of trash and putting occasional finds in its mouth. One of the other Hacan shuffled over and offered me a sip of his beverage, and I took one, to be hospitable. The drink bore the same relationship to the fine sunwine I'd enjoyed on Shilsaad Station that a lump of regurgitated gristle bears to a prime-cut caprid steak.

That said, I'd drunk worse, and enjoyed it less.

I couldn't do much at the moment, so I just waited. When the Coalition thugs departed, I'd figure out what to do next. Azad would likely get out all right – there was an escape route, after all, and anyone who caused as much trouble as she did was probably adept at escaping it. I hoped she'd find me again. Despite our recent disagreements over the best way to proceed, we still had a common goal, and she was a resource I could use.

If she didn't come back, I supposed I would try to make my way to one of my hidden caches – I'd always considered the possibility that life might turn against me, and had prepared contingencies, after all – and just lay low for a while. But I had higher hopes. I wanted to find out who'd destroyed my life. I wanted to destroy *theirs*.

I took another sip. "This is marvelous," I said, and handed the bottle back to my new friend.

CHAPTER 13
AZAD

"Of course I don't have any breathing apparatus," Lonrah said. "I can breathe fine underwater."

Azad looked at the pool of black water in the floor. They were in a tiny concrete-lined space hidden behind a false panel in the back of the server room – they'd had to move a rack of machines just to get access. What they'd gotten access to looked a lot like drowning to death. "Yes, but you deal with all sorts of chemicals, so you must have *something.*"

"I have various filtration systems, but none that would help you breathe down there. I have an attachment dome for my exo-suit that I can fill with air or water, and I use that sometimes when I work with especially volatile materials, but even if we could cram you inside the bubble, it wouldn't fit in the escape tunnel."

"Great. How far is it to the other end?"

"About five hundred meters."

Azad tried to do some math – how fast could she swim underwater, how long could she hold her breath – and gave up because even without all the variables the answer was obvious. "Five hundred meters is very far. I will die."

"I *said* the usefulness of this route depended on how long you could hold your breath."

"No human can hold their breath that long. Or a Hacan either!"

"It's not a water pipe," Lonrah said. "It's an old smuggler's tunnel that flooded. It's not full of water the whole way – there are places where the roof caved in, with air pockets, so you can pop up and get a breath here and there."

"I don't suppose you have a map or a list of the precise locations of these pockets?"

"I've tried this tunnel exactly once, Azad, and I just swam through it. I didn't make a map. There are no branches or anything."

"Right. That's something, I guess. At least I won't take a wrong turn." She looked at the still pool. "The alternative is staying here, and probably dying at the hands of *Felix Duval*, and I can't abide that. Better to drown like a rat. OK." She was prepared to swim, wearing a tank top and shorts and shoes that were pretty much just extremely tough socks. She checked her belt and the vest she'd strapped on, its waterproof pouches full of the cure and her other possessions, such as they were. "Thanks for all your help, Lonrah."

"I didn't do it for you. I did it for Terrak. And also for science."

Terrak. At least Azad didn't have to listen to him complain about the swim. She hoped he was OK. He was savvy enough not to wander into the middle of a commando raid, anyway, and with luck he was laying low nearby instead of running as far and fast as he could. If he was still in the vicinity, she'd find him. Assuming she survived her escape. "That's still very noble, Lon. I pretty much only do stuff for money."

"I'm ... surprised you didn't kill me."

Azad cocked her head. "Why would I do that?"

"To keep me from telling those soldiers up there what you're doing. You didn't even make me promise not to tell."

"Why make you tell a lie? Of course you'll tell. But killing you wouldn't be very good manners, after all the help you've given us. Listen, though. The puppetmasters aren't as polite as I am. You should run. In fact, you should swim, along with me, right now. Show me where those air bubbles are."

Lonrah said, "My whole *life* is in this place, all my research, everything–"

And Terrak had said she was an agoraphobe. Oh well. Azad had tried. Sometimes people didn't understand the danger they were in until the danger fully closed around them. "Suit yourself. But you might end up locked in a place a lot less pleasant." Azad gave a little wave, took a breath, and dove straight down.

The water was cold, which was unpleasant. Azad hadn't done a lot of swimming growing up – it wasn't a common form of recreation in orbit around Meginstjarna – and though she'd learned to move in the water well enough during her military training, being underwater never felt good or natural, even when it *wasn't* cold and dark.

Once Azad kicked her way down into the tunnel proper, she was glad she hadn't bothered with a careful calculation of lung capacity and swim speed, because conditions in the field were worse than anticipated. For one thing, the tunnel was narrow, and her hands slammed against the sides, slowing her progress; she mainly propelled herself by kicking. She swam as close to the top of the tunnel as possible, which meant she bumped her head a lot, but she couldn't risk missing an air pocket. Just when her lungs had transformed into two burning coals in her chest, her head broke through the top of the water. She spun, sticking her face into the dark gap above, and sucked in deep breaths. The air was scented with stone and water. Better than sewage, anyway. She took another breath and went down again.

She proceeded that way, rapidly losing track of how far she'd gone. After that first long stretch, the crumbled spaces at the top of the tunnel were more frequent, and then the water level gradually sank as the tunnel angled upward, which helped. She walked the last dozen meters, the water dropping from neck deep to chest to waist to knees. There was light ahead of her, just a faint glow filtering down from above. The water was only ankle deep when she reached a rusty maintenance ladder, the bottom rungs slick with mildew, and climbed up. There was a hatch on top, but it was just made of wood – hence the light, filtered between the slats – so she was able to heave the cover up and out of the way.

She emerged in an empty lot full of weeds, looked around, and laughed out loud. It was the same field where they'd captured the old Hacan, though he'd moved on, apparently. She clambered out, soaking wet in the bright sun. After stretching for a moment, she turned her earpiece back on. She was hooked into Lon's intercom and could hear the audio from her lab's surveillance system. Mostly what she heard was various thumps and screeches. Not terribly informative.

She went looking for Terrak. He was annoying just lately, but overall, he'd been more help than hindrance. If he was telling the truth about being able to get them a ship, she'd even forgive him for throwing their spores away. As long as it was a ship with good heating.

CHAPTER 14
FELIX

Ggorgos pried the hidden elevator shaft open, but there was no elevator car there, of course. "We should have brought antigrav harnesses or something," Felix said, peering down into the depths.

A panel popped open on the back of Ggorgos's shell, and a spool wrapped with black cable topped with a folding grapnel emerged. "Secure the end," she said, pulling some of the line loose and handing the hook to Calred.

The security officer dutifully wrapped the cable around the utility box and hooked it into place, giving it some hard tugs to make sure the grapnel would hold. "All set."

"Give mother a hug," Ggorgos said, opening her arms wide, her tone so entirely deadpan that it took Felix a moment to realize she was making a joke.

"You're being funny now?" he said.

"Descending into the lair of my enemies puts me in good spirits. Come." She beckoned again, and Calred and Felix awkwardly stepped into her embrace. Felix didn't like the idea of clinging to a large tortoise being lowered into a pit – the chances of slipping and falling seemed too great – but her shell shifted, panels popping open to reveal molded carbon handholds. "Grab on tight," she said, and once they assured her they were secure, she stepped into the shaft.

The cable unspooled steadily, lowering them to the bottom of the shaft – it wasn't that deep, in the end, more basement-level dwelling than proper subterranean lair. Ggorgos used the same cutting tool that had opened the ground-level doors to cut through the roof of the elevator car and dropped down. She opened the doors – that only required pushing a button – and rushed out into a long, narrow room lined with shelves full of bottles and jars. Calred and Felix came behind her, weapons up, Calred holding an energy rifle, Felix a kinetic sidearm. There was nothing and no one to shoot at, but also no trip wires or exploding things, so Felix decided to call it a win.

Ggorgos dispersed her drones, and they went zipping through the space, disappearing through an open doorway at the end of the room. After a moment, she grunted. "One hostile present. Not Terrak or Azad."

"Azad was *here*," Felix said.

"Was I?" Azad's voice crackled over the intercom. "Or was I just broadcasting remotely? Go easy on Lonrah. She was just doing a little business. And Felix – listen to what she says about the conspiracy, OK? You're on the wrong side, which isn't unusual for you, but this time, you're even wronger than usual."

"Azad, damn it, where are you?" Felix glared at the ceiling, but no one answered.

A Hylar in an exo-suit stomped in, escorted by a buzzing group of drones. "Hello, unthinking tools of state-sanctioned violence."

"Where is Terrak?" Ggorgos demanded.

"I have no idea. He left a little before you all showed up, to run an errand. I expected him back by now, but… I imagine he saw you, or the hole you put in my elevator doors, and decided not to hang around."

Ggorgos cursed, and several of her drones zipped back up the shaft. "I'll search the local area. Duval, see what useful information you can get out of her." She returned to the shaft and zipped back upward on her line.

I hope the elevator still works, Felix thought. He turned to Calred. "Why don't you see if you can get into her security system, take a peek at the archive, and make sure Azad and Terrak aren't hiding under a floorboard or something?" Calred gave a lazy salute and pushed past Lonrah, moving deeper into the lab.

Felix smiled at the Hylar. "So, Lonrah. What's all this I hear about a conspiracy?"

CHAPTER 15
SEVERYNE

A message came in from Immental, in text form this time: *Our targets have evaded capture. They may attempt to leave the moon in an unknown vessel. Be on alert.*

"Oh, good, we're looking for an unknown vessel," Severyne said. "There's never any shortage of those." She sent back a reply: *Acknowledged.*

The *Grim Countenance* was the sort of ship people tended to notice, so they were hiding in the shadow of an uninhabited satellite, with unostentatious probes dispersed to keep watch over Huntsman's Moon and relay sensor data back to them.

How was Severyne supposed to find the right ship? Stop them all and search them? The local authorities wouldn't be happy about that, and neither would the *Temerarious*, once they noticed she was here.

She notified the bridge crew. "Monitor all traffic from Huntsman's Moon. Our fugitive may try to depart soon, and we don't know what vessel he'll use. Hack the local traffic control system and look for anything anomalous – departures ahead of schedule, reports of vehicle theft, life sign readings that don't match crew manifests, *anything*. If our quarry gets away,

I will be very upset, and you all know what happens when I'm upset." Severyne had encouraged the rumor that if any of her subordinates displeased her, she would take them down to the training deck, turn off all the lights, and hunt and kill them for sport.

The rumor wasn't true, of course. She never actually killed any of them. That would generate far too much paperwork.

THE FAITHFUL VIII

Fleet Captain Harlow – retired leader of the Mentak Coalition raider fleet, renowned politician and military strategist, and one of the first to be blessed by the sacrament – lay unmoving in her bed.

Her two longtime, devoted aides stood by her bedside. "I don't see how she'll be able to attend the summit," Callis said. "She's supposed to be right up there on the dais, as one of the architects of the Greater Union, but there's just less and less of her here every day."

Wallich nodded. "I caught her wandering in the garden yesterday. That's why I strapped her down. She almost fell into the fishpond. She seemed to think she was back in the battle of Tegenaria, on the bridge, and the fish were Letnev ships. She couldn't understand their fleet formation, she said. She thought it was some new tactic."

"She doesn't seem to be in any pain, at least."

Wallich shook her head. "No, of course. The guides would never allow her to suffer."

Callis and Wallich had been a devoted couple before they joined the faithful; now devotion to anyone but the guides seemed pointless. Callis oversaw the grounds of Harlow's estate, and Wallich oversaw the house, and they shared a cottage that was nicer than any home they'd lived in before joining Harlow's staff. The three of them were the only sapient beings in residence on the entire continent of this remote, automated agricultural world. The place got lonely sometimes, but Harlow had wanted a quiet retirement after a career filled with political and literal battles.

The isolation made hiding Harlow's decline easier, of course. The fleet captain had always been sharp, quick-witted, decisive, and hilarious. Even in retirement, she'd had a thousand hobbies and projects. She often said that after devoting her career to conflict, she wanted to spend her last years learning the pastimes of peacetime. Her favorite activities ranged from word puzzles (she excelled at them) to logic games (even better) to painting (she was very bad) to sculpture (she was worse) to cooking (she had Wallich make edible meals afterward), and there were always new books and media streaming into the database as she sent out requests for material to help explore her latest interests.

Harlow kept up an extensive correspondence, too, maintaining the myriad connections she'd made in her career – the same connections that had made her so valuable to the guides. Keeping *those* communications going without raising suspicion was the hardest part of Harlow's decline. Wallich had found a program that could scan a database of material and produce plausible new entries in a series, and they'd used that on the captain's vast archive to generate new letters, but every one of them had to be reviewed and tweaked and personalized. Wallich forestalled video and voice calls with claims of mild illness or technical difficulties, but they both wondered how long the charade could last. "Someone will come to check on her," Wallich said. "She's supposed to arrive early for the summit on Moll Primus, and when she doesn't show up, someone will come, no matter what excuses we make."

"We have a little sacrament put aside," Callis said. "Enough to bring an unwelcome visitor or two into the fold."

"What if there are more than one or two?"

"Then… the guides will tell us what to do. Won't they?"

"Of course," Wallich said. "Of course they will."

It was hard to worry much, when the sacrament was doing its work to ease their minds. They were both so happy the fleet captain had taken them into her confidence and allowed them to join her communion. Callis had screamed so much, when she saw Wallich twitching and spasming on the ground, but she simply hadn't understood what was happening. She'd sobbed, later, when she gave thanks for the blessing of the guides.

Still. Seeing the captain decline like this – first forgetting things, then going blank for longer and longer stretches of time, and finally lapsing into delirium and catatonia… it was disturbing enough that occasional spikes of unease broke through the comfort of the sacrament.

Wallich reached out and found Callis's hand, their fingers entwining out of the habit of years. "Trust in the guides," Callis murmured.

CHAPTER 16
TERRAK

Azad squatted down next to me. She'd acquired an old brown coat from somewhere and jammed a tattered hat down tight over her ears. "Thanks for not fleeing the moon without me," she said. No one glanced twice at her, though everyone in the camp had surely noticed her arrival. She was the only human here. Hiding your true feelings and reactions can be a useful survival skill. Excessive curiosity was probably not an advantage in this sort of place.

"I saw those soldiers..." I trailed off. I was going to ask, "Did you kill them?" but I didn't actually care much about that. "Is Lonrah all right?"

"Last time I saw her, yeah. I was slipping out the back door, which was really more of a filthy tube full of water, but any exit is better than none. I doubt the Coalition goons will rough her up much. I know the leader, a little, from a past operation, and he doesn't have the stomach for real nastiness. She'll be questioned, but nothing worse."

"You're assuming this leader you know is still the person you *used* to know," I said. "What if he's been co-opted, too?"

"In that case, bad news for Lonrah," Azad said. "But as far as I can tell, the puppetmasters are targeting people with high-level political or military connections. Felix Duval is a field operative. He doesn't usually get close enough to anyone important to spray spores in their face, either. He may have been turned before being sent after us, I guess, but it's hardly necessary – the cover story about you being a remorseless murderer is perfectly adequate justification for pursuit."

"Poor Lonrah," I murmured. "I never meant to get her into trouble."

"She's definitely got trouble. That said… I called the local authorities and told them Mentak Coalition soldiers were conducting unauthorized operations in the city. I sent them some of Lonrah's footage of soldiers in tactical gear, cutting into private property. I imagine the Rantula security forces will be along…"

Three ships screamed overhead, just black-and-white streaks, moving low, making trash swirl around the alley and provoking curses and shaken fists from the people in the camp.

"…right about now," Azad said. "That should keep Lonrah from getting *immediately* murdered, even if there are spore-zombies in her lab. If she has any sense, she'll run before the puppetmasters can get to her."

I hoped she would, but she hadn't left her lab in years, and I was afraid inertia would overcome good sense. There was nothing I could do about it. We could only move forward. "Do you have the cure?"

She patted the side of her coat. "Sure do. Your plan is still the least bad option. We should move away from the nexus of police activity. You said you could get us a ship?"

"I can. But first: tell me where we're going? Who's the nearest subject we can test the cure on?" I still didn't like the idea of injecting people with an untested cure, but at least our future subject was *already* infested with mind-control spores, and it was worth the risk if we could save them.

"I've been giving that some thought. From here we can most easily reach a wormhole leading to Barony territory. There's a Letnev captain who's been really vocal about supporting the Legion, despite a career spent as a frothing xenophobic warmonger, extreme even by Barony standards. If someone like *that* starts talking about the need for a strategic alliance with filthy aliens, important people will listen, because things must be serious. I'm about ninety-nine percent certain he got turned, and he was just on the other side of that wormhole, last I heard... but I don't like our odds. He'll be tough to reach without more guns or connections. I don't suppose *you* have secret allies in the Barony?"

"No. It's hard to make friends with the Letnev. They are not a friendly people." I'd encountered a few in my diplomatic career. They were not, as a rule, charmed by my sparkling wit.

Azad smirked. "Oh, you might be surprised. Under the right circumstances, some of them can be very friendly."

I firmly decided not to ask any follow-up questions. "Do we have another option?"

"We're not too far from another wormhole that leads to a Mentak Coalition system. It's kind of a backwater... but there's this one Coalition fleet captain there. Retired, so she's not on a battleship or locked away at the center of some facility bristling with energy weapons. She's just enjoying her dotage on a colony planet. We think she was one of the first people the puppetmasters compromised, because she quit fishing or quilting or whatever she was doing down there, and started calling in favors and taking meetings with various colleagues who were still active in politics. She would have been easy for the puppetmasters to reach and turning her would open a lot of doors. Not long after her sudden return to politics, the whole Greater Union thing started to gain momentum, and she's considered one of the architects behind the idea."

I mulled that over. "She does sound like a better choice. I still can't understand why the conspirators would try to create both the Greater Union and the Legion. They're oppositional forces – the Legion only came about because the Letnev are paranoid and assume the Union exists to target them."

"Both sides are planning big summits, one on Moll Primus and one on Arc Prime. You know how these things are, they can fall through or get postponed infinitely, but it looks like they're both going to happen, and soon. That means a bunch of very important people, including heads of state, will be all together in a couple of concentrated areas."

"So, the conspirators want to compromise them as well? If you could pull the strings of the rulers of major nations..."

"Sure, you could do some stuff with that. But even absolute tyrants have limits on their behavior. If the Baron of Letnev suddenly said, 'Hey, let's throw our support behind some other random faction for the throne on Mecatol Rex', he'd probably have a terrible accident the next day and some cousin would step in to steer the people back to the old path."

"Assassination, then," I suggested. "The conspirators put agents in place to kill all those leaders at the summits, so they can take advantage of the resulting chaos?"

"My bosses give that scenario a pretty high degree of probability. I'm not an analyst. I just steal things and blow stuff up. Maybe if the cure works, we can get some answers out of this fleet captain. She's become a lot quieter recently, like her part of the plan was done."

"Tell me about her retirement home. We can get to her there?"

"Oh, sure. She's on a planet called Entelegyne. Fertile and boring, mostly home to automated agricultural systems. The place produces food for a bunch of Mentak Coalition worlds. It's close to a wormhole, convenient for shipping, but it'll take us a few days or a week to get there, depending on what kind of ship we get."

"Which wormhole is it?" I asked. She told me. "I think I can get us a ship there."

She rubbed her hands together. "Good. I'll drive."

I laughed. "About that ..."

CHAPTER 17
AZAD

"It will be fine," Terrak insisted. "I've used this method to transport various items before." Azad started to object, and he held up his hands. "Don't worry, no one local knows about the arrangement, not Lonrah, or the Facilitator, or my importer/exporter friend. It's all arranged remotely with a dispatcher I have a deal with. Even *she* doesn't know when I'm putting contraband into a given shipment."

They were in the belly of a mostly automated cargo ship, inside a pressurized container that was half-filled with live plants housed in transparent cubes with their own inbuilt light sources and water systems. They hadn't talked to anyone on the way here, just crept to the spaceport, where Terrak had used various codes to get them through the security gates and onto the ship. That part was good. The part Azad didn't like was the idea of traveling as cargo.

Terrak kept trying to convince her. "This vessel is going in the right direction, and in six days it's stopping near the correct wormhole to drop off a delivery. We'll need to pick up another ship to traverse the wormhole and reach Entelegyne, but by then we won't have such... fervent pursuit... and will have more options." Terrak pulled the container doors shut, and they sealed with a hiss.

"This is a wonderful plan that won't work at all," Azad said. "We've got no supplies, or access to any. We don't have water, so a few days into this six-day journey, we'll be dead. We also don't have any food, unless these plants are edible, but hey, starving takes longer than dying of thirst, so I'm less worried about that."

"Humans die after a few days without water?" Terrak said. "My people evolved on a desert world; we can do rather better. But that's not an issue. Why do you think I looked in three other containers before choosing this one?" He knelt by one of the plants and used one of his fingernails – rather stronger than a human's – to pry off a back panel of the containment cube. He twisted something, then removed a bulb-shaped reservoir with a tube sticking out of it. "Pure water, for the plant's internal irrigation system. There are gallons and gallons in here." He slurped on the tube and grinned, pleased with himself.

Azad wasn't so pleased. "Fine, so we won't die of thirst. We have bigger problems."

"As for food–"

"I'm sure you have some solution," she interrupted. "Maybe one of the five hundred other containers in here is crammed full of raw seafood. I don't *care*. Being alive and well is actually our problem. There's only supposed to be one living person on a ship like this! The backup redundancy pilot, and he's only along for the ride in case the automated systems have a catastrophic failure. If Duval's crew or anybody else is in orbit looking for us, they're going to scan for life signs and compare the findings to crew manifests, and then flag any anomalies for investigation. We're anomalies. Even if we get past them, we're still going to hit a couple of customs checkpoints on this route, and the authorities there *will* scan for life signs, *because* ships like this get used for smuggling."

Terrak looked at her patiently, and Azad suddenly found herself wondering about him and his capabilities. She'd determined early on that Terrak was in over his head and unwilling to admit it to himself. She'd pegged him as a reasonably canny merchant and diplomat who foolishly thought his social and negotiating skills had equipped him for life on the run. Among people of all species, there was a tendency for older, successful people to believe that, because they were experts in a given field, that made them experts in *every* field. Such people tended to blunder around in clouds of hubris. Maybe Terrak was doing that, and his confidence was totally unfounded, but he was certainly looking at her like he had a handle on this situation. How could that be? Someone like him shouldn't be comfortable in circumstances like this.

"If you're done assuming I'm a fool," Terrak said mildly. "no one is going to detect our life signs." He reached into a pocket and removed two capped auto-syringes. "I had Lonrah mix these up for us. I've used this technique when I've needed to... help people reach distant places without being noticed."

Azad groaned. "Are those stasis drugs?"

"They'll drop our body temperature and slow our heartbeats and other electrical activity enough for standard life sign scans to miss us, *and* we won't need to eat or drink while we're in hibernation. These doses are calibrated to keep us down for five days, which will give us a day of consciousness to rehydrate before we need to do anything too active. The ship is stopping to make a delivery at a small station where they won't care about anomalous life signs, or anything else, as long as you pay your fees, so we can get off there and find our next mode of transport."

"I apologize for misjudging your competence," Azad said. Apologies were the kind of thing diplomats cared about, right? It didn't cost her anything to say some words. But then, Terrak was proving he wasn't an average diplomat. Her intel said he was a little shady, but she was beginning to wonder if he wasn't downright criminal. The skillsets of professional thieves and smugglers often overlapped meaningfully with her own, after all. She hated any plan that involved loss of control, but they weren't exactly swimming in options. "I don't know about being unconscious here, though. It's a perfectly good plan, assuming nothing goes wrong. If somebody does board this ship looking for us, we won't be able to run or fight."

Terrak spread his hands. "I am open to alternative suggestions. But decide soon – this ship is scheduled to depart shortly."

Azad sighed. "Fine. Hibernation it is. I can't believe I'm injecting myself with mystery juice some squid gave to a guy I barely know. But I've done stupider things for a mission. Let me call my bosses and tell them I'm going to be out of contact for a few days."

She pushed her way through the plants until she reached the far end of the compartment and sat with her back against the wall. She closed her eyes and waited for the connection to click into place. "Hey, boss," she said into the expectant silence. "I'm going to be out of contact for a little while…"

CHAPTER 18
TERRAK

Azad mumbled to herself at the other end of the cargo container as I moved the plants around to clear some space for us to stretch out. I prefer not to sleep on metal floors, but at least I'd be so profoundly unconscious that I wouldn't be uncomfortable... until I woke up. If you've ever experienced decreased circulation and felt that pins-and-needles sensation when you move the affected limb... imagine that in *every* muscle of your body, and you'll have a sense of what it's like to emerge from this sort of stasis. It's not pleasant, but this was the best solution I could come up with in the time I had. You have to be adaptable and willing to improvise if you want to succeed.

Azad returned, and I said, "How are things back on Jord?"

"I wouldn't know. I don't usually talk about the weather or local politics."

"Are your handlers on board with the new direction our mission is taking?"

She laughed and sat on the floor, leaning back against a couple of plant boxes, looking instantly at ease. "They're results-oriented. They let me run things as I see fit, with their full support, as long as that support is completely deniable and untraceable. The moment I fail, they stop being happy with me, and I pretty much cease to exist as far as they're concerned. They've arranged for me to get my funds replenished when we hit the station by the wormhole, though. I don't have any useful contacts in that area, so I'm not sure how we'll get a ship, but money will help."

"Oh, I know some people," I said. "I know people almost everywhere. That's why you keep me around, isn't it?"

"Also for the titillating conversation and the access to exciting drugs."

The ship rumbled around us, and there was a lurch as we lifted off. Traveling through the atmosphere and pulling out of a gravity well was always a little bumpy. "We'd better get sedated," she said. "In case anyone is lurking in orbit scanning for life signs."

I complied, removing a small case that held two syringes, one marked with Azad's initials, and one with mine. I didn't want to mix them up. Hacan and human physiology differ, and I am a *lot* bigger than Azad. "Don't accidentally kill me," she said. "Don't kill me on purpose either, now that I think about it. We're probably the only hope to save the galaxy, and also I'd like to get paid."

"We are in accord." I handed her the syringe. "Do you know how to use this?"

"I've had to take my share of combat drugs in the field. Nobody's even shooting at me right now. I can manage."

I took my syringe, and we settled ourselves as comfortably as we could among the plants. I watched Azad until I realized there was no way she was going to inject herself first. She probably wanted a few minutes to rifle through my pockets before she went into hibernation, to see if I had any *other* surprises hidden away from Lonrah's lab. That was fine. I'd expected as much, and there was nothing on me that I didn't want her to see. I seated the needle in a vein, depressed the plunger, and winced at the sensation of cold that flowed into me. Then I put the needle away and settled onto my back. "See you in a few days, Azad," I murmured, already feeling myself pulled down, down, down.

CHAPTER 19
FELIX

"Conspiracy," Lonrah repeated. "I thought you were going to ask me where Terrak and Azad went."

Felix said, "Do you *know* where Terrak and Azad went?"

"No."

Felix shrugged. "I didn't expect you would. It hardly seemed like they'd tell you their plans and then leave you behind to tell someone else. So, instead, you can tell me the things you *do* know."

"Are you a spore-zombie?" Lonrah said. "You don't seem like one, but then… I'm not sure I'd be able to tell."

"What, exactly, is a spore-zombie?" Felix was aiming for an earnest and curious tone. He was not a professional interrogator, but he vaguely remembered something about the importance of building rapport and a sense of trust. In this case, that meant humoring a very strange Hylar.

"You have no idea what's going on here, do you?" Lonrah said. "Or else you do, and you're pretending… Ugh. This whole situation is so exhausting."

"Consider me clueless." Felix leaned against the doorframe and crossed his arms. "I'd love to be enlightened. Maybe you can spare yourself a charge for aiding and abetting a fugitive if you help me out now."

"The Mentak Coalition has no authority in the Rantula system! We're independent."

Felix shrugged. "Such things can generally be worked out. This system does have trade relations with the Coalition, and with trade comes diplomacy. I'm sure the local authorities would hand you over if we asked nicely. But it doesn't need to come to that. I've heard rumors about a conspiracy that Terrak is involved in. If he's not working alone, that would be useful information–"

"Terrak isn't working *for* the conspiracy, he's working against it. Only because they gave him no choice, by framing him for murder."

Felix considered for a moment, then said, "Let's say I believe you. Terrak is innocent. He was framed because he stumbled onto some secret. What *is* that secret?"

"How much do you know about the Arborec?" she asked.

The answer was… almost nothing. The Mentak Coalition was the most diverse of the major polities, with numerous alien species sharing citizenship and a common culture, but there were no Arborec involved. He only knew what he'd learned at the academy and picked up in passing. "They're telepathic plant creatures. I've never met them… it… one of their representatives, though I hear they're a bit gruesome. Why?"

Lonrah's pseudopods fluttered nervously as she spoke. "After Terrak started asking questions about his friend's odd behavior, someone broke into his room and tried to spray him in the face with a canister. I examined the contents of that canister and found spores similar to the ones the Arborec use to create their Dirzuga – the walking, talking corpses they use to communicate with other species. Terrak and Azad believe someone has altered those spores to allow them to work on *living* people. Either to brainwash them into compliance, or to outright control their minds, turning them into puppets. Azad rescued Terrak and stole the canister of spores because she's investigating who's behind the whole thing. She believes the conspiracy has compromised agents in most of the major polities, both in the Greater Union and among the Letnev and maybe other members of their Legion."

"That's… quite an accusation," Felix said. It was a totally ridiculous story, but the fact that it was so ridiculous almost made him more inclined to believe it; surely a liar would come up with something more plausible? "Do you have any proof?"

"I have my analysis of the spores."

"Could I analyze them myself? Or have one of our people do it, rather?"

She flushed the color of dismay. "The samples were destroyed."

"That's convenient."

"No, it really *isn't*, because there's an armed man in my lab demanding them. I don't have the spores, but I do have the recipe for a possible cure, provided by Azad's bosses."

Felix whistled. "That is… all extremely interesting." What would Jhuri make of this story? It sounded outlandish, but then, Felix had discovered to his dismay that sometimes outlandish things were all too true.

"It's more than interesting, it's *terrifying*," Lonrah said. "Unknown individuals are controlling the actions of powerful people all over the galaxy, for reasons we don't understand!"

"I do recognize the gravity of the situation," Felix said.

"That's nice. I wish that made any difference. Knowing about this conspiracy won't help you."

Felix frowned. "I'll contact my superiors, and we'll look into your claims–"

The Hylar spasmed her limbs in what Felix recognized as a

laugh. "Then you'll get murdered or turned into a spore-zombie yourself. Terrak basically just said, 'Does anyone know why my old friend is acting funny?' and hours later the old friend was dead and Terrak was wanted for murder. If you ask your superiors to launch an investigation, you'll be next."

Felix sat down on a crate. "Well. When you put it that way…" He enjoyed chasing fugitives through space, matching wits against villains, and concocting stratagems to best enemies in battle. Why didn't he get to do more of *that*? Why did he always end up in these strange, gray, complicated, mysterious situations? "I suppose I'll have to investigate these claims myself."

"That's a good idea. But… do you trust your crew, captain?"

"Of course." To say Felix trusted Calred and Tib with his life would have been an understatement. Tib was his best friend from childhood – they'd grown up together on space stations, joined the military together, and apart from an interval when Tib was undergoing special training in infiltration, they'd even served together. He hadn't known Calred as long, but they'd been on the *Temerarious* together for years, and the Hacan had proven an invaluable ally, bold and brave and willing to improvise. But then… there was Ggorgos. "Mostly."

"Mostly may not be enough." Lonrah sounded almost sad about it. "And even someone you trust completely could have caught a face full of spores in some dark alley. Your crew might not be the people you knew anymore. They may have different loyalties."

Felix shook his head. He didn't want to believe that, and decided he'd think about it later. "Enough. Give me the data on this supposed cure."

"Planning to pre-emptively inject it into the veins of your crewmates?" Lonrah said. "Not a bad idea… except the antidote hasn't been tested yet. We didn't have any infected subjects."

Felix frowned. "Then… assuming your story is true… Terrak and Azad must be going to find test subjects. Do they have a list of supposedly compromised people?"

"Probably, but they didn't tell me where they were going, and I didn't ask. I think I've come to the end of my usefulness, captain." She offered him a small data stick. "This contains the information on the pathogen I found, and the formula for the possible cure. I don't know what good any of that will do, but I wish you well."

Felix slotted the data stick into his tablet, revealing an array of tables and charts and a terse report. There was also a photo: a small vial, filled with little green specks. Could those tiny green flecks really – what? Rewrite your brain? Make you into a puppet? He put the data stick away. "We'll be out of your way soon, Lonrah. Thanks for your cooperation. I think our official involvement can end now."

Felix went looking for Calred and found him working at a console. "Turn up anything useful?" he asked.

Calred sighed. "Nothing. Lonrah has a security system, but large swathes of it have been wiped. Amina Azad covering her tracks, I imagine." The big Hacan looked away from the screen and down at Felix. "Did you get anything useful out of the squid?"

Felix hesitated, but just for a fraction of a second. "I'm afraid not. I–"

"This is the police!" An amplified voice boomed through the lab. "Come out with your hands up!"

"Oh, dear," Felix said. "I think it's time for diplomacy."

THE FAITHFUL IX

Canner wasn't exactly frustrated; it was impossible to be frustrated with the guides, as they were the source of all that was good and worthwhile in the universe. But at times they seemed to have difficulty grasping matters that seemed simple enough to him. "No, it's not an issue of tissue degradation. The physical structures of the brains of your faithful are essentially unharmed by your interventions."

<*Then we do not understand. The faithful gradually lose efficacy after receiving the sacrament. In some, the progression is slower, and in others faster, but in every case, decline has proven inevitable. Our earliest converts are bedridden now, and almost entirely insensible.*>

"As I said, it's a matter of overstimulation, great ones." Canner sat at the desk in his medical office, buoyed by the constant cloud of happy chemicals that had suffused him since his conversion. He had files of brain scans and blood test data before him, all gathered through the network of the faithful and sent to him for analysis. Their fellowship boasted many politicians and members of the military, but very few scientists, and Canner had been tasked to deal with the intractable problem of mental decay among the faithful.

"Your sacrament provides bliss when we please you, and a

constant sense of well-being, and the sure knowledge that our service is meaningful and essential. The experience is *glorious*. But… the brains of humans, Hylar, Hacan, Xxcha, the Letnev, all the species you have seen fit to bless – they are adaptable things. Neural pathways can be rewired, new pathways created, and we *are* rewired to better serve you… but there are trade-offs. There are troubling long-term changes, but even short-term… surely you've noticed that even new converts seem to lose a certain degree of creativity, and the ability to adapt to unforeseen situations? Thinking very deeply, without getting distracted, becomes harder for us, too."

<*The faithful look to us for guidance. Perhaps… slightly more than is ideal.*>

"I would never presume to say so, guides!" Canner spoke with absolute sincerity. "In addition to those very mild deficits, however, your followers also develop a tolerance to the effects of the sacrament, and that resistance intensifies over time."

<*Resistance? Do you suggest that the faithful wish to defy us?*>

"Not consciously, guides!" Canner was terrified of offending his benefactors. "I'm sure all the faithful, like myself, are delighted to serve you. The path forward has never been so clear, and when I think back on my life before, I see only a gray haze of poisonous ambition and resentment. Now everything is bright and clean. You have our minds. But our *bodies*… those are, to an extent, autonomous things, beyond the direct control of our minds. Our brains become resistant to specific forms of pleasure, when those pleasures are experienced too frequently and intensely. Hormones become depleted and take time to be replenished. Receptors can become overwhelmed and cease to bind to chemicals as strongly as they once did. Our bodies also have myriad methods to resist what they perceive as, ah, invaders."

There was no answer from the guides, but there was a sort of expectant silence.

"As time goes on, and the impact of the sacrament begins to wane, the faithful become… less faithful." A distant part of Canner's mind was shouting at him: *Listen to this, listen to yourself, don't you* understand? That part of him was easy to ignore. He hadn't been faithful for very long and had only experienced the positive effects of the sacrament. "They begin to return to their old selves – their flawed, terrible, selfish selves – and as a result, the sacrament increases its efforts, in order to prevent the faithful from straying, and regain the lost equilibrium. The growths in their brains create analogues to the hormones and other chemicals that have been depleted and increase stimulation in other areas of the brain as well. As a result, the faithful do remain devoted, but then, they develop a tolerance to that *new* level of stimulation… and so the stimulation must increase again. As the chemical interventions grow more powerful, mental functions diminish."

<*Why do they diminish?*>

Canner sighed. "Basically, their brains become so flooded with bliss-inducing chemicals that other functions are overwhelmed. Motor control begins to fail, first on a fine level, and then a gross one. Their underlying personalities and skills vanish beneath a rising tide of chemicals. Eventually all that is left is a vague and hazy sense of compliance and well-being, but without the ability to make independent decisions." Or, indeed, casual cocktail party conversation. "The autonomic functions persist, so they breathe, and their hearts beat. They remain faithful, too, of course! The sacrament sees to that. Their faith just… isn't good for much anymore." *That same decline will happen to me*, Canner thought, and a spike of clarifying terror flooded his mind before being washed away by the release of counteracting chemicals to keep him calm. He sighed contentedly.

<*We understand,*> the guides said. <*How can this problem be dealt with?*>

Canner shook himself out of his brief, blissful reverie. "What? Oh. I can't think of a way, really. You could counteract the soporific effects with stimulants, I suppose, but that will also make the faithful more resistant to the sacrament's soothing effects. Essentially, all of the faithful are on intense doses of recreational drugs, and long-term users of those sorts of drugs ... generally suffer ill effects. In the absence of the sacrament, even the most far gone of the faithful would improve, and with time and therapy and medication most would recover fully. But, of course, their lives would be empty and meaningless, and none of us would wish for that."

<*No solution,*> the guides murmured. <*That is unfortunate. But we have time. If the plan is not interrupted, we have time.*>

"Will you tell me, guides, what is the nature of the great work?" Canner had never been more eager to know anything. "What is the glorious future we are helping usher into being?"

<*You will see, faithful one. The old stars will be extinguished, and new stars born, and the void itself will seem to burn.*>

"Beautiful," Canner murmured, and sank into the blissful haze of a job well done.

CHAPTER 20
SEVERYNE

"Nothing, captain," Voyou reported, face impassive on her screen. She was in her office, and he was reporting from the bridge. Everyone worked better there when she wasn't obviously watching them. She made most of her crew nervous. She even made Voyou nervous, but at least he'd gotten better at not visibly wincing when he had to give her bad news.

Severyne made a sound of disgust and leaned back in her chair. "What about that cargo ship? It's big enough to hide an entire pride of Hacan."

"We detected only one life sign, and we confirmed that was the pilot," Voyou said. "There's no sign that the fugitives have left the moon."

"The admiral's reputation does not suggest a great tolerance for failure, Voyou."

"No, captain. It does not."

"Hmm. What are the Coalition forces doing now?"

"They've just returned to the *Temerarious*. They did not appear to have any prisoners with them, and they were escorted off the moon by local security forces – there was some jurisdictional argument there, it seems."

Severyne smirked. That was amusing, at least.

Voyou continued. "We're monitoring communications from the *Temerarious*, and they haven't sent any messages out of the system. If they'd succeeded in capturing or killing Terrak, I'm sure they would have sent word back home by now."

"Give me *something*, Voyou, or you'll find out the admiral isn't the only woman who doesn't like failure."

"I was already aware of your feelings in that area, captain. We did find the place where Terrak and his escort landed on the moon. We were able to obtain security footage from the port, including one fairly clear image of the human assisting Terrak, though she did a remarkably good job of avoiding the direct view of the cameras. We're going to run her through our databases. Perhaps if we identify her, we can better understand Terrak's plans."

"Let me see," Severyne said.

Voyou's face vanished from her screen, replaced by a still image of a human woman's face, half turned away.

Severyne stared. She hadn't seen that face in some time, but it hadn't changed much. Her features were sharp, and her expression faintly amused, like the world was a joke only she truly understood. "I know her." Severyne's voice croaked, and she cleared her throat before continuing. She'd never expected to see that face again. She ruthlessly suppressed the feelings that welled up when she did. "That woman is a Federation of Sol covert operative named Amina Azad. I have crossed paths with her before."

"The Federation is helping Terrak escape?"

"It makes sense, if Terrak is one of our operatives, attempting to defect," Severyne said. "Of course he would go to our most hated enemy for help."

"But, ah…" Voyou clearly didn't want to say, 'but we thought the admiral was lying to us' on a Barony communications channel, even a supposedly private one like this.

"Yes," Severyne said. "But." What was going *on*? Why was Azad involved? And – Severyne did her best to suppress a flutter at the thought – was she going to see her again in person before this was all over?

Severyne sat back and drummed her fingers on the arm of her chair. Finding out Azad was part of this had briefly knocked her mind off track – the woman *did* have that effect on her – but she was still Severyne, so she almost immediately began to calculate angles and points of leverage and ways to turn this information to her advantage. After a moment, she smiled. The admiral would not approve of her idea… but the admiral would approve of success, by whatever means. As long as you won, nobody really cared, after the fact, *how* you'd won.

"Desperate times," she murmured. "Voyou, open a channel to the *Temerarious*, would you? Tell the captain an old friend would like to have a word with him."

"Are… you sure?"

"Have you ever known me to be unsure, Voyou?" she said, still gazing at the image of Amina Azad's face, nowhere near as clear on the screen as it always was in her mind.

CHAPTER 21
FELIX

Felix was in his cabin, tucking Lonrah's data into a locked drawer, when Ggorgos appeared on his screen, transmitting from the bridge. "We are being hailed by a Letnev cruiser," Ggorgos said. "Why are we being hailed by a Letnev cruiser?"

"How would I know? What does the message say?"

"It is from a Captain Dampierre of the *Grim Countenance*," she replied. "Requesting to speak with you personally."

Felix would have been only slightly more surprised if he'd heard it was the ghost of his dead grandmother, but he didn't let that show. He was having to hide a lot of things just lately, and he didn't like that. "Why don't you put her through and I'll find out what she wants?"

"You would simply... converse with an enemy?" Ggorgos radiated disapproval.

"Was there a formal declaration of war between the Mentak Coalition and the Barony of Letnev that I don't know about?" Felix asked. "I don't always read my memos very carefully, I confess, but I think I would have heard about that. Besides, conversing with an enemy is one of the best ways to learn things about them, Ggorgos."

Ggorgos didn't scowl, or blink, or anything at all. "If you receive any information pertinent to the mission, you will share it with me at once."

"We share everything, don't we, Ggorgos?"

The reptilian face vanished from the screen, replaced by the hard features of Severyne Joelle Dampierre. Felix hadn't seen her in years, since the disastrous Thales expedition ended, a mess they'd somehow all managed to walk away from alive. "Sev!" he said with as much bonhomie as possible. "Still zipping around on the old *Grim Countenance*, I see, and with a face to match. This must be homecoming week, because I *just* spoke to–"

"Amina Azad," Severyne interrupted. "I received reports that she was in this system. You've had contact with her, then?"

"I've been fine, Sev, thanks for asking."

"Amina. Azad. Tell me what you know about her location and trajectory, and I will be on my way."

Felix shook his head. "Why are you looking for her?"

"She is wanted for crimes against the Barony of Letnev. When we received reports that she was sighted in this system, I was nearby, and was dispatched to retrieve her."

"Huh. I thought after Thales completely failed to revolutionize space travel, you and Azad parted as friends. Or, if not as friends, then at least not as hated enemies who would pursue one another across the galaxy–"

"The Barony is not forgiving, Duval. Neither am I. Why are *you* pursuing Azad?"

"Ah, well, you know, the same reasons you are, probably–"

"Hmm." Severyne glanced off to the side. "I have received additional information. Azad is in the company of… an escaped murder suspect, one Terrak, who killed a diplomat at a Greater Union summit." Her face stopped being impassive. Now she was doing her version of a smile, which was even worse. "Did someone disrupt a meeting of your little club, Duval? And they sent *you* to bring the killer back? They must not want him very badly. But why is Amina Azad helping this Terrak? She works for the Federation of Sol, which, as I recall, is a *member* of the Greater Union. Could your entire alliance be falling apart, riddled by factions, plotting against one another? The Federation *is* treacherous – we could have told you that. Humans seek only their own advancement and dominance in the galaxy–"

"Unlike the loving altruism of the Barony of Letnev, yes, yes." Talking to Severyne was exhausting. He'd enjoyed spending years not doing it. If only there were a clear way to get rid of her now. "I can neither confirm nor deny that I'm in pursuit of Terrak, but you're an intelligent person and secure in your own judgment, I'm sure."

"I have no interest in the Hacan," Severyne said. "You, I assume, have no particular interest in Azad."

"She *is* aiding and abetting a fugitive, but… she is a secondary target at best, I will admit." Felix could see where this was going, and he didn't like it, and he especially didn't like that he was probably going to agree to it.

"Then we will join forces," Severyne said. "Share information and resources. When we capture the fugitives, you will take this Terrak, and I will take Amina Azad. I trust these terms are acceptable?"

"I'll… have to run them by my superiors," Felix said. He would, but it was all just going through the motions. Severyne was relentless, and it wasn't like she'd stop going after Azad if he told her she wasn't allowed. If he agreed to a partnership, at least she'd be less likely to shoot at his ship *too*.

Severyne snorted. "They keep you on a short leash, then,

Duval? I have authority to complete my mission in whatever way I deem most expedient."

"Then I'll leave you to revel in your freedom for a little while and get back to you soon, all right?"

He'd barely cut the connection when Ggorgos reappeared on his screen. "Well?" she demanded.

"The Letnev are in pursuit of Amina Azad. Which, before you object, does make a degree of sense – Azad was involved in an operation a few years back, one I have firsthand knowledge about, where she crossed paths with the Barony. Captain Dampierre has a personal grudge against Azad." A personal something, anyway. Their relationship was complicated in ways Felix preferred not to think about, but he figured it was best to keep it simple for Ggorgos. "Dampierre suggested we join forces to track down Azad and Terrak – she'll take custody of the former, and we'll get the latter."

Ggorgos said, "This proposal is–"

"Not yours to allow or forbid," Felix said. "This is a joint mission, and while you were given the lead, I do get some input. I'm going to contact Jhuri now."

It took a few moments for the automated assistant on the other end of the line to track down Jhuri, who appeared to be peering into a portable terminal in a hallway somewhere, the view bouncing around. "Felix! Did you get him?"

"Negative. Terrak has either gone to ground on the moon, or he's escaped. The local authorities are doing a thorough search, but… if you ask me, they're gone, offworld and on to their next destination."

"What destination? Those contacts in the Rantula system were our only lead!"

"Maybe not our only one." Felix had given this a lot of

thought. He had to trust *someone*, and Jhuri – despite being a professional liar and spymaster – was someone he trusted. After all, Jhuri wouldn't have mentioned a theory about a conspiracy if he was part of said conspiracy, would he? "I questioned the Hylar chemist Terrak and Azad met with, and she told me quite a story…"

Felix filled Jhuri in about the spores and Lonrah's claims. The view on the screen stopped bobbing as Jhuri ducked into an empty conference room. "If this is true, Felix… I've had to deal with double agents before, but this is beyond that. No amount of poring over financial records can uncover someone who's been compromised by mind-control spores instead of money." He considered. "I *can* sift through some databases looking for anomalous behavior, at least among high ranking Mentak Coalition personnel. There's no point in controlling someone's mind if you don't make them do things they *wouldn't* normally do. The trick will be mining that data without anyone noticing what I'm up to."

"You believe this conspiracy idea could be true, then? Not just paranoid fantasy?" Having someone he respected say this *wasn't* insanity would go a long way toward assuaging Felix's own doubts. It sounded like a delusion, but if so, it was an increasingly widespread one. Morever, he'd once seen a hole ripped in the fabric of space-time, revealing monsters from another reality on the other side, so he'd learned not to dismiss even outlandish ideas out of hand.

Jhuri gestured uncertainly. "Nothing Terrak did makes any sense, and I can't see why Amina Azad would be involved… unless this conspiracy business is true. Then events begin to form a pattern. The conspiracy theory is certainly worth looking into, with extreme caution. Trust no one else with this information.

Send me the data on this supposed cure via an encrypted channel."

Great. The worst-case scenario had just gotten a lot worse. Now they had to uncover and uproot a vast conspiracy? The "vast" part would presumably make it easier to uncover... but harder to uproot. "Will do. There's one other thing. I was recently contacted by Severyne Dampierre on the *Grim Countenance*. She's in the Rantula system. She says she's after Amina Azad, pursuing her for crimes against the Barony, and she asked to join forces since we're in pursuit of a different member of the same duo."

"Her arrival right now is awfully convenient," Jhuri mused. "If she's part of the conspiracy, she could be after Terrak too, to silence him."

"Jhuri, how do you know *we* aren't part of the conspiracy, even unwittingly? What if we were sent after Terrak to silence him? We don't know much of anything about Ggorgos, beyond the fact that she's terrifyingly competent. What if the Xxcha insisted she come along because they needed someone compromised by spores on my crew, to make sure Terrak has an accident before he can tell us what's really going on?"

"I have considered the possibility," Jhuri said grimly. "For the time being, we *all* have the same goal: get our hands on Terrak and Azad. So... sure. Team up with Dampierre. We know she has a history of cooperating with her rivals to achieve a common goal – her partnership with Azad caused you enough trouble during the Thales affair. This time *you* can enjoy her company. If she gets any leads, follow them. I'll start sifting through the data here. If Terrak and Azad need test subjects for their cure, they'll be looking for someone they believe is compromised, as close to the Rantula system or nearby wormholes as possible."

He flushed the Hylar equivalent of a resigned sigh. "It's a good thing I am extremely good at data mining."

"Be careful, Jhuri. If there is a conspiracy, there are people on Shilsaad Station who are part of it. They tried to turn Terrak and destroyed his reputation when they couldn't. Don't let them get to you too." Lonrah's suggestion that someone on Felix's crew could theoretically be compromised had stuck with him and made him worry about literally everyone he knew and trusted.

"I have years of practice at being paranoid and mistrustful, Felix. Don't worry about me. Keep *your* eyes open. If Lonrah's story is true, anyone could be infected, even people you've known your entire life."

"When I became a secret agent, I didn't think it would involve quite *this* many secrets," Felix complained.

CHAPTER 22
SEVERYNE

Duval contacted Severyne directly on an encrypted line she'd provided. "All right, you have a deal." His face looked slightly less smug than she was accustomed to, which pleased her. "We have reason to believe that Terrak and Azad have left the moon."

"Why were they on the moon in the first place?" Severyne said. "We understand they met with a chemist. Why?"

Felix hesitated, briefly, but long enough to make Severyne suspicious. "Just making contact to acquire supplies, as far as we can tell. We questioned the chemist. She didn't tell us anything useful."

"I see." Out of the screen's view, Severyne tapped out a message to Voyou on her wrist gauntlet: *Secure the chemist and bring her here. Quickly and quietly.* "Do you have any idea where our fugitives might be headed next?"

"Nothing definite. This is the only system of any significance that's reachable without traversing a wormhole. The closest wormhole leads to Barony territory – I'm guessing that's where you came through. The next nearest leads to a region that's a mix of independent systems and Mentak Coalition space. Terrak and Azad are probably headed to one of those. I can cover one, and you can cover the other? I guess it's obvious which of us should do which."

"You want us to stand watch over wormholes? That's not much of a plan, Duval." Not that she was surprised. Duval was adequate in a fight and capable of following a straight line to the end no matter how arduous the journey, but he didn't have her skill at thinking around corners.

Felix winced. "You're not wrong. I'm hoping for a more solid lead soon. Our analysts are working on the problem, and if they come up with something, I'll let you know. You'll do the same for me?"

Severyne showed her teeth. "Of course. We're partners now." She would share anything it benefited her to share, of course. She trusted he would do the same on his end.

"That is an outlandish story," Severyne said to the Hylar across the table in one of the *Grim Countenance*'s more pleasant interrogation rooms. (This one didn't even have a drain in the floor, and there were no alarming stains on the walls.) Some people said that outlandish stories were more likely to be true because a liar would try to come up with a more believable tale, but Severyne assumed that liars were aware of that interpretation, and willing to take advantage of it.

Lonrah said, "Agreed. I'm getting pretty tired of telling it."

Voyou, sitting beside Severyne, shook his head. Most of his experience was in annexation, and he was often the officer sent to break the news to the denizens of a given planet or moon that they were part of the glorious Barony of Letnev now, and by the way, their taxes were extremely overdue. He could switch between veiled and overt threats with ease, which made him better at talking to people than Severyne was. She generally dispensed with the veils entirely. "You really expect us to believe there's some spore-based conspiracy, not just in the Greater Union, but in the *Legion*?" Voyou said.

"I don't expect you to believe anything. The fact that you scooped me up when I was trying to flee for my life might lend my story some credence, though." The Hylar sounded totally defeated. That, more than anything, made Severyne inclined to believe her – or at least to think the Hylar believed her own story. "Look, I can only definitively tell you two things: what Azad and Terrak told me, and what I saw when I did my analysis of the spore sample."

"A spore sample you conveniently no longer possess," Voyou pointed out.

Lonrah undulated. "People keep saying that's convenient. It is *less and less* convenient. I gave you my analysis. That's the best I can do. The spores themselves were incinerated."

"You told all this to Duval?" Severyne asked. She wasn't surprised Felix had kept this conspiracy rumor from her; she was just surprised she hadn't realized he was hiding something. Perhaps he was improving at the "covert" part of being a covert operator.

"I'm not good at keeping secrets from people with a lot of guns," the Hylar said. "So yes."

Voyou turned to Severyne. "I don't suppose Duval gave you any hint of this conspiracy story, despite our so-called partnership?"

"No," Severyne said. "But then, he hardly would, since I might well be an agent of said conspiracy. I would be cautious in his position as well." She thought about the situation, then turned her attention back to Lonrah. "It is irrelevant whether the conspiracy is real or not."

The Hylar waved her pseudopods in a gesture that Severyne

assumed was meant to convey outrage or disbelief. "What? If the leaders of major polities, including your own, are being manipulated, that's *irrelevant*?"

"For my purposes, yes. I am chiefly interested in trying to find Amina Azad." That was true; it just wasn't the whole truth. Severyne preferred her lies to contain as few falsehoods as possible. She was in fact *deeply* interested in whether the conspiracy theory was true or not, and talking to Amina Azad would help her figure that out. Azad was a professional liar, but Severyne knew her better than most, and was confident she'd be able to judge Azad's sincerity. "That is my mission. What matters to me is, does *Azad* believe in this conspiracy? You think she does?"

"She's absolutely committed," Lonrah said. "She has no doubts. She even kidnapped a Hacan vagrant to infect with the spores so she could test her cure, before Terrak stopped her – he's the one who destroyed the spores. That's why they need to find another test subject, someone who they already know, or strongly believe, is compromised."

"Did they tell you their candidates?"

"No. I assume they discussed it after they escaped. Assuming they even did escape together. I don't know where Terrak went."

"Azad is quite capable," Severyne said. "If she wished to find Terrak again, I'm sure she did. Hmm." She waved her hand. "All right, put her in a shuttle back to her little moon, Voyou."

"Should we, ah, really…"

"Release her? She has been cooperative. Killing those who cooperate discourages future cooperation."

"Of course, but if she spreads this ridiculous tale…"

"What do we care?" Severyne asked. "The galaxy is full of conspiracy theories."

Voyou nodded. "As you say, captain."

"I'm not interested in talking about this anymore anyway," Lonrah said. "Don't worry about that. If I never hear the word 'spore' again it will be too soon."

Severyne got a priority call from Admiral Immental not long after Lonrah was gone. "Report," the admiral demanded.

"It's been an interesting few hours," Severyne said, and filled her in completely, omitting no detail. Her doubts about Immental had taken on a new heft and seriousness, and Severyne wanted to see the admiral's reaction to the conspiracy theory. When she finished, she said, "It's quite a delusional notion, isn't it, admiral?"

"I'm not interested in some squid raving about spores." Immental scowled through the screen.

Dismissing the whole idea out of hand, then. Interesting. You didn't become a Barony admiral without being paranoid, and if Immental was… uncompromised… Severyne would have expected at least a few follow-up questions about the supposed conspiracy. Still, there was a lot going on. Perhaps the admiral was simply preoccupied. The information was inconclusive.

Immental said, "I'm more concerned about this alliance you've formed with Duval."

Severyne sniffed. "'Alliance' is a strong word for our arrangement. I will use him as long as he is useful and discard him the moment he ceases to be. Unless you forbid our association?"

Immental sighed. "I was warned your methods were unconventional… but effective. I won't stop you if you think Duval can be useful. In fact, I can see how he might be. We have recently received intelligence suggesting that Terrak is headed for a Mentak Coalition colony world, on the other side of a wormhole near your location. If Duval accompanies you there, he can smooth things over if any local authorities notice your presence."

"Where did we acquire this new intelligence, admiral?" Severyne asked. If there *was* a conspiracy, one that had agents among the Barony *and* the Mentak Coalition, there would, presumably, be sharing of information among them... but the admiral had many sources, including legitimate spies. Still inconclusive.

"We have many sources," the admiral snapped. "It doesn't matter. All that matters is, the tip is credible. Contact Duval and let him know, if you insist." She closed the connection.

Severyne lay down in her bunk and gazed at the ceiling. The time had come to work this through as far as she could.

Assume there was a conspiracy; make that an axiom upon which to build a theorem. Suddenly, her superiors had a lead, when there was no lead before. How? Had members of the conspiracy received word that Terrak and Azad were looking for a victim to test their cure on, and figured out the most likely nearby candidate, someone who was compromised and probably on Azad's list? That seemed plausible. The puppetmasters didn't need to bother with data mining or behavioral analysis or anonymous tips. They already *knew* who the closest compromised people were. So: how did the puppetmasters know that Terrak and Azad had a cure they needed to test? Someone must have told them.

Severyne ran down the list of possible sources. Lonrah knew; Severyne and Voyou knew; and Duval knew, as did anyone else he'd told. That's where her list had to break down. Lonrah might have told others, after all. And Duval had probably told his handler, at least. Had he also told his potentially compromised crew? Or had one of them learned it independently? Duval hadn't been alone in Lonrah's lab, after all. Someone could have overheard them or monitored the conversation.

Disappointing. Severyne possessed insufficient data to make a solid determination. Anyone, other than herself, could be the leak; even Lonrah could be compromised, and engaged in some elaborate double-bluff. That was the problem with vast and shadowy conspiracies. If you believed in them, they made every shadow into a threat, which rendered accurate threat assessment impossible.

The more pressing question was still whether Immental was part of this conspiracy, or if she'd simply received information from a compromised source, without understanding its nature. The admiral could be a great ally, or her most dangerous enemy. If there *was* a conspiracy, and it stretched *that* high, the Barony itself was under threat. Severyne couldn't allow that. The Barony was not just her beloved homeland; it was the theater for her career and personal success.

Severyne would have to proceed without trusting anyone… except, hilariously, Duval himself. Not that she intended to be fully open and honest with him, but she was at least fairly sure he didn't have a brain full of spores.

Ah, but no, Felix wasn't the only one she could trust. There was Amina Azad, too: she was fighting the conspiracy, not part of it, though Severyne didn't doubt Azad had her own personal agenda.

Severyne's feelings about Azad were the most complex she had about anyone or anything. Azad had saved Severyne's life, and threatened it; made her growl in frustration, and cry out in ecstasy; and, in the end, altered Severyne's entire conception of herself. In a sense, her brief, tempestuous relationship with Amina Azad had made Severyne into the person she was today:

an officer working out in the field, rather than a bureaucrat manipulating her way up the chain of command on some remote Barony science compound. "Perhaps I'll get the chance to thank you in person before we're through, Azad," she murmured.

She sent a message to Duval: *We have a lead.*

He replied promptly: *Really? I wonder if it's the same one we just received…*

THE FAITHFUL X

Mmaranor, the head of the Xxcha delegation on Shilsaad Station, double-checked that the doors of his suite were locked before reaching out to his masters. "Wise ones, your suspicions have been conveyed to Captain Duval through channels he will not find unusual. The *Temerarious* will make all due haste for Entelegyne and apprehend these vile criminals. They should reach their destination in a few days."

<Terrak must not be permitted to use his poison on our faithful.>

Reading the tone of the guides was difficult – telepathic communication was very strange overall, though, oh, it felt so *good* to be spoken to by the wise ones – but Mmaranor thought they seemed... concerned. "Is it truly possible to break our holy connection?" Mmaranor asked. "I can think of nothing more terrible."

<Our power is great, but the forces arrayed against us are fiendish. We will not take chances with the great work. If Terrak does poison the fleet captain, and turns her against us, she might reveal crucial details that could yet be disrupted. The plan must proceed until the final summits are held.>

"I will do all I can to assure its success."

<There is something else on your mind. What troubles you?>

"Wise ones," Mmaranor said. "Earlier today, I was in a meeting, and my... my mind wandered. I lost track of time, and over a minute passed before I returned fully to myself. Everyone stared at me, waiting for me to answer a question I hadn't even heard. I am somewhat worried–"

<*Worry not, for you are faithful,*> the guides said, and waves of bliss obliterated all Mmaranor's concerns.

CHAPTER 23
TERRAK

I opened my eyes in the shipping container. The interior wasn't dark, because of the lights shining in the containment vessels of the plants stacked all around us.

I groaned as I tried to sit up and turn my head. Every joint resisted me, like the hinges of a rusty grate. I was surprised not to hear an audible squeal when I moved. Eventually I managed to roll over on my side, fumble one limp hand toward the bulb of water I'd set aside and maneuver the straw into my mouth. I took small sips, resisting the urge to gulp the fluid down, knowing I'd only give myself a sick stomach if I overindulged now.

After that I spent long minutes on my back, waiting for my muscles to stop complaining. I finally gave up on that hopeless wish and started gently massaging my sorest parts instead, even though my hands were plenty sore themselves. After a long time – longer than last time I took hibernation drugs; age was creeping up on me – I got to my feet and went to look at Azad.

She was resting on her back, looking like a fresh corpse. Her skin was waxy, and she didn't appear to be breathing. I hoped she wasn't actually dead. She had skills I could use, but it was more than that. I wasn't exactly growing fond of her, but I was certainly getting used to her, and having her around was better on many metrics than being alone. I can work by myself, but I don't relish solitary struggle – not the way I used to. Another symptom of getting old, probably.

I'd had Lonrah configure Azad's dose differently from my own. I told her to keep Azad down for five days. For me? Four and a half. Hibernation drugs aren't exact, and I knew that time could shift in either direction by a few hours, but I'd get at least a small interval when I was awake, and Azad wasn't.

I searched her. She had a standard earpiece, for local comms, but that was all. How had she called her handlers in the Federation of Sol (or wherever) before we took off? Sure, her comms could be routed through a ship or a station's system to reach more distant contacts, but not without leaving a trace, and there was no way she would have risked piggybacking on the container ship's system to make a call. Did she have a more sophisticated comm system implanted in her skull? Such things weren't unheard of, but they weren't likely for an undercover agent, who might be subject to scans that would reveal the tech.

It crossed my mind that maybe Azad wasn't talking to her handlers at all. Maybe she didn't *have* any handlers. Maybe she was mentally ill, with a persecution complex and delusions of grandeur, and she'd dragged me along into her insanity, convincing me her worldview was real. That was a depressing idea to contemplate. I didn't *really* believe it – the conspiracy explained too many otherwise inexplicable things, and Lonrah's data on the spores supported that interpretation – but I couldn't shake the image of Azad just sitting in a corner, talking to herself, lost in labyrinths of the mind.

I shook off the idea and continued my search. Azad really didn't have much on her – just what she carried in that vest of hers and at her belt. The drugs from Lonrah. Her folding tranquilizer gun, and an energy pistol. Credit and data sticks. A wicked folding knife, lockpicks, a handheld codebreaker, and a lighter. The only item that seemed remotely personal was a small and much-folded printout of a photograph of a Letnev woman's face. It looked like a frame grab from a security camera. I frowned at it for a long time. I had no idea who the woman was. The Federation and the Barony were ancient and implacable enemies, so perhaps the woman was Azad's nemesis? She seemed like the type who might have a nemesis.

Well. That all turned out to be basically pointless, but I had to try. I've gotten as far as I have in life because I am always keen to acquire useful information.

I put everything back just the way I'd found it. Then I settled down, and thought, and dozed, and generally waited for Azad to wake up. She finally did, a bit earlier than I would have expected. Once her groans were sufficiently loud, I made a few sounds of waking myself. "Good morning," I said, pretending to yawn. "How did you sleep?"

"I feel like I just plummeted into the atmosphere without a ship or a suit." Her voice was a dry rasp. "And my mouth tastes like some kind of animal took a crap inside it."

"Wasn't me," I said. "Though I will have to relieve myself at some point, once I get this water into me."

"Water. Yesssss." She rolled over and groped for the bulb she'd prepared before going to sleep, and slurped hungrily. After a thoughtful belch, she stood up and went through a series of stretching exercises. Her movements appeared much more effective than my own attempts to work the kinks out had been. "So, I've been thinking," she said.

"When? In the five minutes since you regained consciousness?"

"My mind is always working, Terrak, even when I'm sleeping. You've never woken up with the solution to a problem just waiting there for you on the top of your thoughts?"

"I suppose I am familiar with the phenomenon. What solution did slumber afford you?"

"Mmm, the details are still a little hazy. Let's talk over our situation, and maybe the fuzzy bits will clear up. So. Lonrah probably told everything she knows about us to anybody who asked, right?"

"I am sure she cooperated with the authorities, yes," I agreed. "We are friendly, but not so friendly she'd risk imprisonment or worse to protect me."

"So, she told them all about the conspiracy, the spores, the cures, everything."

"Hmm. She probably told them we believed there was a conspiracy, at least. I don't know if she believed us, honestly, and she probably wouldn't have admitted it if she did."

"She more than likely told somebody who's been compromised – there might even be somebody on Duval's crew. The puppetmasters have to be following your case pretty closely, so if that information got passed on anywhere, I'm sure they picked it up." Azad did a series of moves that involved squatting and flinging her hands out in front of herself over and over. Just watching her made me tired. "So much for the element of surprise. All the bad guys knew before was that you were on the run, with help from a mysterious benefactor. I'm usually more of a mysterious malefactor, but this role works for me too. Now, though, we have to assume the puppetmasters know we're onto their scheme, and actively seeking to oppose them. That changes the whole nature of the relationship."

"Really?" Terrak said. "We were being relentlessly pursued anyway."

"Now we're being relentlessly pursued with malice, and, I hope, just a little bit of desperation." She switched to jumping jacks. "Assume they know we have a possible cure and need to test it. You don't become an interstellar puppetmaster by being stupid, so they've probably guessed we're going after the fleet captain. At the very least, they'll know it's a possibility, and take precautions."

"Not necessarily. They don't know about your data mining, the anomalous behavioral comparisons, or that you have a list of people who've likely been compromised."

"Probably not, but they know there's an opposition now, and an organized one, so I'm sure they can guess. We whipped up a cure fast, which suggests a certain level of competence on our part. The Mentak fleet captain is the nearest person who's gotten weird recently. Trust me, they'll be keeping an eye on her. That's the way to bet, anyway. I doubt we can just stroll in, snatch her up and inject her full of the cure."

"I must admit, I'm glad you didn't realize all these problems earlier," I said. "You probably would have killed Lonrah to keep her quiet."

Azad snorted. "Of course I realized all this earlier. The only reason Lonrah is still alive is because just killing her wasn't sufficient, and I didn't have time to cover our tracks. Duval's Devils showed up at her lab, and I had to flee. I could have blasted Lonrah after she showed me her escape hatch, but I didn't have time to wipe her data banks or clear out all her surveillance footage, so there was no point. The puppetmasters would have found out about us and the spore sample and the cure anyway." She smirked. "Lonrah actually asked me why I didn't kill her. I said it was bad manners." Her face went serious again. "I hope she took my advice and ran as fast and far as she could, though. Maybe the cops barging in gave her enough time."

"Calling them was an actual kindness," I said. "It made me like you better."

She waved a dismissive hand. "Nah, I was just sowing discord and confusion among my enemies." She grinned. "Which is basically my idea for how we'll get our hands on this fleet captain."

"Do tell," I said.

"First, give me some more information about this station we're sneaking onto."

CHAPTER 24
AZAD

Chelicera Station catered to travelers going in and out of the wormhole, which meant it specialized in supplies, food, booze, and entertainment, the latter encompassing everything from immersive holo-suites to dancing to prizefighting to intimate companionship (and sometimes combinations of some or all of the above).

The station was independently operated, run by a protégé of the infamous Sagasa the Disciplinarian, a Hacan crime boss whose tendrils expanded into numerous systems. Azad had dealt with Sagasa in the past and was confident that someone schooled in his business methods would nurture the kind of environment where she could do business.

Sneaking off the ship wasn't difficult – everything was run by autoloaders, so they just walked out of the cargo bay past the robot forklifts and onto the bustling docks. Azad stopped at a public terminal and refilled her credit sticks with the promised funds from her employers, then tossed a handful of sticks to Terrak. "That should cover your part."

Terrak frowned. "I have concerns about your plan."

"What do you mean? My plan has *two prongs*. That's one more prong than I usually bother with. Confusion to our enemies is always a solid tactic. You go ship-shopping and make the recording. I'll get busy recruiting."

She sauntered off in search of a couple of desperate idiots. There were always plenty of those on a shady station like this. She went to the closest bar and looked around but didn't see what she needed. Fortunately, there were other bars. She needed a human woman and a male Hacan, the kind of people who'd accept a windfall without questioning why their garbage luck had finally turned…

Three bars later, after marking a few possibilities, she found something she hadn't dared hope for: an existing set. Way in the back, a Hacan and a human sat together in a booth, looking extremely glum. She decided to give them a shot; if it worked out, she'd only have to make her pitch once.

Azad slid into the seat next to the woman and said, "Let me buy you two a couple of drinks." The Hacan was older than Terrak, with a scar on his muzzle, and the woman was younger than Azad, but they were both close enough at a glance.

"We don't have any money for you to scam off us," the woman said. "We can't even afford our port fees."

"Then you should be happy I'm buying you drinks." She gestured to a passing server and said, "Two more of whatever they're drinking, and something twice as expensive for me." She tapped the server's ring with her own and winked. "Plus a little something extra for your efforts."

"What do you want from us?" the Hacan rumbled.

"We won't do any weird stuff," the woman said.

"Well…" the Hacan said. "I mean…"

"Nothing weird. I want you to leave this station on a better ship than the one you arrived in, that's all."

"You want us for your crew?" the woman said. "You don't even know us."

"I am hiring a crew, but I won't be on the ship with you. I just want you to deliver something for me."

"Smuggling? Why pick us?"

"Because my known associates all got compromised, and you're total strangers, who can't be traced back to me. I'll pay you ten percent up front, and the other ninety percent on delivery."

"Ten percent of *what*?"

Azad grinned. By the time people started asking questions like that, you had a deal; it was just about nailing down the details.

After Azad concluded her business, she went over to the bar and picked up a napkin. "Do you have something to write with?" she asked the bartender.

CHAPTER 25
TERRAK

Buying a small, fast ship was surprisingly easy. After some discreet inquiries, I found a captain with significant gambling debts sitting in a public corridor, staring blankly at a wall, and offered to solve all his problems. He took me to his vessel, the *Vermilion*. The ship was a smuggler's dream, small and swift and sleek, with more cargo space than you'd expect, and faster engines, too. He transferred ownership to a false corporate identity Azad had already prepared.

I went into the *Vermilion's* cockpit, fiddled with the controls, and figured out how to make a recording. Once I was sure the screen showed everything I needed it to – Azad had been very specific about the background we required – I gazed directly into the camera, and I told my story.

When I was done, and all the necessary arrangements were made, I joined Azad on the station. "I wish we could have taken the *Vermilion*," I said, watching the sleek machine depart through one of the station windows, a dart made of night.

"What have you got against the *Nine-Tenths of the Law*?" Azad said. "It's... well... it has a working propulsion system. And seats. There's a window. Who could ask for anything more?"

"I could." I turned and looked down at her. "How long before the message starts to broadcast?"

"I programmed it to launch for an hour from departure, and it'll run on a loop after that until it gets out of range of the station here. Sagasa's cousin is happy to amplify and rebroadcast basically any signal we want, for a price. He didn't even ask what we were planning to transmit. I love the free market."

The *Temerarious* lurked in space, as stealthy as could be, between the wormhole and the nearest inhabited object of any size, Chelicera Station. They'd been here for two days, and Felix was getting antsy.

Having Undercommandant Voyou on board didn't help. The Letnev officer was unfailingly polite and formal, but there was a current of mockery running underneath every interaction, like Voyou thought he was better than the Mentak Coalition crew – which he doubtless did, since a sense of superiority was the Letnev national pastime. Voyou strolled around the ship, making conversation, inquiring about everyone's work and pasts, and somehow managed to never reveal anything at all about himself. "Oh, I'm just a cog in the great machine, doing my part to serve my captain and country."

"You're a hostage," Ggorgos rumbled at him. They were all in the galley, where crew members without immediate duties tended to congregate during the "interminable waiting" phase of any operation.

"And here I thought I was a spy." Voyou turned around in his chair. "Tib Pelta, didn't you say I was a spy?"

"You can be both," Tib said from a corner, where she was ostentatiously cleaning a gun.

"Then Calred, back on the *Grim Countenance*, is he a hostage, or a spy, or both?"

"I prefer to think of it as a cultural exchange program," Felix said. "Gaining a greater appreciation of one another's worldviews. We're all learning, and also, we're all having fun."

Voyou smiled. "*I* certainly am."

The decision to exchange Voyou and Calred was the only solution they'd found to the problem of forming an alliance with someone you found basically untrustworthy. Severyne and Felix had agreed they should take up positions on either side of the wormhole, to double their chances of capturing Terrak and Azad – if the fugitives slipped past one, the other could catch them. They'd argued back and forth over who should wait on *which* side of the wormhole, though, and finally they'd literally used a random number generator to decide who went where. Felix rolled an odd number, so he was here, the first line of defense. He didn't much like this position, but he wouldn't have totally liked the alternative, either. If he was on the Mentak Coalition side of the wormhole, he'd be able to respond at a moment's notice if a cry for help went up from Entelegyne. But on this side, he could monitor traffic heading into the wormhole, allowing him to leap on any ship that seemed like it might contain their quarry.

Obviously Severyne couldn't be left on the other side of the wormhole unattended, where she might snatch Terrak *and* Azad and fly off into the darkness. Severyne couldn't abide leaving Felix unmonitored on *his* side, for the same reason, even though Felix was basically an honorable guy, within the boundaries of his duties. Their solution was the exchange: Severyne got Calred, and Felix got Voyou, bridge officer for bridge officer. Felix thought Severyne had the better end of the deal. Calred was *much* better to play cards with.

"We're receiving a transmission." Tib was looking at the small screen on her wrist. She swiped her fingers across the gauntlet and put the transmission up on a larger wall screen.

A tired-looking Hacan said, "Greetings."

Felix whistled. "Terrak is reaching out to *us*?"

"Not us specifically," Tib said. "This message is going out wide, transmitted from… let me see… Chelicera Station."

"Let's get to the station then!" Felix leapt to his feet.

"No, strike that, it's being *relayed* through the comms system at Chelicera Station. Terrak is broadcasting remotely, let me see if I can find–"

"Perhaps we should listen to what he's *saying*?" Voyou offered, not very loudly, but very pointedly.

They all turned their attention to the Hacan's speech.

"…is Terrak," he said. "I am – or rather, I was, before dark forces conspired to destroy my reputation – a special trade ambassador for the Emirates of Hacan. I have a long and distinguished career, spanning decades, and while I have made my fair share of enemies over the years, as anyone does in business and politics, not even my most vociferous detractors would call me a *killer*." He shook his head dolefully, mane swaying. Felix thought he looked very convincing; he had a lot of gravitas.

Terrak said, "But killer is what they call me now, throughout the inhabited galaxy. The authorities claim I murdered one of my oldest friends, and when asked why I would commit such a terrible crime, they make vague comments about 'personal disagreements'. There were no disagreements. I loved Qqurant like a sibling. No, my friends, I have been falsely accused in an attempt to silence me, because I have uncovered a terrible truth. A truth that threatens us all. A truth I will reveal to you now."

"There's a stencil on the wall over his left shoulder," Tib said. "Part of a ship ID number I think, hold on…"

Terrak kept talking, growing more impassioned and lively as he did. "I attended a summit on Shilsaad Station and noticed my dear friend Qqurant was acting strangely. I approached him and found him confused and disoriented. He walked away, and avoided me, so I asked friends if they'd heard anything to explain this strangeness – had the poor fellow suffered some tragedy, was he distracted, had I offended him in some way? No one had an explanation, but the question was out there in the world, and people were wondering. That night, when I returned to my rooms, I was *attacked*."

Terrak described being assaulted by an unknown Yssaril, who tried to spray him with a mysterious canister. "After I fought off the craven assailant, and they fled, I received a call from Qqurant himself, asking me to come to his room. When I went to meet him, I found him dead, slain with my own ceremonial spear, stolen from my closet. Security rushed in just moments after I arrived, tipped off, I'm sure, by the real murderer. Since their gambit with the canister failed, they chose instead to ruin my reputation… and worse. They took me into custody, and I would have died in an 'accident' the next day, if not for the intervention of a human operative investigating the very conspiracy I had unwittingly stumbled into."

Well, that fit with what Felix had gathered from the Facilitator. If there was a conspiracy afoot, Terrak was lobbing a bomb at them by talking about it publicly. There was sure to be a reaction… and that reaction might *reveal* the conspiracy. Either way, Felix had to get to Terrak. He was either a deranged fugitive or a whistleblower whose life was in danger, and Felix wanted him locked up safely in the brig while he figured out which.

Terrak took a deep breath. "What I have to tell you is deeply troubling. A leading chemist analyzed the contents of that canister – the one these villains tried to use on *me* – and discovered it contains fungal spores stolen from the Arborec and weaponized to sap the will of victims. Those who breathe the spores are made puppets of the as-yet-unknown conspirators. We have been investigating the conspiracy and have discovered that highly placed members of the military and governments of several major polities have been compromised. Their minds are not their own, and they are acting against their own interests, and the interests they are sworn to serve. My poor friend Qqurant was one of their pawns, and we believe his strange behavior was caused by the spores – the effects of mind control seem to cause those very minds to deteriorate. The analytical data the chemist gathered can be downloaded here–"

"The *Vermilion*!" Tib shouted. "That's where he's transmitting from! It's a trading vessel, recently sold to a dummy corporation, and it departed Chelicera Station an hour ago. I got some security footage from the docks, showing the crew board, and they were wearing hoods, but it's clearly a Hacan and a human woman."

"Set an intercept course for this *Vermilion*," Felix said.

Ggorgos, who'd been silent up until this point, nodded in agreement. "Yes." She cocked her head and looked at Felix. "What is all this nonsense about *spores*? I knew Terrak was a murderer. I did not realize he suffered paranoid delusions."

"The Hacan is talking about you, now, Felix," Voyou said.

Felix snapped his attention back to the screen. "…and his crew of Mentak Coalition clandestine operatives have pursued us relentlessly. We have created a possible cure for those affected by the spores and had planned to test it on a victim we've identified… but the wormhole we need to pass through has been blockaded by the *Temerarious*. Is this Duval compromised by the spores, in league with the conspirators, or just an unwitting dupe? In any case, we fear we'll be captured, and have chosen to release what we know before we can be silenced. We only want you to consider: has someone close to *you* changed recently? Begun to behave in ways that are wildly out of character? Furthermore, ask yourself, who's *really* behind the formation of the Greater Coalition, and the opposing force created by the Barony of Letnev, the Legion? Call your representatives. Ask them to investigate–"

"Aren't you supposed to be a covert operative, Captain Duval?" Voyou said. "But there's your name, broadcast all over the system. Probably beyond, if anyone finds this interesting enough to pass along, and someone certainly will. Everyone loves a juicy conspiracy."

Felix groaned. Jhuri wasn't going to like this. Felix didn't like it much either. They needed to capture Terrak and wrap this up *fast*. "Just… catch that ship. I need to make a call."

"I do, too," Voyou said. "Supraluminal, to the other side of the wormhole. I'm sure my captain would love to know about all this."

THE FAITHFUL XI

<*Disaster!*> the guides cried in Immental's mind. She clutched her head, waves of nausea pulsing through her. She was only glad she was alone in her quarters, and not in a conference or appearing before the Baron.

She collapsed, curling into a ball, and then forced herself to speak through the pain. "This... Terrak's transmission... it can be contained, guides. All is not lost. We will capture the fugitives. Duval is en route to intercept their ship and stop the broadcast. We will discredit Terrak or bring them into your communion and make them recant."

<*The summits on Arc Prime and Moll Primus must go forward as planned! The great work must proceed!*>

A burning sensation washed over her, like ants biting every bit of her exposed skin. "Guides!" she cried. "I... cannot... serve you... if... I feel such... pain..."

<*Fix this, or this pain will feel like nothing at all.*>

The agony did not cease immediately, but it tapered off. Sadly, it was not replaced by a corresponding intensity of bliss, just a neutrality. Her sense of obedience felt suddenly less like a pleasure and more like a shackle. Immental was no longer being tormented, but she realized she would not be rewarded unless she did something worthy of reward.

CHAPTER 26
TERRAK

"It would be nice if that transmission alone could make a difference," I said. We were sitting in the cramped cockpit of the *Nine-Tenths of the Law*, watching the bomb I'd just dropped on the galaxy.

"Ha," Azad said. "The idea that just releasing some horrible truth to the public automatically leads to meaningful change is a fairy tale. Little kids and the occasional university student are the only ones who believe it. Most people will just think you've gone insane, and the really clever ones will think you're *pretending* to be insane to try and prove diminished capacity and save your own ass in a murder trial. Fortunately, we're up against secretive, paranoid forces who are terrified of having their plans brought to light. Who knows? Maybe the message *will* freak out a few people in high places, make them nervous, and jam up the works a bit. I'd welcome that. But what matters is, the puppetmasters are terrified of the mere possibility of exposure. Look at how they reacted when you asked some friends at a cocktail party a few questions. And now, you just – put it all out there! The conspirators will drop everything they're doing to chase down the *Vermilion*."

That was the hope, anyway. It wasn't much of a plan, but it was something. Azad was a great believer in the power of sowing confusion. "I hope they don't just destroy the vessel," I said. "Those people you hired to fly the *Vermilion* may not be innocent, exactly, but they don't deserve to die."

"I think the bad guys would rather capture us and fill our brains with spores at this point. They'll want you to recant this transmission, and say you made it all up, and they'll want me to tell them who's funding me, so they can figure out who else they need to co-opt or silence."

"If they do manage to capture us, they can force us to do whatever they like," I said.

"Best we don't get caught, then. I don't want to be backed into that particular corner. I've never been a big fan of those hollow teeth full of poison. Frothing and twitching is not the way I want to go out."

"Better than living with a brain full of fungus," I said.

"No argument there." She flicked switches and toggles on the control board. "Let's see if we can slip past Felix and company in the chaos."

CHAPTER 27
FELIX

"We're in pursuit of the *Vermilion*," Felix said. "They're fast, but we're faster. We should be able to overtake them in a couple of hours." He was beginning to have his doubts – could it really be this easy? What if this was some sort of ruse created by Terrak and Azad? He tried to tell himself Terrak was a lazy diplomat and Azad was a blunt instrument who favored violence, not subterfuge… but diplomats had to be clever, and while Azad was crass, that didn't mean she was simple. Still, he had to assume they were on board. If they let the *Vermilion* go, and the fugitives *were* on board…

"I want this finished, Felix," Jhuri said. "It's dragged on too long. Let me know as soon as Terrak is in custody."

"Of course."

Jhuri started to turn away from the screen, and Felix said, "Wait! Where are you going?"

The Hylar flushed colors of annoyance. "I'm rather busy here, Felix. I have to go brief the Xxcha on your current status, even though Ggorgos has probably already told them everything you told me. I swear, information flow only goes one way around here—"

"Boss. The *video*. Terrak was talking about the conspiracy! The… the whole thing I've been secretly investigating!" Not that Felix had gotten very far in said investigation. In fact, he'd gotten nowhere at all. But still. "If that video isn't total confirmation of your theory, it's at least a strong suggestion that you're on the right track."

Jhuri sighed. "Felix, forget about all that. The conspiracy idea is nonsense. I don't know what I was thinking."

Felix stared at the screen. "Jhuri… What's with the sudden shift?"

"I thought it was possible there might be a small cabal of people opposed to the Greater Union, maybe drugging people or trying to discredit rivals," Jhuri said. "That's the kind of political idiocy that happens from time to time. But these claims Terrak made? That people in all the major factions are being mind-controlled by *space mushrooms*? It's absurd. Put it out of your mind. Just apprehend Terrak and bring him to justice." Jhuri switched off the transmission.

Felix put his head in his hands. *They got to Jhuri.*

CHAPTER 28
SEVERYNE

"Join the pursuit!" Immental shouted from the screen. "Transit the wormhole and go after this *Vermilion*!"

"I will do so if that is your order," Severyne said calmly. "I would, however, advise against such an action."

"Capturing Terrak is your only priority! What *else* should you be doing?"

"Waiting for Amina Azad to show up on this side of the wormhole, admiral."

Immental frowned. "What do you mean?"

"I know Azad. She would not reveal her position this way. Appeals to the good will and good sense of the public are not in her nature."

"But the Hacan – Azad can't necessarily control him. He could have done it on his own. Maybe he even left Azad behind when he got this new ship."

"I acknowledge the possibility," Severyne said. "Which is why I am happy to let Duval rush off in pursuit of the vessel. I do not, personally, believe Azad and Terrak are even on the *Vermilion*. Perhaps I am wrong, and Duval will capture them – if so, Voyou will see to it that our interests are secured, and nothing will be lost. But if I am right ... if this transmission is part of a scheme, and a distraction ... we should not leave the wormhole unguarded. I think Terrak and Azad are still on their way. They know about Duval's forces – Azad spoke to them from Huntsman's Moon. They don't know the Barony is involved, though. They will never expect us to be waiting here, ready to pounce when they appear."

"That ... may be so," Immental said. "And I suppose by the time you caught up with the *Vermilion*, everything would be over anyway. Assuming Duval can even intercept the ship."

"I believe his competence will extend that far, admiral. His ship is quite swift; I've used it myself. I will remain here, with your permission, and report if we detect any sign of the fugitives."

"Very well." Immental started to turn away, then looked back at the screen. "Captain Dampierre ... Severyne ... you haven't asked me about the contents of that video. The Hacan spy's outlandish claims."

"It seems self-evident to me that Terrak is either suffering from paranoid delusions or making up an outrageous story to distract from his own guilt. Is there reason to think otherwise?"

"No," Immental said. "That is our assessment as well."

"At least he didn't tell the *actual* truth – that he's secretly a Barony agent. That would have been embarrassing for us. As it stands, Terrak has only embarrassed himself."

"Yes," the admiral said. "Indeed. Well said."

Severyne affected a slightly confused look. "I am curious, though – do we know why Terrak and Azad *actually* want to visit this Coalition colony world? If there is no conspiracy, no cure to administer, what business could they possibly have with Fleet Captain Harlow?"

Immental said, "I ... should think it's obvious. Terrak committed a murder at a summit, doubtless intended to disrupt the Coalition. Now, he plans to attack Harlow, an architect of the Union, to further throw the proceedings into chaos."

"Ah. Yes. That *does* make sense. But admiral... if their aim is to weaken the Greater Union... why are we trying to *stop* them?"

For just a moment, Immental's expression was disturbingly blank. Then she narrowed her eyes and said, "Terrak is a rogue Barony asset, and your mission is to capture him, not to speculate about his plans, or the infinitely more complex and subtle plans of your superiors."

"Of course, admiral. My apologies."

"Get Terrak. I'll await your report."

The screen flickered off.

Severyne swiveled back and forth in her chair. Such nervous habits were unseemly in an officer of her rank and distinction, but there was no one here to see it, so she indulged. She was surprised to discover she missed Voyou. They'd gone through a lot together, including surviving a deathtrap created by an ancient alien tyrant, and as a result, he was one of the few people in the galaxy she felt comfortable talking with. Having someone to share ideas with was helpful in developing new and better ideas. She had so much to think about now. Like the fact that the admiral seemed to be–

Someone knocked at her door. Actually knocked, instead of calling ahead. She frowned, slid open a drawer, and wrapped her fingers around the grip of a pistol. "Come," she called.

The door slid open, and Calred stepped in, ducking his head so he wouldn't hit it on the way through. Severyne found the presence of a Hacan in her ready room as incongruous as seeing a toad on a dinner plate. The two of them had shared a ship before, when he was her prisoner, and she'd liked him better when he wasn't allowed to wander about. Sadly, locking him up now would only strain her partnership with Duval, so Calred retained his irritating liberty. "What do you want?" she said.

"Just to talk over recent events." He sat down in a chair without asking permission. The top button of his uniform jacket was undone. The Mentak were so *slovenly*. "I heard about the *Vermilion*. You think it's a trick, right? Amina Azad doesn't leave a trail that wide and easy to follow."

Slovenly, yes, but quicker on the uptake than Admiral Immental, which was the problem. Immental was reckoned the finest tactical and strategic mind in the Barony. That was the reason her support of the Legion initiative was so successful, even though such an alliance went against basic Letnev principles of superiority and self-reliance. A ruse like Azad's shouldn't have taken the admiral in. She'd lost a step. The question was, why? The pressures of the upcoming summit on Arc Prime? Or something more sinister? She was increasingly concerned that the admiral was compromised, and if that were true, it meant a great many *other* things were probably true, too.

Severyne didn't say any of that. She said, "The beads woven into your mane look very stupid."

Calred chuckled. "I'm eager to take fashion advice from the Letnev. I understand the bold new look on Arc Prime this season is a splash of dark gray to accent all the black. So. We're going to stay parked right here and wait for Azad to wander into our clutches, I assume?"

"That is my intention. Will you tell your captain that he's almost certainly off on a pointless adventure?"

The Hacan crossed one leg over the other, getting even more comfortable in a chair that was designed to make comfort as difficult to achieve as possible in the absence of literal spikes. "Nah, I don't think so. Someone has to check the *Vermilion* anyway, just on the off chance Terrak and Azad *are* on board, and if I told Felix I thought it was a fool's errand, I'd just sap his enthusiasm. Felix does better work when he's fully committed."

"I can't tell if you're being loyal or disloyal to your captain," Severyne mused.

"I'm being practical, which is usually better than either of those. How about all this mind-control-spore stuff Terrak spouted? What do you think about it?"

"I think it's irrelevant to my mission."

Calred snorted. "You can do the obedient-little-Letnev routine with me if you like, I don't mind, but we're in here alone, Severyne, and I've seen you try to murder people with a *stick*. You can talk freely with me."

Severyne allowed herself to smile. "Our shared history as enemies creates a degree of closeness between us, then? In some ways, we are closer than friends? I have heard that position espoused before. I think believing it is a good way to get knifed in the back. But I will assume you speak in good faith, and offer my answer in greater detail: I have no reason to believe that a secret conspiracy is using weaponized Arborec spores to mind-control people in order to manipulate galactic politics. It is the sort of extraordinary claim that I will not credit until I see real evidence." She left unspoken her determination to *discover* that evidence, if it existed.

"Sensible Sev," Calred said. "How long do you think before Azad pops through the wormhole?"

"If I were her, I wouldn't wait long. I'd begin the journey as soon as the bait was released and your captain went racing after it. She's probably on her way now."

"We need our guy alive," Calred said. "So, no blasting them out of the sky, right?"

"I also wish to recover my target intact."

"Right. What was I thinking? You wouldn't kill Azad from a distance anyway. You'd want to do that up close, right?" He showed his teeth. "Though you'd probably have a hard time deciding whether to kill her or kiss her, if the way you two looked at each other last time is any–"

"You are dismissed, Calred. I will let you know if your services are needed further."

He gave her a lazy Mentak-style salute and sauntered out.

Severyne went back to swiveling in her chair. A conversation with Calred wasn't as good as talking to Voyou, but it was better than talking to herself, and had, indeed, clarified certain factors in her mind. She had a mission to fulfill… but she also had a *responsibility*, to serve the best interests of the Letnev people, and, of course, to look after her own future prospects. It would be a delicate balance, but Severyne thrived in dynamic situations.

CHAPTER 29
TERRAK

Azad piloted the *Nine-Tenths of the Law* to the wormhole, paid the toll, then let the automated systems handle the actual transit. We emerged on the other side, near a space station that was larger and rather less scruffy than Chelicera, equipped to handle the vast freighters the Mentak Coalition sent to the local colony worlds. The automated traffic control system scanned us, but we were legally owned (by another fake corporation) and didn't send up any red flags, so the system waved us through without requiring a manual inspection.

"It's a pretty short trip from here to Entelegyne," Azad said.

"Assuming this ship doesn't fall to pieces before we get there." I was in the co-pilot's seat, though I wasn't doing any co-piloting. There just weren't any other seats, only a couple of tiny bunks that were really just slots in the bulkheads.

"Hey, I looked the ship over pretty well. My best estimate is that it'll fall apart slightly *after* we reach our destination, so that's fine." She consulted the scanners. "This planet we're going to is really just... wow. There's basically nobody there. It's all automated farms, and even the supervisors use telepresence bots, with only occasional visits in person. The fleet captain has a pretty sweet little bungalow on the southern continent, with a staff of just two people. Talk about getting away from it all. It's possible she's got some extra personnel hidden on the grounds, since the puppetmasters suspect we're coming, but my guess is they don't want to let anybody they don't control near Harlow. She's supposed to be an honored guest at the summit on Moll Primus, but I'd be willing to bet she's barely able to string a coherent sentence together now, if she's been under the influence as long as we think."

"Is she really the best candidate for the cure, then?"

"What, because she might be a vegetable with a brain full of vegetables? She might be the best candidate. If the cure works on her, then it *really works*, you know?"

I grunted. "What if it doesn't work? If we go to all this trouble, and the cure simply fails, or kills her?" The idea of going to all this effort, making these hairsbreadth escapes, expending such ingenuity, only to *fail*, was troubling. We were being hunted, and we wouldn't escape our pursuers forever. We needed to make progress.

Azad was less concerned. "If it doesn't work, I'll tell my bosses what happened – seizures, frothing, death, nothing at all – and take some blood and tissue samples, and we find another scientist to do some analysis, and my bosses send a tweaked recipe, and we try again. Nobody ever said science was easy or pretty. That said… the people I work for are smart, and they'd already done a lot of work on finding ways to disrupt Arborec communication. I'm hopeful that what we've got here will do the trick."

We sailed through the star-speckled void, and eventually an orb appeared in the distance, growing in size in the screens until it became a green and cloud-streaked planet. "Entelegyne. Looks pretty from up here. You just know it's all bugs and allergens and mud when you get to the surface though. Ugh."

I frowned, gazing at the screen. "Azad… something just occluded one of the stars to the left of the planet."

"What are you talking about?"

"There was a star, visible *there*, and then, it went dark."

"Are you sure?" Azad pulled up an overlay of the local star chart on the screen, and all the matching stars turned green. One dot stayed stubbornly red, with no corresponding light source in reality. "Huh. You're right. Could be an asteroid, or space junk. Anything, really."

"It could be a ship. It could be the *Temerarious*."

"No way. They're off after the *Vermilion*, I'm sure of it. Duval is a dog – you throw a stick, and he's going to chase it. He might worry he's being tricked, but he's not going to let it go, or delegate it, either. He's got personal feelings about me, and they are negative." She manipulated a few switches and buttons, then sighed. "Damn. I wish the sensors on this ship were better. We'll have to get a lot closer before I can see what we're dealing with."

"There." I pointed at the screen. "The star is back. Whatever that object is, it's *moving*, and I think it's most sensible to assume it's a vessel that's looking for us."

Azad made a little growl in her throat. "Maybe the Mentak Coalition sent another ship out here, just to cover the contingencies. I really thought the puppetmasters would try to keep the circle small, to contain things… but maybe we changed their math when we spilled the truth all over the spacewaves. They could dispatch uninfected people to capture us now without worrying we'd give something away, since we *already* gave it away, I just didn't think they'd have time to mobilize crews. Maybe there was a ship in the vicinity already… Well, whatever, we deal with what's in front of us. We're on the right trajectory to reach the planet, so I can cut our power and we'll just keep sailing along. If they notice us at all, they'll think we're just a passing asteroid–"

The control console buzzed. "Incoming call," I said. "Heavily encrypted, too. They don't want anyone overhearing."

Azad sighed. "I guess it would be rude not to answer."

CHAPTER 30
SEVERYNE

Calred pounded on the door this time, and Severyne opened it with a scowl ready and waiting on her face. "I am not *Felix*," she said. "You don't bang on my door and demand my attention."

"I'm not allowed to use the onboard comms, Severyne. The rest of the crew literally ignores me when I talk to them. This is the only way I can get your attention."

"You're a *hostage*, Calred, only here in order to compel Duval's cooperation. None of us want or need to talk to you. Now if you'll excuse me, I'm required in the hangar bay."

Calred tried to loom over her. He could do so physically, but she was not intimidated. If he even breathed on her more heavily than she liked, she would have his knees removed. She'd agreed to return him to Felix alive, not unharmed. "That's why I'm here!" he shouted. "I heard someone mention a landing party. Why are you landing? Correction – why are *we* landing? You agreed I'd be included in this operation, remember?"

"I was about to send for you," Severyne lied. "We're landing because a ship is approaching the planet, and I believe Terrak and Azad are on board."

"So, capture them!"

"What a clever idea," she said flatly. "We ran simulations. Attempting to take them in space is too dangerous. If we try to disable their ship, we might inadvertently destroy it, and boarding parties are also chancy. Azad is a great fan of traps and ambushes, and there's no need to send my crew into harm's way. Fire could be exchanged, and their ship is frankly a flying piece of trash, so accidental decompression could result as well. We know where Azad and Terrak are going. We'll simply land and capture them on the ground."

"Do you think the fleet captain will take kindly to a group of Letnev soldiers appearing on her doorstep?"

"I do not. Which is why we will land quietly and proceed carefully. And, if we do make contact, why, we'll have *you* there to smooth things over, won't we? An officer in good standing in the Mentak Coalition Navy." She patted Calred on his immense bicep. "Come along."

"I'll need a weapon. I will not face Amina Azad without a gun in my hand. I don't even like being around *you* when I'm unarmed."

"Of course, Calred. You're one of the team, and my team *always* comes prepared."

Severyne, Calred, and four Barony marines in black armor and blank face masks boarded a shuttle and dropped from the *Grim Countenance* to the planet. Their vessel bounced through the atmosphere, plummeted to within a few hundred meters of the surface, then skimmed over a wide, grassy plain toward the fleet captain's estate.

The shuttle settled down in the shadow of a rock formation, and the group disembarked. Two marines went first to make sure the area was clear, then Severyne followed with Calred at her side, followed by the other marines. There were no dangerous fauna on this continent, so there was no fence or other real barricades around the estate – just ornamental stone walls, low enough to step over.

Severyne squinted at the sky. She envied her troops their light-filtering masks as they marched around her with their guns at the ready. "Sunshine. Appalling. I've never seen the point of it. I know, everyone says it helps the plants grow, but we grow things just fine in the dark back home."

"I'm just happy I can finally see," Calred said, rifle resting over his shoulder. "It's so dark on your ship I keep banging into things."

"That is because you are a gargantuan oaf."

"Could a gargantuan oaf do this?" Calred brought his rifle down and discharged an energy burst into a pile of rocks, scorching the stone and making Severyne turn and stare at him. All her troopers trained their guns on him, just awaiting her order to turn him into charred meat.

Calred held his rifle pointed at the sky, held his free hand up, and smiled a wide smile. Hacan could smile very widely indeed. "Please, be calm. I just wanted to make sure the weapon worked. I used the lowest setting, and it hardly even made a noise. I just had this silly idea you might give me a rifle with no charge and wanted to ease my mind."

"Giving you an inoperative weapon would violate the terms of our partnership."

"You're the one who said I was just a hostage."

"That's because you were annoying me. I trust you're satisfied now?"

"Very."

"Good. Don't fire that weapon again without my explicit orders, Calred, or I'll have my marines shoot your feet off and leave you and your cauterized stumps in the bushes. We want our quarry alive. The guns are for purposes of intimidation or unexpected resistance."

"Yes, ma'am." He offered another lazy salute. That was probably the only kind a Mentak Coalition soldier knew how to give. It was astonishing to her that such a rabble had risen to become a galactic power.

They continued moving slowly and carefully across the grounds of the fleet captain's estate. It was so… so… *pointless*. There were little arched wooden bridges over trickles of water already narrow enough to step across. Severyne spied tiny stone buildings nestled among bright flowers. They paused near an octagonal structure with a peaked roof and sides that were open, apart from railings. "What is *that*?"

"It's a gazebo." Calred sounded amused.

"Why would you want a structure like that? It's completely indefensible."

"That's true. I can't think of a single time in history a gazebo withstood a siege."

"And this is aquaculture, I suppose?" Severyne went to the rocky edge of a large fishpond, connected to other ponds on the grounds by narrow channels spanned by more tiny bridges. "I can see the appeal of fresh seafood, but really, it's needlessly ornamental."

"Nobody eats these fish, Severyne. They're just here to be pretty and make you feel peaceful. They're bred to be decorative. See, their scales are silver, orange, ooh, there's one that's all white."

"And I suppose that… damp structure… isn't meant for irrigation?"

"It's a fountain. You must have seen fountains before."

Severyne clucked her tongue. "The Mentak Coalition is decadent. You sicken me."

"The feeling is mutual. The sickening, I mean. Not the decadence. Nobody would accuse you of having any fun."

"Decadence doesn't mean *fun*–"

"Hey, Sev," a voice called. It seemed to emerge from behind a pile of mossy boulders, doubtless arranged with great precision for no particular purpose. Severyne stiffened her spine, and she found herself, improbably, wondering if her collar was straight or her hair was mussed. "And Calred! Wow, what a big happy fancy fun reunion."

"Azad," Calred growled, and swung his rifle down.

THE FAITHFUL XII

Jhuri ended the call with Felix. "That… didn't feel right," he said.

Kote Strom – someone Jhuri had considered an annoying incompetent, before the gift of the sacrament revealed them to be partners in the great work – scowled from her seat, just out of view of Jhuri's screen. "What didn't feel right? You don't think Duval believed you?"

"I don't know," Jhuri said. "I tried to be as convincing as possible, but the guides insisted I be firm and direct and scornful, to mock the whole idea of a conspiracy. Given that I recently told Felix to *investigate* a conspiracy, I worry that wasn't an effective approach."

Strom was chilly now: "You question the wisdom of the guides?"

The idea sent a shudder of visceral horror through Jhuri's entire nervous system. "Of course not! That's not what I meant. It felt… wrong to lie to Felix, instead of bringing him into the fold. We have a member of the faithful on board the *Temerarious* already, so it would be easy enough to offer Felix the sacrament–"

"The guides say no. The guides say it is important to have agents who are unaware of their existence."

"But why?" Jhuri said.

"They did not say." Kote Strom looked briefly stricken. "But I think it's because – because we *decline*, we lose our ability to–" Her eyes rolled back in her head and she fell off the stool.

<*Because not all are worthy to partake in our glory,*> the guides whispered into Jhuri's ear.

"Oh," Jhuri said. "Yes. That makes sense."

Kote sat up, touching the side of her head and wincing.

<*You will both attend the summit on Moll Primus,*> the guides whispered. <*To help ensure all goes smoothly. Arrangements have already been made.*>

"To make sure what goes smoothly, guides?" Jhuri asked. He didn't *want* to question the guides, but he was head of Coalition covert operations; being nosy was basically part of his DNA, and the question just came out of him by reflex.

<*All will be revealed in time,*> the guides said, and for some reason, Jhuri found that answer perfectly satisfying.

CHAPTER 31
TERRAK

When the mysterious ship hailed us, Azad pushed a button on the ship's console, and a Letnev woman's face appeared on a screen. I recognized her immediately as the same person from Azad's much-folded photograph.

"Sev!" Azad said. "What in the hell are you... oh. Oh, no. You haven't gone green on me, have you, Sev?"

"I have been dispatched to capture your associate, Azad," the woman said, face completely expressionless. "I am told that he is a Barony intelligence asset, now attempting to defect to the Federation of Sol."

I snorted. "Ridiculous. There's no point in cooperating with the Barony. They're even stingy when it comes to bribes."

"No, no, it all makes perfect sense," Azad said. "Terrak is, what, a triple agent, and I'm exfiltrating him after a botched operation. Wait. Why am I exfiltrating him to a Mentak Coalition colony world? I forget. I'm sure there's a good reason."

"I am merely reporting the substance of my orders," the Letnev woman said.

"Did you see our blistering expose, Sev? Either you've already

236

got spores on the brain, or you're at least a little bit suspicious that your superiors might."

"Your allegations are outlandish. I would require real proof in order to take them seriously."

"We're a little short of proof at the moment," Azad said. "That's kind of why we're in this system."

Sev sighed. "Yes, Azad. I know. So, let's go down to the planet and *get* the proof, all right?"

Azad cackled. "You mean it? Really? The old gang is getting back together again?"

Still no mirth from the Letnev. Did Azad just enjoy needling her? Did the *Letnev* woman enjoy it, and just didn't show it? If they'd ever been a couple, it was hard to imagine an odder one.

Sev said, "If you're lying, or mistaken, you will be taken into custody and handed over to my superiors. If you are telling the truth... that would interest me. I would have to reconsider my options."

"I'll meet you on the ground, then. My bosses sent me a sketch of the captain's estate. There's a bit on the western side, away from the main house, with a pile of boulders and a fountain and a gazebo and a fishpond – really, this place is a *lot*. I'll meet you by the fountain, all right?"

"Gazebo. Fountain. Hmm. As you say. I will organize a landing party. Be advised – Calred, from the *Temerarious*, is with me. He will not be informed of our arrangement. He is likely to be hostile when he encounters you."

"That is... some strange bedfellows you've got going on there, Sev. How'd that happen?"

"I am cooperating with Duval to capture you both. He took one of my bridge officers, and I took one of his, to ensure that both parties obey the terms of our partnership."

Azad grunted. "The Barony and the Mentak Coalition working together on an operation? Does that seem like something that would happen naturally, or something that might, say, be organized by a malign fungal intelligence—"

"We will find out one way or another soon, Azad. I will see you at the rendezvous point." Her image vanished.

"I gather that was an old friend of yours?" I asked.

Azad leaned back in her chair, shaking her head and smiling. She seemed genuinely wonderstruck. "That was Captain Severyne Joelle Dampierre of the Barony warship *Grim Countenance*. She's… an ex. Ex-ally, ex-enemy, ex-lover, ex lots of things."

"It sounds like your relationship has gone through many permutations." Azad had made a suggestive comment about a Letnev when we first met. I assumed this Sev was she. I could see how the woman would make a strong impression.

She chuckled. "It sounds that way, but to be really accurate, Severyne was ally, enemy, and lover all at the same time. The puppetmasters probably sent her after me because we have history. She's the closest thing the Barony has to an expert on Amina Azad. Lucky for us she has a wild disobedient streak, huh? Any other Letnev soldier would have just bagged us and tossed us in a cell as instructed."

"You trust her, then?" I asked.

"Oh, I absolutely trust Sev. I trust her to do what's best for her. Being the pawn of a vast conspiracy is not what's best for her. Once we show her we're telling the truth… she'll help us out, and come up with a way to cover herself in glory in the process."

"I very much hope the cure works, then."

"What with our lives depending on it, you mean? Yeah. We should be careful, though. Sev probably hasn't gone green – I don't think she'd bother with this level of subterfuge if she was working for the bad guys, especially since she could take our little ship with her big one easily enough. But she'll be traveling with a Hacan who likes shooting stuff, and her personal guards too, and who knows whether any of them have been compromised?"

"I will continue with my policy of trusting no one," I assured her.

"It'll be good to see Sev again," Amina said. "If me and her start to make out or something, just avert your eyes until we're finished."

The humans sometimes said "opposites attract", but that only made sense to me when talking about magnets. "You baffle me, Azad. I have seen evidence of your competence, but you don't seem to take *anything* seriously."

"I'm always serious, big guy." She leaned back, looking pleased with herself. "In my line of work, every day could be my last – sometimes every second. But that means I'm also serious about enjoying myself as much as humanly possible. And humans are *good* at enjoying themselves."

CHAPTER 32
SEVERYNE

"Don't point that thing at people, Calred." Severyne pushed the barrel of his rifle down until it was aimed at the ground. He scowled but didn't resist. "Azad, Terrak, come out where I can see you."

Azad strolled out from behind the pile of rocks and stood on the far side of a small wooden bridge from Severyne. Her hair was mussed, her grin wide, and her clothes rumpled. She remained one of the most arresting things Severyne had ever seen. She opened her arms wide. "Are we hugging? We're hugging, right? I was never a hugger before I met you, Sev, but something about your warmth and openness, it fundamentally *changed* me."

"We are not hugging," Severyne said. "We are here to settle a question."

"Hugging after, then?"

Severyne only sighed.

Calred looked from Severyne to Azad and back again, and finally growled, "Someone had better tell me what's going on."

"Hello, cousin." A Hacan stepped out to stand behind Azad. He was older than Calred, with gray in his mane, wearing a plain gray robe.

"I'm not your cousin. I've got plenty of cousins, and none of them are murderers."

Terrak tilted his head. "Really? I was speaking figuratively, but among my cousins, there are at least, hmm, three murderers, though two were ruled self-defense–"

"Shut up!" Calred said. "We're here to take you into custody for your crimes against the Mentak Coalition and the Greater Union and the Kingdom of Xxcha!" He swung his head around to Severyne. "*Aren't* we?"

The Hacan was behaving intemperately, but that was no surprise. As long as he didn't try to actually shoot anyone, she could tolerate his irritation. "Sounds like a bit of a jurisdictional tangle," Severyne said. "I can't see why I'd do anything for any of the factions you mentioned. But, yes, we were sent to apprehend you and your partner. First, though, let's settle the outstanding question of this conspiracy."

"You're not…" Calred groaned. "You said their mushroom mind-control story was ridiculous!"

"You have such a lazy mind." Severyne shook her head. "What I *said* was, I would require real evidence in order to believe such a thing. They propose to offer such evidence."

"Sure do," Azad said cheerfully. "One of you hold the old woman down, and I'll give her the cure, and we'll see what happens."

Calred shook his head, beaded mane swaying. "You can't inject an unknown chemical into a Mentak Coalition fleet captain! She might *die*!"

"I regret to inform you that the Barony of Letnev is not overly concerned about the well-being of Mentak Coalition military officers. Even retired ones."

Calred whipped his gun up and squeezed the trigger repeatedly as he swept the barrel across Terrak, Azad, and Severyne in a single rapid maneuver.

That was clearly the idea, anyway. Since the rifle didn't fire, it was an ineffective approach. Severyne's troopers pointed their weapons at Calred and took the gun away from him while he stood looking baffled.

Severyne held up her hand, revealing a small black fob with a single button in the center. "This is a remote safety. We use them sometimes in training. I was afraid you might… react badly to this turn of events. The question is, did you fire on us because you were outraged by my plan as a Mentak Coalition officer, or because you were terrified as a puppet of the conspirators?"

"You won't get away with this," Calred said.

"I will refrain from shooting your feet off, in case you *are* uncompromised," Severyne said. "But we'll have to bind you and leave you here under guard."

Calred closed his eyes for a moment, and shivered, and then whimpered. He said, "I'm sorry," and then another word – "gods", perhaps? – before launching himself at Severyne, claws out.

CHAPTER 33
FELIX

The *Temerarious* caught up to the *Vermilion* and ordered it to halt and prepare to be boarded. The ship complied right away, which caused a sinking feeling in the depths of Felix's gut. There was no way Amina Azad would just surrender like that.

Felix and Ggorgos boarded, and they found the ship's occupants on their knees in the cargo area, hands behind their heads, as ordered. They still had their hoods up. Ggorgos pointed her weapon at them – an energy rifle equipped with a grenade launcher under the barrel and a bayonet above – while Felix approached. He pushed back the woman's hood, already knowing what he'd see. She had dark hair, and she was human, but that was as far as her resemblance to Amina Azad went. He pushed back the Hacan's hood, and he was older than Terrak, with a big scar down his muzzle. Their scans had turned up no additional life signs, so Azad wasn't hiding in the crawlspace with a pistol in each fist. These two were all they'd get.

Felix sighed. "Why did you broadcast that message?"

"What message?" The woman seemed genuinely bewildered.

"What is your relationship to the fugitives Terrak and Amina Azad?" Ggorgos said.

"Who?" the Hacan said. "Is one of those the woman who hired us?"

Felix pulled up images of the fugitives on his tablet, though he was just going through the motions. Azad had tricked them. He knew it. He accepted it. He took some small comfort from the fact that she probably hadn't expected to encounter Severyne on the other side of the wormhole, so maybe *she'd* gotten a nasty surprise, too. "Was it her?"

The woman nodded. "Yeah, she hired us to transport… something. We don't know about any broadcast."

"Transport what?" Ggorgos snapped.

"Can I?" The woman gestured, and Ggorgos gave assent. She went to a locker, opened it, and removed a small box wrapped with a purple ribbon. She brought it over and handed it to Felix.

"Scanning," Ggorgos said. "The package does not contain explosives. I detect no devices at all. It seems to be empty."

"I thought it seemed kind of light," the woman said.

Felix tore off the ribbon and opened the box.

It wasn't entirely empty. There was a napkin, the sort Felix had seen a million times underneath his drinks at bars. Someone had scribbled a drawing on the paper: a caricature of a human (probably meant to be Felix, what with the mustache) who had curving devil horns on his head. "Happy hunting!" was scrawled across the bottom, and then, "Your friend, AA." She was the *worst*. He hated her, only slightly more than he hated himself. Azad had set out some tempting bait, but he'd been the one to chase right after it. Except, what *else* could he have done?

Felix showed the drawing to Ggorgos. To his surprise, the Xxcha ground out a laugh. "This Azad is an audacious character, isn't she?"

"I thought you'd shout and blow things up." Felix put the napkin in his pocket. "I didn't expect you to appreciate her wit."

Ggorgos said, "There was always a chance this was a ruse. It had to be checked out anyway." That reassured Felix, mildly. "No matter. The *Grim Countenance* is watching the other side of the wormhole. We will call them from the ship and ask if they've seen our quarry." Ggorgos stowed her rifle on a magnetic rack that jutted out of one of the facets on the back of her shell. She turned to the crew. "We apologize for the intrusion. Check your comms – you'll find you've been broadcasting a ... rather strange message on a loop."

"Ah ... thank you?" The woman looked at her Hacan partner. "We get to keep the ship?"

"I don't see why not," Felix said. "It was lawfully purchased, and you were hired to fly it. Just, in the future ... refrain from making deals in bars with shady characters?"

"Yes, sir," the woman said, and didn't even bother to sound sincere about it.

As they headed back to their ship, Voyou started shouting into their comms: "They're on the *planet*! We have to go back!"

"How do you know where they are?" Felix asked suspiciously. He knew he was seeing conspiracies everywhere, but in his defense, there probably *were* conspiracies everywhere.

"It ... just stands to reason." Voyou's tone was sulky. That was new; his emotional range had previously seemed limited to "supercilious" and "bored." "If Azad and Terrak aren't here, then they must be on Entelegyne."

"A reasonable supposition," Ggorgos said. "We will proceed with all due haste. With luck, the Letnev ship has intercepted them, or will soon."

"Surely they would have mentioned it," Felix said, suddenly

with new things to worry about. "Sev might pretend she forgot to call, but Cal would tell us." He hailed Calred on his crew's personal channel – Duval's Devils only, no Ggorgos allowed – and received no answer. He called Tib instead. "Hail the *Grim Countenance* for me and ask for a situation report."

"Will do."

Felix and Ggorgos returned to the bridge and began making their way back to the wormhole. By the time the *Temerarious* had left the *Vermilion* well behind, Tib said, "The communications officer on the *Grim Countenance* says Captain Dampierre is in a meeting, and Calred is unavailable for comment."

That sounded like a cover story, though a cover story for *what*? Felix looked at Ggorgos, who was, as usual, totally expressionless, and then realized she hadn't heard any of that exchange. "Tib can't reach Calred or Severyne." Frustration bubbled up inside him. "What are they *doing* over there?"

"I am unsure," Ggorgos said. "But I now believe we should proceed with *excessive* haste."

CHAPTER 34
TERRAK

Calred launched himself at Captain Dampierre, clearly intending to deliver a killing blow. I was too far away, across the creek, to do anything about it. I didn't know either of them, but in a group like this, with so many divided loyalties, violence had a way of multiplying and spreading out, so I prepared myself to flee or fight as needed.

Severyne seemed to expect the attack, however, stepping deftly aside as two of her guards moved forward in tandem, almost as though they'd rehearsed the move. The soldiers hit Calred from either side with shock-sticks, and he went down, spasming and groaning. They stood over him, clearly awaiting further instructions. Severyne said, "Hmm."

"Safe to say the big guy has fungus on the brain, wouldn't you agree?" Azad stepped across the creek, ignoring the ornamental bridge, and threw her arms wide again, as though to embrace the woman. Severyne stepped deftly aside from *that*, too, keeping her hands clasped behind her back and appearing to not even notice the overture. She was the sort of woman who could look down her nose at someone a meter taller than her. You almost had to admire it.

"Calred seems to be compromised, yes," Severyne agreed. "That was as good as an admission."

"We could test the cure on him," I said.

Azad grinned at me. "What, no mercy for this Hacan? Is it because he's not down on his luck like the last guy?"

I sighed. "I objected to infecting an innocent person with mysterious spores, Azad. This poor man is already sick. If we can help him, we should."

Calred rolled over, moaning. "No." He tried to rise up on his elbows, but another jab in the shoulder with a shock-stick put him down again. "Please… don't… the guides… they won't let you take me, we have orders, and without them, nothing means anything, everything is gray, please."

"I quite like gray," Severyne said. "Proceed with the cure. Guards, hold him if he struggles."

Azad knelt beside the Hacan, humming to herself and plucking things from the pouches on her vest: a syringe, a vial, a small silver flask. She unscrewed the latter, took a swig, then splashed some of the alcohol on the crook of Calred's elbow. The Hacan tried to rise again, but a pair of guards held him down. Azad peered at Calred's arm, found a vein, slipped in the syringe, and depressed the plunger. She removed the needle, capped it, and put it with her supplies. Then she looked down at her… patient? Calred was muttering, "No, no, no", and "I'm sorry", and the like. It was pitiful and horrible and all I could think about was the fact that I'd nearly been like him, infected and compromised and lost to myself.

"How quickly can we expect a reaction?" Severyne sounded impatient, though I was beginning to gather that was how she always sounded.

Azad looked up at her. "Should be pretty fast, according to

the lab notes. My bosses think the spores activate various happy-chemical receptors in the brains, so first off, the cure will mess with those. Keep the chemicals from binding or make them bind better or whatever will cause the effects to diminish. I'm not a neuroscientist. Then the antifungals will start to take effect, killing off whatever's growing in there. The neural regeneration stuff will take a lot longer, could be hours or days before the victim returns to full functionality–"

Calred rolled over on his side and threw up a thin stream of mostly bile, then coughed pitifully.

"I half-expected to see little mushroom caps floating in his vomit," I said, trying to make light of a situation that was anything but. No one was amused. Everyone stared at Calred, desperate to see what he'd do: die in convulsions, try to kill us, scream in defiance–

Calred began to weep. He covered his face with his hands, and Severyne's guards moved to shock him again, I suppose just on general principles, but she stilled them with a gesture. "Wait." She didn't look sympathetic, but she no longer looked murderous, either.

"He's... not dead," Azad said. "That's a good sign." She elbowed me. "See, we could have injected the old guy after all, he would have been fine."

I growled at her. She didn't seem particularly intimidated.

"I'm sorry, I'm sorry, it was... I was in a fog." Calred's voice was muffled. "I feel so empty now, but... but the guides, I don't hear their voices anymore. I'm sorry–"

"Save your apologies for later," Severyne snapped. "We need information now. Who are these guides? Your handlers in the conspiracy?"

Calred struggled to sit up, and managed, just about, though his posture was slumped. There were tears shining in the corners of his eyes. "It's not like that. The guides are more like… mentors. They want what's best for us. They want to create a better world, and when you take their sacrament, they show you how you can help. It feels *good* to help."

"Great, but who actually are they?" This from Azad, who positively vibrated at the prospect of obtaining hard information from one of the compromised.

"I don't know, and I never thought to ask." Calred wiped his mouth on the back of his hand. "Stars, there are really spores in my *brain*–"

"Focus!" Severyne snapped her fingers in front of his face. "Surely you have some information we can actually use?"

"I…" His eyes widened. "Oh. One thing. They know you're here."

"Who does?" I asked. "The fleet captain?" I looked around, but there were plants and ornamental bits of stone everywhere, enough to hide a dozen of the infected. I felt horribly exposed.

Calred shook his head. "I get the impression the fleet captain is pretty far gone, but she has employees – two of the faithful." He winced. "That's what the guides call us. Faithful. I sort of… connected up with Harlow and her staff when we landed. I can't feel them anymore… They must think I'm dead. Or cured. Not being connected to the other faithful, or to the guides, it's like having my head sealed in an iron box–"

Azad knelt down and looked into Calred's face. "What do you mean, you connected with them? Like, telepathy?"

"Not exactly. I can't read their minds, but I can – I could – sense the presence of other faithful, and tell how close they are, and whether they're awake or asleep or in pain, things like that. It's only the guides who speak in my mind with actual words, but we can share information through them – if I tell them something, they can inform the other faithful."

"You were in constant contact with these guides?" Severyne asked.

"No, not really. We always have our standing orders, and the sacrament keeps us blissed out, but in terms of actively communicating, the voices of the guides get weaker and stronger and sometimes fade entirely. Here, though, I could hear the guides clearly – there must be a node in the house, like the one on the ship."

"*What* ship?" Severyne snarled, just as Azad said, "What's a node?"

"Your ship," Calred said to Severyne. "Though there's one on mine, too." He looked to Azad. "A node is… it doesn't look like much. The faithful who recruited me gave me one, when I was on a rest and relaxation trip, right after they sprayed me with spores. The node was barely even a seed then – it looked like a speck of green. I put it in a little water and gave it a little blood and it grew into a sort of mushroom, with a red flower on top. The guides said the node would help me communicate with them and connect with the other faithful, and I was supposed to harvest the spores and grow nodes and hide them everywhere I went, to extend the network."

Azad grunted. "That node sounds like a miniature version of a Letani. The whole point of those is to allow the Arborec to communicate when they're away from their home planet – every Letani generates a local spore cloud that lets the creatures with them communicate. It's like they carry their own communications network with them."

"You put one of these nodes on my ship?" Severyne's eyes widened in outrage, like someone had insulted her dignity, or maybe beat up her best friend. It was the most emotion I'd seen her display so far. Some captains are like that with their ships.

Calred shook his head. "No. But only because I didn't need to. There was already one on board."

Severyne went completely still. "Who on my crew is compromised?" The guards started glancing at each other and taking careful steps back, giving themselves room. My claws slid out of their pads without me consciously intending them to.

"Voyou," Calred said. "We thought it was funny, the way you had us swap ships, when we both shared the same true loyalty."

Severyne swore. It was quite a good curse, in an Emirate dialect. She must have liked Voyou, to react so strongly. "Where did you learn to say *that*?" I asked.

"She's met Sagasa," Azad said. "That's one of his favorites."

"We should move," Calred said. "The fleet captain's caretakers will come looking for us. They'll be able to find the spot where I… went offline. If we stand around, they'll shoot us from cover."

"Yes, fine," Severyne snapped. "We'll proceed with caution and take a roundabout route to the house." She gestured, and the guards formed up, a couple still staying within striking range of Calred. I didn't think he was faking his recovery, but we couldn't really be sure. We couldn't be sure of much of *anything*, could we?

While we walked, Severyne called her ship. "Get in touch with the *Temerarious* and tell them that Voyou is compromised." A pause. "What do you *mean* you can't reach them?"

CHAPTER 35
FELIX

"What do you mean the comms are down?" Felix said.

"There's a fault in central processing," Tib said. "No idea what's going on. I'll go down and take a look. Calred is the engineer, though, so if it's more complicated than a loose cable, I don't know what I can do about it."

"Your efforts are appreciated." After she was gone, Felix sat in the captain's chair on the bridge and considered the trajectory details on the screen. Even at top speed, it would be almost two hours before they reached the wormhole, and then they had to transit and get to the planet, and who knew what they'd find once they got there? In space, everything took forever except the things that happened very fast.

Ggorgos came onto the bridge and walked over to the tactical board, though there was nothing for her to shoot at just then. She was very good at being expressionless, but Felix detected a hint of frustration or impatience on her beaky face.

"This is going to be a very tedious few hours, isn't it?" Felix said. "I hate waiting. Is there anything worse than being bored, when you know there's action happening somewhere else?"

The Xxcha merely grunted.

Then Tib spoke over a private channel into his ear: "Captain, I'm down in central processing, and it's not a loose cable. The communications system has been sabotaged."

I guess that's worse, Felix thought.

THE FAITHFUL XIII

TX138 was eating some kind of still-wriggling small crustacean, crunching through the tiny creature's exoskeleton, but without apparent pleasure. It was like watching a miniature crushing machine at work. The L1Z1X liaison swallowed, then turned her red eyes toward Captain Tournasault, twenty-year veteran of the Barony fleet and relatively new member of the faithful. TX138 said, "Would you like some?" She pushed a bowl across the table. The things in the bowl were trying to escape.

"I am quite all right, thank you," Tournasault said. "Why did you summon me to your quarters? You were ordered to induct your superior into the faith, but you and I are the only faithful I can sense on the ship." And, to be honest, TX138 seemed a little... *faint*, compared to the other faithful Tournasault had met. The L1Z1X had definitely taken the sacrament, but the connection was fuzzy.

"I will do as ordered, I think," TX138 said. The L1Z1X were deeply distressing creatures, horrible amalgamations of the biological and the mechanical, their red eyes glowing with devastating zeal. They were odd, and secretive, and their relationship with reality seemed tenuous at best. For one thing, they thought they were the rightful rulers of the empire, when in reality they were twisted perversions of the once-mighty race who'd *lost* an empire. Tournasault hated being around them, as a rule, and even with TX138 felt only a shadow of the usual connection he felt in the presence of other faithful.

"You think? You must! The summit is only days away. Soon we'll reach Arc Prime, and your leader hasn't even committed to signing the treaty yet."

"There are some points that do not yet satisfy us," TX138 said. "Certain crucial details remain unclear. When, precisely, will the other members of the Legion pledge fealty to the undying empire of the L1Z1X?"

Tournasault groaned. "Never. That isn't what's happening. As we keep *telling* you."

"How very strange. You continue to deny objective reality. That is unacceptable."

"Listen." Perhaps Tournasault could make a connection, faithful-to-faithful, despite the profound strangeness of this creature. "The guides have explained their plan to you, haven't they?"

"Unity," TX138 said. "They strive to create a better future… but any better future is, by definition, the dominion of the L1Z1X Mindnet. The future belongs to us. We are attempting to reconcile these discrepancies." TX138's red eyes flashed, and she shuddered. "Mmm. More positive reinforcement. How pleasant."

<*They are… resistant to our efforts,*> the guides whispered in Tournasault's mind. <*These creatures are so cybernetically altered that our sacrament is not as effective in them as usual. They have extensive voluntary control of their own endocrine systems… You must convince her to serve, faithful. You must.*>

Tournasault thought furiously. Thinking deeply and coming up with tactics and stratagems had once come so easily to him, but more and more it seemed a struggle. Finally, he said, "TX138, your superior – LV286, isn't it – is he very wise?"

"He speaks for Ibna Vel Syd, the greatest ruler in the galaxy, heir to all the stars, yes. LV286 is great and good."

"Then... wouldn't it make sense... to give LV286 the sacrament? Surely his wisdom would enable him to reconcile these... troubling details... you're struggling with?"

TX138 sat perfectly still, her face – if you could call it a face, with so many tubes going in and out, and all that metal – perfectly blank. Then she smiled. It was horrible, but welcome, nonetheless. "That is an excellent suggestion."

Tournasault sat back, and the guides rewarded him with an incremental increase in bliss.

CHAPTER 36
AZAD

"The guides probably told Voyou to take out the communications system when I went offline, knowing I might be compromised," Calred said, limping along behind Azad. "The guides have been really worried about this cure. They think you're a threat to the great work."

"Oh, there's a great work," Azad said. "Maybe you should tell us about that." She was annoyed. She'd had this idea that once she managed to cure one of the mushroom zombies, she'd actually get answers, and be able to tell her employer those answers, and get paid – well, paid more. But so far, the only new thing they'd learned was existence of those nodes, little vegetative communications satellites hidden on ships and stations all over the galaxy.

Calred sighed. "All I know is there *is* a plan, and I was a small part of it. I was supposed to keep an eye on my boss, Jhuri, and neutralize him if he got suspicious about the conspiracy. Then I got sent on *this* mission, to capture Terrak, and my main job then was updating the guides on our progress. And..." He swallowed. "Killing or compromising you and Terrak, before you had a chance to tell anyone what you'd found out."

"It would have been funny to see you try," Azad said. "You don't know anything about the bigger picture?"

"Just that the guides are eager for the Greater Union to succeed. They didn't want anything to disrupt the treaty process. Maybe the guides really *do* mean well, and they just want to promote peace and harmony in the ..." He trailed off. "No. I suppose not."

"Seems unlikely," Severyne said absently. "Wait." She held up her fist to halt the group, then peered through tiny gaps in a stand of tall reed-like plants that formed a natural barrier. "I can see the house. So many windows, how can anyone stand it? Useful for surveillance, though ... I don't see movement. Where were the faithful when you could still sense them, Calred?"

"All three of them were in the house, but when I got disconnected, I'm sure they freaked out. The fleet captain might still be inside – I don't think she's very mobile. She just gave off a vague impression of blissed-out confusion. The other two were sharp, though."

"Still, there are only two of them. We can handle that," Severyne said.

"Only two that we know of," Azad said. "There could be uninfected mercenaries or something, and they'll shoot us just as dead as the faithful would."

"The guides didn't mention anything about outside contractors," Calred said. "I think they wanted to keep the fleet captain's condition a secret. An architect of the Greater Union descending into rapid dementia would be bad for the project, probably. The guides thought between Severyne and Felix, the situation was pretty well covered."

"Then let's take the house." Severyne nodded to her troops, who fanned out and disappeared from view around both sides of the reed wall. Severyne took a small cylinder from her belt, twisted her wrist, and snapped the cylinder out into a pole nearly two meters long. She looked at Azad and Terrak. "I know *she's* armed. Are you?"

"Only with my natural attributes." Terrak showed his fangs.

"Can you shoot?"

Terrak shrugged. "I have been known to, at a firing range."

Severyne tossed a sidearm, and the Hacan caught it, almost fumbling the weapon. Azad rolled her eyes. Amateurs. "Try not to let anyone take that away and use it on you," Severyne said.

"I love this take-charge thing you're doing, Sev," Azad said. She hadn't expected to ever see her again, and it was making an enjoyable mission even better. Everything was always more fun with her, and sure, Sev was looking her most strait-laced right now, but she inevitably loosened up and got more impulsive after they spent a little time together. This time they were even on the same *side*. "Maybe when this mission is over, you and me could find a little private time to do a thorough debrief. Not that I'm actually *wearing* any briefs–"

"Please focus on the task at hand." Severyne cocked her head, listening to something on her comms. "My troops have made entry through a back and side door. They've located the fleet captain's quarters and have the area secured. They've seen no sign of the caretakers as yet. Perhaps they're out wandering in the garden, but just in case they're hidden elsewhere in the house… I'll take the side entrance there. You and the honorable ambassador can go through the front." She walked away without waiting to see if Azad and Terrak agreed.

"Don't you love a woman who knows what she wants?" Azad said, watching the Letnev disappear around the side of the house. "What she wants other people to do, I mean. I wonder how she'd react to a little saucy insubordination?"

"I have resisted this question, but... what exactly is the nature of your relationship with Captain Dampierre?" Terrak asked.

"What, now you're curious, when I don't have time to share salacious details?" Azad said. "Let's just say 'complicated'. That's the best kind of relationship, don't you think?"

"It's certainly the word I'd use to describe ours," Terrak said.

"We're differently complicated." Azad led him around the reed wall, toward the front entrance of the house. Viewed from above, the house was shaped like a star mashed together with a pentagon, but seen from the ground, the structure was low and rambling, made of thick timbers and expanses of glass, with rooms jutting out at unusual angles. The front doors were dark wood, elaborately carved with images of vines and spaceships, which Azad thought was pretty muddled, conceptually and aesthetically, but she was hardly an art critic. There were glass panels on either side of the doors, not even foggy or tinted, giving her a clear view of the vestibule beyond. There was a round table in the middle of the foyer, with a crystal vase full of drooping flowers on top, and a coat rack on one side of the door, with several pairs of shoes lined up neatly in a row beneath it.

"I don't see any machine gun nests or land mines or caltrops, so in we go." Azad tugged on the door handle, expecting resistance, but it opened smoothly. "I guess when you're the only people on the planet you don't worry too much about burglars." She slipped in, scanning the space beyond the vestibule–

Someone landed on her head and shoulders, driving her to the ground. Azad tried to get up, but a limb clamped around her throat, pulled tight, and cut off her air. She rolled onto her side and twisted violently around, but couldn't dislodge the attacker. She caught a glimpse of the rafters above – the caretakers must have been hiding up there, waiting to pounce.

It was definitely caretakers plural – the other one was busy trying to kill Terrak, and *that* one, a human man with wispy gray hair, was armed with a large carving knife. Terrak should have died right away, despite the size differential, because corrupt old trade ambassadors weren't famed for their ability to fend off ambush knife attacks. And yet… the Hacan had somehow avoided getting stabbed in the neck in the initial assault and was even now easily dodging the man's wild swipes. Terrak dropped and spun and swept the assailant's legs out from under him. Terrak aimed his sidearm while rising and fired a pulse into the man's chest, as casually as if he did it every day. The fallen man went still.

Azad watched, her vision beginning to fill with black spots, as Terrak picked up the knife, squinted, and threw it at her head. She couldn't even squawk in terror because she had no breath–

And then the weight on her screamed and vanished, and Azad rolled over, gasping. Terrak fired his pistol again, past Azad this time. She turned her head and saw her own assailant fall – a woman, equally gray-haired, with a knife buried in her shoulder, eyes rolled back in her head.

"Sorry for the knife-play," Terrak said. "My pistol was on the stun setting, and the charge will transfer to anyone the target is touching, so I thought it best to get her off you first–"

"You're not a trade ambassador," Azad gasped. "Not with moves like that. What are you *really*?"

CHAPTER 37
TERRAK

I helped Azad to her feet and tried to brush off her question. My entire career, my entire *life*, is based on keeping certain secrets. She wasn't willing to let it go, though. "You've had training in combat," she insisted, "and there's *nothing* in your background about that. It's not the sort of thing you'd hide – you'd act all faux-humble about it but make sure everyone knew – so tell me the truth."

The truth. Ah, well.

"I do work for my government," I said. "Just… not in the capacity you assumed."

I have not been entirely honest in this account, and this part can never be released. Any truly honest memoirs I recorded could never be published, even posthumously.

I *am* a trade ambassador. Every bit of documentation in my life attests to that fact. The rumor mill says I am also a favor trader, and just corrupt enough to be useful to a wide range of people, without being so corrupt that I bring unwanted attention or unforeseen difficulties. That is, functionally, an accurate description of myself and my work.

Both those identities, however, are covers.

I was recruited into the Emirates of Hacan clandestine services right out of the Collegium. I showed certain attributes that were useful in a potential field agent: mainly charisma, a gift for manipulation, the capacity to put matters of conscience aside when necessary, and a certain adeptness at swift acts of violence. (As I've gotten older, I try to minimize the need for the latter. There are usually better ways.) I spent my early career working for various trading houses engaged in inter-system commerce, making valuable connections and passing on intelligence to my government whenever possible. Eventually, it became plausible to endow me with diplomatic credentials, which meant less time skulking in alleys and breaking into embassies. Instead, I was invited to parties at the same embassies, which made stealing documents so much easier.

So, yes, I'm a spy, if not exactly like Azad, then at least not radically dissimilar. I've had a long and varied career, but this was, by far, the strangest assignment I'd had, and not just because of my unlikely partner.

Azad groaned. "Don't tell me you were you investigating the conspiracy too?"

I shrugged, then offered a hand to help her up. "My superiors had some suspicions, though they didn't go nearly as far as yours did. We'd received reports of a few people acting strangely, and one of them was an old colleague of mine, Qqurant, so I was dispatched to investigate. I did not anticipate such a… swift and aggressive response to my preliminary questioning. I was trying to figure out how to get word to my handlers, to avoid being murdered in custody, when you appeared. And since you seemed to have better leads than I did, when you proposed our collaboration…"

"You *got* me!" Azad crowed. I'd expected her to be furious, but she seemed delighted. "Do you know how long it's been since somebody *got* me? I thought I was using you, and all this time you were using me. Respect, Terrak. If that's even your real name."

"I prefer to think we have been engaged in a partnership."

"Ha, sure, right." She prodded one of the fallen caretakers with her toe. "Guess we oughta jam them full of the cure. But first. Severyne!" she shouted. "Sev, come here, we got them!"

I winced. "I would prefer it if you didn't share the truth of my–"

Azad waved away my concerns. "Don't worry, Sev and I don't whisper secrets in one another's ears. You and me can be covertly covert *together*."

"It's not unheard of for the Emirates and the Federation of Sol to take part in joint actions occasionally," I said.

"Right, see? We're practically sanctioned."

Severyne appeared, with a guard at her shoulder. She looked over the bodies and nodded. "Come along. The fleet captain is here. She is insensible. Perhaps your drugs will help." She turned and walked away.

Azad sighed and grabbed one of the caretakers by the ankles. "Can you get the other one?" she asked. "Who knows how long spore-zombies stay down when they're stunned?"

CHAPTER 38
SEVERYNE

Severyne sat by Fleet Captain Harlow's bedside, glancing up only briefly when Azad and Terrak entered, dragging the unconscious caretakers with them. Calred was sitting on the other side of the bed, his chin on his chest, lightly snoring. Being flooded with anti-fungals and neural regrowth serum was apparently tiring. "Bind the captives," Severyne said to her guards, then beckoned Azad over. "Look at this woman's eyes. They're green."

"Some humans have green eyes, Sev… oh." Azad leaned close. "There are green specks in the *veins* in her eyes. That is bizarre."

"You think she was an early convert to this conspiracy, yes?" Severyne said. "If so, the long-term effects are debilitating. She has mumbled a few things, about guides and faith and the sacrament, but she is largely unresponsive to stimuli." She poked the woman in the cheek, hard, eliciting no reaction.

"The chromium woman of the raider fleets," Terrak said.

Severyne frowned at him. "What?"

He inclined his head toward the woman in the bed. "Her name came up occasionally in meetings once the Greater Union idea took hold. She was a powerful force in the Mentak Coalition, guiding the agenda of their raider fleets for years. She chose her targets not just opportunistically, but in order to support long-term strategic goals of the Mentak military *and* trading interests. Her attacks helped the Coalition secure monopolies on certain commodities and allowed them to apply pressure when it came to negotiating treaties in disputed border areas. She was brilliant, and by all accounts retired only because she felt it was time for her handpicked protégés to shine. To see her like this..." He shook his head.

"Let's see if we can snap her out of it." Azad took out her syringes and vials. The fleet captain was already hooked up to an intravenous line – presumably because she was so far gone that she couldn't drink or eat on her own – so introducing the cure into her veins was easy. Severyne watched with interest. The cure had worked on Calred, but Harlow was much further gone.

The fleet captain stirred and moaned shortly after the cure was injected but didn't wake. Azad said, "The lab notes say that for subjects who've been under the influence of the spores longer, the process might take extra time. Terrak, do you think you can shoot her maid and butler full of juice? The dosages for humans are written on the printout there."

"What will you be doing?"

"I need to make a call."

Terrak agreed, and Azad left the room. While he was busying himself with the drugs, Severyne said, "Is Azad contacting her handlers?"

"I assume she's letting them know the cure actually works," Terrak said.

"Hmm. She's working for the Federation of Sol?"

"I assume so. Do you have reason to think otherwise?"

Severyne shook her head. "I have simply learned to take nothing for granted when it comes to her."

"Probably a good policy." The Hacan finished administering the cure, then said, "What will *you* do now? Report the conspiracy to your superiors?"

"I have not yet determined my next course of action," Severyne said. "I was sent to capture a Barony operative attempting to defect to the Federation. I was deceived. The question is whether the people giving me the orders were also merely deceived ... or if they were compromised."

"Maybe when Harlow wakes up, she can tell us something," Terrak said.

"How wonderful," Severyne said. "I'm putting my future prospects into the trembling hands of an unconscious, drooling human."

CHAPTER 39
FELIX

Felix held a gun on Ggorgos. "Take off your shell."

Voyou and Tib Pelta were hanging back. Tib had a gun, too; Voyou just had a smug look on his face.

Ggorgos seemed untroubled. "You are making a mistake, Duval. I did not sabotage your communications equipment. Why assume I am responsible, and not the Letnev?"

Felix shook his head. "Voyou hasn't been on the ship long enough to account for all the things that made me suspicious. I know everything, Ggorgos. I know you were sent to my ship as an agent of the conspiracy."

"What *are* you talking about?" Voyou said.

"Everything Terrak said in that broadcast is true," Felix said. "Jhuri told me to investigate, but then he told me to *stop*, and I think it's because he's been compromised, too. This ends now."

"Have you been sleeping enough, Duval?" Ggorgos said. "Perhaps you are dehydrated. Here–" She took a step forward, and Felix took a step back.

"Take off your shell and get in the cell, Ggorgos."

"I am not a conspirator, Duval. I am here to catch a killer. Terrak's paranoia has infected you."

Felix ground his teeth. "If you are compromised, it's not your fault, and you can probably be cured. There's an experimental medication. I just need to contain you until we can confirm the cure works, and then we'll administer it, all right? But I can't have you running around my ship with that arsenal on your back."

"You will regret this, Duval." Ggorgos pressed a few spots on her shell, in a deliberate sequence, and the armor hissed and separated into two halves. Each half extended telescoping legs that allowed them to stand upright by themselves. Ggorgos stepped out of the divided shell, and it was all Felix could do not to avert his eyes. He'd seldom seen any Xxcha without an exocarapace before, and she seemed weirdly vulnerable. Ggorgos walked into the cell with great dignity, and Felix slammed the button that powered on the forcefield barrier.

"We're going to fix you up, Ggorgos, don't worry." Felix beckoned Voyou and Tib, and they all returned to the bridge. "Tib, get us through that wormhole." They had prior authorization to transit at will, so their inability to communicate with the wormhole station wouldn't get them blown to bits, at least.

"Could I do anything to help, captain?" Voyou said. "Since you're down *two* crew members now."

"Sitting down and shutting up would be wonderful."

"Those are duties at which I excel, as it happens."

The *Temerarious* passed through the wormhole uneventfully. Felix was trying to imagine what kind of report he could send to his possibly-mind-controlled superior. *Having dead comms is a benefit in some respects,* he thought. *That makes explaining myself a problem for future Felix.* "Let's get to the planet as fast as we can, Tib."

"I wasn't planning to dawdle, captain." She entered the course. "So, this conspiracy thing…"

"It's true, Tib." Felix tapped the screen on the arm of his chair. "There. I gave you access to my notes. Read them, and you'll know as much as I do. I'm sure you'll reach the same conclusion I did. Ggorgos has been passing information to her *real* employers. They've known every step we've taken. Ggorgos must have sabotaged the comms to keep us from finding out what's happening with the fugitives and the *Grim Countenance* and the fleet captain. I just wish I knew *why*."

Tib scanned through the data. Felix watched their trajectory slowly unfurl on the screen until he couldn't stand being still anymore, then rose and paced up and down on the bridge. Voyou sat quietly but looked smug about it. The Letnev were always happy to revel in the misery of humans, even when they were on the same side.

"That's ... interesting stuff, captain." Tib raised her eyes from her console. "I'm not sure what to make of it all, but yeah, locking up Ggorgos was probably a good call. Better safe, and everything. We're approaching the planet. Without comms we can't tell the fleet captain we're coming, or contact the *Grim Countenance*, which is still lurking around here somewhere, so..."

"I'll take the shuttle down to the estate," Felix said.

"You'll take me with you, I trust?" Voyou said. "You *did* promise Captain Dampierre that I would be included in all mission-critical activities—"

Felix rubbed his face. When had he last shaved? "Yes, fine, you can come, just do as you're told and keep working on that sitting quietly thing we talked about."

The shuttle comms were dead, too, of course, the wires yanked out from beneath the console and left dangling, but the other systems were intact. Felix set a course for the fleet captain's estate. The journey was remarkably swift, as planetary travel always was, compared to the relatively slow passage through the vastness of interstellar space.

They glided over a low plain… and soon saw another shuttle parked on the ground, this one of Barony design. "Severyne must be down here already," Felix muttered. "But why?" He'd *finally* gotten a handle on things to his satisfaction, and now there were new unknowns to baffle him.

"Something is wrong here," Voyou said.

Felix looked over. The Letnev's superciliousness had vanished – he was chewing his lip, brow furrowed, eyes darting back and forth as though searching for something in the long grass. "What do you mean?"

"I… I don't know. It's a feeling."

"I didn't realize the Letnev believed in intuition."

"My instincts are finely honed, captain." The boast seemed unusually hollow.

Felix settled his shuttle down near the Letnev one, then disembarked, Voyou at his side. Felix checked the other shuttle, but it was empty. He and Voyou moved slowly onto the grounds of the estate, on the lookout for hostiles – or friendlies, or the ambiguous – and saw no one. "It's all too *quiet*," the Letnev said, almost moaning.

Had Voyou never been in a combat situation? Trust Severyne to send him a useless officer. "Shh. I prefer quiet to small arms fire or explosions," Felix said. They reached the front doors of the estate, which were standing wide open. Felix pointed at dark smears on the floor just inside the foyer. "Blood. Be careful."

"Felix!" a voice boomed. Calred appeared in a hallway, pointing at Voyou. "Grab him!"

Felix had been through fire with Calred, and didn't hesitate, immediately seizing Voyou and wrenching the man's arms behind him in a submission hold. Severyne appeared behind Calred – along with Amina Azad and Terrak. The latter was holding something in his hand – something like a squashed mushroom, with a drooping red flower on top.

"Having trouble talking to your guides, Voyou?" Severyne said. "We found and destroyed the local node."

Voyou struggled in Felix's arms, so he wrenched the man's arm up harder. "Would someone please explain to me what's going on?" Felix demanded. "I'm ready to start shooting things I don't understand."

Azad stepped forward, holding a syringe. "We're going to fix up Voyou real quick, and then we're going to talk to the fleet captain. She just woke all the way up. You've got pretty good timing for once."

"What… what do you mean, fix me up?" Voyou's voice was high and panicky.

"We will eradicate these spores in your system," Severyne said. "You will be cured–"

Voyou snapped his head back, even though doing so meant dislocating his shoulders, and slammed his skull into Felix's face. Felix stumbled back, his nose a concentrated burst of pain, and Voyou raced out the door.

"Don't let him reach a shuttle!" Calred shouted. Through eyes blurred with pain-tears, Felix watched Severyne race off in pursuit.

CHAPTER 40
SEVERYNE

Voyou didn't get to a shuttle. He was crouched beside a fishpond, shouting, in a vicious argument with himself. "I know my orders, but I… I can still be useful, I can still *fight*, they won't turn me, my devotion, it's… it's… I can't… I *must*."

With a final cry of anguish, he lay down on the bank and plunged his head into the fishpond. As she ran toward him, he began to thrash, but didn't remove his face from the water. He was still by the time she was close enough to drag him out. She attempted resuscitation, but to no effect. He'd drowned himself.

No, that wasn't right. These "guides" had driven him to the act. They'd ordered him to die rather than be turned – rather than allow Severyne and her allies to save him. The guides had put the mental equivalent of a secret agent's hidden cyanide pill into her undercommandant's mind. The guides had murdered Voyou, not out of anger or cruelty, but in a cold calculation to deny Severyne's alliance another asset.

Severyne sat beside his body for a moment. Voyou had been with her during the annexation of Darit. He'd remained loyal and steadfast throughout the Xing affair. They'd survived the World of Light together. He was perhaps the closest thing she had to a friend in all the galaxy.

Severyne did not cry, but another part of her already stony heart hardened.

Then she rose, and went back inside, to see what would come next.

THE FAITHFUL XIV

Jes'Gald was a G'hom, a member of the elite Tekklar unit, the most fearsome and ferocious warriors of the Sardakk N'orr. He had been chosen to accompany the Envoy and select members of the Veiled Brood to the Legion summit on Arc Prime. Jes'Gald was fearsome even by the standards of his order, and accustomed to seeing humanoids cower in his presence. There was no better feeling than scuttling forward with his brothers to war for the glory of Sardakk, the Queen Mother, and grinding lesser beings beneath his scything forelimbs and spiked legs.

The Letnev in his quarters stood perfectly at ease, though, and why not? They were both numbered among the faithful, a bond that transcended petty concerns like species. Captain Palesque had inducted Jes'Gald into the faith shortly after their first meeting, when Jes'Gald had been assigned to make sure the "honored guest" didn't wander off or get into any trouble. Now they were on board the finest ship in the N'orr fleet, making their final preparations for the summit.

Or that was the idea. At the moment, Palesque was trying to explain why the mere sight of a N'orr made so many species scream and flee. "It's because you look like bugs, you see." Palesque gestured with a glass. He was sitting on a mound of resin on the floor of Jes'Gald's curved, cavelike quarters. "A lot of species have a basic fear of insects. They're small, they infiltrate, they infest, they can appear when you aren't looking, they have too many eyes, too many limbs, their presence suggests squalor and disease... I'm not saying that perception is *fair*, mind you, and I'm sure there are Letnev and humans and so forth who adore bugs, but generally... humanoids, especially, find bugs worrying. And you're *immense* bugs. What are you, four meters long?"

"Your system of measurement is barbaric," Jes'Gald said.

"It works well enough for us. Anyway, that's why so many species have a negative visceral reaction to your lot. You're giant versions of something we find disturbing even when it's small. I don't suppose you have any particular instinctive feelings about bipedal primates?"

"Such creatures never evolved on our world," Jes'Gald said. "It is a shame. They would have been a valuable form of protein. Thank you for your insights. Should we discuss the next steps?"

"Hmm? Oh, yes, of course. Sorry. It's easy to get distracted, when the voices of the guides are this faint."

"Their voices become *stronger*?" Jes'Gald was astonished at the idea. The whisper of the guides had already convinced him that loyalty to the Queen Mother and her envoys was of secondary importance and should be set aside in favor of devotion to the great work. If that voice grew stronger...

"Oh, yes. You can't imagine." Palesque smiled. "Won't it be wonderful to share the sacrament with your envoy?"

The N'orr were a collective race, though not in the way many other species assumed. Their strength came from their unity of purpose and a capacity for cooperation that other races could only dream of. Some fools thought they were a hive mind –

that the soldiers of N'orr were mindless drones – but they were wrong. The N'orr were individuals, bound together by common goals and values, and were all the stronger for it. "I want to share this joyous purpose with *all* my people," Jes'Gald said.

"To the Legion, and the guides, and our glorious future, then," Palesque said, raising his glass.

CHAPTER 41
FELIX

Felix used the communications system in the admiral's house to call up to the *Temerarious* and told Tib to set Ggorgos free. "It seems Cal was the leak all along. He's OK now, though. Their cure works."

Tib swore at length. Felix let her finish, then said, "I couldn't have said it better myself. I feel like an idiot *and* a bad friend *and* a bad officer. He just… seemed like Cal to me."

"It's fine that he fooled you," Tib said. "I'm furious that he fooled *me*."

Felix almost smiled. "As for Ggorgos… she's exactly what she seems to be. I don't know if she'll ever forgive me, but I'll settle for her not stomping me into a puddle of goo."

"Here's hoping," Tib said.

"I know we hate to leave the ship unattended, but I think you and Ggorgos should both get down here."

Once he was finished, he returned to the fleet captain's room. Harlow was awake now, though not speaking much. She was mostly sipping clear broth from a cup and glaring at everyone around her. Her newly cured caretakers were fussing over her, fluffing pillows and checking her vital signs.

"Don't beat yourself up for not figuring me out, Felix," Calred said. "I was extremely convincing. I didn't have instructions to do anything I wouldn't normally do, except... report on all our comings and goings to the voices in my head." He groaned. "Am I going to be court martialed? I'm not fully versed in all the nuances of our military code, but I seem to recall that treason is bad."

"You're a great actor," Felix said. "I can believe I'm a dolt, but Tib didn't notice either, and she's professionally suspicious."

"As for treason, I'll put in a word on your behalf," Fleet Captain Harlow said, her voice a croak. "Unless I'm up before the tribunal right beside you." She shooed her caretakers away and sat up in bed, wincing. She gazed at the group gathered around her bed and laughed, a sharp bark of a sound. "So, this is the salvation of the galaxy – two Coalition operatives, a Federation of Sol assassin, a fugitive trade ambassador, a Barony warship captain, and her shock-troops?"

"There's also an Xxcha who's unusually gifted at violence on the way, and my Yssaril first officer, too," Felix said. "But... yes. I think that's about it. I can't speak for Severyne, but I'm pretty sure my boss is compromised."

"Jhuri?" Harlow clucked her tongue. "I hadn't heard. If so, he's a recent convert. In the Barony, though, yes – Admiral Immental was one of the last recruits I heard about before things got... hazy for me." She ran her hands through her hair, frowning. "I must look a mess. How long have I been out? When is the summit on Arc Prime?"

"It's scheduled to begin in four days, fleet captain," one of the caretakers said.

Harlow jolted like she'd been slapped. "Four *days*? Then we're about four and a half days from all-out interstellar war."

They all looked at one another, wide-eyed. When Felix had contemplated worst-case scenarios for the conspiracy's plans, he hadn't even considered something that bad or that rapid.

"Explain what you mean," Severyne said to Harlow.

"Before you explain anything else," Azad said, "would you just tell us who is *behind* all this? Or are you just as clueless as every other puppet we've talked to today?"

"Oh, no," Harlow said. "I know who organized the conspiracy. I helped them *plan* the conspiracy." She smiled at Calred. "So, as you can see, your little treason is nothing compared to mine."

CHAPTER 42
TERRAK

I listened to Harlow's story just like the rest of them: with mounting dread. Here's what she told us, as best I can remember. I will omit Duval's moans of dismay, and Severyne's hisses, and Azad's admiring whistles, to focus on the essentials.

"Last year, I received a visitor," Harlow explained. "An old bridge officer of mine named Grisham, who was serving in the diplomatic corps. They'd upset someone in a position of power, so Grisham got assigned to deal with the Arborec. Nobody likes being the liaison for that faction – negotiations can be frustrating, because we don't share a lot of fundamental assumptions with the Arborec. Even if we manage to make substantive progress, you're stuck negotiating with dead-eyed, blank-faced corpses, puppeted around by vegetable intellects. I'm Mentak Coalition through and through. I grew up surrounded by all sorts of species and am as comfortable as anyone in the company of aliens ... but even I find dealing with the Arborec off-putting. Anyway, this associate of mine was sent on a mission, and they met with a Letani – you know about those?"

"Ambassadors of the Arborec," I said. "Each one carries a sort of copy of the central consciousness."

"Oh, an individual Letani isn't capable of carrying a whole *copy* of the hivemind," Harlow said. "Each Letani is at best a portion of the Symphony, specialized for a given task – some are focused on trade negotiations, others on information gathering, others warfare. They're individual enough that they actually have names of their own, though mostly for the sake of communicating with creatures like us. My protégé met with one of the Letani, called Ohseroh, in a neutral area, to discuss matters of a ... sensitive nature. Specifically, the exchange of certain weapons."

"We trade weapons with the Arborec?" Felix said.

"Not officially. While they were talking to the Letani's Dirzuga mouthpiece, one of the other ... lifeforms on the Arborec ship, a sort of ambulatory assemblage of slime molds, swarmed around Grisham's ankles and pinned them in place. Then the Dirzuga coughed in Grisham's face, and ... that poor soul became the first of the faithful."

"The *Arborec* are behind the conspiracy?" Azad seemed genuinely shocked. "But ... they don't do stuff like that. They don't just abstain from playing the great game, they don't even seem to know there's a game going on! I've never heard of them trying to turn a double agent or anything."

"If you let me continue, the situation will become clearer," Harlow said sternly. "Grisham was their first experimental subject. The Letani, Ohseroh ... worked on them for a while, until my friend was under their complete control, but could still function, and pass for a person with free will. Ohseroh did a lot of damage as they perfected their process, though, and not long after Grisham came to see me – to *recruit* me – they died. Something very bad happened to their brain. Grisham suffered an imbalance profound enough to disrupt their autonomic systems. It was very sad, but at the time, I *wasn't* sad, because I just saw them dying for the cause of the guides, and that was the only cause that mattered." She shook her head. "I was a fool. I had no choice, but that doesn't make me feel much better."

"Why were you chosen as the second recruit?" I asked. "Just because you were the most influential person their patient zero could plausibly visit?"

"Yes, but... my influence might be larger than you realized. I was a good choice. Here, help me out of this bed." Her caretakers assisted her in getting to her feet, and then she shuffled over to a chair by the window and sat in a shaft of sunlight through the window. "I suppose there's no harm in telling you this, since we've now formed a conspiracy of our very own – a counter-conspiracy, if you will. I wasn't just a fleet captain. I was also the longtime head of special projects. I used to be your boss's boss, Felix."

Azad cackled. "You ran Mentak Coalition covert operations? Oh, that's beautiful. No wonder the puppetmasters wanted you."

"I was quite a catch," Harlow said. "The Letani who flooded my brain with chemical devotion didn't just want me for my political connections, or for the secrets I knew. Grisham told it about my real position, and after that, the Letani wanted my *advice*. Ohseroh had figured out how to do one thing very well: take control of people's minds and coerce their loyalty. What the Letani didn't know how to do was use that ability to achieve its goals. For that, it needed expert counsel – someone who understood the way all these baffling creatures made of meat actually think, and the ins and outs of our social and political systems. I was a perfect candidate. Ohseroh and I spent countless hours discussing possibilities, refining the details, and running scenarios. I betrayed my nation, and I was ecstatic to do it, because nothing felt as good as obedience. Even now, everything

feels ... muted, dim. You all look like you're behind dirty glass ..."
Her attention started to drift, and she visibly forced herself to
focus. "At any rate. The guides – Ohseroh, that is, who tends to
talk about itself in the plural, probably out of old habits – and I
came up with the great work together."

"What great work?" Felix asked.

"The plan to achieve total war," Harlow said.

There was a moment of profound silence at that, as you
might expect, with the requisite groans, hisses, and whistles. I
contributed a moan of dismay myself. I suppose if you have a vast
conspiracy in your control, it doesn't pay to think small.

Harlow continued, "As close to total war as we could engineer,
anyway. I explained to my new god that the really impressive
wars were never limited to just two nations facing off against
one another. The biggest ones involved *multiple* nations, bound
together by mutual interests, and usually also by treaties. 'Imagine,'
I said, 'if we could get several of the most powerful factions in the
galaxy to form an alliance, opposed to another, equally powerful
alliance. If we could engineer a conflict between even a couple of
major players in those respective treaty organizations, the chains
of obligation would drag *all* the factions into a conflagration.
Many of the lesser states would inevitably become entangled and
forced to choose sides, spreading the devastation further."

"The Greater Union versus the Legion, with a side of
everybody else," Felix said.

"Yes, obviously," Severyne said. "Do try to keep up."

"OK, but for what possible purpose?" Felix said. "How does
all-out interstellar war help the Arborec?"

"Confusion to your enemies," Azad said. "It's never a bad plan."

"A war like that would clear the field," Severyne added. "If
the Arborec can goad the Legion and the Greater Union into

attacking one another, that would plunge the galaxy into open chaos. Untold billions would die. The devastation is incalculable. And from the ashes... the Arborec would rise, unified and triumphant."

"Ashes make good fertilizer," Azad said. "Plus, with spore-zombies in all branches of the military services and in the government, they'd get plenty of good intel they could use to keep the war going. They could make sure nobody makes peace or gains a decisive advantage. But like I said, the Arborec don't *do* stuff like this. I don't get it."

"It's *not* the Arborec," Harlow said. "It's just Ohseroh, acting alone. One Letani, budded off from the Symphony of the hivemind. Specifically created to ponder the problem of conflict with we strange biological creatures and determine whether trading weapons with us was sensible or not. We wanted to trade with the Arborec, for their technology, which is impressive and strange, entirely at right angles to the sort of tech other factions develop. Not even the deepest, darkest Hylar labs have bioweapons like the Arborec can make with ease. But what did we want those weapons *for*? What was the point of it all? The Arborec understand competition for resources, because they dealt with that problem before they completely took over their home world, but when our conflicts go beyond such simple terms – into ideology, and revenge, and honor, and all those other bizarre alien concepts – the Arborec lose the thread. They just don't comprehend any of it. So they made Ohseroh, a Letani stranger than most, more individual than most, and told it to talk to those of us who desired weapons of war and come up with a plan for how to deal with us, and to protect the interests of the Arborec."

"The Arborec wanted this Letani to figure out how to prevent war," I said. "And instead, it determined the best course of action was a very *large* war?" I was unprepared to deal with an enemy like this. I could understand those motivated by avarice and lust for power, but the Arborec were *different*.

Harlow nodded. "Ohseroh sent word to the hivemind back home. It explained how the Arzuga fungus could be altered to allow the Arborec to take over living bodies of many species – the Embers of Muaat are immune, and of course the Creuss, and some others – and proposed an ambitious plan to infiltrate and destroy. The Arborec refused. Not out of compassion, or any great regard they have for the other species, but just because the plan was too risky. If anyone realized what the Arborec was doing, all the peoples of the galaxy would band together to destroy their homeworld and silence the Symphony forever. Even if the plan worked, the galaxy would be a nightmare for generations, torn apart, impossible to govern, and difficult to put back together. The possible rewards didn't merit the risks."

"So… what?" I asked. "The Letani took initiative? They aren't supposed to do that. They're just extensions of the will of the Arborec."

"Yes," the fleet captain said. "But this Letani was created for an unusual purpose, as I said, and there must have been… flaws in its cultivation. Ohseroh went rogue. It became convinced its plan was worthwhile and refused to rejoin the Symphony and be subsumed into the overmind. Instead, Ohseroh stole a ship, and set out to enact its plan. Ohseroh believes that, if it succeeds – when it succeeds – the overmind will welcome it back, and hail it as a hero. Even though the Arborec don't really *do* heroes."

"It's a bad plan, and I don't like it," Azad said. "A little chaos is tasty, but I like living in a galaxy that's not completely on fire."

Ggorgos and Tib walked in just then. "We are up to date," the

Xxcha rumbled. "Felix kept us patched in on the house comms system."

Felix cleared his throat. "Ggorgos, I'd like to apologize–"

The Xxcha held up a hand. "You did what you thought best with the information in your possession. We will speak of it no more." She addressed the fleet captain. "I concur with the human criminal. It is a bad plan. How do we stop it?"

Harlow said, "I don't know if we can. The summit on Moll Primus is in *four days*? Then the Legion meeting – that's scheduled for roughly the same time, yes? I know there was more back-and-forth there."

"Our new allies like to squabble," Severyne said. "But, yes, it was decided that to hold the summit *after* the Greater Union's would make it appear that we were reacting out of fear of that organization, so our meeting is scheduled to begin one hour earlier."

"That is so petty," Azad said. "I love it."

"I've been lost in the fog for a while," Harlow said. "But this next part was the linchpin of the plan, so I doubt it's changed." She took a breath. "There will be coordinated attacks on both summits. A crew of the faithful, in a Mentak Coalition warship, will attack the meeting on Arc Prime. At the same time, a crew on a Barony warship will assault Moll Primus."

That was an astonishingly audacious plan, the sort of terrorist attacks that would live in infamy for generations, but–

Felix spoke up with my objection before I could. "A single ship won't do much damage, especially on such heavily protected worlds."

"We – *they* – have compromised people in key positions to let the attacking vessels get closer than you'd expect," Harlow said. "But the point isn't really the damage they can wreak.

Ohseroh isn't interested in assassinating the Baron or the Table of Captains or the Headmaster or any of the other leaders. They just want to make a brazen *attempt* on the lives of those leaders and position the opposing alliances as existential threats to one another. With their leaders personally attacked, the people will be outraged, and support war between the Union and the Legion. Plus, getting all the leaders together in a Moll Primus bunker or an Arc Prime vault is a good opportunity to infect the ones who remain unconverted, which will make this whole elaborate puppet theater of a war even easier to orchestrate."

"We must stop those ships before they attack," Ggorgos said.

"Sure," Azad said. "But we also have to stop the Letani."

"I concur," I said. "Kill the puppetmaster, and you needn't waste time cutting strings one by one."

"We must achieve all three of those objectives, while acting in direct opposition to the orders from our compromised leaders," Severyne said. "If we fail…"

"If we fail, we've got bigger problems than court martials," Azad said. "And if we *win*, think what that could do for your career, Sev?"

The scythe-like curve of a smile appeared on Severyne's face. "I have been thinking about just that."

Felix cracked his knuckles. "OK, then. Let's go save the galaxy."

CHAPTER 43
FELIX

"Our plan has *three* prongs," Azad said gleefully. She was sitting across the room from Felix, talking to Terrak, but, of course, she was very loud. "That's so many prongs! I can't decide who has the best prong. Maybe us? But also, the other ones sound pretty fun. Do you think we'll get to destroy a spaceship? I'll be upset if we don't get to destroy even *one* spaceship."

Felix was glad his prong didn't overlap with Azad's. This was going to be hard enough without contending with her unpredictable exuberance. He was standing with Calred, Tib, and Ggorgos. They were going to take the *Temerarious* and burn hard toward Arc Prime and try to intercept this Coalition warship. The trip was going to be a little tricky, since Felix was fairly sure they were going to be declared rogue and hunted down as fugitives themselves... and the Letnev wouldn't be happy about a Coalition ship zipping around space they controlled... but what was the alternative? Sending the *Grim Countenance*? Having a Barony ship shoot down a Coalition ship was just asking for an international incident, while sending a Coalition ship to do so could still be incredibly messy, but less likely to end in just the kind of war they were trying to prevent.

At the same time, Severyne would take her hideous ship toward Moll Primus – the very idea was horrific to Felix; that was the homeworld of his people – and intercept the Barony vessel.

Meanwhile, Terrak and Azad would take the fleet captain's personal ship and track down this rogue Letani, following a lead the fleet captain had provided. They would, ideally, eradicate *that* part of the threat.

If even one of us fails, everything *fails,* Felix thought. If either one of the Legion or Greater Union summits were attacked, it could still spark a war. If Ohseroh wasn't neutralized, the Letani would just continue its conspiracy, infecting new people, and probably taking better precautions against being discovered. The stakes were *so high.* It was terrifying and exhilarating and he was doing something that *mattered.*

"We should get moving," Felix said. "We're going to be cutting it close, and that's assuming the planned flight paths of the attack vessels haven't changed during the fleet captain's, ah… time offline."

"I will not be going with you," Ggorgos said. "I will accompany the Letnev woman instead."

That was unexpected. "Why would you do that?"

"She has lost her most trusted lieutenant," Ggorgos replied. "I believe she could use the support. She is also tasked with protecting the summit where the leaders of my kingdom will be in attendance. My greatest loyalty is to protect my people. I will do so."

"I don't think that's the best–" Felix began, but Ggorgos was already stomping across the room toward Severyne, who was standing with her shock troops, making sharp slicing gestures with her hands as she spoke to them.

He looked at Tib. "That's because I made her take her shell off and locked her in the brig, isn't it?"

"It is a thousand percent because of that, yes," Tib said. "I can't say I'll miss her, exactly, though."

"She was growing on me," Felix said. "After I figured out she wasn't part of an evil conspiracy, especially."

"I could tell you were suspicious of her." Calred was monotone, washed-out, and low energy. Azad said the condition should improve in time as the cure worked to repair the damage done to his neural tissue, but that he was going to be chemically depleted in the meantime, and prone to anxiety, anhedonia, and depression. "I … seeing you look at her that way made me happy, because it meant you weren't suspicious of *me*, and my directive from the guides was to go unnoticed."

"You're OK now." Felix clapped him on the shoulder. "And, hey, we're back to the original Duval's Devils, together again."

"Except our handler probably has a brain full of spores," Tib said. "Once Cal gets the comms working again, we're likely going to have some very unhappy messages from Jhuri."

"Maybe don't make fixing the comms a priority," Felix said.

CHAPTER 44
SEVERYNE

Severyne heard the stomping behind her and turned to watch the Xxcha's approach. Ggorgos was an alarming sight, with her armored shell and glowing eyepiece, but Severyne made a point of never letting alarm show. "May I help you?" she asked instead, in a tone that suggested she hoped not.

"I will accompany you to destroy the Coalition ship."

Severyne arched an eyebrow. "Oh, will you? I do not require oversight from–"

"I am not offering oversight, but assistance. I am very capable."

"I can believe that," Severyne said. "But the Xxcha hate the Letnev. There was that… unfortunate business… with your planet being destroyed."

Ggorgos grunted. "Current problems concern me more than ancient crimes. The enemy of my enemy is my temporary and contingent ally."

Severyne didn't laugh, but she did let a smile through her barricades. "Even so, I assure you, I am more than capable of completing this part of the mission myself. Go back to your fellows."

The Xxcha looked around the room, then took a step closer to Severyne, lowering her head to speak quietly into the Letnev's ear. "You have to get me away from Felix Duval before I finally lose my patience and punch him through a bulkhead."

Now Severyne did laugh, a brief burst of delight that made Azad look over at her curiously. (She was always aware of where Azad was looking.) "Very well," she said. "I think we can find common cause. Welcome to the crew of the *Grim Countenance*. Shall we begin?"

THE FAITHFUL XV

Jhuri and Kote Strom perambulated through the grounds of the Mentak Coalition capitol on Moll Primus, watching workers erect stages and set up chairs as harried organizers of various species rushed around shouting into earpieces. "This looks like the sort of chaos that eventually resolves into something impressive," Jhuri observed. "I still can't believe all the parties are on board. I really thought we'd lose the Kingdom of Xxcha."

"The guides managed to reach the right people there," Kote said. "The Greater Union will go forward, and glory will follow."

"I don't suppose you know the goal of the great work?"

"The guides have not seen fit to share the wholeness of their vision with me. Only that the formation of the Greater Union is key to the plan."

"Mmm, yes. They told me the same thing. Have the guides seemed... troubled to you, lately?"

"Perhaps a bit preoccupied," Kote allowed.

"I hope it doesn't have anything to do with Felix and the hunt for the fugitives. My operatives haven't reported in for a while, and the guides refuse to discuss the subject with me."

"I doubt it's anything as mundane as *that*," Kote said. "The guides have more on their minds than your small operation. Preparing for our glorious future takes a lot of attention."

"You seem a bit preoccupied, too."

Kote winced. "Is it apparent? I have been given an assignment. I have to select some volunteers, and… well… Jhuri, in your official capacity, you have access to explosives, don't you?"

"When it comes to armament, I can lay my pseudopods on just about anything short of a dreadnought at a moment's notice."

"I'll let you know what I need. The guides say everything is going well, but that it's important to have backup plans."

Immental emerged from the meeting with her cousin, the Baron. She had a splitting headache that the guides, in their wisdom, had opted not to soothe. She usually enjoyed the company of the Baron, who appreciated someone who could match wits with him, but he'd just declared her "dull company" and said, "I hope you return to your usual self after all this tedious business with the summit is done." She'd been looking for an opportunity to give him the sacrament, but there were guards and advisers and toadies and other cousins all over the reception room, and there was never a chance.

The Baron *would* sign the treaty – he was already being hailed as a visionary, ready to take the Letnev into the future they deserved. That was all thanks to the efforts of the state propaganda machine, guided by a few of the faithful in the right positions. But Immental was the one organizing the summit itself, and there were so many moving parts! The N'orr envoy was not among the faithful, and now she had reports that the L1Z1X were giving the captains assigned to them trouble, and of course the Gashlai couldn't be inducted into the faith at *all*, but had to be brought along with ordinary inducements, like preferential trading terms and the promise of violent death to their enemies.

The Baron was putting the entire burden of the summit's success on her, since she'd been the one who convinced him of the Legion's importance, and while she could delegate, it wasn't as if anyone else were *competent–*

The guides spoke to her. She stopped in the hallway, glanced around to make sure she was unobserved, and then said, "*Bombs?* Why do we need bombs, wise ones?"

CHAPTER 45
TERRAK

Azad and I had to wait a little while for the fleet captain's personal ship to be made ready, and for a few other preparations to be completed. Harlow's vessel, the *Darkest Mercy*, was no warship, sadly, and I didn't like the idea of going up against the leader of a vast conspiracy with nothing but our wits. Harlow did have a collection of personal armaments she'd collected, stolen in raids, and won in battle, though, and offered us our pick. Azad was having a merry time sorting through the vault, exclaiming over bits of deadly kit, while I contented myself with borrowing a variable-output energy pistol and a Muaat fire knife (with a modified handle so creatures who *weren't* fireproof could hold it).

"Whoa, this is a Creuss rifle!" Azad held up a device that looked more like a bit of curving silver abstract art than a weapon. "They call it a ghost gun – I've heard they can shoot through walls without putting a hole through them, fire around corners, and do all kinds of other weird stuff that shouldn't work, unless we have some fundamental misunderstandings about the laws of physics." She sighed. "No charge though." She tossed it aside and turned back to the wall of weapons in the captain's vault. "Hylar repeating rifle, no, they're too fussy and over-engineered, prone to breaking… good old Federation of Sol issue pulse rifle, super boring, I practically grew up with one in my hand… Yssaril shame-knife, those are nasty, but I don't think an evil plant is going to be bothered by a scar that won't heal… Sardakk bracers, I kinda don't think they'd fit on my wrists and I doubt they'd work right if I strapped them to my thighs… Ooh, hello. You'll do." She picked up a machine gun that bristled with attachments. "This is some classic Mentak Coalition ridiculousness right here – a bunch of mostly stolen technology cobbled together into a whole that somehow more or less works." She fiddled with some switches near the grip. "I can swap between kinetic and plasma loads, there's an inbuilt grenade launcher, and if you overload this here you can do a one-time electricity discharge that's lethal… ha, there's even a tiny little localized EMP, and get this: a no-fuel flamethrower!"

I frowned. "How do you make a flamethrower with no fuel?"

"It's not a totally accurate name – there is fuel, it's just a small quantity of water instead of a large quantity of something more flammable. It uses hydrolysis to split the water molecules into hydrogen and oxygen, then uses *those* as the accelerant."

"That actually works?"

"So I'm told. Until you run out of water, and it's heavy to haul around too much of that. But it does mean you don't have to carry a tank of accelerant around and risk turning yourself into an incendiary grenade if you catch a stray round. This is the gun for me. I'm going to name her Sev."

"Why?"

Azad posed with the gun at a jaunty angle. "Because she's versatile, and deadly, and more fun than she looks."

"You really want to tell me the story of your relationship with the Letnev captain, don't you?"

"I mean, we're going to be on this ship for a few days, and we have to talk about *something*." She took a last glance around the vault and nodded to herself. "Let's go see if the cook and the butler have our supplies ready yet. We should get hunting."

CHAPTER 46
FELIX

"Calred showed me where the Letani node was hidden," Tib reported. "Behind a panel on the lower deck. I sent in a maintenance robot to bag and incinerate it and kicked up the air filters to their highest setting to clear out any remaining spores. Cal says the spores produced by the node don't actually infect people, it's just biological communications gear, but why take chances?"

"Good work," Felix said. "How are we doing on the cure?"

"The chemjet printers in the infirmary are creating as much as we've got reagents for. Should be enough for eight or twelve doses, depending on whether we're sticking it into humans or Hacan or Yssaril or what."

"The people on board the *Sly Mongoose* aren't criminals or terrorists or conspirators. They're victims, and, if at all possible, I want to cure them rather than kill them."

"It would be nice if we could just put the cure in gas grenades instead of injecting it into people one at a time," Tib said. "I'd rather douse everyone at once."

"I gather the dosage is important," Felix said. "I have a whole chart with species and weight ranges that Azad gave us. If we just gassed everyone, they'd probably mostly die."

"That would be somewhat counterproductive," Tib admitted.

Calred's voice spoke from the PA system. He was still pretty low-energy. There were combat and focus drugs that led to that kind of mood crash, but they *did* pass, eventually. Felix hoped this would, too. "Comms are back online, captain. Voyou made a big mess with the wiring, but the damage wasn't that deep. And… yeah, lots of messages in the queue from Jhuri."

"I should go deal with that." Felix trudged back to his quarters. There were thirty-seven messages waiting from Jhuri. His superior had never been one to micromanage – Felix checked in more often than Jhuri liked, honestly – which only bolstered Felix's certainty that the Hylar had been compromised. The messages were all variations on "what the hell is going on?" and "where the hell are you?" Felix composed a brief message, text only, and sent it via an encryption protocol that would bounce across half a dozen systems before landing in Jhuri's inbox:

Comms damaged in fight. Calred lost. Terrak and Azad escaped. Headed toward the Jorun asteroid field. In pursuit. Updates to follow.

Jhuri wouldn't know where they really were and wouldn't know where they were really going… but, hopefully, he wouldn't send anyone to apprehend them. Claiming Calred had died would explain why he was out of contact with his fungal superiors and might allay Jhuri's suspicions to a degree. As far as any of them knew, the rogue Letani didn't know what, exactly, happened on Entelegyne, and couldn't necessarily distinguish a cured servant from a dead one. But Ohseroh's puppets would probably all be on high alert.

Two days passed in travel. They transited a wormhole controlled by an independent trading conglomerate, using false documents and a faked transponder signal. As covert operatives, they were good at staying hidden – even from their own government, as it turned out. In another day they would pass into Barony-controlled space, and then, they'd have to hide even better.

The Letnev home planet, Arc Prime, was an anomaly: a planet without a star to call its own, sailing on a strange course through the void, surrounded by a constantly shifting cloud of ships and stations. Felix sat with Tib and Calred in the galley of the *Temerarious* and watched Barony-controlled propaganda broadcasts about the upcoming summit. There were images of the Baron, or one of his body doubles, dressed in a military uniform that dripped with medals and sashes and chains, waving from behind a forcefield. Admiral Immental, who Severyne said was a spore-zombie, did most of the actual talking, appearing behind a podium and using very un-Letnev-sounding phrases like "a new era of cooperation" and "in unity, there is strength" and "working together to forge a better tomorrow". There was a lot of footage of the meeting space, too, which Felix watched with morbid interest. It was entirely too easy to imagine it being blown to bits by the *Sly Mongoose*.

The Legion summit wouldn't actually be held on Arc Prime, where all the cities were subterranean – apparently the Embers of Muaat had balked at the idea of being trapped underground with their new friends. The going theory was, the Embers were the only people involved in either of these alliances who *weren't* being controlled, to some degree, by Ohseroh – the energy-based physiology of the Gashlai made them immune to the spores. They'd agreed to join the Legion because they hated the Hylar and liked the idea of ganging up against them. The conspiracy had to make allowances to accommodate an uninfected species, and Felix hoped they were having a terrible time with it.

Since Arc Prime wasn't an acceptable location, the summit was being held on the prototype of the Barony's new Dark Star weapons system – the Barony's answer to the infamous Muaat War Suns, only even bigger. The Dark Star was basically a city in space, a mobile weapons platform that, according to Letnev propaganda, would "forever secure the supremacy of the Letnev, and their allies in the Legion, across the whole of the galaxy". Even accounting for Barony exaggeration, the idea of such a weapon in their hands was sobering.

"That sounds bad," Calred said.

"I've seen some of our intelligence reports about that prototype," Tib said. She had lots of friends elsewhere in the clandestine services. "Everyone says the Dark Star looks impressive – bristling with cannons, the usual ornamental spikes, enough engines to move a moon – but it's pretty much a hollow shell. The Letnev engineers are having a horrible time with the electrical systems. They're having trouble dealing with their waste heat, they need multiple gravity generators for something so big and calibrating them to work together is tricky... we reckon the Letnev are years from having a Dark Star that actually works. Using it as a prop for the summit is probably the most use they'll get out of it for a while."

"They'll get even less use out of it if the *Sly Mongoose* manages to blow it up," Calred said.

"I think the idea is just to fire on the Dark Star, and make some noise, and then die as glorious martyrs to the vegetable cause," Felix said. "They wouldn't want to actually kill any of the highly placed puppet people. But even firing on the summit is enough to start a war, so let's make sure it doesn't come to that. When do we rendezvous with the zombie ship?"

"Not long, if Harlow was right," Tib said. "The *Sly Mongoose* was chosen because they were able to turn its whole crew into the faithful, and because it was out on a long-range secret reconnaissance mission on the edge of Barony space anyway, and nobody would notice if it shifted course a little. But Harlow's brain was basically soup for a while there, and plans might have changed. We just don't know. If the ship is on the course she predicted, we should intersect in about twelve hours."

"I'll just be sitting here staring at the clock until then, I suppose," Felix said.

Fourteen hours later, there was still no sign of the *Sly Mongoose*. The Legion summit was scheduled to begin in roughly eight hours, and the Greater Union summit in nine. All the dignitaries were already present or would be soon. Maybe the *Sly Mongoose* was already deeper than expected into Barony space, where the *Temerarious* couldn't hope to follow without being noticed, since there were no puppets clearing a path for them. Maybe they were too late. They had to face the possibility.

"Total war." Felix sat on the bridge with Tib and Calred. He felt as despondent as Cal looked. "How will it start, do you think?"

"From the edges, moving in," Tib said. "The Legion will hit Greater Union colony worlds near its own holdings first. We'll do the same to the Legion colonies."

"We could send the Letnev a warning," Calred said. "Tell them an attack is coming."

Felix shook his head. "They wouldn't take a message from a Coalition ship seriously. They'd think we were just trying to disrupt or delay their event." He sighed. "I sent an anonymous warning anyway, though. Didn't get a response. They treated it like a hoax bomb threat, I'm sure."

"Harlow said the conspiracy has good information control," Tib said. "Ohseroh is super paranoid about people learning its plans, as demonstrated by their whole framing-Terrak-for-murder thing. I'm sure they're monitoring communications, especially after that tell-all broadcast."

"I did a little searching about the speech, hoping it might have changed things," Felix said. "The consensus on the networks is that Terrak is trying to set up an insanity defense, making it seem like he's suffering from paranoia and delusions of grandeur."

"This is one of those cases where the truth is indistinguishable from paranoia," Calred said. "We–"

The main screen lit up, revealing a tiny blob of heat in the cold of space. Their sensors would never have detected that signature if they hadn't been looking for it and looking hard; recon ships were stealthy. Felix shot to his feet. "Is that the *Sly Mongoose*?"

"Looks like it." Tib slid the controls on a console. "They're on the expected trajectory, just a little behind schedule."

"What kept them?" Felix said. "I can't imagine Ohseroh likes tardiness."

Tib shrugged. "Could have been anything – engine trouble, avoiding a Barony patrol, who knows? But they're here now, and I don't think they've noticed us yet."

"All right," Felix said. "Let's make our pirate ancestors proud and take that ship."

They didn't dare risk a disabling shot – in theory, they could damage the *Sly Mongoose*'s engines and leave the ship drifting and otherwise unharmed, but there was always a risk of breaching the reactor and causing an explosion. Felix wasn't about to let this conspiracy claim any more Mentak Coalition lives. Instead, they launched boarding pods at maximum range.

The *Temerarious* was equipped with six pods, and they sent all of them, three managed remotely by Tib from her pod (she was exceptionally good at multitasking), while Felix and Calred piloted the other two. The breaching vessels were tiny, barely bigger than escape pods, just big enough for a couple of crew, but their exteriors bristled with equipment. The pods were draped in every bit of stealth tech the Mentak Coalition navy had developed or stolen, and since they were much smaller than a cruiser, that tech was more effective – the pods didn't produce much in the way of heat, radiation, or other energy signatures compared to a full-sized vessel.

The pods approached the smooth bulk of the *Sly Mongoose* – the cruiser was actually the same model as the *Temerarious*, but newer – and matched velocity. Felix nudged the controls in his pod and gently attached himself to the larger ship's hull with magnetic clamps. The other pods settled in at different points on the ship, like leeches on a swimmer. Duval's Devils didn't risk talking to each other now – using comms this close to the ship would risk detection – but they knew what to do.

One of the uncrewed pods, stuck to the side of the *Sly Mongoose* halfway down its length, extended an array of manipulator arms, tipped with torches, saws, and grasping claws, and began to very noisily and obviously tear into the skin of the ship. The other two empty pods were doing the same thing, at different locations.

While the unoccupied pods were making as much noise as possible, Felix's pod very quietly sliced away at the hull beneath it, cutting a small circle from the skin of the ship and moving it aside. The bottom of the pod irised open, allowing Felix to clamber into the hole. He wore an environment suit specially designed for boarding hostile vessels, so it was more limber than most, but at the expense of a limited air supply and decreased thickness; basically, if he snagged on a sharp piece of metal, he'd probably die.

Felix crawled into the hole, just beneath the outer layer of the hull, and waited in claustrophobic darkness. The space was barely big enough for him to kneel in, but he only had to wait long enough for the boarding pod to replace the cut-away portion of the hull and seal it back in place above him. Once he was no longer exposed to vacuum, Felix used a portable cutting torch to slice through a much thinner inner surface, and then dropped into a narrow maintenance tunnel. Now he was actually *on* the ship, instead of just being stuck in its skin like a splinter.

Felix had chosen his position carefully; knowing the basic layout as well as his own helped. Now he was in the pressurized atmosphere of the ship, but he left his tight-fitting helmet on anyway. This was a ship full of spore-zombies, so breathing around them seemed inadvisable.

There were klaxons wailing, which suggested a certain amount of chaos. Felix checked his pistol, confirmed it held a full load. They weren't sure how many people were on board. Harlow had estimated six crew, but there might be more. They'd brought enough darts to take down twice that many.

Felix peered through a vent, into a corridor, and watched the legs of a human crew member rush by. Once the way was clear, he opened the access hatch and stepped into the corridor. The running crewperson disappeared around a corner, and Felix loped after her, selecting the appropriate load on his pistol as he ran. Just like with the cure, the dose of tranquilizer you needed to take down a human was different from that needed for a Hacan or an Xxcha or an Yssaril.

Felix lifted the pistol and fired a dart into the woman's back, right between her shoulder blades. She stopped and began clawing at her, but she couldn't reach the dart. The part of your back you couldn't reach to scratch by yourself, Felix remembered, was called the "acnestis". Funny, the things that went through one's mind in the heat of combat. Well, not combat, exactly…

The woman spun toward Felix. She had short, blonde hair and wide, staring eyes. She rushed toward him, stumbling but clearly determined. He waited for her to fall… but instead, she said, "Guides, give me strength," and then jolted upright, as if a surge of electricity had passed through her.

Felix knew the Letani sacrament worked by hacking a victim's brain chemistry and flooding them with chemicals that created a sense of love, devotion, and bliss. But there was no reason it couldn't *also* flood them with adrenaline and cortisol, perhaps even enough to overcome the strength of a sedative in the system.

The woman launched herself at Felix, and since she wasn't wearing a spacesuit, she was a lot faster and more agile than he was. She plowed into him, knocking him down, and pinned his body with her own. She tried to tear his helmet off, snarling at him, and he struck her in the face with his pistol once, twice, three times. She didn't appear to feel pain, though. She was beyond all that. She was in the throes of devotion.

Calred lifted the woman off Felix, stuck a stun gun in the side of her neck, and triggered the jolt. He dropped her, twitching, to the floor of the corridor. "Hello, captain," he said on their suit comms. "I find my former colleagues in the great spore religion very annoying."

Felix took the hand Calred offered and got to his feet. "Did you secure the rest of the ship already?"

The Hacan shook his head. "We took out two other crew members. There are at least two more barricaded on the bridge."

"Nice of them to gather together for our convenience. Let's get down there."

Calred picked up the woman and slung her over his shoulder. They walked down the ship's corridors, and just as they reached the secure door to the bridge, the alarms and klaxons stopped. The door slid open, revealing Tib on the other side. Her boarding pod had attached itself near the command deck, and as an Yssaril, she was adept at moving invisibly. There were two unconscious crew members, a Hylar lieutenant and a Hacan wearing captain's insignia, on the floor behind her. "The *Sly Mongoose* is ours, captain."

Calred found and destroyed the *Sly Mongoose*'s node, jettisoning it from an airlock, while Tib and Felix oversaw things in the infirmary. They administered the cure to all five members of the crew – including a second human and an Yssaril – and waited for them to come up out of their sedation. Felix was surprised it all went so smoothly... but, then again, people mind-controlled by the guides didn't become tactical geniuses or unstoppable fighting machines. If anything, they were slower to improvise and react and more easily distracted. The strength of the conspiracy was in its numbers, and its reach into the halls of power, not the prowess of its individual puppets. Now that they knew how to cut the strings, Felix and his allies had a chance.

The captain, a Hacan named Karlon, was the first to blink his way to consciousness. He covered his face with his hands and wailed. "No, no, what have we *done*!"

"You failed," Tib said. "You're welcome."

"We were going to attack *Arc Prime*!" he said. "Because... for the future... to make the galaxy better, but..." Tears welled from his eyes. "None of it makes any sense."

"It's OK." Felix put a hand on his shoulder. He didn't know how it felt to unwillingly betray his people, but he knew how it felt to know you'd failed your crew, and he sympathized. "You're OK. We're going to take you home."

"I…" He looked beseechingly into Felix's face. "What will happen to us there?"

"Well," Felix said, "I figure either we'll be celebrated as heroes, or we'll be executed for treason. It's all a bit of a coin flip, really. Depends on how things go in other places. But at least you'll live and die as your own person, and not a puppet for someone else."

"Living would be preferable," the captain said.

Felix walked to the far side of the room to stand by Tib. "Well, we saved the Baron of Letnev from the indignity of an attack. Hurray. I wonder how Severyne and Ggorgos are doing with *their* part of the mission?"

CHAPTER 47
SEVERYNE

Severyne told the crew of the *Grim Countenance* that they were going dark, cutting off all communications, and fulfilling a secret mission on behalf of the Baron. She told them she would not be taking any questions, especially not regarding the identity of the peculiar Xxcha who had accompanied her up from the planet; the nature of Ggorgos's involvement was deeply classified. Her people were sufficiently loyal, overawed, or terrified of her that they complied without complaint. Only Voyou would have dared to ask any questions, and… well. There was no time for sentimentality now. There was too much at stake.

To her surprise, Severyne discovered that she quite liked Ggorgos. She'd always thought of the Xxcha as weaklings, devoted to diplomacy even when it was clearly a losing proposition, but Ggorgos was different. Severyne almost said, "You are Xxcha with the soul of a Letnev," but refrained, afraid it wouldn't be taken as the compliment it was intended to be.

The two of them discussed strategy, briefly, on the first night of their journey, but that didn't take long; the two of them were remarkably in accord when it came to finding the best way forward.

For the following days, as they moved to intercept the rogue Barony cruiser *The Soldier of the City* before it could penetrate the heart of Mentak Coalition space and launch an attack on the Greater Union summit, Ggorgos and Severyne just... talked. Sometimes they talked while playing the traditional Letnev game Spiralstone, or a somewhat similar strategy game the Xxcha played called The Hidden Shell, and sometimes they talked while sipping small cups of Barony liquor (fermented from the finest lichens), and sometimes they simply sat in Severyne's ready room and gazed out the windows at the stars and discussed the places they'd been and the things they'd seen and the people they'd killed there. She missed having Voyou to talk to, and carefully avoided looking into the empty space his absence opened inside her but having Ggorgos for company made that space less of an abyss.

They also complained about Felix Duval. At least they didn't have to talk *to* him at all; the three teams of the counter-conspiracy were siloed off to make sure Ohseroh couldn't intercept any information about their plans. Their mission could only succeed if their strikes were unforeseen and simultaneous.

Roughly ten hours before the summit was scheduled to begin on Moll Primus, they caught *The Soldier of the City* emerging from an asteroid field. The *Grim Countenance* sat, patient as a spider, and waited for the prey to pass within range.

"Would you like to do the honors, Ggorgos?" Sev asked, standing beside the Xxcha on the bridge, watching the dot on the viewscreen that represented the rogue Barony ship.

"That's unusually magnanimous of you," the Xxcha asked.

"Oh, no. It's just that I won't derive any satisfaction from sparing the Mentak Coalition from an attack, and I thought you might."

"I will."

"Ggorgos has tactical command!" Severyne snapped at the bridge crew.

"Target locked," the soldier at the tactical board said.

"Destroy that ship," Ggorgos said.

The *Grim Countenance* rumbled, faintly, as it launched multiple fusillades of torpedoes.

After a moment, the glowing dot on the screen ceased to exist, its fragments joining the debris in the asteroid field.

"Target destroyed," the soldier said.

"Well done," Severyne said, to Ggorgos and to the bridge crew in general. A compliment from her was only slightly less rare than sunshine on Arc Prime.

Ggorgos said, "How much do you want to bet that Duval pointlessly made his part of the mission more complicated than ours?"

Severyne chuckled. "As long as he gets the job done, his inevitable lapses in judgment are tolerable." She nodded to one of her bridge officers. "Take us back to Barony space, helmsman."

"I hope Azad and Terrak have as easy a time as we did," Ggorgos said.

"Mmm, not that easy," Severyne said. "Azad will be disappointed if things aren't at least a little bit nightmarish."

THE FAITHFUL XVI

<We have lost contact with the Sly Mongoose,> the guide whispered to Immental. <You must engage the failsafe protocol.>

Immental closed her eyes. She was in a meeting room on the Dark Star with the L1Z1X ambassador, and this was *not* a good time to get the worst possible news.

The L1Z1X leader, Ibna Vel Syd, had not come to the summit, the only explanation being that his "current form is temporarily incompatible with standards modes of travel". Instead, the Barony welcomed his proxy, LV286, a red-eyed maniac with metal sticking out of his face from beneath his mysteriously stained robes. LV286 was not one of the faithful… or at least, not completely so. The guides said that the L1Z1X were "resistant to the sacrament", though not fully immune like the Gashlai were. The L1Z1X had taken so much cybernetic control over their biological systems that the guides couldn't control them as easily as other species. (It was odd that Immental could understand *how* she was being manipulated, without that knowledge conferring even the slightest bit of resistance to the manipulation. It really served to show how perfect and powerful the guides were, didn't it?)

"You are distracted," LV286 said.

"I am merely frustrated, ambassador," she said as smoothly as possible. "The summit is mere hours from now, and you have yet to commit to joining our Legion."

"You have yet to agree to take on a subservient role to the Mindnet."

"The whole point of the Legion is that we are a partnership of equals."

The red eyes twinkled. "But we are not equal. We are the rightful rulers of the galaxy, and you are the descendants of rebellious scum." This was said with no apparent rancor, or even awareness that it was insulting. "We are generously offering to take you under our protection, yet again. Ibna Vel Syd is baffled by your refusal to embrace his largesse. The guides also refuse to direct their power toward the restoration of our rule. We would empty your skins and fill them with wonders, yet you rebuff us."

"Your offer is… very kind, and as I've said, I will be sure to tell the Baron, but again, the nature of this particular alliance is one of–"

A bolt of pain shot through her head, like a spike driven through her temples. *<Prepare the backup plan!>* the guides shrieked.

"Ambassador, forgive me, I must… I have an urgent matter I must attend to."

"The guides are calling?" The monster tittered. "Too many masters to serve, admiral, too many, better to serve only the L1Z1X." She rose from the table, and LV286 looked at her with those intent, glittering eyes. "Wonders," he said. "Think on them, and tremble, with ecstasy and dread."

"I certainly will." She turned and left the conference room, ignoring the beeps in her comms – everyone had an emergency today, and everyone wanted *her* to solve them, but her first allegiance was to the guides, as they'd just... strenuously reminded her.

If the *Sly Mongoose* wasn't coming to fire on the summit and start a war, that meant Immental had to distribute her stash of high explosives to members of the faithful. Several had been chosen to pretend they were Greater Union double agents, sent to sabotage the meeting. Just as the dignitaries prepared to sign the treaty, those faithful would declare their allegiance to the Union, detonate their bombs, and destroy large, nonessential portions of the Dark Star – along with themselves. One of the faithful would have a malfunctioning bomb, so she could be taken into custody and interrogated, allowing her to repeat her cover story as often and loudly as necessary to convince everyone that the Greater Union was an immediate threat.

When it came to starting a war, a coordinated suicide bombing was nowhere near as good as a Mentak Coalition warship opening fire on the station – acts by individuals could too easily be written off as the work of radical terrorists, not official actors – but then, if it had been a *better* idea, it wouldn't have been the backup plan.

Immental wondered if she would be called upon to detonate one of the bombs herself. If so, she would die secure in the knowledge that her life had served the great work: ushering in a single galactic community, overseen by the wisdom and beneficence of the guides. But she vastly preferred the idea of living to see that future personally.

CHAPTER 48
TERRAK

I was reclining in one of the plush armchairs on Fleet Captain Harlow's personal vessel, the *Darkest Mercy*, when the call came in. The ship was a pleasure craft built by one of the shipyards in the Federation of Sol, either bought by the Mentak or captured by their raider fleet. It was the second-nicest ship I'd ever traveled on: there was a chandelier in the galley, a palatial shower (spacious even by my standards), plush carpets, actual beds, and every other conceivable comfort of home and beyond. The ship was also incredibly fast and quiet. It was possible to forget you were on board a spacefaring vessel at all, at least until you looked out a window and saw stars instead of trees or the sea.

The comms chimed pleasantly with an incoming priority call, and I answered from a console in the chair's arm. "I have the details you requested on the *Crystal Stair*," the message from Catriona said. "I'll charge it to your account."

An encrypted data packet downloaded, then unspooled itself across the screen. I pushed the information to Azad's tablet, highlighting the coordinates of our target ship's last known location. (Azad was in the library, where there were actual paper books, looking for anything that had dirty pictures in it, probably.

On our first day of travel, she told me about her affair and rivalry and partnership with Severyne Dampierre, and now there were dirty pictures etched in *my* mind. Since I don't find hairless primates particularly attractive, those were most unwelcome. That's what I get for finally giving in to my curiosity.)

Harlow had a high degree of certainty that our rogue Letani was on board the *Crystal Stair*, a two-generations-old Mentak Coalition cruiser that was supposedly decommissioned and sold off. "Ohseroh couldn't remain on board its original ship, not after going rogue," Harlow told us. "The Letani managed to keep its crew – an array of the various lifeforms that live on the Arborec home world, all bound together by fungal symbiosis – under its control, but the ship itself was too easy to track by the Arborec. With the help of some loyal puppets I helped Ohseroh recruit, the Letani faked an accident and destroyed the original vessel in a bid to convince the hivemind back home that Ohseroh was dead. We rerouted the *Crystal Stair* away from its destination in the scrapyard, made sure the relevant paperwork was destroyed, and loaded Ohseroh and its helpers on board. There are a couple of faithful on board, too, a Letnev and a human, in case they ever need faces to present to local authorities. The ship has been cruising around ever since, under independent trader colors, with its movements disguised as much as possible by our confederates, erasing logs and so on. Ohseroh travels back and forth between Mentak Coalition and Barony space, where it has the highest concentration of loyalists and nodes. As it goes, it seeds additional nodes in moons and ships and planets and stations wherever possible. That increases Ohseroh's range and ability to directly communicate with its adherents. Think of the *Crystal Stair* as the Letani's mobile command center."

"I know you were the key to infiltrating the Coalition, but how did Ohseroh make such progress in the Barony?" I'd asked.

Harlow explained, "I had a double agent among the Letnev back when I ran covert operations, and I was able to set up a meeting so Ohseroh could infect them. From there, the faithful worked their way up through the Barony, almost to the very top."

Azad wasn't thrilled with the information. "'Somewhere in Barony or Coalition space' isn't much help when it comes to tracking down a ship, Harlow."

"I believe I can narrow it down," I assured her, and so I had. A ship that travels so much needs to be regularly restocked with fuel and supplies, even if most of the crew does consist of plant-creatures, and no one can cover their tracks perfectly. I reached out to Catriona, my data analyst par excellence, who wasn't at all concerned about my status as a wanted fugitive. She pored over data from the known locations Harlow could provide for the *Crystal Stair*, and then worked her usual magic. She'd just come through with coordinates: a ship matching the description of the *Crystal Stair*, with a registered name that proved to be false when Catriona investigated, had been seen yesterday departing the Nicodemidae system. That was in Barony space, not a terribly long journey from Arc Prime itself.

Azad strolled into the lounge and dropped into the chair across from mine. "Looks like Ohseroh is planning to oversee the Legion summit from close range, huh?"

"It makes sense," I said. "Harlow says the Gashlai are immune to the spores, and the L1Z1X are resistant, so the Legion meeting is more likely to hit snags that need smoothing over."

"They have no idea what kind of snags they're in store for," Azad said. "I'm going to set a course. You start sharpening your claws."

"I prefer to prevail with sharp wits, as a rule."

Azad snorted. "Good luck using your charm on an insane mushroom bent on galactic domination."

"I do love a challenge." I paused, before deciding to broach something that had been worrying me. "Do you think Harlow's theory is right? That stopping Ohseroh will free those in its thrall? If not... what happens to a bunch of mind-controlled puppets when there's no one to pull their strings?"

Azad shrugged. "I'm not an expert or anything, but I remember hearing once that the largest single living organism on Jord is a big mushroom colony. It looks like thousands of individual growths, but underground, it's all connected by a single mycelium. The Arborec homeworld is bigger than *that*, and even so, it's a single symbiotic organism. It's possible that Ohseroh is connected to all the puppets, and if we kill it, we cut the strings. Otherwise..." She sighed. "We'll have to inject a *lot* of spore-zombies with the cure. While they're being driven insane with grief for their dead god. So. Let's hope... not that."

CHAPTER 49
AZAD

Azad was terrible at waiting, which was a bad quality in a covert operative, but since she was excellent at every *other* part of the job, she generally managed. She spent the journey to the Nicodemidae system disassembling and reassembling her new gun, exercising, starting arguments with Terrak, fantasizing about past debaucheries, enjoying the contents of the fleet captain's exceptionally well stocked liquor cabinet, enduring Terrak's culinary experiments with her equally well stocked spice rack, and reading. (Everyone was always surprised when they found out she liked to read. She loved reading. Reading was how you learned everything you couldn't learn by doing.)

They finally reached the *Crystal Stair*'s last known location, and then picked the most logical route to reach Arc Prime. Azad figured the Letani wouldn't get too close to the actual summit, just near enough to monitor the situation, and since it had such a high concentration of spores in Barony space, it wouldn't have to get all *that* close. There was a promising asteroid field where you could easily hide a ship of the *Crystal Stair*'s size, and keep an eye on the proceedings through conventional means as well as fungal tech.

The *Darkest Mercy* approached the asteroid field, and Azad made final preparations. While Azad bustled around, Terrak sat watching the live broadcasts about the Greater Union summit – the footage from the Legion summit preparations on Arc Prime was all state propaganda anyway, and a lot more boring. The capital city of Moll Primus was all polished and shiny, hung with banners, the streets and stadiums filled with cheering people. It felt less like a diplomatic meeting than a festival, with various games and contests and musical exhibitions held all over the city, featuring the most skilled and talented people from all the invited systems. "Ohseroh didn't plan for all *this*," she said, leaning over Terrak's shoulder to watch. "It can't possibly give a crap about cultural exchange."

"No, but there are plenty of people involved in the planning who haven't been mind-controlled, and this… is just what people do."

"Any excuse for a party." Azad toggled the main viewscreen to show the approaching cloud of rocks before them. The asteroid field was many thousands of kilometers across, dense and deep, perfect to conceal a vessel. "The *Crystal Stair* is hiding in there somewhere. I'm sure of it."

"How do you intend to find it?"

"Easy." She opened a short-range communication band, the sort used for ship-to-ship communications. The transmission was strictly local and wouldn't be picked up by anyone outside of the immediate area. She turned on the camera and grinned into the lens. "Hello, Ohseroh," she said. "It's Azad and Terrak. We need to talk to you." Time to see if the Letani was capable of curiosity.

The sensors lit up, and there was the ship, barely a thousand kilometers away, hidden in the thick of the asteroids… except it wasn't trying to hide anymore.

The image flickered. A Letnev man appeared on their screen. His eyes were glazed, and there was some kind of moss hanging from his chin. The air around him was visibly full of floating particulates. "We should kill you." The voice was monotone.

"Why?" Azad said. She'd only given it fifty-fifty odds the Letani's puppet would answer at all, so she was feeling good about things. "We've seen the error of our ways. You're clearly going to win this war – you're smarter than *we* are. We've met some of your faithful, and they're all happy and fulfilled and sing your praises all day long. We can't possibly defeat you, and everyone says we'd be fools to even try. So, we've come to beg forgiveness. Let us join your fellowship."

"This is a trick. This is subterfuge."

"No, it's not. I would never. You want us to recant all that stuff Terrak said on his broadcast, right? We'd be happy to–"

"That is no longer necessary. Our plan is on the cusp of success."

"Really? Because–"

The *Crystal Stair* fired on the *Darkest Mercy*. Despite being decommissioned, Ohseroh's ship still had weapons, courtesy of its various fungal loyalists. The fleet captain's unarmed pleasure vessel was an easy target.

"That was rude," Azad said, after turning off the comms. But not unexpected, of course.

She and Terrak had sent their message from a shuttle, far enough away from the *Crystal Stair* to avoid the debris field, but close enough to relay their comms through the larger ship, to make it seem like that's where the message originated. "So much for throwing ourselves on the mercy of the spore-lord."

"Ohseroh won't see us coming now, at least," Terrak said. "Your plan worked."

"I've benefited greatly over the years from people thinking I was dead."

The shuttle moved slowly through the asteroid field, careful to keep itself obscured from the *Crystal Stair*, though the ship didn't appear to be on particularly high alert – there was no sign of the vessel using active sensors. They'd settled back into a position of concealment over caution. "Is it really so easy to trick Ohseroh?" Terrak murmured.

"Don't forget, the evil mushroom needed Harlow to come up with an actual plan," Azad said. "Ohseroh is really good at a couple of things, and not so good at others. That's the downside of specialization, and why I prefer to be a generalist."

They settled in behind a large asteroid within visual range of the *Crystal Stair*, then suited up. "Remember, helmets stay on, even when we board," Azad said. "There's no telling what kind of stuff is floating around in there." She strapped her huge gun onto her back. This mission had involved a lot of annoying sitting around and going to-and-fro, but this was the fun part. She was glad to have the Hacan along for company too. Sure, she was a covert operator, but that didn't mean she didn't appreciate an audience. "Ready?"

"No," Terrak said. "But off we go anyway."

CHAPTER 50
TERRAK

I hate extravehicular activities. My greatest strength is talking to people, and that isn't nearly as much use when tumbling around in the black. We had personal propulsion devices, so we were unlikely to go flying off hopelessly into the void, but it's still disorienting to float in the vacuum, even more so when there are rocks all around. The smallest asteroids were as big as houses, and the largest as big as ships. I grew up on a planet, and I find it fundamentally surreal to see pitted stones just hovering around me.

Azad launched herself toward the dark bulk of the *Crystal Stair*, maneuvering with air jets, and I did the same. She was better at checking her speed with counteracting bursts of air; I just bumped into small rocks, certain I'd rip a hole in my suit and die. We did reach the airlock of the enemy ship eventually, though I thumped against the side of the *Crystal Stair* so hard I was sure someone would hear the bang and come to investigate.

No one did. Azad pried open a panel beside the airlock with a flat-edged tool, then hooked up a small device to the wires inside. Harlow had given us override codes for this generation of ship, and our boarding plan hinged on those still being functional.

I hated this plan, but at least it was better than the alternative, which involved breaching charges, and would be a lot noisier and attention-getting. It had been a long time since I'd been on an infiltrate-and-execute operation, and I really hoped the moves would come back to me.

I'd asked why we couldn't just blow up the entire ship and then go for a drink, but Azad said we didn't have enough firepower to be sure we'd kill Ohseroh, and also we had to confirm the Letani was actually on board, and also also, wouldn't infiltration be more *fun*? "I like to look my enemies in the face before I destroy them," she said.

I told her, "Letani don't *have* faces. They just have a sort of red flower on top—"

"Then I want to look her right in the bee-hole," Azad said.

The airlock door popped open, and Azad grinned at me through her helmet's faceplate.

Her grin turned into astonishment when vinelike tentacles whipped out of the opening and yanked her inside the airlock.

CHAPTER 51
AZAD

Azad had never really dealt with the Arborec before. She knew they were a conglomeration of various ambulatory plants, but that hadn't mentally prepared her for being attacked by a sort of vine-octopus stuck to the wall inside the airlock. She'd had the vague idea that the plant things would need air to survive, but apparently not this one – it was anaerobic, maybe, or had its own dedicated air sacs, or who knew what? She wasn't a xeno-botanist. She wished she was. They would know how to kill a thing like this.

Azad struggled as the vines drew her toward something that looked disturbingly like a mouth at the center of the growth. The maw wasn't big enough to swallow her whole, but that wasn't reassuring, really; it meant the thing would have to swallow her in pieces instead. What a way to go. Ugh. Only one way out now, and maybe she wouldn't get paid if she went that way, but at least her enemy would lose too, which was a comfort. She reached behind her for the discreet button on the bottom of the hilt of her gun, the *real* reason she'd chosen that weapon–

Then Terrak was there, too, also wrapped in a vine and getting yanked in, but *he* had a knife, and when he hit a discreet button on the hilt, the dull gray blade glowed with white fire. Terrak slashed at the vines holding them, severing them and causing spurts of dark gray fluid that floated in gross little globules.

Azad reached out for the pistol on Terrak's hip, tugging it loose from the holster and toggling it to plasma ammo. She shot a few rounds of superheated goo at the vine-monster until sufficient portions of its body were blackened and glowing, and then it stopped waving its tentacles around. The recoil slammed her into a wall, but that was OK. She could handle getting a little bruised, and she'd taken the best of the combat drugs Lonrah had made for her before they left the shuttle, so pain was currently a problem for Future Amina.

Azad handed Terrak back his gun and gave him a little salute, then pulled the outer airlock closed. Getting through the inner door was easier – you just hit a button and waited for the pressures to equalize. The gravity generator kicked in, too, making the globs of fluid fall and splash on them. Even more gross. She pushed the door open when the light went green and ducked her head as she stepped into the corridor.

The interior of the ship looked like a rotten fruit. The walls, floor, and ceiling were covered in greenish-gray molds and lichens. There was another vine-monster stuck to the ceiling off to the right, but no other visible life forms. Or maybe there were. Maybe the blanket of moss was a whole *person*. If so, it didn't seem to care she was walking on it, so never mind.

She wondered if the vine-monsters sensed vibrations or body heat or something to find their prey. Probably not worth trying to sneak by. These creatures were all psychically linked, and since they'd killed one, the others would know they were coming. She slung her rifle around to ready position, turned on the flamethrower function, and sprayed a line of fire at the vine-monster. It charred, smoked, and blackened, vines waving wildly as alarms began to blare. Spaceships really hated fire. Suppression foam sprayed from the ceiling, but not very well, because everything was covered in moss and mold up there. Fortunately, the blanket of slime was too damp to burn well, though it smoked abominably, and Azad was glad she had her own air source. Sometimes she really did have the *weirdest* job, but she wouldn't have it any other way.

She beckoned to her partner, then sprinted down the corridor, Terrak at her heels. Harlow said Ohseroh was in a large cargo area near the engine room, so that's where they were headed. They passed closed doors, gummed up with slime molds, and she wondered if the lifts would even work. If not, there were always ladders–

Terrak screamed, and when she turned, there was a *thing* on him. It looked like a compost heap with roots for legs, and it was engulfing him, and also tearing off his helmet in the process.

CHAPTER 52
TERRAK

I thought the thing that attacked me was just a heap of vegetable matter on the floor, until it rose and sent me stumbling, and then tried to consume me. I slashed out with the burning blade, and that helped, until it extended thick tendrils and pinned my arms. Then it got my helmet off, the reek of rotting leaves in my nose, and I knew, I just *knew*, that it was going to jam its foul body into my mouth and down my throat.

Azad came back for me, jamming her rifle's barrel into the bulk of the thing and pulling the trigger. The heap shuddered apart, falling to fragments around me. "Sonic pulse," Azad said. She gave me my helmet and I put it back on after brushing some goo off the faceplate. "Do you feel mind-controlled?" she asked.

"I do not." We'd both taken shots of the cure before boarding – Azad said her bosses were "pretty sure" it would have a prophylactic effect and keep them from getting compromised. "Like, eighty percent sure."

I had not been reassured by that number, but either the mind-control spores weren't airborne here, or the cure did its job.

Azad looked at him with narrowed eyes. "You'd say that even if you were compromised, though. How about you walk ahead of me?"

I couldn't argue with her logic, so I took the lead, making my way more carefully now, though I sensed her impatience. We reached the elevator, and amazingly, it still worked – I'd assumed it would be jammed with vines, but upon reflection, I realized this wasn't wild growth. Everything that grew here was cultivated and deliberate under the care of Ohseroh, and it wouldn't impair the ship's vital functions.

I didn't need Azad to tell me to stand to one side before the lift doors opened, so neither of us was caught in the gunfire that sprayed out when they did. Azad tossed a flash-bang inside the elevator car, and after the noise and the burst of light, she dodged in and dragged out the Letnev man we'd seen on the screen earlier. He fought wildly, biting and scratching and clawing at her suit, until she finally banged his head against the wall hard enough to make him stop… which was, unfortunately, also hard enough to break his skull. A spray of spores shot out of the crack like it was under pressure, and she shuddered and dropped his body to the floor.

We descended silently to the engineering floor. The other known puppet on board the *Crystal Stair*, a human woman, opened fire as soon as the doors opened, but we were lying flat on the floor against such an eventuality. Azad shot the woman's legs out from under her.

Overall, our mission was going well, and I hated that "going well" in this case involved so much blood and death. "I wish we could have saved them," I said, after checking the woman's vitals and failing to find any.

"Can't save everybody," Azad said.

"We can try. The whole point of the work we do should be to save lives and minimize suffering, Azad."

"You must have *way* different kinds of handlers than I do." She gestured for me to take the lead, and we made our way to the engineering storage bay, where replacement parts and supplies were stored… usually.

When the doors opened for us, we saw the space had been cleared to make way for something else.

In its basic shape, the Letani was just like the little nodes we'd rooted out. They were something like a mushroom, crossed with a carnivorous plant, crossed with a squid, topped with a red flower, and this was the same… only Ohseroh was immense, filling the bay, bobbing flower towering above us. Its root-tendrils extended all over the cargo area, many stuck to the walls and ceilings, others free to move and curling toward us. The immense flower lowered down toward us, almost like a head looking at us, though I knew that was entirely the wrong paradigm.

A figure shambled forward, connected to the Letani by a series of vines that terminated in the back of its head. It was a human, or had been – now it was a corpse, flesh gray, features slack. A Dirzuga, in the tatters of a Mentak Coalition uniform. I wondered if it was Grisham, the protégé Harlow had mentioned, possessed so long by the Letani that their body had given out, and been repurposed for this. Such a waste, and such a horror. Treating people like objects or tools was the greatest crime I could imagine, and it was even worse, because I'd done it myself, often enough.

At least we could stop Ohseroh from doing it anymore.

"Terrak," the Dirzuga said. "Azad. You have come. You have come to make my new Symphony into cacophony instead. But you are too late. You have stopped my ships, but I had other plans, always other plans–"

Azad shot the Dirzuga in the face, making its head explode in a cloud of blood, brain matter, and spores. Then she launched three grenades straight into the middle of Ohseroh's flower, projectiles disappearing into the cup of the blossom. She spun and ran from the hangar, and I followed, booms filling the air behind us and making the deck vibrate.

"I gave it a frag and a couple of incendiaries!" she shouted.

"You just *killed it*?" I shouted. I'd somehow imagined a longer stand-off, perhaps an exchange of banter, or the Letani pleading with us to join its cause – Azad seemed to thrive on such drama, after all.

"I said I wanted to look it in the bee-hole!" Azad yelled. "Not that I wanted to talk to it! What would I talk to an insane *plant* about?"

She grabbed my arm and dragged me toward the engine room itself. "We can't be sure it's dead, though. Who knows how hardy these things are, or if they can regenerate from a twig or something, you know?"

"We could burn the entire cargo area," I said. "Turn it all to ashes. Or vent the remains into space. Or–"

"Or just blow up the whole ship."

"You said we didn't have enough explosives."

"We didn't have enough explosives to blow up the ship from the *outside*. From the inside, though..." She took her rifle off its strap and looked around the control room. "This will do." She held up the gun and grinned at me. "When I enumerated the features of this rifle, I left one important function out. This all-purpose mayhem machine is sometimes called a 'scuttle-gun'. The Mentak Coalition raiders use them when they need to... well, scuttle something. You can set a timer, here." She twisted a dial. "Then you press this button, here." She depressed a spot under the hilt. "Then you put the rifle as close to the magnetic bottle housing the fusion reactor as you can. When the timer runs out, the gun sets off a burst designed to breach containment, and then... you get a brief uncontrolled fusion reaction. And, subsequently, no more ship." She leaned the rifle against the engineering console.

I took an instinctive step away, which was foolish. It was like backing up a little to avoid being hit by a nuclear explosion. *Exactly* like that, in fact. "That seems extreme."

"We can't leave any of those mind-control spores laying around for someone else to pick up," she said. "That's one of my fundamental mission parameters. Gotta burn it all. Cleansing fire scenario. I'm just glad I found the scuttle-gun. It would have been tricky to rig the ship to blow remotely otherwise. This way, we have time to get back to the shuttle and out of the blast radius, and I don't have to convince you to stay behind to make the ultimate sacrifice."

"You are not that convincing," I said.

"That timer isn't *infinite*, so let's move."

We moved, back to the airlock, past the dead we'd left behind, and into space again. We reached the shuttle, boarded, and made our way as rapidly as possible out of the asteroid field.

Not long after we cleared the area, a bright light filled our screens as the *Crystal Stair* became a cloud of dust and spores. I have never seen such a beautiful and welcome moment of destruction.

"We did it," Azad said. "Look at us. Saviors of the galaxy over here. Who would have thought, a couple of old spies like us, doing something pretty much totally unambiguously on the side of good for once?"

"It's an unusual feeling," I agreed. "I am a bit troubled by Ohseroh saying we were too late, and that there were other plans in place…"

"Maybe we ruined those other plans by blowing everything up. That's the assumption I'm going with. Makes me a lot happier."

"In the absence of verification, I suppose we might as well be hopeful," I said. "But… what do we do now? Both the available ships have been destroyed. We won't make it far in this shuttle."

"I'll call and get us a ride."

"What, send a distress signal? The *Barony* will pick us up. That would be bad. We don't even know if the puppets have been stopped. Even if they have been neutralized, I'm sure it will take time for the truth of what happened here to be understood by the powers that be."

"You act like this is my first time destroying things in a hostile system," Azad said. "My bosses have an exfiltration team on standby. Don't worry. We'll give you a ride to a nice neutral moon where you can wait until this all gets sorted out."

"Where I can wait? Where will *you* be?"

"To make my final report, and collect my bonus," Azad said.

THE FAITHFUL XVII

Immental stood beneath the viewing dome at the top of the ship, the dark orb of her homeworld beneath her, and another dark orb, etched with fiery lines of red, floating above her. She had envisioned a Gashlai War Sun above Arc Prime before, of course, but only in her nightmares. Now, its presence was a symbol of her imminent triumph. There were N'orr ships there, too, like the nests of those foul insects on a vaster scale, and a L1Z1X flagship, an old imperial design embellished with grotesque technological extrusions – not unlike the L1Z1X themselves. The guides had finally exerted sufficient chemical pressure to bring those monsters into alignment with their plans. These were the members of her Legion. The galaxy would burn, the guides said, under her command, and from the devastation, a better future would blossom.

They just had to get through today.

<Are the bombers in place?> the guides asked. There was a sense of urgency in the chorus of voices that Immental had never heard from them before.

"Yes, wise ones. Just after the last signatory ratifies the treaty, a coordinated attack–"

<No. No no no.>

"No, guides? A change in plans?" Immental hoped so. Setting off bombs on board the Dark Star was a dangerous proposition. It wasn't like bombing the surface of Moll Primus, where there was air to breathe; if the destruction was greater than intended here, they'd all be vented into space.

<No. Proceed. There are… distractions. Our focus. Is split. The plan. The plan must not fail. I must return to the Symphony. I must prove that I am right, and I am good. No, no, my voice, they took my voice.>

"Guides? I don't understand what…" Immental swayed, and then fell to her knees, a great burst of pain going off behind her eyes. What… why… what was *happening*, where were the guides, where were her–?

"No." Oh, no, by the dark, what had she done, what had she been doing? Her head spun like she'd downed too much mushroom liquor, and she fell from her knees onto her side. Something was trickling out of her nose, and her ears, and the corners of her *eyes*… she touched her face, and her hand came away bloody, but the blood was flecked with tiny green specks. The sacrament. Purging itself from her body. She was relieved and disgusted and horrified and enraged.

The guides were gone, and… and they were never *guides* at all, they were enemies, controlling her mind, pushing her toward abominable acts. And now… what had stopped them? She wondered if Severyne had something to do with this. The woman had dropped all contact, and Voyou had gone dark, so maybe she'd discovered the conspiracy, and somehow, impossibly, moved against it.

Such speculations suddenly seemed irrelevant as a black pit of despair opened inside Immental. She knew what the guides were now, that they'd controlled her, and used her, but still, their absence was a howling void within her. She had to fill that void somehow.

The only thing she could think to fill it with was duty.

Immental struggled upright. If this was happening to her, it was happening to all the faithful. N'orr, and L1Z1X, and Letnev, falling and frothing and bleeding – she activated her comms. "Get the Baron off the station!" she shouted. "Now, now, now!"

What would the L1Z1X and the N'orr do when they realized they'd been compromised this way? Who would they blame? Would they think it was a Barony plot?

She began making more calls, frantically spinning a cover story: "We are under biological attack, our enemies are attempting to disrupt the Legion, get everyone to safety, send the dignitaries back to their ships, now, now, *NOW*!"

Immental staggered into a wall, her balance failing her. It was hard to hold herself up, but she *had* to. She had to fix this. Immental looked up, through the dome, her vision tinged with red from her bloody tears, and watched the War Sun fire its engines and depart the skies of Arc Prime.

When Jhuri opened his eyes and struggled up from the puddle of disgusting goo surrounding his body, he realized pretty quickly what was going on. The bombers assembled in the capitol basement were starting to moan and get up too, their faces covered in blood flecked with specks of green. *I see*, he thought.

Jhuri looked over at Koté Strom, who was openly weeping in the corner, and said, "Pull yourself together. Get those bomb vests deactivated. Do something *useful*, you little toad." It was probably irrational for Jhuri to be furious at Kote for spraying him in the face with spores – Kote had been a victim of the guides, too – but Jhuri wasn't at his most rational. He wanted to crawl into a hole and pull the hole after him and sleep for a year.

Instead, he activated his comms. "Put me through to the Table of Captains immediately," he barked at his least favorite executive secretary. "Yes, I know people are falling over and bleeding from their eye sockets – I'd like the opportunity to tell our leadership why."

While Jhuri waited to be connected, he thought, *I wonder if Felix had something to do with this.* If so, the man was going to be even more smug than usual. But, if Felix had... by the seas... really just *saved the galaxy*, well, he deserved to feel a little smug, didn't he?

CHAPTER 53
TERRAK

Thus ends my chronicle. I went to my superiors and told them I didn't want any accolades or rewards… except one. I wished to retire from covert operations, and from my ambassadorship. "This is the high point of my career," I told them. "I will never again save the entire galaxy. I'd like *that* to be the note I end on, not some squalid backroom deal. Let me go out on top."

My superiors don't like letting people like me retire, but they'd already seen me make one transmission spreading secrets throughout the galaxy, and I think they were afraid, if they refused, that I'd do the same with some of *theirs*.

I bought a vineyard on a pleasant Emirates colony world. For the remainder of my days, I will sit on my villa's porch, and I will sip, and I will look at the stars.

My boss asked me: "Do you really think you can stand to be idle, Terrak? Do you really think you can *retire*?"

I told him I absolutely could, and I meant it.

Of course, on occasion, some friends might visit me.

Maybe, sometimes, I'll arrange for a favor, or two. Make an introduction. Help someone out when they need it.

I'm only retired, after all. I'm not dead.

CHAPTER 54
FELIX

Jhuri was waiting in the anteroom of the reception hall on Moll Primus when the crew arrived. Felix sauntered over to him while Tib and Calred ordered drinks from a floating servitor. "Hey there, boss," Felix said. "All done puking up green goo?"

"I wish I had expelled that foulness by vomiting." The Hylar shuddered. "It oozed out of me in far more unpleasant ways."

Felix winced. "Never mind. Sorry I asked. How are you feeling? I hear some people take the comedown pretty hard."

"I have never been more depressed and anxious in my life, thank you, but I am on medication to take the edge off, and I am assured my brain will return to something resembling its usual operations in time." He gestured with a tentacle. "I'm proud of you, Felix. You've earned this."

"Medals of commendation all around, and a promotion to admiral for me?" He couldn't help but puff out his chest. "Well, it's a start. I never thought I'd be a flag officer, that's for sure. I sort of figured myself as terminal at captain."

Jhuri chuckled. "Don't worry, they won't actually put you in charge of a fleet. You're still part of the Special Projects division. You'll just get more money and more respect on those rare occasions when you mingle with your fellow officers. But

342

you'll mostly keep flying around in the dark, fighting off the monsters. There are *lots* of monsters, and we're facing them alone, as usual."

"The Greater Union is done, huh?" He hadn't been terribly invested in the idea, but it was still a shame. Uniting even a *chunk* of the galaxy in a peaceful fashion was a lovely dream.

"When many of the invited guests at a summit start to ooze green-flecked blood from every orifice in their heads, it tends to diminish enthusiasm for the whole process," Jhuri said. "We're just lucky our brief allies didn't fully turn on one another. The fact that people from every faction demonstrably suffered was helpful. Our cover story is that we suffered a biological attack from terrorists and are pausing plans for the Greater Union while we sort out the security situation. Those who were infected know the truth, of course, and the leadership in all the factions have been informed as well. They're all understandably furious with the Arborec, but Fleet Captain Harlow's testimony made it clear the Arborec aren't even *truly* to blame, any more than our government is responsible for every fringe group or bomb-throwing radical who happens to have Mentak Coalition citizenship. We are getting some very juicy Arborec technology in the way of apology... although, unfortunately, so is every other faction involved, including those in the Legion."

"Have you heard anything from Ggorgos? I know she succeeded in her mission, since Moll Primus wasn't attacked, but I haven't heard anything from her." They hadn't exactly parted on the best terms, what with him locking her in the brig and all, but he'd hoped she would forgive him. It had been a confusing time. Of course, it was possible she wasn't thinking about him at all.

"I received a report on her report," Jhuri said. "Ggorgos and

Captain Dampierre engaged and destroyed the *Soldier of the City.*"

Felix winced. "They just blew it up? They didn't try to cure the crew?"

"Are you surprised?"

He sighed. "I guess not. Disappointed, of course. We saved *ours*. They made it home safe, though?"

"Dampierre dropped off Ggorgos in a shuttle near a Coalition station and then, presumably, returned to the Barony to get her own medal, or else get imprisoned for embarrassing her superiors by being more competent than they are – you never know how the Letnev are going to react to things like this."

"We can hope for imprisonment, anyway," Felix said. "Any word on Terrak and Azad?"

"Terrak was picked up drinking Hacan firewine on a neutral moon and being modest about his very small role in saving the universe. As for Azad? Gone. No idea where. We made inquiries with the Federation of Sol, who claim she wasn't even working for them, and hasn't been on their payroll since she left the navy. We know *that's* a lie – she was definitely a deniable asset for Federation covert operations for some time after her discharge – but we don't know if she still is. The Federation seemed as shocked and horrified to learn about the conspiracy as the rest of us, which suggests they didn't know about it any earlier... but then, humans are good liars."

"Well, we try," Felix said. "It all turned out well, honestly, don't you think?" There was no use dwelling on the horrible parts. They'd get to him in his dreams, and he didn't want to give them any more waking attention than necessary. Moving forward was the best way to get past something.

Jhuri rolled one eye toward him. "Apart from revealing the

horrifying flaws in our security, exposing our vulnerabilities to exploitation, and bringing the entire galaxy to the brink of war? Yes, I'd say, other than that, everything is marvelous."

"That's the spirit," Felix said, and then it was time to go accept his accolades. All's well that ends well, after all. If you didn't think about all the people who'd been killed along the way, at least.

CHAPTER 55
SEVERYNE

Severyne had never been in the Baron's presence before. Few Letnev ever were, as he preferred to govern from a distance, but now she was in the palace, deep beneath the surface of Arc Prime, marching to the throne room between a pair of towering guards in full regalia, complete with ceremonial pikes. She was wearing a freshly tailored uniform, with her new rank insignia on the shoulders, and boots so shiny they could have been black mirrors. She was, she supposed, happy. The sensation was strange but not unpleasant.

The Baron sat in a chair made of stone and metal, his own uniform dripping with medals and braid, with a sash across his chest. His face was noble and composed. "Severyne Joelle Dampierre. Welcome to the presence."

She gave a small bow. "Your lordship. You honor me."

"The honor, this time, is ours." The Baron leaned forward. "You singlehandedly uncovered a conspiracy in the highest echelons of our society, organized a resistance, manipulated our ancient rivals into serving our cause, and saved our society from ruin."

Severyne had, in her report, slightly exaggerated the importance of her own role. And why not? There was no one in the Barony who could plausibly contradict her. "I did what any loyal Letnev would, your lordship."

"Loyal. Yes. You sent a query through the viscount, asking after Admiral Immental. Why this concern?"

"She was my superior officer, your lordship, and so sorely afflicted by the foul attack on our sovereignty. I hope she has recovered."

"Your concern does you credit. My cousin is… recovering. She has, of course, been relieved from duty. Can anyone, once compromised, truly be trusted?"

"Your wisdom is great, my baron," Severyne said. She'd heard the old man couldn't quite get his head around the fact that the spores couldn't really be resisted – that succumbing to them was inevitable, not the result of poor willpower or lack of true Letnev fiber. But Severyne didn't really mind. She could use the Baron's prejudice to her own advantage, after all.

"I have decided to grant you a boon, Severyne."

She thrilled as much at the familiar form of address as she did at the substance of the comment – which she'd been expecting, thanks to the viscount's hints, but was still delighted to hear confirmed. "You are too kind, your lordship."

"Any posting, any command, any crew you wish – you have proven that you will serve the Barony above all, and you may choose in what capacity you fulfill that service. I will say, this offer includes the opportunity to take Immental's place as an admiral and become my close advisor."

"That is very tempting, your lordship." Interminable meetings with the Baron and his cousins, all of them looking down on her from their lofty seats of ancient privilege? No, that wouldn't do. "But, if I consider my qualifications with a clear eye... I think I could best serve you as head of the clandestine services."

The Baron leaned back, which Severyne interpreted as surprise. "Really? Retire my cousin Dieudonne? I suppose he has been in the post for a long time, but why?"

"With all due respect to his long service and many accomplishments, Baron... a vast conspiracy infiltrated our society, and Dieudonne was wholly unaware. I would never suggest that he has become complacent, but I feel I would bring a certain level of... youthful zeal and attention to the post."

"I am inclined to grant your desire, Severyne. But you *do* know, to take on a role like this, such a lofty position, so early in your career... you will be subject to great scrutiny. Some may resent you. There will be all sorts of challenges you cannot foresee. And failure... failure will not be tolerated."

"Nor should it be, your lordship." Severyne was secure in the knowledge that she'd never yet met a failure she couldn't turn into a success... at least for herself.

"Your formal appointment will be made in two weeks," the Baron said. "There are certain matters that must be attended to first." Like firing that doddering fool Dieudonne. "In the meantime, we have taken the liberty of securing you a suite on one of our finest pleasure planets, in the famous crystal caves. Enjoy yourself, Severyne. You have the gratitude of your Baron, and of your nation."

"I live to serve," she said.

Severyne slept for most of the trip to the crystal caves. She was fresh and rested when she arrived. She shooed off the various handlers and assistants who escorted her to the resort's lobby, sending them back to the ship. There was no reason for any of *them* to enjoy all this luxury. They hadn't saved the Barony from disaster.

When Severyne entered her gorgeous, lavish, palatial suite, she was surprised to find someone waiting for her there.

CHAPTER 56
AZAD

After a long journey with some extremely boring people, Amina Azad was finally ready to receive her reward.

She'd left Terrak behind and set out on a battered old trading vessel, but two ship transfers later and she was deposited onto a ship made of forcefields and linked crystalline structures. Her hosts assured her the name of the vessel could not be accurately translated for human understanding but might be simplified as the *Lineaments of Gratified Desire*. Azad annoyed the crew by consistently referring to the ship as "Lenny."

Azad was escorted down the boarding ramp by a pair of male Naalu. They were, in essence, humanoid from the waist up, and serpents from the waist down, though Azad was sure a xenobiologist would have pointed out all the reasons why that was a hopelessly inaccurate way to describe them. Her escorts led her down and out and into a glittering square on the Naalu homeworld of Druaa, which she'd heard described as "a paradise of crystal spires". She looked around. Fair enough. Lots of shiny buildings, certainly. She was warm enough. The air had a faint, dry sort of scent that made her think of deserts for some reason. She wouldn't want to live here, but she could see why it appealed to people who liked this sort of thing.

Her escorts hadn't brought her to some remote outpost or back alley, as she'd expected – this was a city center. There were random Naalu slithering around, down streets and up ramps, but none of them gave her a second glance, and very few bothered with a first one. The place was oddly quiet. She was used to a certain amount of background noise in a city, but then, the Naalu didn't talk much, not where the average person could hear.

Her escorts took her to a building that might have been carved from a single large emerald. A door shimmered open when they approached, and inside was a grand anteroom, with a polished opalescent floor and ramps spiraling up into the heights. "I guess you don't do stairs," she said. "They'd probably be tough on the old soft underbelly, huh?"

"S'zakith will see you now." One of the escorts gestured toward a corridor. Azad gave a jaunty wave and strolled where he'd indicated. She wasn't afraid, exactly, but she was keenly aware that if her bosses wanted to make her disappear instead of paying her, they could do that. She'd taken precautions, of course, but precautions against the Naalu were tricky. It was hard to outsmart people who could manipulate your mind and erase your memory.

Azad hadn't known a lot about her bosses before they contacted her. She knew they were isolationists, and thought they were better than everyone else; that they had native telepathic abilities, augmented with technology to the point where they could be weaponized; and that people who looked into Naalu affairs too closely had a tendency to vanish, or worse. She'd worked with a guy, back before she left the Federation of Sol's service, who was sent to do some recon in Naalu space, and when he finally returned, he didn't remember her name, and even had to be reminded of his own every couple of hours.

So, when the Naalu asked her to investigate the conspiracy, she'd laughed. "I thought controlling the minds of lesser races was a *Naalu* thing."

It is, S'zakith had whispered into her mind. *That's why we are so unhappy to learn someone else is doing it, and in such a clumsy way.*

"Why hire a mercenary like me?" she'd asked. "Don't you have little spies with whispers in their brains embedded here and there who can do this for you?"

Independent freelancers are best for this sort of work, S'zakith said. *Those who are under our influence for too long develop a sort of... learned helplessness. They become so accustomed to serving our will that they start to lack personal initiative. We need someone who can think quickly and react to changing circumstances without waiting for our guidance.*

"That's me, all right," Azad had said. They'd agreed to her price so readily she wished she'd doubled it.

S'zakith was waiting in a dim room hung with glowing purple crystals. She was coiled behind a table with a single glass and a decanter resting on it. When Azad entered, the Naalu poured a measure of golden liquid and handed the glass to Azad.

For a job well done, she said.

Azad toasted her, sniffed, and took a sip. It wasn't her preferred form of whiskey – she doubted they grew much corn here – but it was something in the same family, a hint of sweet and a hint of burn and a lot of fruit and wood. "Thank you."

I have told you, you need not speak aloud. You can simply direct your thoughts toward me.

Azad shrugged. "Then we're both staring at each other in total silence, and I know that's an ordinary Saturday night for your people, but it would make me start to giggle, or else think we were about to kiss." She looked around for something to sit on – there was nothing, of course – and settled for leaning against a fluted pillar. "Why did you bring me all the way here? I know you were shadowing me for most of the mission – your telepathy doesn't have infinite range, but you were always there, whenever I mentally reached out to give a report. You must have been distracting minds and wiping memories the whole way to cover your tracks. I figured you'd just transfer me to your ship for the final debrief."

I did, for the most part, stay close, she acknowledged. *Though not as close as you imagine. The range of our telepathy might surprise you, especially with technological augmentation. I wanted to be available in case you needed resources, but you were remarkably independent.*

"I'm famous for that. Still, you could have used your amazing brain powers to smooth the way for me here and there. Make a guard look the other way, hide me from sight, stuff like that."

Azad detected a strong sense of amusement. *Are you so sure I didn't?*

"Ha, all right, you've got me there. Maybe my luck isn't as good as I thought. Still – why am I here?"

Very few humans are permitted to visit Druaa. I thought you might enjoy the experience.

"I'm always happy to see new places, though it's less exciting when I can't tell anyone I've been here. But come on, really, why?"

Because the rest of the galaxy is filthy and vile, and I wanted to come home, S'zakith said.

"Now that, I believe. So. The debrief–"

I have read your mind. Thoroughly. The debrief is done.

Azad grinned. "You're making me wish my old commanding

officer had telepathy. She would grill me for hours about every little detail. So. Do I get paid now, or is this a 'murder the help' type situation? Because if it's the latter, you should know, I took precautions–"

In the event of your untimely death, documents will be released revealing that we hired you, and that we knew about the conspiracy, and that it interfered with our own conspiracy, and so forth, S'zakith said. *Yes, I know. I told you, I read your mind. Your plan would not be effective in the end, but it is also unnecessary.* She placed a small black bag on the table.

Azad picked up the bag and looked inside. There were glittery things, worth a lot and negotiable in many places. There were data sticks, and the information on those was worth a lot more. The Naalu had an excellent intelligence network, and they were happy to offer Azad information on other factions that she could sell to the top bidder. It was possible everything in the bag was fake, but if they were going to cheat her, they wouldn't have done it at the payment stage. The Naalu were plenty rich. "Excellent. And… that bonus we talked about, if I wrapped up this whole affair before the Greater Union and the Legion signed their treaties?"

You did meet the terms of the agreement, S'zakith said. *It pleases us to have the rest of the galaxy fragmented and at odds with one another. You said you wanted our help to get you into a place someone like you could not normally enter?*

"I did. My original plan was to use your mind-games to clear a path so I could stroll right into the Federation of Sol central reserve and do some untraceable embezzling from an all-access terminal. Set myself up for life and screw over my former employers at the same time, you know?"

We know. We are only asking as a courtesy. Again, I can read–

"Yeah, yeah." Azad waved her hand, downed the rest of the whiskey, and put the glass down. "I changed my mind. Now, for my bonus, I want you to smuggle me in someplace else…"

CHAPTER 57
SEVERYNE

"You can't be here," Severyne said.

Azad smiled at her, that self-confident, self-satisfied, self-indulgent smile that always made Severyne forget everything else. "Here, under your sheet? Here, in your bed? Here, in your rooms? Here, at your exclusive fancy Letnev resort?"

"*All* of those!"

"This isn't even all that impressive. I had a plan to sneak into your quarters at the Baron's actual palace, but when I heard you were coming for a week of rest and relaxation, well, I thought, what better way to relax than with me? You can forget about getting any rest, though."

"This... Azad... *Amina*..." Severyne sat on the edge of the bed. It was clear that Azad was naked under the sheet, and that made it hard to think about anything else. "Is this some operation? Some secret plan? Are you trying to make me into a double agent for the Federation, or something?"

"These are fair questions." Azad reached over and put a hand on Severyne's thigh. "I'm pretty sick of conspiracies and secret agendas and treachery and all that, though, Sev. I was hoping for something a little simpler right now. You and me, we can't be together. Not really. We wouldn't even halfway work. But I figured, sometimes, occasionally... maybe we could *get* together." She sat up and murmured in Severyne's ear, "I hear the Baron promoted you. That you got everything you ever wanted." That hand on Severyne's thigh moved. "How about now you get everything *else* you ever wanted?"

The right thing to do would be to summon guards and have Azad hauled away – she *was* still wanted in Letnev space – and interrogated and imprisoned. But then, obeying Immental's orders without question would have been the right thing to do as well. Severyne hadn't gotten where she was by doing the right thing, but by doing the right thing for *her*.

"Oh, all right," Severyne said. "Your human depravity intrigues me."

"You know what you are?" Azad said into Severyne's ear, some time later. "You're my *bonus*."

EPILOGUE
THE INFORMATION
BROKER

On a remote station in the orbit of an icy planetoid, the mysterious information broker known to some as the Nomad sat in a small room before a screen. A call came in, a call they'd been waiting for. The Nomad turned on the screen, which revealed the features of a Naalu female with mesmerizing green eyes. (Many would be mesmerized; the Nomad was not.)

"Yes?" The Nomad's voice was heavily filtered, and their features and form were obscured in an elaborate environment suit. The Naalu were desperate to know their true identity and purpose, but then, so was everyone else who'd ever heard of the Nomad.

"It is done," the Naalu said. "The conspiracy is broken. A rogue Letani was behind it all, and the creature has been eradicated."

"Good."

The Naalu said, "There will be some… inevitable disorder among the affected factions, of course. But we have averted the widespread war and chaos you warned us about."

"I'm glad," the Nomad said. "If the conspiracy had been

allowed to continue… Let's just say I didn't like where it was going. You wouldn't have, either."

"How did you *know* about the conspiracy?" the Naalu said, clearly frustrated at having to ask the question, instead of just forcing the Nomad to tell, or plucking the knowledge from their mind. "You told us someone was using a new form of mind control practically as soon as the conspiracy began."

The Nomad said, "Information is my business. I pick up bits and pieces, here and there."

"We have our own plans in place, Nomad," the Naalu warned. "More subtle and elegant than the plot we just thwarted, to be sure, but still… just because we cooperated with you against this threat does not mean we will tolerate you meddling in *our* stratagems. Be careful about using any 'bits and pieces' you pick up regarding our Collective."

"Threat received," the Nomad said calmly, and ended the call.

The Nomad stood and walked to a window, looking out at the sparkling lights in the immense darkness. As always, they thought about the future.

About all the things they had yet to do, in order to make sure there would still *be* a future to think about.

ACKNOWLEDGMENTS

Thanks as always to the whole Aconyte team, especially Lottie Llewelyn-Wells, who deftly edited this volume in addition to all the other things she does. I'm grateful to the Twilight Imperium creative team for letting me play in their world. Line up this book next to the earlier two, and you can see the full triptych of artwork by cover illustrator Scott Schomburg! I've never had a triptych before. It's a delight.

Thanks to my agent Ginger Clark and her associate Nicole Eisenbraun for handling the business things so I can focus on words.

My wife Heather Shaw and our kid River are endlessly supportive of my weird job and its strange hours. Thanks to my nearest and dearest, Ais, Amanda, Emily, Katrina, and Sarah, for making life brighter and less lonely.

Thanks to all my supportive writer friends. I wish I could see you in real life again, but hey, at least we have the DMs. My gratitude to my boss Liza and my co-workers at *Locus* magazine, the best day job a writer can have.

My greatest thanks go to you, the readers, who've come on this journey with me. I hope you enjoy the conclusion of the trilogy. As Shakespeare basically said, "Journeys end in lovers meeting and titanic space battles".

ABOUT THE AUTHOR

TIM PRATT is a Hugo Award-winning SF and fantasy author, and finalist for the World Fantasy, Sturgeon, Stoker, Mythopoeic, and Nebula Awards, among others. He is the author of over twenty novels, and scores of short stories. Since 2001 he has worked for *Locus*, the magazine of the science fiction and fantasy field, where he currently serves as senior editor.

timpratt.org
twitter.com/timpratt

ZOMBICIDE™

The zombie apocalypse is here – and you're stuck in the middle of it!

TERRAFORMING MARS™

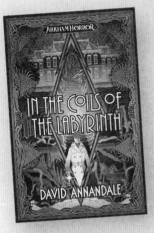

ARKHAM HORROR™

Riveting pulp adventure as unknowable horrors threaten to tear our reality apart.

Something monstrous has risen from the depths beneath Arkham, Miskatonic University is plagued with missing students and maddening litanies, and a charismatic surrealist's art opens doorways to unspeakable places.

A web of terror lurks in the jungle, a director captures unnameable horrors while making his masterpiece, and a thief stumbles onto a necrophagic conspiracy.

Legend of the Five Rings™

Brave warriors defend the empire while battle and political intrigue divide the Great Clans.

EVAN DICKEN

MARIE BRENNAN

DAVID ANNANDALE

Follow dilettante detective, Daidoji Shin as he solves murders and mysteries amid the machinations of the Clans.

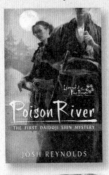

THE FIRST DAIDOJI SHIN MYSTERY

JOSH REYNOLDS

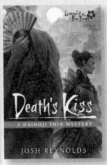

A DAIDOJI SHIN MYSTERY

JOSH REYNOLDS

A DAIDOJI SHIN MYSTERY

JOSH REYNOLDS

The Great Clan novellas of Rokugan return, collected in omnibus editions for the first time, with brand new tales of the Lion and Crane Clans.

DESCENT
LEGENDS OF THE DARK

Epic fantasy of heroes and monsters in the perilous realms of Terrinoth.

Legends unite to uncover treachery and dark sorcery, defeat the darkness, and save the realm, yet adventure comes at a high price in this astonishing world.

WORLD EXPANDING FICTION

Do you have them all?

ARKHAM HORROR

- ☐ *Wrath of N'kai* by Josh Reynolds
- ☐ *The Last Ritual* by SA Sidor
- ☐ *Mask of Silver* by Rosemary Jones
- ☐ *Litany of Dreams* by Ari Marmell
- ☐ *The Devourer Below* ed Charlotte Llewelyn-Wells
- ☐ *Dark Origins, The Collected Novellas Vol 1*
- ☐ *Cult of the Spider Queen* by SA Sidor
- ☐ *The Deadly Grimoire* by Rosemary Jones
- ☐ *Grim Investigations, The Collected Novellas Vol 2*
- ☐ *In the Coils of the Labyrinth* by David Annandale
  (coming soon)

DESCENT

- ☐ *The Doom of Fallowhearth* by Robbie MacNiven
- ☐ *The Shield of Daqan* by David Guymer
- ☐ *The Gates of Thelgrim* by Robbie MacNiven
- ☐ *Zachareth* by Robbie MacNiven
- ☐ *The Raiders of Bloodwood* by Davide Mana *(coming soon)*

KEYFORGE

- ☐ *Tales from the Crucible* ed Charlotte Llewelyn-Wells
- ☐ *The Qubit Zirconium* by M Darusha Wehm

LEGEND OF THE FIVE RINGS

- ☐ *Curse of Honor* by David Annandale
- ☐ *Poison River* by Josh Reynolds
- ☐ *The Night Parade of 100 Demons* by Marie Brennan
- ☐ *Death's Kiss* by Josh Reynolds
- ☐ *The Great Clans of Rokugan, The Collected Novellas Vol 1*
- ☐ *To Chart the Clouds* by Evan Dicken
- ☐ *The Great Clans of Rokugan, The Collected Novellas Vol 2*
- ☐ *The Flower Path* by Josh Reynolds

PANDEMIC

- ☐ *Patient Zero* by Amanda Bridgeman

TERRAFORMING MARS

- ☐ *In the Shadow of Deimos* by Jane Killick
- ☐ *Edge of Catastrophe* by Jane Killick *(coming soon)*

TWILIGHT IMPERIUM

- ☐ *The Fractured Void* by Tim Pratt
- ☐ *The Necropolis Empire* by Tim Pratt
- ☑ *The Veiled Masters* by Tim Pratt
- ☐ *The Stars Beyond* by Tim Pratt *(coming soon)*

ZOMBICIDE

- ☐ *Last Resort* by Josh Reynolds
- ☐ *Planet Havoc* by Tim Waggoner
- ☐ *Age of the Undead* by C L Werner